Praise for *What*

'A road trip takes three siblings
landscape that faces them all, the
of family and memory. Heartbreak...g, ...

Sarah Winman

'A truly gripping and moving exploration of siblings and the secrets we keep from the people closest to us . . . The characters are so richly developed, the sibling dynamic so realistic, the glimpse of America so insightful. I was hooked'   Libby Page

'This sweeping novel takes us on a journey of heartbreak and hope across a hidden America, and kept me enthralled until the very last page'   Rowan Coleman

'A poignant, affecting novel, both intimate and sweeping in its range . . . A deeper meditation on third culture children navigating the intersection of race, identity and politics. A timely, confronting conversation starter of a book'   Wiz Wharton

'I loved this book. It portrayed the multilayered experience of being an immigrant and the child of immigrants, of loving your country and yet never quite feeling as if you belong there. It was heartbreaking and hopeful and it spoke to me deeply'

Julie Cohen

'A timely journey that is vast in character and emotion, all the while capturing the ever-changing landscape of America in all its troubling and beautiful intricacies . . . Winnie M Li manages that tricky balance of capturing the frustrations of sibling relationships and the warm, all-forgiving embrace of family'   Kristen Perrin

Praise for Winnie M Li

'Like the best filmmakers, Li draws you to the edge of your seat and keeps you there... Harrowing, timely, and thoroughly book club worthy' *The New York Times*

'Bold, brilliant, dazzling and devastating. Winnie M Li writes with pure heart and effortless style' Chris Whitaker

'Taut with suspense and drama... Ultimately speaks to the power of the human spirit' Bernardine Evaristo

'Highly recommended' Joyce Carol Oates

'An important and moving book' Cathy Rentzenbrink

'Defiant... conveyed with skill and emotional force' *The Guardian*

'Brave, raw, strikingly original, it is a story that will resonate for many years' *The Daily Mail*

'Li does a fine job exploring how one incident can change the course of a life in this astute psychological study' *Publishers Weekly*

'Such convincing, compelling clarity' *The Times*

'Complex and rewarding' *Stylist*

'Fantastic and fascinating... I really want lots of people to find it and read it' Sara Pascoe

'A remarkable book to read in this time' A.L. Kennedy

'A fine debut from an exceptional talent, and an important study of the human cost of violence' Stuart Neville

'Li infuses each character with an equal humanity' *The Chicago Tribune*

'A spellbinding novel'   *The Irish Times*

'Visceral and timely ... Li's novel is a way of acknowledging the women whose stories have been heard, and those who haven't'
The Observer

'Unflinching and addictive'   *Publishers Weekly*

'Totally compulsive. Truly gripping and unexpected'
Kirsty Capes

'[A] rollercoaster read'   *Elle*

'A must-read'   *Stylist*

'A masterful example of the slow-burn thriller ... Also an ode to the power and beauty of storytelling. I loved it'   Araminta Hall

'Complicit deserves every superlative that has been lavished upon it'   *The Belfast Telegraph*

'Winnie Li is a rare talent with an explosive and timely story. Do not miss it'   Marti Leimbach

'Literally couldn't put this one down ... a really gripping page turner'   Jan Carson

'Timely, entirely believable and feverishly readable'
Trevor Wood

'Fearless, fascinating, a gripping story'   Kate Williams

'A novel for our times but also for the ages'   Kia Abdullah

'Compelling, courageous, and brutal in the best possible way'
Liz Nugent

'Totally intoxicating ... I can't recommend this enough'
Laura Jane Williams

Winnie M Li is an American author and activist who has lived in the UK, Ireland, Qatar and Singapore. A Harvard graduate, she previously wrote for travel guide books, produced independent feature films and programmed for film festivals. Her debut novel, *Dark Chapter*, won *The Guardian*'s Not the Booker Prize, was nominated for an Edgar Award and translated into ten languages. Her follow-up *Complicit* was a *New York Times* Editors' Choice and shortlisted for the Royal Society of Literature's Encore Award. A survivor and advocate against gendered violence, Winnie holds an honorary doctorate from the National University of Ireland in recognition of her work and a PhD from the London School of Economics. She lives in England with her partner and young son and is an Assistant Professor in Creative Writing.

Follow Winnie on X @winniemli and on Instagram @winniemli

Also by Winnie M Li

Dark Chapter
Complicit

What We Left Unsaid

Winnie M Li

ORION

First published in Great Britain in 2025 by Orion Fiction,
an imprint of The Orion Publishing Group Ltd.
Carmelite House, 50 Victoria Embankment
London EC4Y 0DZ

An Hachette UK Company

The authorised representative in the EEA is Hachette Ireland,
8 Castlecourt Centre, Dublin 15, D15 XTP3,
Ireland (email: info@hbgi.ie)

1 3 5 7 9 10 8 6 4 2

A CIP catalogue record for this book is
available from the British Library.

ISBN (Hardback) 9781 3987 0511 1
ISBN (Export Trade Paperback) 9781 3987 0512 8
ISBN (eBook) 9781 3987 0514 2
ISBN (Audio) 9781 3987 0515 9

Typeset at The Spartan Press Ltd,
Lymington, Hants

Printed in Great Britain by Clays Ltd,
Elcograf S.p.A.

www.orionbooks.co.uk

To my Mom
Who has given us as much as she can
For as long as she can

Prologue

1991, Somewhere in Arizona

What Alex mainly remembers is the dust. Or maybe, it is somehow easier and safer to ignore the memory itself, shrouded in the haze of her childhood, and think only of the inescapable dust. Getting up her nostrils, under her fingernails. Sifting in through the car window when she rolled it down a crack to peer at the blue sky beyond.

She was eight years old, and they had stopped the car at some gas station in the middle of the wide, flat desert. Back then, her family drove a beige station wagon. The kind of color they don't make cars in anymore, or the kind of shape, either. It wasn't a car that inspired great love or adoration in any member of their family – although she hesitates now, wondering if her thirtysomething mom and dad had swelled with joy when they'd handed a check over to the salesman at the car dealership sometime in the 1980s and received a set of keys in return. At the time, it would have been their brand-new family car. At one point, it would have shone, undented. An object of pride.

Like everything in their family now, the car was functional. It got them from A to B, from home to school, to the supermarket, to piano lessons, to soccer practice. And on rare occasions, on longer trips like this, to places like the Grand Canyon.

That day when she was eight, the car had jolted and rolled

1

over miles of interstate, green signs whipping past. Squashed next to her sister and brother in the back seat, Alex had sat through it all, wide-eyed and then later, sleepy-eyed. But always soaking in the miles and miles of emptiness that bordered the highway. Dry, dusty scrubland with nothing to see except for the exit ramps leading to towns she would never actually visit, but occasionally glimpse: a cluster of buildings in the distance, housing subdivisions starting to speckle the land.

Watching all of this, what struck her most was a sense of wonder that there could be so much land. This was America: miles of it rolling in every direction, and however far their car traveled, there would always be more. Sea to shining to sea, as they sang in school. If they kept driving on the interstate, how far would it take them? All the way to the Atlantic Ocean? If they picked any one of these exit ramps, what would they discover? There were probably hundreds of them branching off this highway alone. It boggled the mind, to be confronted with the vastness of this landscape.

Somewhere in Arizona, they rolled off one of these exit ramps and left the interstate. Their beige station wagon joined a stream of other cars on a smaller highway north, and there were signs here and there mentioning the Grand Canyon.

'Not too far now!' Her dad glanced back at them, exhorting them in that embarrassing, singsong voice he used when trying to get them excited.

'Aiya, look!' Her mom tapped the gasoline dial in frustration. She muttered something in Taiwanese, and Alex knew it was a reminder to fill up the gas. The arrow was at less than half a tank.

Then followed an irritable exchange between their parents in Taiwanese. She didn't need to understand it to know what they were saying. Mom always wanted Dad to fill up the gas once it reached halfway. Dad always said that was too soon.

The car trundled along in the desert heat, the sun climbed higher in the sky.

They passed a few gas stations, eyeing the price of gas.

'A dollar twenty-two! So expensive!'

'No, we can find cheaper,' Mom said.

Finally, they saw one where gas was remarkably cheap: $1.14 a gallon. Alex didn't recognize the brand – it wasn't one of those familiar, colorful logos like Mobil with the winged red horse or Shell with the yellow clamshell. Just a dusty, no-name gas station, a hand-painted sign out front, faded in the desert sun.

Dad turned off the highway, the car jolting over ruts and holes in the macadam.

Two men sat out front, and stared at them, unsmiling.

Otherwise, the place was empty.

'Um ... do they work here?' Kevin asked, watching the two men warily. They were white and what you might call 'grizzled': cowboy hats pulled low, blue-jeaned legs splayed out, their boots in the dust. Very unlike anyone Alex had seen in Orange County.

Dad parked the car in front of a gas pump and turned off the ignition. The car keys dangled and swung from behind the steering wheel.

'Well, we fill up the gas anyway.'

He shrugged and started to get out of the car.

The two men continued to stare at him.

Alex watched as Dad motioned to the gas pump and their car.

'I just fill up here, okay?' He shouted this to the two men, who looked back in silence. Alex was very conscious of her

3

dad's accent, his willingness to please. She saw how the two men grinned slowly, as if there were an unspoken joke.

'That's what it's there for,' one of the men shouted back. 'Just make sure you pay for it.' Not mean, not serious. One of those unfunny jokes men sometimes make to fill up the space.

'Oh, ha ha, of course I pay for it.' Dad attempted to laugh back. The sun glinted off his wire-framed glasses.

But Alex felt the fear coursing beneath the glare of the sun.

'We got our eyes on you,' the man said. Again, posed lightly as if it were a joke. Suddenly, she was ashamed. She no longer wanted to be there in that hot, strange gas station, staring through the dusty windshield at the two men.

Dad started to fill up the car. Alex heard the whir and the chug as gasoline poured into their tank. The men kept staring.

'I have – I have to go to the bathroom,' Kevin said, nudging Mom.

'You wait until your dad finish, then you go with him to-gether.' There was a protective note in Mom's voice, as if she too sensed danger in the air.

'I have to go, too,' Bonnie said. 'Do you think the bathroom will be gross?'

'Aiya, can't you wait?' Mom asked.

'No, Mom, it's my . . .' Bonnie looked around, then her voice quieted. 'I think it might come any day.'

'What? What are you talking about?' Alex asked. Why did Bonnie have to be so secretive about things sometimes? Bonnie glanced at her but didn't say anything.

Mom let out an exasperated sigh. 'Okay, okay,' she relented.

Alex still had no idea what Bonnie meant. She hated being left out, when everyone older than her spoke in this mysterious kind of code.

Mom instructed Bonnie. 'You and me, we go together. Kevin,

your dad finish filling the gas, so you and him to go men's room. Alex, you need to go bathroom, too?'

Alex saw her dad hanging the nozzle back on the gas pump, taking a used tissue from his pocket and wiping the rim around the car's fuel tank, before snapping the little door shut. He seemed to hesitate, uncertain about crossing over to the building to pay.

'Yeah, you coming, or you just gonna staaaaaayyyy?' Kevin taunted her as he slid toward the open back door.

'No, I – I'll stay,' Alex said, looking at them.

'You sure?' Mom asked as she got out of the car. She leaned down toward Alex, her face in shadow, her body blocking the sun. 'We not stopping again till we get to the Grand Canyon.'

'Yeah, I'll stay.' Alex nodded. Something in her told her to stay clear of those men. She'd rather be here, in the car on her own. As far from them as possible.

'Okay.' Mom nodded. 'Stay right here. Don't get out of the car.'

She wanted to tell them not to go, too. But the gas had to be paid for, and they needed to use the bathroom.

Alex watched as the rest of her family crossed the broken macadam toward the gas station building. They were four slight figures, and the desert heat rose from the ground, distorting them so they looked wavy.

She pushed down the locks on all four of the car doors. And waited.

Present Day, West of Boston

Bonnie is the first of them to hear it, of course. She is in her expansive kitchen – the New England spring ripening into summer, just outside the floor-to-ceiling windows – when she gets the phone call from her father. It is Sunday afternoon, the usual time for her weekly video call with her parents. What is unusual is the absence of her mother.

When the familiar rectangle flickers to life on her iPad, only her dad sits in front of the camera. He looks bereft, like an empty rowboat adrift.

'Hey Dad,' Bonnie says. She glances outside the window, where Henry and Milo stand on their vast green lawn, forlornly tossing a baseball. Her middle son, Max, rests leopard-like on his favorite thick branch of the maple tree. Choosing to be on his own, as usual.

Dad doesn't say anything for a prolonged moment – or perhaps it's the Wi-Fi signal glitching. Then he clears his throat.

'Dad?' Bonnie frowns at the screen. 'You okay?'

She studies him a second longer.

'Where's Mom?'

* * *

Harold Chu, seventy-five years old, coughs a second time in his home in Irvine, California. He traces a quivering index finger across his touchscreen, as if this already near-magical device could miraculously draw his oldest daughter into his room, to sit right beside him, her warm hand squeezing his. But there's only the hard tap on the scratch-resistant glass, shiny but unyielding.

He summons up the words in English.

'Your mother . . . she's not good. She's had a kind of stroke.'

* * *

Bonnie suddenly stands very still, her kitchen surroundings, the birdsong and sunlight falling away. She leans on the granite-topped island – and it is an island indeed, stranded amid an ocean of rigid surfaces, expensive tiling, and gleaming, high-tech appliances. Offering her a place to lean upright, but little comfort.

Her worst fear. The kind of news she always dreaded would arrive someday.

'What do you mean? A kind of stroke?'

Bonnie's mouth has taken on a life of its own, emitting a series of panicked questions, while her mind arches out on a freewheeling trajectory, imagining the worst. Pursuing a single overriding realization: *I never got to organize that seventieth birthday she wanted.*

Her dad shrugs and shakes his head at the same time – a gesture he has always made, for as long as she can remember. The essence of her dad, resigned and hapless.

'It's a ministroke,' he says, edging around the gap in his language. 'There's a medical term for it, but I don't remember. She stumbled and couldn't speak or move . . . At least we didn't have to wait too long for an ambulance.'

'An ambulance?!' Bonnie curses herself. She shouldn't have

postponed that birthday celebration for her mom. Were the strains of raising three healthy sons in complete financial comfort that taxing on her? What an ungrateful daughter she was. 'Where is she now?'

'The hospital. They're monitoring her until tomorrow.'

Harold Chu opens and closes his mouth a few times with no utterance, like a beached fish gasping for water.

Keep it together, Dad, Bonnie thinks. *Don't cry on me.* Because it would be too embarrassing if her seventy-five-year-old father burst into tears right now. Not for her. But a further humiliation for him, with his old-world mentality.

Harold Chu's eyes are watering now, and Bonnie can see it through the FaceTime call. 'They're scheduling a procedure...'

Without realizing it, Bonnie has slid down to the cold gleaming floor, her back against the base of the kitchen island. Almost as if she were hiding, out of sight from any adults who might come stalking into the room.

Forty-six years old. Forty-six. She's an adult. With kids of her own. She should be able to handle this. She could handle it when Henry broke his arm falling off his first mountain bike, when Milo had his tuberculosis scare... But with her own mother, the fear is childlike, primal. Undercut with an indefinable guilt.

Get it together, Bonnie. Clients used to be charged hundreds per hour for your expertise. Strategy is your thing.

'Okay, okay,' she says to her dad, nodding and processing. 'Do you want me to fly out? Someone needs to look after you, too.'

'No, no, Bonnie, you can't.' Harold Chu holds up a hand, protesting weakly. Something shifts in him, an attempt to regain some form of authority. He straightens up. 'Mommy wants to talk to all of you tomorrow. A Zoom call. Do you think you can do that?'

'Uh, sure, whatever you want.' Bonnie scrambles to readjust to Dad's laconic demands. 'What time?'

'Two p.m. our time. That's five for you. Can you tell your brother and sister?'

'Wait, you want me to . . . ? Uh, sure.'

Bonnie is taken aback by how prescriptive this all is. Behind the scenes, she can imagine Mom dictating the appointment time from her hospital bed.

'Just like that? That's the time?'

'Yes.' Dad nods, all trace of his previous weakness gone. 'You their big sister. Call them now, tell them to come onto Zoom tomorrow.'

'Sure.' Bonnie nods, ever obedient. As if it were as simple as shouting up the stairs to them to announce dinner's ready.

But the reluctance pours in, thick and deadening.

Her mind flicks ahead, calculating time zones. Kevin's an hour behind her, no problem there. And Alex . . . It must be 9 p.m. where Alex is. If indeed Alex is still in London. Bonnie can't remember the last time she spoke to her younger sister. Or she does, but it's a memory that barely contains any substance, just a faint outline of a conversation.

Alex is like a homing beacon, bleeping fainter and fainter. Bonnie wonders why she's let her drift so far.

* * *

North of Chicago

Thirty minutes. That's all he needed: thirty minutes to escape his wife and kids. To recuperate, remind himself he was a man and that there was a wholeness, an essence to Kevin Chu – that could exist outside his family.

Jessica had been on his case for months now. Years, even. He was guilty of evading her, that much was true. But he felt such a pure, bracing resentment toward his wife, he couldn't explain it.

It wouldn't have been so embarrassing if it weren't such a cliché. The Midlife Crisis of the Asian American Dad. Life in the suburbs. A five-bedroom split-level, 55 percent of its value still being paid by a monthly mortgage that would persist for the next decade or two. Two cars. Two kids. A lawn that demanded regular mowing and watering before the neighbors started to make snide comments, casually recommend a gardening service.

In his teens he had heard about midlife crises, these fabled traumas that prompted gray-haired men to purchase inappropriate red sports cars, ditch the mother of their children for some hot, nubile blond. He was not that pathetic. Plus, sports cars were terribly fuel inefficient. And hot young blond women, regardless of how alluring their bodies and faces were, probably made for mind-numbingly dull conversation. There was no longer any appeal to the stereotypical all-American girl he would have simultaneously lusted for and resented throughout his horny youth.

No, Kevin Chu would not resort to such clichés.

But thirty minutes was all he was asking for. Close your eyes, turn on some good music – something like Phish or Led Zeppelin or heck, even the wailing refrains of Counting Crows, something to remind him of his earlier, carefree days. And divorce his brain from any thoughts of school drop-offs, or emails from his boss, or the grim, unmentionable state of his finances. Thirty minutes in what Jessica snipingly called his 'man cave.' Was that so difficult to grant?

Jessica had started shouting something or the other about an extended family picnic with her parents and siblings that weekend, but he retired to his room, pretending he hadn't heard her.

Just shut the door.

Turn off the lights.

Lean back in the padded bliss of his leather power recliner.

And look up at the stars.

What Brian, his seven-year-old hadn't noticed, and certainly not Jessica – was that he had slyly purchased an identical extra set of glow-in-the-dark stars when they were redecorating his son's room last year. Little did his family know, he had spent a neck-wrenching hour here and there affixing the stars to the ceiling of his den, faithfully recreating the constellations displayed on his phone's astronomy app. Ursa Major. Ursa Minor. Cassiopeia. And good old Orion, the unmistakable three stars of his belt, beckoning from the ceiling of his study, the same way they had from the night sky in his childhood.

Completing those constellations had earned him an unexpected feeling of satisfaction, even more so because none of his family knew. It was his secret universe.

Of course, they didn't look nearly as awe-inspiring in glow-in-the-dark sticker form. But Kevin had learned not to expect genuine awe or rapture in his adult life anymore. The supermarket version, ordered on Amazon Prime, and slid out from its mass-produced plastic wrap packaging, was the best he could hope for these days.

Still, it offered some semblance of respite. Forget the rest of the world. Turn your eyes skyward.

And escape.

But he has only been sitting in the dark for nine minutes (not thirty) when his wife comes knocking on the door. Rap-rap-rap.

He stays silent.

Rap-rap-rap. Then a huffed exhale. 'Kevin! Turn down the music!'

He turns down the music.

'What do you want?' he asks, audibly peeved.

'I've been shouting for you for ages! It's your sister on the phone!'

He pats his pockets in alarm, looking for his phone. He should remember never to leave it in another room.

'She's on the landline!'

Why? Only his parents and scammers call the landline these days. So, either constant remonstrations or swindlers after your money.

A second later he finds his phone (which he's put on silent) and notices three missed calls from his sister. And a few texts. He squints at his screen, too bright in his artificially dark cave.

Hey are you there? Call me. It's urgent.

Then: It's something to do with Mom.

That single syllable, and the deluge of guilt. His mom, whom he should be calling every week at the very least. Whom he should email on more than just her birthday and Mother's Day, the frenzied last-minute surfing of the 1-800-Flowers website, clicking on an exorbitantly priced Luxury Mother's Love Bouquet, because that at least could temporarily quell his remorse about being a bad son.

'What's going on with Mom?' he asks a moment later when he's called Bonnie.

'It's some kind of stroke.'

In moments like these, Kevin regrets not having gone to medical school. He had enrolled in premed courses for the first two years of college, all ready to fulfill his parents' dreams of having a Son, M.D. But the coursework was too much, he grew lazy. And it was the sense of responsibility that intimidated him: the Hippocratic Oath and everything it required of him. One wrong diagnosis, one slip of the scalpel, and a patient's life could be over.

Now, at forty-two, he has friends who are doctors, ranging from esteemed cardiac surgeons at highly ranked hospitals to general practitioners who coddle whimpering babies and doddering seniors alike. He shuddered at his friends' tales of grueling med school rotations, and then residencies that seemed to last forever in various hospital outposts, further and further specializations that demanded more years, more sleep deprivation.

These days, two decades into his career, he likely earns as much money as those doctor friends. But his job as an insurance underwriter doesn't command the same kind of societal respect. And he doesn't have their medical knowledge. The kind of expertise that could prove very handy now, when his own mother sits tubed up in a faraway ICU. At least to understand the situation, to fully grasp the implications and the possible outcomes, instead of plunging into the blind fear that he now swims in.

'Man, we are horrible Asian kids,' Kevin says to Bonnie. '*Three* of us. And not one of us became a doctor.'

'Well, not one of us wanted to be a doctor.'

'Yeah, you wanted to be a lawyer, I wanted to be an astronaut. And Alex wanted to be . . . well, it depended on the day with her.'

'An actress,' Bonnie says, as if to challenge Kevin's sarcasm. She was always leaping to Alex's defense, even now, when Alex lives thousands of miles away, not giving a fuck. 'She always wanted to be an actress. I guess of all of us, she got the closest to her childhood dreams.'

'Not that it matters anymore. I mean, we're the ones who are gonna pay Mom's medical bill,' Kevin points out. 'Which reminds me, do you know what kind of medical insurance they're on?'

'I didn't ask . . . Dad was too exhausted to answer any questions like that. I'll send him an email or something.'

'No, I can do it,' Kevin says, and immediately regrets it. Some filial sense of duty prompts him to say: man-to-man, son-to-father, let's talk about the dry realities of your HMO plan. He is, after all, the offspring who ended up working in insurance. If anyone knows how to thread their way through the bureaucratic labyrinth of deductibles and coverage loopholes to get their mother the right kind of treatment, it's him.

But he dreads being on the phone with his dad: the long gap of silence; his dad's dry, papery voice as he awkwardly stitches the English words together, hesitating even after half a century in America.

Too late. He's already volunteered.

'You sure?' Bonnie asks. 'I mean, that would be amazing. I can't even get my head around my own insurance plan. And I'm sure you understand this much better than me.'

An unusual shred of pride finds its way into his heart. Maybe he can, for once, feel like he has some sense of purpose.

'No problem.' Another pause. 'So . . . how are the boys? All four of yours.'

Bonnie laughs at the familiar joke. 'Chris is good. My other three . . . well, they're boys. It's almost summer. They're restless.'

Yeah, but they have ten acres to run around in. And a private pond with a boat, Kevin is tempted to say. He thinks back to the last time they visited Bonnie in her New England estate. A castle and grounds, a kingdom to itself. Arabella and Brian came back wide-eyed, still disbelieving that all that land belonged just to their cousins. Their tousle-haired boy cousins with their hazel eyes; long, patrician limbs; and their golden-headed father of esteemed lineage. Well, sixteen generations in this country after stepping off the *Mayflower* would allow a family to amass all that wealth.

'Did you see they have a Jaguar?' Jessica commented on the flight home. 'Like a vintage one, just parked in their extra garage.'

He hadn't noticed. He was too busy trying to guess the value of their house and property.

The next day, Kevin looked up Teslas, wondering if he should treat himself to a belated fortieth birthday present. Then he crunched the numbers and decided he probably shouldn't, not while they were still paying their current mortgage rate. Some luxuries remained definitively out of reach.

'Cool, so you'll speak to Dad about the insurance. And to-morrow afternoon you can do the Zoom?'

'Yeah, yeah, I said I would.' A note of annoyance at Bonnie's managerial tone. He pauses, then asks another question. 'You spoken to Alex yet?'

'I will, once I get off the phone with you. Though it's kinda late over there.'

'When's the last time *you* spoke with her?'

'Uh . . . I dunno. Maybe a few months ago?' Bonnie sounds uncomfortable. He guesses it was half a year.

'You know, she's not a little kid anymore,' Bonnie says after a moment. 'Sometimes you have this image in your head where Alex is still a teenager and rebelling at every single thing in the world. She's *forty* now. She actually has a stable job now. And a partner, too.'

This is news to him. Or maybe it's not. He can't keep track of Alex's partners.

'Is the *partner* stable?'

'Yeah, they've been together for a few years.'

'Is the partner . . . a man?'

Bonnie breathes out, her patented exasperated sigh. 'You know, you really have to get over that.'

'Get over what?'

'Your whole attitude about this. I can't believe you've let this go on for so long.'

'*I've* let it?' Kevin can feel the familiar defensiveness rising, anything to counter Bonnie's scolding. '*She's* the one who's always been a complete drama queen.'

'Can you just—' Bonnie sucks in her breath. 'Listen, she'll be on the Zoom tomorrow. Be nice. It's important for Mom. I don't know what she's gonna say, but she won't want to see you and Alex squabbling.'

Kevin feels a drop – but only a drop – of remorse. Alex has had five years to reach out, but she's never bothered, either.

'Yeah, fine,' he agrees.

'I gotta go call her now. See you tomorrow. Two p.m. their time – which is four p.m. yours, okay?'

'Yes, Bonnie, I know how time zones work. Bye.'

He hangs up. Every time he speaks to his sister, it's like they're kids all over again.

Kevin breathes out and sits there in the dark, grateful for the silence. Above him on the ceiling, the adhesive stars glow in their fixed constellations.

* * *

London

Alex is just settling down for the night, idly scrolling through social media feeds, when her phone lights up silently with Bonnie's call. Next to her in bed, Nya has drifted off to sleep. She gets tired easily these days, while Alex is ever the night owl. But why would Bonnie call this late?

And who actually calls these days, anyway? Conversations happen more unobtrusively in the twenty-first century, strung out mutely over chains of text and WhatsApp messages. So much easier to ignore.

Alex clutches her phone and quietly exits the bedroom. She answers the call in a hushed voice.

'Bonnie? What's up?'

'Hey, um, can you do a Zoom with Mom and the whole family at around this time tomorrow? Ten p.m. your time?'

Bonnie, as always, cuts to the chase, but Alex is still taken aback by the brusqueness of it all. 'Uhhh . . . Sure. Hello, by the way! What's going on?'

It is, in many ways, the phone call she has always dreaded receiving. The predestined inevitability that comes from living thousands of miles away from your family, on the other side of the Atlantic. Your parents will grow older and frailer, your guilt will swell with every unanswered email, every Christmas missed. Until finally, one day the phone will ring – and you will be presented with the irreversible.

You need to come home. Mom isn't well.

After Bonnie has explained what she knows, Alex stands in her darkened living room, the dread growing inside her. She could apologize for letting things drift this far, for living a rich and interesting and colorful life in another country and failing to truly share it with her family. But there is no excuse really, except for her own laziness, her own hidden disinclination.

'How are you?' Bonnie asks, and Alex considers how much she hasn't told her own sister.

'I, um, I'm good. Really good. But I . . .' She pauses and leans against the wall, imagines the five of them sharing a computer screen tomorrow and cringes at the thought. 'God, there's a lot I haven't told you. Any of you.'

Bonnie pauses, as if she is about to remonstrate. 'Like what?'

'Like I'm . . . married?'

'What?! To who?'

'To Nya, who I've been with for years. You know about her.' She can imagine Bonnie breathing a sigh of relief. 'We just had a small ceremony at city hall, so it wasn't a big thing or anything.'

'Wow, well, you're still married! Congratulations!'

Alex catches the unintentional slight from Bonnie: 'still married,' as if Alex and commitment are incompatible. Yet there is even bigger news. Alex wasn't expecting to feel nervous, but she is.

'And . . . um, Nya's pregnant. We're pregnant. We're gonna be – I'm gonna be a mother.'

Each of these short, stuttered sentences chipping closer to the final truth. She, Alex Chu, is actually going to be mother. Something she'd never imagined possible. And she still doubts is possible.

She can hear Bonnie's intake of breath. 'Oh my god. That's huge. How far along are you?'

Nearly five months. Five exciting, terrifying months of watching her wonderful Nya reel with nausea, weather the exhaustion, dutifully relinquish wine and coffee and blue cheese toward the future health of their child. She has begun to understand, if only infinitesimally, the necessary sacrifices that mothers undertake, even months before their baby makes it into this world.

'And why didn't you tell any of us?' Bonnie is asking, affronted.

'Well, I—' Alex catches herself, trips over an unexpected jab of emotion. 'After what happened with Kevin . . . I didn't think anyone would care.'

She has migrated onto the sofa now and stretches out on the cool cushions, closes her eyes. The light from a nearby street-lamp casts a yellow gleam into the shadowed room. Somehow it helps to calm her heartbeat.

'Of course we care,' Bonnie says, her voice compassionate, entreating. '*I* care. I would have wanted to know as soon as possible. And Mom and Dad? Of course they'd be happy for you.'

'Mmmm. You think?' Alex emits a questioning hum and leaves it at that. 'And Kevin?'

Bonnie sighs. 'Kevin's just – whatever, don't worry about Kevin for now. But *I* want to know everything. Tell me all about Nya! Tell me about the pregnancy! Are you excited to be a mom?'

'Bonnie, I have no idea what I'm headed into,' Alex confesses, relieved to be able to share this with someone. 'And I'm – I'm kinda terrified of being a parent.'

She says this with a laugh: oh, the irony of adventuring, commitment-phobic Alex finally being saddled with parent-hood. But she doesn't need to explain further. Bonnie gets her and always has. It has been so long since Alex has sunk into a long conversation with her sister that she almost forgot the ease of telling a story to her, the shared idea that can be communicated with a single grunt or phrase. The emotional shorthand that siblings speak in.

Here in London, late on a Sunday night, everybody is sleeping desperately, resentfully, in anticipation of Monday morning. But where her sister is, it is still early evening, and the sun still shines. Alex dwells in that imagined warmth, grateful for this familiar respite.

It's almost like being home again.

At 5 p.m. Eastern Standard Time the next day, Bonnie is sitting in her home office, leaning forward in the luxury ergonomic chair that she bought to get her through all those endless Zoom meetings of the pandemic. She is always slightly anxious before phone calls with her parents. They are equal parts comforting and exasperating in their familiarity, but also a reminder of the frugal, clipped household she grew up in, one that she was secretly ashamed of when she first started dating Chris – and perhaps has tried too hard to forget.

Her family members flicker to life one by one, until they are all there stacked in a neat four-square – centimeters apart on-screen, thousands of miles apart in real life.

Her parents peer into their camera, always slightly mistrusting any pixilated form of communication. They must be sitting in bed together, because she can see their pale blue padded headboard, unchanged for forty years. The iPad on their laps catches their faces at a low, unnatural angle.

Mom in particular looks thinner, paler, a wizened ghost of the tenacious mother she's known all her life – and Bonnie registers this with shock. But she tamps down the gnawing worry and greets her parents with her usual cheeriness.

'How was the hospital, Mom?'

Her mom sniffs and shrugs, revealing that familiar defeatist attitude. 'It was okay. The food was lousy. I'm glad to be back.'

This is a grumpier version of Mom, shorn of all softness or pleasantness.

'Are you . . . is there a procedure happening?' Kevin ventures.

22

'I'm sick of procedures.' Mom shakes her head. 'They are doing something else to me in about a month.'

They all nod in silence.

Bonnie notes this is the first time Kevin and Alex have been in the same space (virtual or otherwise) in five years. But with Zoom, they don't have to acknowledge each other's presence. They can just exist, side by side on-screen, never making direct eye contact. Which is impossible anyway with Zoom, Bonnie realizes. You can look at your sister's eyes on-screen, but you'll never know if she's actually looking at you.

Each of them contemplates the unspoken, nodding silently around the fact of Mom's medical condition.

In the meantime, they cycle through some more pleasantries of catching up: how is Alex's job, how are Jess and the kids, Chris and the boys. Bonnie is distinctly aware that Alex's news remains a secret – and that it is not her place to hint at any of it.

'So, Mom, why did you want to have a Zoom with all of us?' Bonnie finally asks, trying to be as gentle as possible.

'Can't I see my children all at once?' Mom jokes, a righteous note rising in her voice.

'No, of course you can.' Bonnie imagines that in ten years, she may be asking the same thing of her sons.

'I never get to see all you,' Mom continues. 'I mean, one by one, yes. But when was the last time we were all together?'

'I think that might have been Christmas sometime,' Bonnie offers vaguely. She shoots a look at Alex, then Kevin, but they're staring straight ahead, offering no assistance. *Thanks, guys.*

'So long ago.' Mom shakes her head sadly. 'What happened?'

Does Mom really have no idea? Something did happen; they were all there to witness it at the dinner table. She remembers Kevin's taunting voice, Alex storming off. Her parents, as always, pretending like nothing ugly had happened.

23

'We just sort of . . . got really busy,' Kevin says lamely. 'Raising two young kids in lockdown, that was nuts.'

'I know,' Mom says. 'I raised three of you. All while your dad was working to support us. I know what it's like.'

Whatever Mom says, it always lodges a shard of guilt deep inside Bonnie.

'I'm sorry,' Alex finally speaks up. 'I've been really terrible at keeping in touch . . .' She trails off, takes a breath, and Bonnie wonders if this is the moment when Alex will share her news, as startling and revelatory as it is.

But before Alex can continue, Mom launches into a deep, hacking cough, the phlegm gurgling in her throat, and Bonnie shudders. *How long has she had that cough for?*

'Mom, you okay?' Alex asks.

Mom shakes her head, clears her throat again, reaches for a cup of water.

After she's sipped and recovered, she continues.

'So, I think it's time. I want to see all of you again.'

It's time? There is a terrible finality to the phrase, which alarms Bonnie.

'What, like, now?' Kevin asks. He sounds just like Bonnie's fourteen-year-old. The teenage indignation.

Mom nods. 'Now. This month.'

'This month?' Kevin exclaims.

Bonnie panics. 'Is it that serious?'

Mom shrugs. 'What is serious, Bonnie? A mother wants to see her children after years apart. Isn't that normal?'

Years. Bonnie absorbs this fact. What would it be like to go years without seeing Max and Henry and Milo? Impossible to even contemplate. She wonders if the ache of motherhood subsides with age.

'My procedure is on the twenty-sixth. I want to see you all before then. Together.'

Kevin sighs audibly, and Alex is still quiet – her video frozen for a split second.

'Okay,' Kevin says, ever the obedient son. He glances down – presumably at his phone. 'What weekend?'

'It doesn't matter what weekend,' Dad speaks up. 'We're retired. It's all the same to us. You three work it out.'

'But,' Alex says, then pauses. 'I'll – I'll have to look at flights.'

Mom shakes her head, then explodes into another violent fit of coughing.

'No. Don't just fly here.' Mom gestures toward the screen, as if to admonish them. 'I want you to *drive* together. The three of you.'

Bonnie lurches in shock. 'Drive?! Mom, you live in California, I'm near *Boston* . . .' She does a quick calculation. It would probably take five, six days to drive all the way to the West Coast. Can she be away from her sons for that long?

Kevin's eyes are wide in disbelief, and Alex still appears frozen. Or maybe just in shock, too.

'You don't have to drive the whole way,' Mom argues. 'I just want you to drive *together*. A road trip, like the old days.'

What old days? Bonnie thinks. But then she grasps a memory of sitting in the back seat of their old beige station wagon, the three of them watching the shape of their parents' heads, as miles of highway slid past. There had been road trips, on occasion.

'I want you to drive here to California. And I want you to—' Mom stops and coughs, then resumes. 'I want you to see the Grand Canyon together.'

A strained, unfamiliar feeling of regret curdles within Bonnie.

The Grand Canyon. She lingers on an image: flat, dusty desert rolling endlessly past their car windows.

They had once tried to drive to the Grand Canyon as a family. When she was a teenager. Why they never made it, Bonnie still can't quite understand.

She notices everyone on the Zoom has gone quiet.

'The Grand Canyon?' Alex finally repeats, her voice low.

'Yes.' Their mom nods, uncompromising. 'Have any of you been there?'

'Uh, no.' Kevin shakes his head.

'No. It's a little far,' Alex says.

Bonnie admits that she, too, has never stood on the edge of that great natural wonder, this geological marvel that all Americans instinctively know about, even if they grow up thousands of miles away in New England.

'No, I haven't.'

Mom nods, her argument complete. 'So then go. Drive there, and then here to California.' She pauses before looking straight at the camera, straight at them. 'You owe it to me.'

* * *

They owed it to Mom? They *owed* it? Like it was a debt that could be repaid after all these decades.

A peculiar feeling of anger slices through Kevin when he thinks of the Grand Canyon. How could she claim they owed it to her, when they had only been children, for god's sake.

But Kevin tamps down this resentment, the way he always does with his parents.

'That's a long way, Mom . . .' he starts to say.

'I know it's a long way. That's why we never got to go when you were little.'

Well, we could have. If you hadn't decided to turn around.

26

'I just want you all to spend time together, now that you're all grown-up. You never see each other. You never see your dad and me.'

'I'm sure there's another way we can all see each other,' Bonnie offers, characteristically practical. 'I mean, we just need more time to plan ahead. Like six months, or something like that.'

She trails off. Because they all know that the three of them wouldn't ever get together without their mom's insistence. That's how far apart they've drifted.

The guilt trickles in again, pooling into a dark, secret puddle inside him.

Mom snorts. 'Maybe I don't want to wait six months.'

Maybe she doesn't have six months. That's what goes unsaid.

'Okay, then this month. Before the twenty-sixth,' Kevin finally acquiesces. Always the first to appease his parents, because his sisters have always been too set on having things their own way.

Bonnie sighs, and he can imagine her mentally rearranging her family's upscale social schedule. No more Club Med this year, no more vacationing at Martha's Vineyard.

Out of nowhere, Alex speaks up with unexpected enthusiasm. '*I* think that's a cool idea.'

Alex? She's the one who has to travel the farthest.

Mom's face brightens up on-screen. 'See, I can always count on you, Alex.'

Kevin seethes in silence.

'No, let's do it!' Alex exclaims. He is reminded of the zeal his younger sister always had in childhood: her harebrained ideas for family plays at Christmastime, or an art project for Mother's Day, or an elaborate Easter egg hunt. 'Come on, it'll be fun!'

Fun? And that is so Alex, only thinking of what's fun, never what's responsible or sensible. And can you even say the word 'fun' when Mom's upcoming operation is the real reason for this trip?

'You really want to do this?' Bonnie is asking Alex, as if Mom weren't right there on the call.

'You heard what Mom said. It's been ages since we've all been together. Even longer since we've done a road trip.'

And we all know why, Kevin thinks. *Or maybe you forgot, Alex.*

'Yes, Alex, that's it.' Mom grins. And Kevin has to admit, it's the first time he's seen Mom smile on this call. 'Don't be so serious, like the others.'

'I'm not—' Bonnie starts to say defensively, and then shuts up.

'I know you guys have kids,' Alex says, stating the obvious. 'But maybe you can get away for a week or something? I can fly to Chicago or Texas or wherever, and meet you guys, and we can drive from there.'

Kevin starts a quick mental calculation: Chicago to L.A. How long would you need to drive there, with a stop-off at the Grand Canyon?

'And what am I supposed to do?' Bonnie asks. 'Fly from Boston to meet you guys?'

'Yeah,' Alex answers, nonchalant. 'I mean, I'd be flying from London.' She lets that fact sink in. 'Or you can *drive* from Boston, if you want.'

'That's crazy,' Bonnie says, almost automatically. Which is partly justified for any Alex suggestion.

'What's crazy about it?' Alex asks. 'Rent a car. Get on the interstate. It's not that difficult.'

'Alex, we can't just—' Kevin starts to say. Jobs and vacation

28

time and getting the kids to school, all the stuff Alex doesn't have to think about because she's still not an actual adult.

'Alex, I have three kids!' Bonnie shouts. 'Kevin has two. We can't just leave when we want.'

'No,' Mom cuts in forcefully. 'You can do this. I had the three of you, and I managed to raise all of you, thousands of miles away from my own family, in a new country. With no extra help. Bonnie, you have Chris's family over there. Kevin, Jessica's mom is around the corner. They can all look after your kids. But where is your own mom? All the way over here. You think I don't miss seeing you?'

That shuts them all up. Mom always knows how to lay it on thick.

Kevin watches Bonnie rearrange her face into something corporate and diplomatic. 'All right,' she says. 'I'll speak to Chris and see what I can do.'

'Good, Bonnie, good,' Mom says, like she's praising a loyal dog. Bonnie nods obediently but looks resigned. Kevin has to admit, there is a rare flicker of excitement inside him. A road trip. A whole week away from Jessica and the kids. The open road calling, a welcome distraction from his current misery.

'See,' Mom continues. 'Do it for me. Make your mom happy, okay?'

For the second time on that call, Kevin wonders what exactly they owe their mom. Surely it is something; he just can't name it specifically. Could it be quantified? Repaid that easily through a single road trip?

That was the thing about debt (something that Kevin was now very familiar with). It accrues interest over time. It grows and grows until it burns a deep, irreparable hole in your wallet and your bank accounts and your existence.

Sometimes, it's too late to repay.

* * *

A queasy jolt of excitement courses through Alex when her mom mentions the road trip. There is the familiar adrenaline – what she would normally feel at any mention of travel – but this time it is laced with something more apprehensive.

Of course, the Grand Canyon.

No one in their family has discussed it in all these intervening years, but of course it makes a terrible kind of sense.

She recalls with a surreal vividness the feel of the hot desert sun on her arm as she rode in the back seat of their station wagon. The dust that filtered into the car's interior when they pulled into that gas station and she cracked the window open.

'So you can do it? We'll see you later this month?' Dad is asking now. Looking at his iPad screen, expectant.

'Um . . .' Bonnie answers carefully. 'The three of us will talk offline and figure out our schedules.'

Did she just say 'offline' in a family Zoom? Alex suppresses a snort. She can't remember how long it's been since Bonnie left her high-flying career, but the corporate speak still hasn't left her vocabulary.

'Should we do a deep dive and hammer out the timeline for you?' Alex jokes.

Kevin laughs. It's been ages since he's laughed at one of her jokes.

Bonnie rolls her eyes. 'Ha ha ha, everyone.'

Mom and Dad peer at them perplexed, oblivious to the joke at Bonnie's expense.

'So yeah, we'll be in touch,' Bonnie reassures them.

They nod back – and for once, somehow, pixilated across each other's screens, the five of them seem to be in agreement.

*

When she clicks off the Zoom, Alex lingers for a moment longer in their bedroom. Nya is in the lounge, most likely stretched out on their couch, watching some cozy reality TV competition about baking. Stroking her belly in that protective, maternal way that has become second nature to her in a matter of months.

Alex is relieved to have these moments of silence to herself, to contemplate what was said on the family call. And what wasn't. Her mom could be dying. No one's mentioned it outright; her parents don't like to speak that candidly about things, but it was clearly there in the subtext.

Why else the request for this sibling road trip?

But a dark shadow undercuts that request, a crust of a memory that no one wants to acknowledge.

Alex stands up and peruses her bookcase. There's a framed photograph of herself, Bonnie, and their mother decades ago, at her sister's business school graduation. Alex's hair is still long in this photo, so their resemblance (which people have commented on all her life) is striking. Bonnie appears like a more polished, more successful version of herself, or she the messier, more unsettled version. Their mother's smile is the same as always, poised and practiced, her pride unmistakable – and yet, Alex has always been aware that pride was usually bestowed on her older sister, the one with the perfect life.

She looks around, aware that any photos with Kevin have carefully been removed from her shelf. And Dad – poor Dad – hardly shows up in any pictures, as he was always the one taking them.

Alex buries a seed of bitterness inside her and shifts her attention to the travel guidebooks on the shelf, a testament to the escape she's always sought in far-flung places. Decades' worth of Let's Go and the Lonely Planet and the Rough Guide, spanning the Mediterranean, the Middle East, West Africa,

Southeast Asia, Iceland . . . so many geographies contained within the colorful spines of these books. So many geographies she has eagerly set foot in. Except her own country. There is virtually no mention of the United States, save for a thin New York City guidebook from her trip with Nya four years ago.

Why hasn't she explored her own country? All those states that she's been accustomed to flying over, en route to California – the broad, endless fields; the rugged mountain ranges; the dry desert expanses. All passing silently below her, unknown.

She thinks about belonging. How increasingly, as the years went by, it seemed a foreign notion every time she set foot in America. Until she eventually stopped looking for it.

Maybe it is time, she thinks. She can afford to leave the UK for a week or two. One final hurrah before the reality of parenthood sets in. Nya is nearly five months along, safely out of the first trimester and still nimble enough to get around on her own. So it's not the final call yet on Alex's freedom. They've got time.

When Alex thinks about her own mother, laid up in that bed in California, she realizes they still have time, too. But only just.

It is Bonnie, of course, dutiful firstborn, who initiates the group text message, rounding up her younger brother and sister the way she has done all their lives, wrangling their grumbling personalities to toe the line. She wonders if Kevin and Alex would have done anything at all, without her involvement.

Bonnie scrolls through her phone to find the last group text message between the three of them, sent five years ago. She had sent a couple messages to that thread in the intervening years, and no one had replied. A sadness quivers in her chest when she realizes it's been that long.

Bonnie: Hey guys, reviving this thread. So um, what do you think about visiting Mom and Dad around the second weekend of June?

She places an internal bet: How long will it take for either of them to actually reply? Nothing. She places the phone down, considers if her siblings are really that far gone into their own lives, that uncaring about their mother. To her surprise, it is Kevin who replies first.

Kevin: Um, we really doing this?

Bonnie: Of course. Mom seemed pretty serious. She doesn't usually complain about this kind of stuff

In all her forty-six years, Bonnie has never known her mom to verbalize a demand that places her own needs in front of her children's.

Kevin: I mean, the road-trip part

Nothing from Alex so far. Bonnie frowns and puts her phone down. She reminds herself her sister is five hours ahead of her. Maybe she's having a late lunch.

Bonnie: Alex, you there?

Finally, five minutes later, a message from Alex appears.

Alex: Yes, we should do the road trip

Bonnie: Really? Ok... But from where to where?

Alex sends an emoji: a black-haired woman shrugging. So helpful. Bonnie pushes on.

Bonnie: I mean, should we fly to Phoenix or something, rent a car, see the Grand Canyon, and then drive home?

Alex: I'm open to stuff

What does that mean?

Bonnie: That's maybe the most efficient plan. We can drop the car off in OC & fly back from there

Again, nothing from her siblings.

Bonnie: So we can prob do the whole trip in about 4 days, then???

She sends another question mark.
A long pause. And then:

Kevin: How about we do Route 66?

What the . . .

Bonnie: That's really a thing? Route 66?

Kevin: Yeah. It's a real highway that goes across America, Bon. It's not just made-up

Bonnie: Well, duh. But where does it go from?

Kevin: Chicago to LA

Is he serious? Who has the time for that?

Alex: I'm up for it. We can all meet in Chicago & then drive from there. That sounds cool

Bonnie panics.

Bonnie: How many days is that?

Kevin: You can do it in as little as 3 or 4, but that's not very fun

Fun . . . It's been a while since that word has come up between the three of them. Given the current state of affairs between Kevin and Alex, being shut in a car with them is hardly going to be fun.

Alex: Nah, make it longer. I wanna see stuff

35

Kevin: I was thinking like 6 days maybe

Alex: So like June 9–15 maybe?

Kevin: That could work. We can use my SUV, then we save on renting one

Witnessing her siblings' ongoing dialogue, Bonnie has a distinct sense of things running away from her, out of her control. She suppresses a surge of worry, the very thought of the road trip starts to fill her with dread.

Alex: Bonnie, how does that sound?

What the hell, she thinks. They're her brother and sister. She's known them all their lives. What is she so scared of? Still, it is with a certain trepidation that she types her response.

Bonnie: Yeah, ok. Let me just check with Chris

A pause before anyone writes back.

Alex: Do we think Mom's ok? It seems serious

Bonnie: I think it is serious

Kevin: I've been helping Dad with their health insurance. Complicated, but I think she's covered for this round of treatment

Alex: That's good

Bonnie: Thanks, Kev

And there in the spaces between the on-screen text, between the words that appear and the thoughts that go untyped, between the thousands of miles that stretch between them, the three of them sit, each balancing their unspoken fear with a tentative shared understanding.

Kevin has been reading about Route 66, and now he has a stack of books and maps piled up on his desk, whisked over handily by Amazon Prime at the click of a mouse.

'What are all these packages for?' Jessica had glared at the boxes. Amazon's persistent smiling arrow, branded over and over on the cardboard, grinned at her.

'Just some research,' Kevin mumbled cryptically.

'Research about what?' Jessica probed. But he'd shut the door in her face and didn't answer.

Of course, she was already pissed off. He could have said he was buying platinum jewelry for their upcoming twentieth anniversary, and she would have still found a reason to complain. But his own mother's request, after a stroke and before a potentially life-threatening medical procedure? That trumped any spousal grievances, and both of them knew it.

Kevin stares at a map of Route 66, and he wonders how his marriage has come to this: a series of sniping, passive-aggressive comments traded by the hour, and the routine drudgery of getting the kids to comply to the simple demands of their everyday lives. Wake up, get changed, eat. School, practice, homework, back to bed. Then rinse and repeat, over and over again, until they grow up and you die.

The only difference between childhood and adulthood is that once you move away from home, you have some small modicum of choice in whether or not you're forced to do these things. Unless of course you screw up, get married, and have kids.

There's another knock on the door.

'I said I'm busy for a few minutes!' Kevin shouts on autopilot.

'Dad?' It's his ten-year-old daughter, Arabella.

Oh shit. He gets up, opens the door with a smile on his face. 'Hey Schnopes. How're you doing? Sorry, I thought it was your mom.'

'Yeah, I know.' Arabella slopes in and takes her usual seat, swiveling back and forth on his office chair.

She gazes around the room, taking in his fraternity banner, the painfully dated photo of him and his crew from college, the Route 66 guidebooks on his desk.

'What is it, honey? You okay?'

There is always that way in which a single look from his daughter can floor him, bring to heel all the other mundane worries in his life.

She nods, her black hair sweeping her thin shoulders. She hesitates before speaking.

'Mom's really angry that you're going on this trip.'

Did Jessica put her up to this? he wonders.

'She's not happy with a lot of things I do these days.'

'Like what?'

There's so much he could tell her that would be inappropriate. But there's also a front he has to maintain as a father.

'Maybe Mom thinks it'll be too overwhelming to look after you two when I'm away. But we're moving in your other Ama for the time being. And you're very grown-up these days yourself. I bet you can help look after Brian, too.'

'I can make sure he gets ready in the mornings. And does his homework.'

'I know, you're an awesome big sister like that.' It occurs to him, this is probably what Bonnie was like to him when they were growing up. Responsible, always on his case because she wanted to help their parents, relieve their workload somehow.

He feels a twinge of guilt for all those years he hated his older sister for her bossiness.

'Mom doesn't think you have to be away for so long.'

And of course she wouldn't. Jessica cares little for his parents, and the feeling is mutual. They have always thought her too superficial, too obsessed with designer brands.

And he has to admit, maybe there is some grain of truth in that. Maybe, if Jessica wasn't like this, he wouldn't have boxed himself into this career that he's come to hate. The job necessary to earn the income to pay off the bills and maintain the lifestyle that Jessica expects. Or maybe (if he has to be honest with himself), the lifestyle that he's grown accustomed to as well. Always finding ways to earn more interest, to make his savings work harder. Finding himself in his current situation.

'How long you gonna be away for again?' Arabella now dawdles along the edges of the room, picking up one Route 66 book. She flips absently through it as she returns to the chair.

'Six days to drive to California. Then a few days at Agong and Ama's. So probably a week and a half, maybe two.'

Arabella lingers on a map, and he contemplates what's going through that brain of hers. Is she envisioning what these forty-eight states look like? Trying to understand the breadth of the continent?

'What's Route 66, Dad?'

'Oh, it's this old highway that was built a long time ago. Lots of people drove on it to get to California. So a bunch of cool diners and motels and things to see sprung up along the way.'

He himself can't recall the first time he heard about Route 66. But the mythology of the road seems almost timeless, as if it were always there from the beginning, stretching across to the Pacific, entreating travelers to cross the long, golden miles.

'It's something all Americans are supposed to do at some point.'

'What, like saying the Pledge of Allegiance and paying our taxes?'

Kevin stifles a laugh. 'Well, not as mandatory. And a lot more fun.'

'Are you gonna only fill up gas at Exxons and Shells?'

'That's a good question.' Kevin grins, pleased that Arabella remembered his weird quirk of traveling. 'Probably a smart idea.'

'Because you only want brands you can trust,' she recites dutifully.

For a brief moment, Kevin regrets that he's so inculcated his own daughter into brand consumerism, but there's a deeper reason to his preferences. A more primal one he doesn't like to dwell on.

'Well, I hope you have fun.' Arabella stops swiveling in the chair and tilts her head at him. In that moment she so resembles a younger Jessica that Kevin finds it disorienting, his beloved, one-and-only daughter, couched in the image of his best-avoided wife. 'And I hope Ama will be okay.'

'I hope so, too.' At this mention of his mom, he can almost feel tears welling up in his eyes. A sudden rush of regret that he forgot about her momentarily – she, the very point of the trip – while getting so caught up in Route 66 and his own marital misery.

'Hey Dad,' Arabella shakes him out of his reflection.

'What is it, Schnopes?'

'Are you gonna ever take us on a trip like this? Like me, Brian, and Mom?'

Kevin opens his mouth to answer, but he doesn't know what to say. He knows he should say yes.

He would be lying if he did.

* * *

'At least the three of you can split the driving,' Chris mused, when Bonnie had explained the Route 66 idea to him.

Bonnie said nothing. She smiled and nodded, wondering if that comment was akin to the jokes Chris often made about her driving skills. He usually insisted on doing the driving whenever their family headed somewhere. And Bonnie always obliged, even though she silently winced at his abrupt braking and unnecessary revving of the engine, which surely damaged the car.

But really, that was a minor quibble in their relationship, and she knew she shouldn't complain. After all, most dads wouldn't be okay with the mother of their three children going away for ten days. So, grateful for Chris's blessing, Bonnie researched the transport options, methodically bookmarking web pages and jotting notes in her turquoise faux alligator skin notebook.

Now, Bonnie Chu Prescott sits at the desk in her study and steals a few illicit moments to stare out the window. The window is open, and the fragrant, late-spring breeze wafts through the screen bearing pollen that, every year without fail, makes her sneeze, and her throat itch uncontrollably.

When she first moved out East decades ago, she couldn't understand why her allergies were so much worse. In the dry, sun-baked air of California, the palm trees and desert scrub and frugally watered gardens didn't yield any lethal pollen with the blossoming flowers and warmer days. But she'd since come to accept that living on the East Coast, everything was smaller but more intense. The summers were more humid, the winters frigid and snowy, the vegetation treacherous. The communities were more set in their ways, generations of families layering their legacies on top of each other, residing in old clapboard or brick houses that could date back centuries, long before the first American settlers had even set foot in California.

'How do you know you'll even like it out there?' Nineteen-year-old Alex had asked when Bonnie sat packing her suitcase for Harvard Business School, unsure of what a New England winter required.

'I dunno.' Bonnie shrugged, twisting her long black strands of hair through her fingers, the way she always used to do when she was younger and more unsure of herself. 'If I don't, what am I gonna do? *Not* go to Harvard Business School?'

They smirked, both knowing that was impossible. Not with their parents.

She was twenty-five at the time. She tries to recall what her life had been like before arriving on the East Coast. Before she had tasted Sam Adams beer or heard the strange, open camber of the Boston accent, or found herself living in this close, crafted neighborhood, where everyone was white and the houses white and shuttered, too, and the lawns a rich green, and the plentiful trees boasted foliage that turned aflame in the autumn. Where social calendars hinged on multigenerational family barbecues and kids' sports leagues and summers at the beach and winter ski weekends in Vermont.

It seems strange that there had once been a time in her life when all she had ever known were the four other people in her family, her mom's stir-fry, and Southern California. When she hadn't even realized you could live outside Orange County, or would ever want to, with its balmy, year-round sun and its panoply of Asian restaurants. And yet, a few decades on and here she was, raising three boys, each different in their own way, with their brown hair darkening into adolescence, and her own jet-black hair now streaked unmistakably with gray. Married to a husband who was generous and ambitious and blue-eyed, but who had only ever visited California for cushy vacations or the occasional business conference – and had never once lived a life that was not buoyed by his own family's wealth and influence.

What could Chris possibly understand about her parents, who had emigrated as skinny, studious, nervous twentysomethings to a country where they hardly spoke the language, where they had no relatives, no inroads, virtually no cultural understanding? And somehow, from those improbable beginnings, they had carved out a life, acquired savings and a four-bedroom house with a yard in which to raise their own three children.

Children who then – as soon as they reached adulthood – had moved as far away as possible.

A premature sense of loss ripens within her as she considers a framed photo on her oakwood desk. Her and her siblings in childhood, Mom and Dad, all of them with arms around each other, grinning in front of their house in California. It was taken just after they had moved into that house, which had seemed so new and pristine, with rooms that were vacant, waiting to be filled with furniture and belongings and decades of family life.

She thinks about that house now, home to only her two parents, growing feebler by the years. And yet her mom has kept each of their teenage bedrooms in a state of semi-preservation, ready for her children's return.

'Mom, you know you can repurpose our rooms into something else if you want. Turn one into a study for you, or a painting studio maybe.' Bonnie had said this a year after Henry was born, when they had come to visit her parents.

'You never know, there might be some emergency!' Her mom shook her head, adamant. 'What if Kevin loses his job, or Chris gets injured and can't help you with Henry, or Alex gets into another accident? I want you to know, you will always have a place to stay here.'

'Yeah, but Chris's parents can help with Henry, or they'll hire help . . .' Bonnie began. Then she trailed off, wondering if that might make her mom feel irrelevant, replaced.

'You never know when you might need to come home,' Mom had insisted.

What Bonnie wanted to tell her (but didn't have the heart to), was that maybe California no longer was her home. Maybe that locus had somehow shifted, over time, to Massachusetts.

So those bedrooms had remained largely empty over the decades, only filled a handful of times each year if she or Kevin came home – and at Christmas, the only possible time all three siblings would converge on the family home. In recent years, those annual Christmas gatherings had petered out, too. After she and Kevin had their own kids, they began alternating their Christmases between sets of parents. Then Kevin and Alex had had their feud – and they made sure never to spend the same Christmas in California.

And that dreaded emergency their mother foresaw had never happened – until now.

A twinge of sadness pricks her as she realizes the irony of it all. The ingratitude that she and her siblings have shown, leaving their parents on their own in that California house, thousands of miles from the children they sacrificed so much for.

Was that the inevitable road parenthood sent you down?

That you would invest your all into sustaining these small creatures, raising them into adulthood – but they were always destined to forget you, move on to the excitement of their own

45

lives and only visit you occasionally, when obligated. When you fell into a stroke and could barely communicate.

Bonnie instinctively looks out the window to check on her three sons, romping around in their verdant backyard. Henry, the oldest, taps a soccer ball into place so Milo can kick it. Max, the middle child, rests alone in the shade of the big willow, throwing stones absently into the pond.

She wonders when these three will forget about her and charge ahead into the future, consumed only by their own lives. Hopefully, she still has a few more years with them.

Bonnie hears a sudden shout from below, and sees Chris striding toward the three boys. They all rush together, Chris's blond hair shining in the sun, contrasted with the dark brown of her sons'. As he tells them something, Milo jumps with excitement. In another moment, the three boys, in their gangly, uneven way, run en masse into the house, hollering.

What is it? What did Chris tell them?

Bonnie pokes her head into the hallway and hears the boys rampaging up the stairs toward her.

'Mom! Mom!' Henry is shouting.

Within seconds, Max has barreled into her, Milo wrapping his arms around her knees.

'Is it true?' Milo clamors. 'Dad said you figured out your whole plan for your trip!'

'Are you really gonna *drive* across the whole country?' Max shouts, his arms stretched up high in disbelief. 'Can you do that?'

''Course I can,' Bonnie answers with a smile.

'Are you driving to see Ama?' Henry asks, concern marking his too-adult face. 'Is she still in the hospital?'

'Well, she's going back in for an operation,' Bonnie says, trying to sound upbeat.

'Is Uncle Kevin going with you?'

'First, I'm driving to Uncle Kevin's in Chicago, and then we'll drive together to California to see Ama and Agong. Auntie Alex is joining us, too.'

'Wow,' Milo's eyes are round, disbelieving. 'All the way from London! Daddy was a little worried about it. He says it's a lot of driving for you.'

Bonnie smirks, brushing away a shred of annoyance at hearing this. 'Daddy doesn't need to worry about me. I know how to handle a car.'

'Which car are you taking?' Henry asks. 'The SUV? Because we need that to get to baseball practice.'

'The Lexus has better suspension,' Max offers. He's the one who knows his cars.

'I'll probably rent a car,' Bonnie answers. 'Then I get to pick whatever car I want.'

'Can we see where you're gonna drive?' Milo asks.

But Max has already taken a road atlas down from the bookshelf and opened it to a double-paged spread of the contiguous forty-eight states. He places it in Bonnie's hands. 'Show us.'

Bonnie can't help but grin, and she sits on the thick cream carpet, the atlas in front of her and her three sons gathered around, leaning on her. Their restless energy permeating from their limbs into her own.

She had glanced at a map the night before. But now she is curious to see Route 66 laid out before her in full: the intended route from here to her parents. It seems so improbable that she could simply get into a car here on the East Coast, and with enough time and gasoline, drive all the way across the continent to Irvine, California. Like a board game, but writ large. Her actions no longer reduced to the size of half-inch playing pieces.

'Okay, where's Massachusetts? Milo, can you show us where we are?'

A moment's pause, and his small index finger finds its way to the crooked boot of Cape Cod, then up to the encircled star that is Boston.

'Very good.' Bonnie squeezes Milo's shoulder. 'So then we look for . . . Route 90, and we follow that all . . . the . . . way . . . across to New York and then down through Pennsylvania . . .'

Her finger traces the thick blue line of the interstate, past imagined towns and fields, over state borders.

'. . . Ohio . . .' Milo says.

'. . . Michigan . . .' Max continues.

'. . . over to Chicago!' Henry cheers.

'Yes!' Bonnie jabs the large star fixed on the western shore of Lake Michigan. 'And I'll meet Uncle Kevin there. And probably return the rental car. And then we're gonna drive all . . . the . . . way . . . down this highway.' Without her reading glasses, she squints at the paper.

'The 55,' she continues. 'To St. Louis. And then we'll probably take . . . this highway through Missouri.'

'And then through Oklahoma?'

'No, go through Kansas, Mom!'

'I don't – I don't think there's anything to see in Kansas, Max.'

'Go to Oklahoma! Tell us what it's like!' Milo is shouting, rocking back and forth on her shoulder.

'Well, if we go to Oklahoma, we can also go through Texas,' she explains.

'Whoa, Texas.' Henry's eyes open wide.

'What's wrong with Texas?' Milo asks.

'There's nothing wrong with Texas.' Bonnie puts on her cheery voice, deciding to steer clear of politics.

'There's *a lot* wrong with Texas,' Henry corrects her.

'Have *you* ever been there, Henry?' Bonnie asks.

'No, but I don't have to go to know,' Henry states with confidence. 'They still have the death penalty. Everyone owns guns—'

'Everyone owns guns?!' Milo asks in awe. 'How cool is that!' He spins off, cradling an imaginary machine gun in his hands and targeting Bonnie's framed diplomas. 'Pyew-pyew-pyew!'

'Well, it's not very cool if you're driving through the state unarmed,' Bonnie counters back. 'Probably kinda scary.'

'Then why do you want to go there?' Henry asks.

'Maybe I'm curious.' Bonnie shrugs. 'Plus, it's the fastest way to the West Coast.' She continues on, her finger demarcating the I-40. 'Then probably into New Mexico, and then into Arizona, where we'll stop and see the Grand Canyon. And then . . . all the way to California, where Ama and Agong live.'

She taps the greater conurbation of Los Angeles, recalling the familiar press of freeways, shopping centers, and suburban subdivisions sprawled over the dry brown hills.

'Wow,' Max breathes out. 'That's a long trip.'

'I guess, but your Uncle Kevin, Auntie Alex, and I will take turns driving. So we won't get too tired. And it's important to see Ama right now.'

'That's very good of you, driving all the way across the country to see her,' Henry says this, stroking her hair. Bonnie grins, absorbing this compliment from her own son.

'She is my mom, you know.' Then she pauses. 'If *I* were to get really sick one day, would *you* boys drive all the way across the country to see me?'

The three of them find this funny and dissolve into laughter.

'Only if I get to drive a great big truck!' Milo shouts.

'You won't get that sick.' Max rolls his eyes.

'Of course we would,' Henry answers, ever responsible.

'I hope so,' Bonnie says. 'Otherwise I'd be very sad.' Then she wonders if she's piling on the guilt too much already, as a mother.

'But there's one thing I'd definitely make sure of, if I were doing a trip like that,' Max asserts.

'What's that?' Bonnie asks, her hand cradling his cheek.

'If *I* were going to Texas,' his voice curls upward, speaking with twelve-year-old authority. 'I would definitely be bringing a gun.'

* * *

Alex stands and bends to stretch her right hip while surveying the packing she has laid out on her bed. Shoes: trendy sneakers, hiking shoes, flip-flops, Tevas. That should be enough footwear, but then she debates if she should bring a pair of 'nice shoes' in case they have to go somewhere looking presentable. Then again, what does 'nice shoes' mean to a lesbian like her?

Until recently, she still owned the odd pair of ballerina flats, the last remnant of feminine footwear after slowly, gleefully weeding out all the pumps and stilettos over the years. Gone are the days of having to totter around on high heels, the leather rim of some shoe biting into the skin of her heel, the balls of her feet aching in agony after a few hours in torturous footwear. The shoe industry has a lot to answer for, a massive billion-dollar conspiracy designed to shame women into hobbling themselves for the sake of fashion. But this is what progress looks like. Her female ancestors had had their feet bound up and disfigured so they could appear more ladylike. Fast-forward a century and now liberated Western women were earning large paychecks and spending them on designer heels that similarly

50

mutilated their feet to appease the male gaze. There you had it: capitalism and patriarchy, the twin evils of our time.

If there's one detail she loves about being out as a lesbian, it's no longer having to pretend. No longer having to torment yourself with high heels because they were seen as the appropriate thing to wear to a function. No longer having to put on mascara, bending forward to painstakingly coat individual eyelashes with ink so they didn't clump, so you could take it all off hours later with a cucumber-scented facial wipe.

She didn't mind dressing up for the stage, though. It's been years since she last put on makeup as an actor, but she can still recall the excitement in the pit of her stomach, the pre-stage jitters as she sat in the greenroom before a performance, trying to concentrate on the ritual of her makeup: foundation, blush, eyeliner, eye shadow, mascara, lipstick.

Stage makeup was always heightened. Larger than life. The audience needed to see your face accentuated, to fully absorb the emotions you were trying to project.

What Alex liked – in fact, missed – about acting was the acknowledgment of the artifice. She wore stage makeup, and it was okay that it was exaggerated, because everyone understood it was a performance. You stepped into character and then you stepped out. And that was all expected. In real life, you were supposed to act as if all this artifice – the makeup and footwear and fashion – as if all this was normal, natural. The organic expression of your female personality (albeit a form of self-expression that cost a lot of money and demanded a lot of time). What a ridiculous con – and how liberating to no longer be deceived by that con. Male gaze, begone! Men were beside the point, irrelevant in her world now. They hardly ever factored into her thinking – and she didn't miss their presence one bit.

But now, with this return to the US, she was aware there

were two men she would have to interact with again. Two men who, despite everything, knew her very well: her brother Kevin and her own father.

Or did they really know her? How could Kevin know her and still say the awful things he'd shouted five years ago?

Even now she bristles with unspent fury, recalling his words.

She realizes that until then, her family had only ever seen the performed version of Alex, the 'straight' version she had pretended to be for so long.

But they had known her from the very beginning, before she had even had any understanding of straight or gay. Her father had held her in his hands when she was a screaming newborn, during her very first minutes in this world. Her brother had met her soon after. They had known her in her purest form. Surely they would recognize the integrity of the life she led now: free of playacting, free of artifice.

Surely, they would see that the Alex Chu now was the truest version of herself.

Alex is still contemplating her packing when Nya enters the room, her unruly hair heaped atop her head, even unrulier in pregnancy.

She glances at the packing-in-progress, the half-empty back-pack propped against the bed, and nods her approval.

'Looks good. Sure you didn't forget anything?'

Alex snorts. 'A giant American flag? A healthy dose of xeno-phobia?'

Nya speaks with mock disapproval, her London accent melt-ing into a faux American one. '*That* kind of attitude, young lady, will get you nowhere in the US of A.'

They share an amused look, and Alex recalls their visit to the US Embassy that morning, to renew her expired passport. Nya was curious and wanted to accompany her, so the two of them had stood at the foot of that shiny, futuristic silver building, staring up at an unnecessarily large American flag that flapped in the breeze above them. Also unnecessary (she thought) were the burly security guards, clad in black military gear, carrying semiautomatic rifles. They were efficiently friendly, they even had American accents, but Alex felt distinctly uncomfortable with the tip of that deadly weapon mere inches from Nya's pregnant belly.

Yet forty minutes later, there she was with her emergency American passport safe in her hands. She touches the passport now as it sits on her bed, the US seal emblazoned in gold on the navy cover. Ah, all the untold privileges borne by that small blue booklet. Possessing it allowed one to traverse borders unchallenged, escape danger, access jobs and opportunities, elect a supposedly influential world leader – in a way that another person, born in another country, couldn't. These undeserved, arbitrary privileges.

'Am I really ready for this?' She turns to Nya. 'Driving through all these flyover states? With my homophobic brother?'

Nya shrugs, offers the warm, wise advice Alex always craves. 'Maybe he's not as homophobic as you think. Besides, it's travel, baby. It's what you do best.'

Alex's enthusiasm lifts, coupled with the somber realization that this may be her last bout of travel for the foreseeable future. Her last chance to discover the unknown, even if it's the scary backwater of her native country. Meanwhile, this new unknown, the one that looms ahead of her with Nya's growing belly . . . Alex shudders internally, trying to quell those thoughts.

She turns to her suitcase, picks up a pair of ankle boots. Ones that would constitute 'nice shoes,' but which add another two pounds to her baggage. Twenty-two years of solo travel have told her to always, always keep her baggage to a minimum.

Travel light. Walk freer.

'Screw the nice shoes,' she says, and tosses the boots to the side. They land with a satisfying thump.

She feels lighter already.

* * *

And just like that, Bonnie is off.

Her right foot pedals the gas of a shiny new rental car as she guns down the Massachusetts Turnpike, speeding away from suburban Boston, away from that spacious house surrounded by the maple trees and lawn and lake. Away from her three spirited sons and her less-spirited husband, toward her ageing parents on the other side of the continent.

There is an undeniable feeling of freedom as she switches deftly into the fast lane of the interstate. An escape of sorts. But can you really call it escape if you're leaving one place of family responsibility to return to another?

She glances at the screen of her GPS: a highlighted red line snaking down a pixilated highway, her car denoted simply by a triangular arrowhead, inching along.

Again, the abstraction of her journey is what strikes her. That you can do this so simply. Alex was right: get in a car, turn on the ignition, press down on a pedal – and be on your way; a five-thousand-mile journey back to the place you once called home. Shifting from adulthood back to some strange approximation of her childhood life, with its well-worn family dynamics, a familiar journey she needs no map for.

Chris laughed when he saw the sports car she had rented, but why not? What he doesn't know is that last year, Bonnie had enrolled in a tactical driving course, just for fun. Or maybe just to prove him wrong about her driving. It was something she did on a weekend, claiming it was a girls' trip, when secretly she was learning how to do J-turns and swerves. She could think of no better thrill, the car responding deftly to her slightest touch, the power that roared alive with a simple tap of the gas. She was the only woman taking the course; the others were young men and doughy middle-aged men, seeking some fun in their boring suburban lives. They stared at her, this petite Asian woman who delighted in being behind the wheel. And for once in her life, she didn't care. It felt like the kind of impulsive thing Alex would have done.

The GPS issues a vocal command in a competent female voice.

'Stay on Highway 90 for one hundred and fifty-seven miles.'

One hundred and fifty-seven miles it is.

And then Bonnie realizes she doesn't need to follow any commands or instructions for now. It's a straight shot ahead. All she has to do is reach Chicago by tomorrow night. How thrilling to think that between now and then, she can do whatever she wants. She can veer completely off-path if she wants. She can stop overnight in Buffalo and talk to men at a bar, try to remember what it was like to once be single. The road is hers, wherever she decides to take it.

Kevin pushes open the screen door of his house, his eye on the white mail truck slowly making the rounds of their quiet suburban street. Midmorning and his commuting neighbors have left already. So, too, has Jessica, driving off in her silver Camry with hardly a word after he announced he was working from home today.

He'll do the office thing tomorrow, his final day before the trip. Glad-handing with the guys, a catch-up with the boss, showing the requisite despondency for his mom's medical condition, playing the good, responsible, grown-up son. No one at work knows about the Route 66 plans, and he prefers to keep it that way.

The mail truck drives off from their house, the mailman offering a hearty wave, which Kevin returns. Still wearing his pajamas, he shuffles in his outdoor slippers down the front path to their mailbox.

As always, the unease that weighs his stomach every time the mail arrives these days.

He flicks through the envelopes. Gas bill, phone and broadband bill, home insurance. (Heck, they all decided to arrive today.) An advertisement for a Christian fundraising event, another for a senior living facility.

And that's it. Not the envelope he'd been dreading.

He breathes a sigh of relief but knows it's only temporary. Another letter is bound to arrive soon, and most likely, when he's away on the trip. The unease churns quietly at the back of his mind.

Before heading back into the house, Kevin turns and looks out at their neighborhood, the homes hushed during the day, the green lawns yet to feel the full blast of summer this year. This street, which feels like a trap in its own way, each brown-brick house and triangular peaked roof smothering the lives within. He's glad to be escaping, if only for a short while.

Bonnie will arrive tomorrow evening. She's probably en route right now, cruising down the interstate. The kids and even Jessica were excited to hear she'd be staying the night before they set off on their trip. But Arabella was strangely disappointed to learn they wouldn't also see Auntie Alex, their 'cool auntie.'

Kevin grimaces at his daughter's phrase. Sure, Alex was always 'cool.' And always irresponsible.

Yet even *he* felt a sharp bitterness at this news.

'Alex said she was gonna stay with friends in town,' Bonnie had explained. 'We'll meet her in downtown Chicago with the car and pick her up at the start of the drive.'

Too cool to even see her brother's family, then.

'You know, you could have invited her,' Bonnie said, as if reading his mind.

Kevin scoffed. 'I haven't gotten a direct message from her in years. Why should I?'

Bonnie said nothing for a moment, just breathed her judgmental silence. 'Honestly, I can't believe you guys are in your forties and still acting like this. Grow up.'

But it was Alex who needed to grow up.

Kevin enters the house, kicks off his outdoor slippers, and sinks into the corner of their off-white leather couch. (Jessica had insisted on off-white, and for eight years, he has lived in perpetual fear of spilling something on it – and the resulting tantrum from Jessica.)

He thinks for a moment about his younger sister. What does he actually know about her now?

She moved to London almost twenty years ago, ostensibly to

take some summer course at a fancy British drama school. But then she never moved back. Alex with her pretentious, artsy airs, which she'd had throughout their childhood. She was always drawing and painting, bold and colorful stuff, which grew angry and vigorous as time went on. When she was eleven and Kevin was thirteen, she'd made him sit down for an hour so she could paint him for her school art assignment. It was the most boring hour he could imagine; she wouldn't even let him turn his head or scratch his back or other body parts (he was in the height of puberty here). To make the time pass, he'd had to angle his body in order to obliquely watch some idiotic episode of *Power Rangers* (a show he'd always hated: of course the Yellow Power Ranger had to be the Asian one). Then at the end of the hour, Alex had proudly handed him the thick piece of paper she'd been slaving over, and there he was: thirteen-year-old Kevin Chu, rendered in vivid strokes of orange and blue, appearing glum, a furious scowl on his face. It wasn't flattering in the least, as if Picasso had decided to paint a nerdy Asian kid slumped in the corner. And yet, as much as he hated to admit it, the portrait did somehow capture some element of him – the insecure, sullen part.

'Are you fucking *kidding* me?' he had seethed, so angry he even dared to use the f-word as an adolescent.

Alex was surprised, the pride on her face suddenly shriveling to hurt. 'What do you mean? I-I thought it was good?'

'It's terrible!' he'd shouted. 'It doesn't look anything like me! I had to sit still for an hour so you could make *that*?!'

But just then Bonnie had entered the room, took one look at the homemade portrait, and burst out laughing at how un-cannily accurate it was. Alex's mood turned back to pride. And then, of course, Bonnie had to show their parents, and what had originally been an opportunity for Kevin to shame Alex about her artistic delusions was now another chance for their whole family to celebrate Alex's 'talent' – and somehow, along with it, mock Kevin's own awkward appearance.

That very portrait later won Alex first place in a regional art competition, and it hung in their school lobby for weeks, so their entire student population could jeer at it, jocks and popular kids pointing and saying, 'Hey, that's Kevin Chu!' before collapsing into giggles. He'd hated Alex even more for that: for ensuring the hell of his daily public humiliation.

But even after the school year ended, there was no escaping that portrait.

Eventually, their mom framed it – *framed it*, as if it were some masterpiece you'd buy in a gallery – and hung it above the landing in their staircase, so that every damn houseguest would see it, and their mom could gloat, 'Oh, Alex was only eleven when she painted that portrait of Kevin. She won first place in a big competition . . .'

As an adult, on visits to his parents' house, Kevin would still be confronted with that painful adolescent version of himself, whenever he climbed the stairs on the way to his childhood bedroom. He wished he could tell that boy to stop sulking so much, that life wasn't so bad: he would graduate from school eventually, he would find girls to date, and even marry one. Things would get better someday. But then he remembered that being thirteen *had* been that awful.

So there he was, a grown man, unable to escape that visual reminder of how miserable he'd been decades earlier.

And he only had his precocious younger sister to thank for it.

And where was Alex now, with her preternatural artistic gifts? She'd gone to London and never returned. Their parents had probably wasted thousands on her British drama course. She'd never become an actress – or at least had any notable career.

(Kevin remembered Alex mentioning a TV commercial she'd shot once, and some fringe theater shows, where she never seemed to get paid for her acting.) She'd never sold any paintings or drawings – or even managed to turn that into a reliable career like graphic design.

No, Alex had never been sensible, but that's because their parents had let her get away with being artsy and impractical. For all he knew, they had been funding her ridiculous transatlantic life for years – maybe they still were. Meanwhile, he and Bonnie had had to get normal jobs like everybody else, placate their bosses, and save up their vacation days. Grow old without luxuriating in monthlong backpacking trips, which Alex seemed to do every other year in her twenties.

So yes, he'd always been resentful. Mom and Dad had encouraged Alex's artistic whims, sending her to music camp, to art camp, buying her expensive art sets for Christmas, while he got boring polo shirts and had to become a doctor – and he had failed at that. At least Kevin had sucked up his failures and become a responsible adult. But Alex?

Such little gratitude she'd shown them. Disappearing off to London and never coming back. Everything was always an experiment for her, nothing ever permanent. So yeah, announcing she was a lesbian was probably just a phase for her, an excuse for all her failed relationships, her inability to land a boyfriend, which had always caused Mom to worry.

What did we do wrong? they once asked him. *She's smart, she's talented. Why Alex still single?*

You did nothing wrong, he wanted to tell them. *It's just Alex.*

Alex. Always attention-seeking, never reliable. He remembers now: a specific image of Alex when she was eight, under the desert sun. A ball of misguided energy, howling to the sky. He bets she howls the same way, even now.

1991, Somewhere in Arizona

Kevin is never exactly sure what happened that afternoon. It sits like an unspoken void, occupying the space of that aborted vacation, obscuring any clear view of the past. To him, it seemed like no big deal, just one of those strange, unpleasant occurrences that happens when you venture out into the world, a flinty collision with unpleasant people. But no more than that.

It was only later, when he thought about it, that the unspoken significance of that afternoon dawned on him. He remembered Mom and Dad had been excited about visiting the Grand Canyon for weeks. They'd checked out a library book, which he'd seen Dad perusing from time to time – it sat on the living room table for a while.

They were excited to visit – and then, suddenly, mere hours from actually arriving there, they'd decided to turn around. And they had been close, hadn't they? He remembers Dad driving the car, pointing to a sign and saying cheerfully, 'Grand Canyon, we're almost there!'

Kevin had been very, very bored that entire day. Las Vegas had been exciting, with all the flashing lights; the hotel they'd stayed in, so high, so many levels up on the elevator; and at the top, the incredible view of all the other casinos and strip malls and houses; and receding into the distance, the highways and the palm trees and the low brown hills under the bright blue sky. There were so many things to see and so many people, and all of them so different: tall Black people and fat white people, large families who spoke Spanish and occasionally some very pretty women with long blond hair, so perfect looking that he couldn't stop staring. From time to time he might see some other Asian people, other families who seemed as clueless and lost as Mom and Dad were.

They walked around the casinos at night, when the heat had cooled down. And ate food at a loud, bright restaurant, after which he'd fallen asleep to the lights of Las Vegas casting their flickering colors into the hotel room. (They all stayed in one room. Mom and Dad in one bed, Bonnie and Alex in the other. And he got the fold-out cot that creaked and groaned when you sat down on it and shifted your weight.) But he didn't mind because he got to sleep the closest to the window, staring out at all the twinkling lights of Las Vegas, silent from all the way up here, but still the gold, green, red flashing upward and back down in sequence.

But that was Vegas, and the next day, they bundled back into the station wagon and entered what seemed like a totally different planet.

He can't remember how long they'd been driving for. Because he kept sliding in and out of sleep. Everything blended into each other. He'd wake up and see a flat, dry landscape, and fall asleep, and wake up who knows how much later, and seem to see the same exact landscape again. In and out of that dreamlike fugue state, and the only thing to mark the passage of time was the sun climbing higher in the sky and his steadily filling bladder.

By the time they reached the gas station, he was ready to burst.

He didn't know why Dad was taking so long to fill up the gas and pay for it. 'C'mon, c'mon, Dad. Just hurry up.'

When he finally stepped out of the car, the desert heat hit him full in the face. Mom and Dad had actually turned on the air conditioner inside the car, instead of trying to save money by making them boil. But now, he was exposed to the elements, the sun was strong, the dust sifted into his nostrils.

But his bladder. That trumped everything.

Eventually – finally – four of them left to use the bathroom. Heading toward that faded brown building, with the painted sign creaking in the desert breeze. The two men on the doorstep glared weirdly, almost seemed to grin, as they drew closer.

He remembers looking back, seeing Alex in the car on her own. The car looked so small, dwarfed by the vast, flat land-scape. And Alex looked smaller still. She was just a face, barely recognizable, pressed faintly against the glass of the back-seat window.

He stuck his tongue out at her and kept walking.

Chicago, Illinois

'Hey!' Kevin shouts, his face lighting up. 'How was the drive?'

Bonnie is standing there on his doorstep. Maybe a few more gray hairs and a few more lines around her eyes, but otherwise the same as always. Pretty, tastefully dressed, in control.

'It was good.' Bonnie smiles. 'First time I've done a long drive like that on my own. Kinda liberating, in a way.'

He can imagine. But what would Bonnie ever need to be liberated *from*? A suffocating life of material luxury?

Jessica crowds in behind him and shouts a warm hello to Bonnie. She's very good at maintaining an exterior civility, even though she can be lethal at home.

'Can I get you something to drink? Juice? Water? Beer? Musta been a long two days of driving.'

But Kevin can sense his wife always assessing Bonnie, envying her tasteful designer clothes, the ease and confidence that comes with her wealth. Thinking what did Bonnie do right to end up so fortunate? And concluding that it must have been who she married; she didn't pick some chump like Kevin.

He's grateful when Jessica retreats to fetch Bonnie an orange juice. Just then, he notices the glossy Chevy Camaro parked in the driveway. Black, sleek, sporty. Very unlike Bonnie.

'Wait, is *that* your rental car?' he shrieks, cracking up with laughter.

'Pretty crazy, isn't it?' Bonnie cackles. 'It was only a two-day rental, so why the hell not.'

'No way, what a cool car!' Brian shouts, tumbling out from the hallway.

Arabella follows suit, and the two of them barrel into Bonnie. 'Auntie Bonnie! Auntie Bonnie! You're here!'

'Hey look, my favorite niece and nephew! You two are so grown-up!' Bonnie, of course, is good at everything – and this extends to pleasing kids, too. She always comes armed with gift-wrapped presents – thoughtful, well-made clothes and toys for the kids from some pricey boutique – and she hasn't failed this time.

As she unpacks the children's gifts from the trunk of her rental car, Arabella clings to her aunt's legs, a babyish gesture she hasn't done to her own parents in ages.

'Why isn't Auntie Alex coming, too?'

'Oh, she . . . she couldn't make it.' Bonnie raises her eyebrows pointedly at Kevin. 'She was flying in a long way from London to get here. And we have to leave early tomorrow, but I know she wanted to see you guys.'

'Who's Auntie Alex?' Brian asks again. Kevin realizes with some guilt that Brian was only two the last time he met her. And he's barely mentioned her to the kids since.

Bonnie is shaking her head in disapproval at Kevin, but he ignores her and changes the subject.

'Hey, how's it feel to drive this thing?' Kevin strokes the hood of the Camaro. He imagines sitting behind that wheel, low to the ground, ready to floor the accelerator.

'Badass. Amazing pickup. Made it really easy to pass other

cars on the highway.' She smirks. 'Hey, you wanna have a spin? You can drive it to the rental office.'

'Really? No way!' Suddenly he's fifteen again, and his sister is letting him get behind the wheel in an empty parking lot outside a Southern California shopping center.

'Yeah, so long as you don't crash it. I only registered one driver when I rented it.'

'Awesome! After that, you're gonna have to make do with my Mazda for the rest of the road trip. It'll be a step down. But it has good fuel efficiency,' he teases her.

Bonnie stops to appraise his Mazda CX-5 parked in the driveway. Royal blue, a respectable compact SUV with off-road capabilities he's never used. Cleared now of all the junk that kids accrue inside a car, and waiting to serve as their chariot to the West Coast.

'A Mazda, huh,' Bonnie runs with it. 'I can slum it from time to time, you know.'

They look at each other and laugh.

* * *

The air pressure builds in her ears as the cabin staff make their final announcements. Alex leans forward to catch a glimpse of the Chicago skyline: a cluster of skyscrapers silhouetted against the clouds, the sprawl of the city covering the shore of Lake Michigan. They approach it over the glistening stretch of water, like the opening shot of a Hollywood film.

Here it is: the metropolis. Seen from this height, it appears like a child's playset, but there is still something impressive about the city: how neat and shiny these buildings are, how optimistic in claiming the lakeshore and striving upward. Shooting straight up from the ground, as if those skyscrapers had always been rooted there, commanding the western edge of this vast lake.

Alex tries to imagine the lakeshore in an earlier time, before these buildings, before this great conurbation had taken root. She recently read that the 'Founder of Chicago,' its first known non-Indigenous permanent settler, was a trader of African descent.

'See!' She'd pointed this fact out eagerly to Nya, hoping to somehow prove her country wasn't so racist, knowing how slightly pathetic this made her seem to her Black wife.

But the founding of Chicago had taken place over two centuries ago. The shore was no longer pristine and unsullied. And a lot had changed in America since then.

She tries to imagine what it will be like to bring a Black daughter into this world. To introduce her to Chicago, then explain there are parts of America she'd be safer avoiding. But she still can't even see herself as a mother, as a person responsible for protecting another, more fragile life. She hardly feels capable of protecting her own.

How does Bonnie do it? How did her mother do it?

Alex has never been a mothering type. But is parenthood somehow instinctual? A natural behavior that just kicks in once your child enters this world?

Only one thing has ever felt natural to Alex. And that is travel. She loves the in-between state. The getting from one point to another, staring out the plane or train window and watching the landscape unspool. Not having to be anywhere just yet. She stares at the Chicago cityscape wheeling beneath them, and she has to admit: it's the arriving that always seems most daunting.

* * *

'Where are we meeting her again?' Kevin asks this as he fiddles with the GPS on his Mazda. It's midmorning the next day, and Bonnie sits next to him in the passenger seat, their suitcases packed in the trunk.

'The Sheraton Grand downtown. Think it's right on the river,' Bonnie answers. She has told him that at least three times before, but as with her own husband, it seems she needs to repeat a message multiple times before it actually sinks in.

'Whoo, fancy,' Kevin says. 'She stayed with a friend, right? I can't imagine she can afford the Sheraton.' Bonnie ignores this dig at Alex, as she watches his ungainly index finger jab at the GPS keyboard on the screen, S-H-E-R-A-T-O-N. Impatient, Bonnie almost wants to wrest it away from him, but they are at the mercy of the Garmin navigation technology and its leisurely pace.

They wait as the GPS calculates the route and drive time.

'Woo-hoo, only forty-three minutes. Great!' Kevin seems unnaturally cheery, given they're going to meet Alex.

'Wow, why are *you* so excited?' she teases him.

Kevin shrugs as he reverses out his driveway, his eyes squarely on the screen in front of him, displaying the rearview camera. 'Oh, I dunno, a chance to get away?'

'From them?' Bonnie gestures to Jessica, Arabella, Brian, and Jessica's mother, who have dutifully lined up in front of the house to wave them goodbye. She grins and waves back, and wishes her brother would acknowledge his own family, too.

But Kevin swerves the car eagerly into the street, ready to hit the road. Finally, he rolls down the window.

'Bye! Love you guys! I'll call you tonight!'

She notices he doesn't say any names, doesn't single them out one by one. Just a generalized sort of goodbye for everyone.

'Send us photos!' Brian shouts.

'Bye, Dad!' Arabella says.

'Drive safely!' Jessica calls.

Jessica's mother remains silent, smiling and waving stiffly like a dignitary at a function.

Kevin hits the button to close his window, steps on the gas, and they speed down the road.

He grins at Bonnie, as the car hits thirty miles per hour in a residential zone.

'Yeah,' he answers her question finally. 'Freedom from them. I love 'em, but god, do I need a break.'

Speeding down the I-90, it occurs to Bonnie how unusual it is that she and Kevin are in similar positions right now: secretly delighted to be away from their families and homes, reveling in this unusual sense of midlife liberty.

How come we were never warned about this?

She grew up wanting to get married and have children. Bonnie can't remember these words ever being spoken to her as a directive, but somehow, as if by osmosis, she absorbed an understanding that her life was meant to follow this pattern.

What did little girls learn to chant?

First comes love, then comes marriage, then comes a baby in a baby carriage.

She recalls blank pieces of paper being folded up by nine-year-old hands, little girls pressing and creasing with their fingers to create some makeshift fortune-telling device, which divulged your future to you like a mystical mouthpiece. Ballpoint pens scrawled names of boys you might marry, numbers to indicate how many children you'd have, and then your four options for a future home: mansion, apartment, shack, house.

And next, the giggling as your fate was read out.

You will marry Christopher Prescott. You will have three

children. You will live in a very large house. Some might say a mansion. In Massachusetts.

There is no way her preadolescent self, living in Southern California, could have predicted any of that. She would not travel to Massachusetts for the first time until she was twenty-three. She would not meet Chris Prescott until she was twenty-five. All the years in between would have concealed her destiny.

And yet, here she was with her brother by her side, still four years younger than her, but decades older since their last trip together. Speeding down a highway to escape their spouses and children. Homing back to their ageing parents like world-weary pigeons, winging through the open sky.

Kevin grunts as he flicks through the radio stations, scanning for an agreeable song.

A familiar whine flashes out – and Bonnie, recognizing it, shoots out a hand.

'No wait, go back, go back!' she shouts.

'What, Counting Crows? Really?' Kevin grimaces, even though he secretly wants to hear the song, too.

'Oh, come on, those were my formative teen years right there!'

'I know. You sang that practically every morning, getting ready. Man, I hated it.' Kevin shudders.

'Oh, and what do you listen to now?' Bonnie asks archly. She gestures to the radio. 'Go ahead, find something you want to hear.'

Kevin ignores her and responds by pressing harder on the accelerator. The RPM dial jumps to three, then settles down.

Bonnie grins, teasing. 'I remember that time you bought this Tupac CD and Mom was furious. "Don't listen to that kind of music! Then you become bad! Then you stop doing your homework!"' She imitates their mother's Taiwanese accent.

Kevin can't help laughing. 'God, she nearly grounded me for buying that. As if listening to rap equals criminal degeneracy.'

Bonnie shakes her head and leans back in her seat, seeing green highway signs and concrete barriers flit past.

'Do you know she even asked me if some boys were being a bad influence on you at school, making you listen to rap music... Because clearly, Tupac was the gateway to dealing heroin and going to jail.'

'God, Mom could be so sheltered and prejudiced all at the same time.'

A silence settles upon them as they listen to the familiar music of their adolescence, undercut by the car tires speeding over asphalt. Bonnie watches the Chicago skyline approaching in their windshield, her thoughts on Alex. She's seen photos of Alex and her wife; but she's the only one in the family who knows Nya is Black. She is aware it's not her place to tell anyone else. Alex would be furious.

So Bonnie talks more obliquely, wondering aloud and hoping for a comment from Kevin.

'Somehow, I think Mom and Dad are just scared of what's unknown to them. I mean, when have they ever really interacted with lesbians before, or Black people?' She pauses to consider this. Chris they could accept, because he was white and elite, the perfect poster boy for all-American success. 'So with Alex, I wonder if there's some way we can make it easier for them to accept... where she is right now.'

'And where is that? A failed actress in London?'

'Oh, come on, Kevin. It's not her fault there were like zero roles for Asian actresses in London.'

'Not exactly the smartest choice of career then, huh?'

Can't he be kind for once? 'In case you missed it, she's got an actual job now, does communications for a domestic violence charity. So she speaks to the press and runs workshops. I think that's how she met her partner.'

'What, was her partner a charity case?'

'Fuck off, Kevin! Her partner works with women escaping abusive relationships.'

Kevin has gone quiet. She can't read the expression in his eyes, which remain fixed on the road.

'I dunno,' he finally says after a minute. 'I mean, Alex leads her own weird life. If Mom and Dad have trouble accepting it, that's Alex's problem, right? What's that got to do with us?'

Bonnie flinches at his coldness, and stares at her brother. Why has he always been so uncaring toward Alex?

'Well, we *are* her siblings. And Mom and Dad are a different generation—'

Kevin huffs. 'Listen, Alex gets herself into these situations. She's been doing this her whole life. And I don't see why you always feel like you have to protect her, like, step in and mediate between her and Mom and Dad. I mean, she's forty now. She can take care of herself.'

'Jesus, Kevin – a *situation*?' She forgot how much of a prick he can be. 'This is Alex's life. Her partner for years now.' She steps carefully around the fact of their pregnancy. 'I mean, this is completely different from her getting a DUI—'

'Or that time Dad had to pick her up from that Pasadena house party in the middle of the night, or that time she nearly got suspended from college for her radical feminist art protest.'

'This is completely different. It's who she is!' As Bonnie shouts this, it dawns on her that maybe Alex's rebellious behavior as a teenager was some form of acting out about her sexual identity, her inability to fit in. 'Heck – maybe if Mom and Dad

72

were more open-minded at the time, Alex wouldn't have needed to hide who she was. She wouldn't have been so difficult.'

'Oh, for crying out loud. Are you blaming her behavior on, what, suppressed trauma about her sexual identity?' Kevin wheels the car angrily down an exit ramp, and it jerks to a stop at a red light. 'That is exactly what I fucking hate about this day and age. Everyone's given excuses because they're gay, or they're disabled, or some oppressed minority, or an immigrant or – I mean, look at us. Look at me. Mom and Dad came here as immigrants; I wasn't exactly the most popular kid growing up, but I'm not blaming my present-day woes on being Asian.'

'We grew up Asian in *Southern California*, Kevin,' Bonnie's voice is edged with annoyance. 'In Irvine. Which is fifty percent Asian. We weren't exactly an oppressed minority.'

'Okay whatever, but my point is: I made it through okay. No, I'm not ecstatic about the way my life's turned out, but I'm not gonna say it's all because I'm Asian and everyone's racist.'

'What does any of this have to do with Alex being gay?!' Bonnie glares at him, frustrated.

'I'm just tired of people claiming oppressed-minority status and blaming that on why their life turned out the way it did. You made bad choices, you fell asleep at the wheel. That's why life ends up the way it does. People have to own up to that.' Kevin says this as he powers the car through the final nanosecond of a yellow light. They are now somewhere in the middle of downtown Chicago, and Bonnie wonders how close the hotel is.

'Alex isn't claiming any of that,' Bonnie grumbles. 'Not that you'd even know because you don't even talk to her.'

'No, I don't,' Kevin proclaims. 'In fact, I don't even know what I have in common with her anymore.'

Suddenly, a disgusted rage floods through Bonnie. 'What do

you mean? You're her *fucking brother*!' She thumps her hand repeatedly against the glove compartment to emphasize each word.

Kevin slams on the brake in the middle of the road. The car behind them screeches to a halt and beeps angrily.

'What are you doing?' Bonnie hisses. The three cars behind them wheel into the righthand lane and pass. One of the drivers swears at them.

'Don't hit the glove compartment like that!' he seethes, furious. But there's a strange fear in his voice. Kevin glares wide-eyed at the closed lid beneath her hand, as if it contains something toxic.

'It's just a glove compartment,' Bonnie mutters, her anger giving way to confusion.

Kevin's shaking his head. 'It's what's inside.'

'What are you . . . ?'

And before Kevin can do anything, Bonnie releases the catch on the glove compartment. Inside is a strange black rectangular case. Ignoring Kevin's protests, she opens it, curious – and sucks her breath in when she sees, nestled inside, a handgun. She reaches out with a tentative finger, to make sure the gun is real. Her touch confirms it: the cold hardness of the metal makes her flinch with an implicit fear.

Bonnie stares in shock at her brother. 'You have a *fucking gun* in here?'

But Kevin doesn't need to answer, because she holds the answer in her own hands. Instead, his eyes look forward with a peculiar dread.

'We're here,' he says.

Bonnie follows his gaze out the windshield. Straight in front of them rises the gleaming tower of the Sheraton Grand, looming over the Chicago River.

'Let's go meet our sister,' Kevin pronounces with a flat solemnity.

'What — you're not gonna — ?' Bonnie splutters, the open handgun case in her lap, demanding an explanation.

'Put it *away*, Bonnie.' There's an authoritative edge in Kevin's voice. The hotel valets step forward to greet their car, and for once she listens to him.

'We are *not* done talking about this,' Bonnie says, as she returns the case to the glove compartment and snaps it closed.

A gun. Her own brother has a fucking gun. What kind of person has he become?

Kevin is still in shock when he pulls into the forecourt of the Sheraton Grand, scanning the ranks of uniformed valets and loitering tourists for a glimpse of Alex.

'Did she say she'd meet us out front?'

'Yeah. She should be right here.'

He hadn't expected Bonnie would find the gun *that* quickly. He'd planned to lock the glove compartment, but already he's feeling like he's been caught out by his older sister. A lifelong pattern, repeated. A mild annoyance yammers at him from one corner of his brain. The whole point of owning a gun is to feel powerful, like you can protect yourself, force your way through this world. But now that the gun's been discovered, in such rapid fashion – Kevin only feels exposed. Like he shouldn't be owning one in the first place.

The look of horror in his sister's eyes. And yes: of disgust. Even disappointment.

But what the fuck does she know, living her privileged life in an idyllic slice of the New England countryside? This is Chicago, you need a gun to be safe.

(Admittedly, it's been months since he set foot in downtown Chicago, but whatever.)

So far, in four years of gun ownership, he's never actually had a reason to use his revolver. He's taken it to shooting ranges from time to time. He was even invited by Brad Malloy to go hunting with his boys one weekend in Michigan. But that would have been rifles, and he made up an excuse, knowing how incompetent he'd feel in the woods with them.

A ghost of a childhood memory flashes out: a holstered gun

at the waist of a tall man striding toward him. And a complete sense of helplessness, paralyzed under a desert sun.

Kevin shakes the memory away.

The fact is, you never know when you might need a gun.

So better to be safe than sorry.

'Do you see her? She's right there.'

Bonnie rouses him from his reverie, and suddenly there is Alex standing in front of the car, a wide grin on her face. Jolted from his train of thought, he barely recognizes her at first. On the Zoom a few weeks ago, he'd noticed her short haircut. But now he sees it's really gone, the long black hair she's worn all her life. And she's dressed like a guy: white T-shirt, black jeans, some kind of ugly shoes that Jessica would have laughed at.

He tries not to frown. Why the hell would Alex deliberately want to look like this?

Yet she seems happy, freer and bolder. Or maybe that's just because Mom and Dad aren't around.

Kevin observes all of this from the driver's seat, watching as Bonnie wraps Alex in an excessive hug, their words muted. She then points inside the car, at him. Kevin gives a forced smile and waves through the windshield. Alex smirks, raises her palm in an ironic gesture, like an Indian chief saying 'How' in some outdated TV show.

He pops the trunk, temporarily relieved when they disappear from view to load Alex's backpack. Apparently, she's still traveling like a backpacker after all these years. Not like a normal adult with a wheeled suitcase.

A second later the doors open, the city sounds stream in, and Alex is in the back seat of his Mazda.

'Hey Kev.' She nods at him. 'How's it going?' More of a statement than a question.

He turns slightly, nods back. 'Uh, yeah. I'm good. I'm good.'

For a moment, the three of them sit in the car, while downtown Chicago surges around them. No one says anything. Kevin can feel Bonnie silently shouting at him, and he ventures a look in the rearview mirror.

Alex finally speaks, her usual spikiness on display. 'So . . . should we get this show on the road, then?'

'Yeah, definitely.' Kevin is grateful she broke the silence, and he fires the car to life.

* * *

Fucking Kevin. *'Uh yeah, I'm good.'*

That's how he greets her after five years apart?

Alex sits fuming, too proud to admit her hurt, as the car plies south, over the river and into the complex infrastructure of the Chicago Loop: dirty, smog-choked tunnels layered underneath luxury apartment buildings and urban parks.

But what was she expecting? An open-armed hug? An apology? Diplomacy has never been Kevin's strong suit. He takes after Mom and Dad in that way.

Alex stares out the window, trying to crowd out her feelings by marveling at the towering, shiny facades of the Miracle Mile. Chicago never fails to awe her, with its blue-gray ribbon of river lined by glittering skyscrapers, its friendly, carb-loving crowds. This Midwestern metropolis, unashamedly pulsing with life and ambition and optimism.

Unexpectedly, Kevin pulls the car over after just a few blocks.

'What are you doing?' Bonnie asks.

'This is the start of Route 66,' Kevin announces.

He points to a brown-and-white sign by the streetside. It's fixed to a lamppost and rises like an inconspicuous weed among the jungle backdrop of skyscrapers around them.

Historic Route, it reads, with an Illinois U.S. 66 symbol in between. Above it, a separate rectangular plate announces: BEGIN. As if it were the first square on a board game.

'Come on, let's go pay our respects.' Kevin flicks on the hazard lights and exits the car.

He motions for his sisters to come join him. They hesitate.

'Is it even legal to park here?' Bonnie looks around for a sign.

'What the fuck,' Alex mumbles. 'I didn't fly all the way over here to go on Kevin's stupid scavenger hunt.' She glares out the window.

'Oh, come on,' Bonnie says. 'You love to travel. You'd be totally into this, if it weren't Kevin's idea.'

She's got a point there.

'All right, let's just do this and go.' Alex undoes her seat belt, and the two of them hurry over to Kevin by the Route 66 sign. He's already enlisted a passing shopper to take a photo of them and the sign.

'Are the three of you gonna be driving it together?' she asks in that cheerful Midwestern way.

'Yup, all the way to California,' Kevin says. 'Our parents live there.'

'Isn't that great,' the woman remarks. 'I'm sure it'll be a fantastic trip.'

Alex suppresses a snort.

The woman holds Kevin's phone high while bunching the shopping bags at her feet. 'All right, cheese!'

Alex flashes a grin, one of those superficial ones she has been flashing all her life. As an actor, she's had to do this onstage, after shows, at auditions. But in all those scenarios, she wanted to be there; there was some authenticity to her smile. Here, standing by the Route 66 sign, her brother's arm around her, it's as fake as she's ever felt.

* * *

When the Chicago skyline is finally framed in his rearview mirror, Kevin considers the unusual situation he is now in.

He is on the road for a week with his two sisters, one of whom he can't stand. His mother is ailing on the West Coast, requesting that the three of them *drive* together to the Grand Canyon. His own wife despises him, and the feeling is relatively mutual.

Would he say he's running away?

Because something else looms over all of this, like the unsettling, off-screen thrum in a horror film. The reminders that have been increasing in frequency and intensity over the past few months. Text messages. Voicemails. Emails with fire-red font. And yes, physical letters that he has had to surreptitiously winnow from his mailbox and hide in a locked drawer in his filing cabinet.

Hiding, too, is a gun in his glove compartment. A gun he's never before fired outside the controlled environment of a range, but which he's glad to have with him. Call it a placebo effect, the superficial sense of security it brings him.

And as an insurance professional, he knows that's exactly our psychological weak point in the modern age: our fear that anything can happen. So capitalize on it, charge premiums and deductibles, build an entire industry on that fear.

What lies we live on. Nothing like American ambition, right? Reach for the stars, but at any moment, you can crash and burn. Optimism rooted in a shifting, hollow landscape.

We know it, and yet we still buy into it, brainwashed by the—

'Hey Kevin, what's the itinerary for the next few days?'

Bonnie is looking pointedly at him, and Alex, too, has even bothered to make eye contact.

Frazzled, Kevin snaps into tour guide mode. Over the past few weeks, he at least enjoyed the distraction of planning their Route 66 schedule, poring over maps and guidebooks, losing himself in this retro vision of an earlier, simpler America.

'Oh, um, St. Louis tonight. And Tulsa tomorrow night—'

'That's Oklahoma, right?'

'I can't believe we're actually going to Oklahoma,' Alex mutters.

'Oh, we're going farther than that. Tucumcari, New Mexico, is the next stop. Then we can play things by ear, but the hotel at the Grand Canyon is booked for Sunday night. And Mom and Dad's after that.'

It still sounds impossible that they'll be driving through all those states, to reach their parents in less than a week. But thousands of miles of open road, a full tank of gas, and Kevin can think of no better way to disappear.

Illinois

They speed down the I-55 now, away from Chicago. For a while they pass the nondescript, empty spaces of land that always seem to border highways in America.

Eventually they turn off an exit and find themselves on a two-lane highway, flat as a pan, headed past cornfields and red barns. In the summer light, the fields shimmer green, the midday sun slants directly through the windshield.

Now Bonnie witnesses the Midwest landscape, and how it feels different from the rest of the country. On the East Coast, there are fields and barns and two-lane highways, but on a smaller scale, more manageable. Here she gets a sense the land could roll on forever, endless miles of roads and farms and the occasional lake or river, impossible to keep track of, a vast panorama that would take an entire lifetime, even more, to grasp.

The Mazda trundles through a series of perpendicular turns: cornfields, tractors, wooden farmhouses with covered porches that wrap around three sides of the building. Bonnie is tinged with a strange nostalgia, for a country she's never really known, although she's meant to. This is the kind of farmhouse that Dorothy was whisked away in by a tornado, the pleasant rural Americana where Superman was raised as Clark Kent, where blond children and their parents sighted UFOs in wide starry skies. All the collective cultural memories that come from growing up as an American, even though your own hometown is miles from these Midwestern idylls. Nowhere in these cultural memories did Bonnie ever see children that looked like her and her siblings. It was always girls in blond braids, towheaded young boys astride tractors.

This is America, she was told. Not you or your life.

And in New England, it has been the same for her these past two decades. White clapboard churches, redbrick buildings from the colonial era. Her own sons look a step closer to the American ideal, even though she knows they will never get there. But she bakes brownies for their school fundraisers, waves her flag at the Prescotts' famous July Fourth barbecue, gushes about her sister-in-law's homemade apple pie. She has eliminated nearly any trace of her own culture, except for occasional forays to the Asian grocery five towns over, and stir-fried noodle dinners she cooks on Chinese New Year and other rare instances. There are always appreciative murmurs from her husband and sons, even though Chris sometimes complains about the smell of stir-fry.

But that is it. Mom and Dad would be heartbroken to learn you can lose your heritage that quickly, within the space of a generation. Their own Taiwanese dialect has vanished from her vocabulary, even though she once spoke it as a child, translating to Kevin and Alex, forming the bridge between her parents and her siblings.

So she is familiar with these landscapes, she knows how to fit in. She has now become the acceptable Asian wife and mom in an elite white dynasty. Harvard Business School degree, high-income career, three sons and a nine-bedroom house. She is the success story every immigrant parent would want for their child. But perhaps something of her has become lost in the process.

Bonnie wonders, what would it be like to grow up here, a blond kid, among cornfields owned by your family for generations. To have such wide-open space as your immediate home – and to never question if you belonged.

Maybe one day her sons or their sons will feel that security. But if they do, maybe they will have forgotten that other part of their heritage. Their Ama and Agong, growing fainter and frailer on the far side of the continent, and everything that they represent. That family past Bonnie never tried to connect with, because she only ever wanted to look ahead.

* * *

Barely an hour from Chicago, and Kevin is already slowing the car down, somewhere in a humdrum small town.

'Is there a particular reason we're stopping?' Alex asks. She is still adjusting to the sudden changes in landscape the past few days: London to Chicago, gleaming skyscrapers to quiet, level farmland.

'Yeah, this place,' Kevin answers. 'The Gemini Giant. It's kind of iconic.'

'What's so iconic about it . . . ?' Alex starts – and then she sees the giant astronaut standing thirty-feet tall outside the restaurant. Or at least a large figure of a man, straight from a 1950s sci-fi film, wearing a green suit, a silver space helmet, and silver boots. He's holding a rocket – or maybe it's a missile. An American flag streams behind him.

'Cold War propaganda,' Alex mumbles.

Kevin parks the car at the foot of the statue. 'This is considered one of the must-see landmarks in the early stage of Route

66. People used to come here in droves to eat hot dogs and look at the Gemini Giant.'

'That's it?' Alex asks sarcastically. 'I mean, you just look at the statue and chomp on a hot dog?'

Kevin yanks open his door and steps outside. 'You guys are fucking terrible. Do you have *any* respect for this country's history?'

Alex follows him, a rabid dog gunning for a fight. 'How is this history? It's what, fifty years old? It's just crass commercialism. Ooh, a giant statue of an astronaut, so you can come here and buy our hot dogs.'

'Speaking of which, I could use a hot dog right about now,' Bonnie chirps, getting out of the car, her purse in hand.

Alex sighs and stares at the outsized spaceman. He's wearing a space helmet and a green, short-sleeved T-shirt. A T-shirt? Hardly proper attire for an astronaut. She grumbles.

'Do you think they have anything here for vegetarians?'

Inside the Launching Pad restaurant, they sit under painterly renditions of all the sights awaiting them on Route 66. Alex chomps morosely on her lunch.

'I am literally eating a pickle dressed up as a hot dog.'

A large pickle sits nestled in her bun, drizzled with mustard, ketchup, and sauerkraut. Bonnie cringes. 'Sorry, I'd have thought they'd at least have tofu dogs or something.'

Alex catches a glimpse of what the next few days will be like for her: french fries on repeat – and if she's lucky, a limp garden salad.

'Grilled cheese sandwiches,' Kevin says through a mouthful of chili hot dog. 'That's the way to go.'

Alex looks at him and shrugs. 'Guess so.' It's the first time on this trip that Kevin has addressed her directly, aside from the basic formalities. At least he's attempting to be helpful.

They chew in silence for another minute, listening to the sixties classics playing on overhead speakers and chatter from the local teenagers behind the counter, who sneak looks at them from time to time. They are three middle-aged Asians in a Midwest town. Nothing to see here, people.

Alex swallows a mouthful of pickle, the vinegar stinging the back of her throat. Okay, then. If she doesn't try to break the ice, Kevin clearly won't.

She takes a deep breath. 'So, um, Kevin, you know I'm still with Nya, the woman I've been with for a while, right?'

Kevin looks up, feigning innocence. 'Oh, you are? Yeah, Bonnie said you were. That's nice.'

Not so fast. Alex keeps going. 'Yeah. I'm actually married to her. Nya and I got married during the pandemic.'

Kevin stops chewing, and Alex studies his face closely, daring him to frown. He's doing a remarkable job of keeping his face neutral. 'Oh, I didn't . . . I didn't know that.' He glances at Bonnie, a *why-didn't-you-tell-me* look, but Bonnie simply nods with a smile.

'That's, uh . . . Wow. Do Mom and Dad know?'

Congratulations. Alex glares at him. *Are you gonna offer me congratulations?*

'No, I haven't told them yet. I wanted to tell them in person. But I wanted to tell you first.'

'Oh, okay.' Kevin looks blankly at her and nods. 'That's – that's good you told me. So . . . it's been a few years, then?'

Alex sharpens her glare. 'Kevin, I'm *married* to her. This is for life. It's not just a phase.'

Her brother seems to wither under her gaze. 'Okay, then, I guess it's not.'

He's not getting away with it this easily. She slows down,

weighing her words with a deadly seriousness. 'But you *remember*, right? You remember what you said the last time we saw each other.'

Kevin's eyes widen, but he still avoids eye contact. His voice is small. 'I don't . . . what did I say?'

Jesus Christ. Refusing to take responsibility for his words.

She slows down even more. Now is when you deliver the clincher in a theater scene. You give each word space to resonate with the audience.

'You said maybe me coming out was just a phase. Another way of getting attention.'

Alex has rehearsed this confrontation countless times to herself. She had thought she was prepared, but now, she can feel tears gathering in her eyes, the back of her throat swelling. There is still pain, underneath all her anger and resentment.

Don't. It's too early in this trip for tears.

'Did I say that?' Kevin asks. He must know it's a rhetorical question, but he grins sheepishly. 'Well, clearly, it's not a phase! I'm glad you're married now. Congratulations.'

That's it? No apology?

Alex looks to Bonnie, who shrugs. Better than nothing, right?

Alex nods. He did say congratulations. 'Thanks,' she says flatly, and watches as Kevin goes to toss out their used hot dog trays and napkins.

She sighs, already exhausted. She stares at Kevin, his khakis and white sneakers as he buses his tray by the trash can. Call it a work in progress.

* * *

I really did not need that, Kevin thinks as he returns to the driver's seat, waiting for his sisters to finish using the bathroom. Alex being spiky as usual, always occupying her idealistic high horse. Needling Kevin for some reaction, some display of his caveman ignorance.

So she's fully embraced her lesbian lifestyle. Fine, good for her. Good luck not causing Mom to have another stroke with that news.

He immediately regrets that last thought and mentally utters a very quick prayer to God in apology. Not that he 100 percent believes in God, but just in case. *Huh*, maybe Jessica's pious habits are starting to rub off on him.

Mom, he reminds himself. They're doing this trip for Mom. Just focus on that.

The dread within Kevin has deepened, but he regains Route 66, distracting himself with these sleepy little towns, often no more than a collection of houses, and sweeping tracts of farmland.

Somewhere halfway across the state of Illinois, they drive into a one-stoplight town. The Main Street is exactly one block: one cafe, one general store, one museum/town hall/police station. In the summer heat, the murals painted on the town walls shimmer: a colorful tableaux of pioneers crossing the prairies, workers building a railroad, Abraham Lincoln addressing a nineteenth-century crowd. Pride of place is given to another giant figure of a man, this time in red shirt and jeans, bearing a giant hot dog.

'Route 66 sure likes their towering white men,' Alex mutters. 'Holding some kind of phallic symbol.'

Bonnie laughs, and Kevin has to suppress a giggle, too.

'I think that's supposed to be Paul Bunyan,' he says, remembering something from the guidebook.

'The folk hero? Was Paul Bunyan known for having a giant hot dog, or is that just advertising?'

'I think he had a giant ox, right?' Bonnie says.

'Probably just advertising,' Kevin admits, leaning out the window. 'It *is* pretty kitschy.'

Alex snaps a photo on her phone. 'Speaking of white men,' she says. 'How's Chris holding up? Do you think he'll manage looking after three boys when you're away this whole time?'

Bonnie shrugs. 'He's a grown man. He can figure that out himself. But, uh, he also called for backup. I think his mom's moving in when I'm away.'

Alex snorts. 'Classic.'

'Jessica's mom is staying over for a few days, too,' Kevin says. 'Thank god I won't be around.'

'Oh, great,' Alex says, sarcastically chipper. 'They can do Bible study every day with the kids, then.'

Bonnie tsks. 'Don't be mean.'

Alex holds her hands up like a guilty criminal. 'Okay, I repent. But Kev, is Jessica still dragging you to church every Sunday?'

'The kids still go,' Kevin replies. 'But I think she's given up on me.'

Then again, he doesn't blame her. As his sisters laugh, he internally kicks himself. He deserves it, anyway. He would have given up on himself ages ago, too.

Staunching any further thoughts of his marriage, Kevin turns the Mazda away from this antiquated Main Street. He feels the urge to floor the accelerator, to put as many miles behind him as possible. Time to find the interstate again.

* * *

Late that afternoon, the car crosses the broad brown expanse of the Mississippi River, leaving Illinois and approaching St. Louis. Bonnie rouses herself to stare at the famous Gateway Arch that rears up on the western bank. In the summer light, it is unexpectedly graceful but also colossal; a tall, gleaming loop balanced beside the wide, flat river. Dwarfing the city buildings, the warehouses, and barges at its feet.

A landmark she has always associated with St. Louis, but only now does she see how elegant it is, astonishing in its simplicity.

'I've never seen this in person before.' Bonnie gapes.

She is surprised, too, at how big St. Louis is. The highway seems to roll on and on past the sprawling city. A stadium, a vast park, warehouses, churches, office buildings, neighborhoods, all in great numbers. Occupying so much more space than Boston, which is packed into its close-knit peninsula.

'It's your first time here, right?' Kevin asks.

It is for Bonnie and for Alex, who is now reading St. Louis facts off her phone. 'Okay, so. Recently voted one of the most dangerous cities in America. But before that . . . Founded in the 1760s as a center for fur trading . . . Slaves worked the waterfront . . . Rapid growth after the Civil War . . . Fourth largest city in the US by the 1890s . . . Hosted the World's Fair in 1904.'

'The fourth largest?' This is news to Bonnie.

In all her forty-six years as an American, St. Louis has rarely crossed her mind. It amazes her that a city this big, with this kind of history, could thrive right here on the banks of the Mississippi, sustaining the lives of millions of people – and for all her advanced degrees and supposed sophistication, she knows virtually nothing about it.

How narrow has her existence become? Such a small radius Bonnie now traverses, depositing her kids at school, picking them up, and in between, shopping, yoga, paperwork, lunches with friends. Even her vacations have become so routine: skiing in the winter, Martha's Vineyard in the summer, often intertwined with Chris's larger family. Their trips away are cushy and relaxing, and yet, just that tiny bit too predictable.

Her heart crumples at the thought of all the cities she's never explored, the landmarks she's never visited, simply because she was too busy being a suburban mother.

The teenage Bonnie would have laughed at how tame and unexciting her life now is. What happened to that high-flying, jet-setting career woman she'd set out to be? The one who crisscrossed oceans and continents for her job – the one whose world was only ever expanding outward.

1991

What was there to say about that afternoon?

She was almost fifteen and had only started getting her periods the year before. Chrissy Yang was twelve when she first got hers, and Jen Peterson the same year, too. But Bonnie had had to wait an entire year after them, wondering if there was something wrong with her, half-relieved that she didn't have to deal with the blood yet, but half-ashamed that it still hadn't happened to her. That she was so much a child, compared to everyone else.

When she did finally get hers, she didn't realize it would hurt so much. A weird, hollow pain low in her stomach. Nothing like a stomachache – and she'd had some bad ones, like that time she'd had the raw egg in the huo guo for Chinese New Year and had spent the entire night writhing on the couch. No, this kind of pain didn't make you want to writhe, just curl up in bed, cuddle your stuffed animals (even though she knew it was childish to still hug stuffed animals), and whimper.

She'd grown to dread the monthly arrival of her periods. The constant fear of not knowing exactly when the bleeding would start, and oh the terror, of what might happen if you bled through all your clothes, so everyone else would see – would *know* – that you were on your period. Once, Sharon Acosta had bled through her white jeans. She'd bent over to put her lunch tray on the table, and the entire cafeteria had started to gasp and giggle when they saw the telltale red spot. And Sharon just kept on eating her curly fries, oblivious to all the silent sniggering behind her.

Bonnie lived in fear that the same thing might happen to her, so she was extra cautious when she thought her time of month might come. Kept going to the bathroom to check the bleeding hadn't started. But she didn't want to put a pad in too early, because you couldn't waste pads, they were expensive. Mom always clipped coupons for Always multipacks, so she knew you should only buy them on sale.

Bonnie dreaded the stained bedsheets that often came with her period, and the way her fingers froze in the cold water every time she had to rinse the blood out.

Mom had warned her: 'Never use hot water to wash it out. Always cold.'

Meanwhile, other girls spoke of tampons and squealed about the ickiness of having to put them in, but Mom just shook her head at the thought. 'No. You don't use tampons. Just pads. Much easier and safer.'

Bonnie was relieved. Pads were manageable, almost reassuring. The last thing she wanted was to prod and poke down there, to have to *insert* something. She shuddered at the thought.

But as the day of their Grand Canyon trip grew closer, Bonnie realized with a sinking feeling that her period was supposed to start around then. She couldn't really enjoy Las Vegas because she was worried the bleeding would begin any minute, and the next day, as she sat watching the monotonous flat desert roll past, she worried that she would start bleeding and stain the car seat. Already, she could feel the cramps starting to creep into her abdomen. As soon as Dad stopped the car somewhere, she would need to run to a bathroom and check.

And yet, she couldn't say this outright, not with Kevin in the car. Because any mention of a period, and he would automatically make fun of her. And Dad would just be awkward, and Alex would just ask annoying, clueless questions. So it was really only Mom she could talk to about it, and only when no one else was around.

So when Dad was filling up the gas and Kevin announced he needed the bathroom, this was perfect. She would just hint to Mom what was going on, why she needed a bathroom, too, and Mom would understand right away.

Bonnie was glad when Alex and her stupid questions stayed behind in the car, and when Kevin and Dad went into the little gas station store. With the two of them gone, it was just her and Mom. She wouldn't need to hide anything.

'Maybe there's no key. Let's just check first,' Mom said as they edged around the corner of the building, toward the back where gas station bathrooms normally were.

Bonnie was very aware of the two men sitting on the doorstep, staring at them. The same way they'd been staring at the car ever since they pulled in, but now their stares were trained on her and Mom. She even thought they looked at Mom's legs, which were bare – Mom was wearing those outdated plaid shorts of hers. And the way they were looking at Mom's legs made Bonnie feel creeped out. Made her wish she wasn't wearing shorts, too, but she was, the thick black ones. Black in case she started to bleed.

'Howdy,' one of the men said, grinning, as she and Mom walked past.

Who says 'howdy'? Bonnie thought to herself. Like it was

something only cartoon cowboys said on TV. So she didn't respond. And neither did Mom, who just kept marching past, stone-faced, staring straight ahead.

She was relieved when they turned the corner and the men were out of sight.

'Not very friendly of you,' one of the men called out. Almost like he was singing.

Even the sound of his voice made her shudder, following them around the corner.

St. Louis, Missouri

At the hotel reception in St. Louis, an efficient young woman greets them, her hair in an elaborate swirl of braids. Her name tag says Asia, which Kevin finds ironic, since she is Black.

'Hi, I'm a Diamond Member. I have two rooms booked for tonight under Bonnie Prescott.' Bonnie says this with the ease of someone accustomed to a certain level of treatment. Ah, Bonnie, always quick to show off her status. First it was her straight-A report cards, then all those clubs she ran in high school, now all her elite loyalty memberships with their points programs.

'Sure thing.' Asia nods. 'So the room with the king bed is for ... Mr and Mrs ... Prescott?' She looks slightly puzzled, but glances at Kevin and Bonnie, expecting a confirmation.

There's an awkward silence as they stare back at her, horrified.

'Oh god, no,' Bonnie exclaims. 'No, we're not — this is my brother.'

'Blech.' Kevin visibly cringes. 'I am not — I am *not* Mr. Prescott.' Did she think they were husband and wife just because they're both Asian?

Alex cackles behind them, intensely amused.

Asia apologizes profusely. 'I didn't mean to — Oh, I see the resemblance now. Brother and sister, I get it. No, so then the two queens are for . . .'

'My sister and I,' Bonnie explains, gesturing to Alex.

'And the king is for you.' Asia nods at Kevin. 'Okay, I got it now.'

Kevin hadn't thought this far ahead, but of course this is a handy benefit to traveling with Bonnie. A king-sized hotel room all to himself, paid for by Bonnie's Diamond Membership points. If he were younger – say, his kids' ages – he would celebrate by bouncing up and down on that king-sized bed all by himself. Up and up into the air until he was breathless, laughing. He has a vague memory of that unbridled joy from childhood vacations.

But now that he's forty-two, he just wants to throw himself onto the bed and sleep.

* * *

'Ah, veggie burger to the rescue.'

Alex grins as her dinner is set down in front of her, the exhaustion from the day finally subsiding into a gentle calm. They are seated at a busy open-air sports bar on their hotel rooftop, overlooking Busch Stadium (home to the St. Louis Cardinals). Baseball. Burgers and beer. She still finds it slightly surreal how suddenly she's been planted in the American Midwest. On the other side of the bar, the Gateway Arch looms, illuminated a bluish-purple, like a sleek alien design.

She has to admit, St. Louis has a lot more going on than she'd expected. As Kevin described, it was simultaneously the northernmost Southern city of the US, the southernmost Northern city, the westernmost Eastern city. But still squarely, undeniably in the Midwest.

Kevin is on his third beer, and Bonnie has ordered a bottle

of pinot noir. 'I got this,' she said casually, as they perused the menu. For nearly a decade, that has been the default policy: Bonnie covering the more elaborate bills, because they all know she is the wealthiest among them. Kevin would always put up a battle, a custom they'd long witnessed among Asian aunties and uncles squabbling over the honor of paying for a group meal. But Bonnie would only relent for the more affordable meals, still assuming most of the financial burden, while allowing Kevin to save face by occasionally footing the bill.

'Thank you.' Alex smiles at her. 'But . . . for the rest of the trip, should we split the costs somehow?'

Bonnie shrugs. The shrug of someone who never has to worry about money. 'Honestly, it's fine. We can take turns paying, but it doesn't have to be an exact science. I'll get whatever you guys don't feel like covering.'

She takes out a fancy-looking thick Mastercard: a muted rose-gold color. Alex wonders how much monthly spend you need to qualify for such a distinctive card.

Alex takes another gulp of pinot and leans back to look up at the night sky, the metallic loop of the arch.

She thinks of her years of backpacking, carrying the lightest possible knapsack around Southeast Asia, getting by on fifteen dollars a day, wads of local currency stashed in her money belt. What a very different form of travel this is.

When the veggie burger is consumed and she is sufficiently buzzed from the wine, Alex decides it's time to resume that conversation with Kevin.

A work in progress, she reminds herself. *Take it in baby steps, and maybe he won't drive you too crazy.*

She drains the rest of her wineglass and sets it down with a clunk.

'So, Kevin.' She uses her theater voice, training it on him with a focused intensity. Kevin looks up, a shadow of dread on his face.

'I'm going to reveal a series of announcements about my life. It may take you some time to accept all of this, so I won't dump it all on you at once. But it's important to me that you know these things, because this is my life now. It's not "just a phase." '

A frown briefly crosses Kevin's brow, but she continues on. He has no choice.

'Okayyy...' Kevin drags the syllable out, the way he did in adolescence.

'So first of all, Nya and I are married. We have been since 2020.' This is simply restating a known fact, but she needs to establish it again. It's the next one that should surprise him. She clears her throat for emphasis. 'Number two: we're pregnant. Nya's pregnant, and we're going to be mothers. The baby's due in October.'

Kevin's eyes bug out. 'You guys are gonna have a kid?'

'Yeah. Is that shocking for you?'

Kevin stammers. 'Well, I – I guess the thought of you as a mother...'

'Fills you with despair?' Alex jokes. And yet, some queasiness simmers inside her.

Kevin laughs nervously.

'Kevin,' Bonnie cuts in. 'It's okay; I had a similar reaction when I found out you were gonna be a dad.'

'Well, that's different,' Kevin says.

'Why? Because you're not gay?' Alex keeps pushing.

'No, I mean – Well, yeah, I guess,' he stammers.

Alex decides to save him from his floundering. 'It *is* different. The thing about being a lesbian couple and trying to get pregnant is it's all very intentional. You don't just *happen* to become parents. A lot of planning goes into it. Sometimes a lot of money. So you have to really want this path in life.'

Kevin nods, perhaps more out of apprehension than comprehension.

'Do you – know if it's gonna be a boy or a girl?' he asks hesitantly.

Alex skips the lesson about gender being a social construct, and simply says: 'A girl.' Truth be told, she and Nya were somewhat relieved when they learned they wouldn't have to raise a boy and educate themselves in young male anatomy.

'That's great!' Bonnie enthuses. 'A girl cousin for Arabella, finally!' She elbows Kevin, who echoes with an appropriately upbeat, 'Yeah!'

'So you guys had been trying for a while?' Bonnie asks.

'We'd tried once or twice before, and it didn't work. And then we fooled around again, and suddenly – there you go, Nya was pregnant.'

Bonnie and Kevin nod politely. They are clearly holding back a deluge of questions, which amuses Alex to no end.

'So you fooled around . . . with IVF?' Bonnie ventures. 'Or you didn't use . . . IVF . . . ?'

Her question peters out, and it's all Alex can do to stop herself from laughing, seeing her sister so awkward.

'So how did you two . . .' Kevin trails off, then blurts it out. 'How did you two get pregnant?'

Ah Kev, Alex thinks. *The question you've been dying to ask.*

'You know.' She smirks. 'Lesbians *can* spontaneously reproduce if they're in an environment without any men.'

Bonnie laughs and Kevin rolls his eyes. 'Very funny. Ha ha.' He takes a slug from his craft beer. 'But what, you don't want to tell us? Is it some secret?'

100

'No, it's not a secret. I just like how uncomfortable it makes you.' She grins, while Kevin grimaces. 'Okay. Okay, fine. There's two ways of doing it. There's the expensive way, with IVF. We did it the budget way. A male friend of ours donated some sperm when Nya was ovulating and we just ... applied it.'

' "Applied it?" Like a topical cream?' There is an undeniable horror in Kevin's voice. 'But obviously not topical...'

'Kevin.' Bonnie smacks him on the shoulder. 'Stop probing so much.'

Alex smiles. 'We used the turkey baster method. Just sort of ... got the good stuff up there.'

Kevin and Bonnie sit blinking at her.

'Doesn't sound very fun,' her brother remarks.

'IVF isn't fun,' Alex retorts. 'Nor was getting pregnant for the majority of women in arranged marriages throughout human history. Last time I checked, it's mainly only *men* who enjoy ejaculation.'

'Here we go again with the feminism,' he mutters.

'Kevin,' Alex's voice takes on a sharp tone. 'Shut up sometime. Yeah, I'm a feminist. It's a pretty fundamental part of who I am, so just accept that and move on. You can also *maybe* congratulate me on being a future parent?'

'Congratulations,' Kevin croaks. 'Who's the sperm donor? Is your kid even gonna look Asian?'

Alex stares in shock at him. 'What difference does that make? He'll still be my kid, mine and Nya's. Or does he not count as family if he doesn't look Asian? Is that how narrow-minded you've become?'

'That's it.' Kevin stands up drunkenly, and his chair skids back a few feet. The people at the table nearest them look up. 'I'm not taking this anymore. I was just asking some questions.'

'Hey hey hey,' Bonnie rises, too, and lays a placating hand

on Kevin's shoulder. 'Mom just came out of the ICU, and you're picking a fight with Alex over this stuff?'

'*I'm* picking the fight?!' Kevin looks incensed. 'I was simply curious about their pregnancy. And then Alex had to turn it into her usual feminist soapbox.'

'There's no soapbox. It's just my belief system.'

'Guys,' Bonnie persists. 'We haven't even been on the road twenty-four hours and *already* you guys are bickering? Can't you two just act like mature adults for once?'

'I dunno,' Alex says sarcastically. She glares at Kevin while stabbing a fork at the last of her french fries. '*Can* we?'

* * *

'*Is your kid even gonna look Asian?*' Alex mimics Kevin, casting her voice whiny and petulant. Angry, she whips a hotel pillow repeatedly onto her queen bed, and Bonnie watches.

'How am I gonna last through the week on this road trip with him?' Alex turns to her sister, pleading.

Hmm, maybe Kevin's right. She is a bit of a drama queen...

Bonnie exhales. 'Listen, I know Kevin's not the most... woke about some things.' She's rarely used the word 'woke' before, but now seems to be the right kind of context. 'But I don't think he's deliberately trying to be malicious.'

'*Just a bit of a dinosaur,*' Alex offers an excuse with air quotes. 'Well, it gets exhausting having to school him all the time.'

Bonnie sits down on the bed next to her sister. Thinks of what she would say to one of her boys at a moment like this. 'I know. But you're trying, right? That's what counts.'

'I guess I am, yeah.' Alex punches the air half-heartedly in front of her. 'But is he?'

*

Bonnie thinks about the incident that caused all of this, that Christmas five years ago. Was it just that single argument, or was that the culmination of years of continental drift, her brother and sister destined to clash in a fiery eruption?

It was at Christmas Eve dinner, with the kids appeased in the den, watching holiday specials. Alex had waited until they were all there in one room – she liked an audience after all – and announced that she was seeing women now. Mom and Dad were slow to comprehend what this meant. They just looked at Alex, their faces unchanged. But Kevin had rolled his eyes and uttered that infamous statement: *Maybe this is just another phase. Maybe you should grow up for once, stop experimenting. Become a responsible adult.*

Even Bonnie had flinched hearing Kevin's words. He'd always been harsh on Alex, but saying this? In front of everyone else?

Alex went nuclear. She flung everything at Kevin. How he was always so intolerant, it was no surprise he was a homophobe on top of everything. Did it ever occur to him some people might just be different? But no, he would never understand; he led the most unoriginal conformist life; he was content to hold a boring nine-to-five just to pay the bills, and how was that working out? Kevin responded with a list of everything Alex had ever done wrong, all the worry she'd caused Mom and Dad over the years, her utter selfishness.

Bonnie tried to step in, but they ignored her. They ignored their parents' pleas and growing mortification. Mom ended up in tears, forced to watch her youngest two rip each other apart. Kevin used this as an example of the kind of hurt Alex caused, so maybe she should just leave. And Alex, being Alex, stormed off.

They watched her backing Mom's car out of the driveway,

and no one saw her again until late that night, when Bonnie heard the key in the lock, saw Alex stumbling in after midnight on Christmas morning.

She came up to hug Alex, wondering if she might smell alcohol on her breath. But Alex must have anticipated her suspicions.

'Don't worry,' she said, her hand held up to ward off any questions. 'I sobered up before I drove back.'

No one apologized to Alex. Kevin ignored her for the rest of the visit, Mom and Dad acted like nothing had happened. Bonnie wanted to check in with her, but the next day was Christmas and her three boys were rambunctious, too eager to open presents, demanding all her attention. From time to time, she would glimpse Alex on the sidelines, watching pensively as the kids tore the wrapping off their Christmas gifts.

Bonnie thought it odd that she, Kevin, and Alex had once been like that at Christmas, children united in their joy. Quickly appeased by items you could purchase and put in boxes. If only happiness was that easily attainable for adults.

Really, it was only ever kids who seemed to enjoy Christmas.

*

Photo Message sent, 8:54PM, Central Time.

We started Route 66 today! Here's us in Chicago. We're in St. Louis, Missouri now. Headed up the big Arch tomorrow morning. Love you.

Bonnie sends this to Chris, knowing he'll show it to the boys in the morning. She sends the same photo, and virtually the same message, to Mom and Dad.

* * *

Alex sits watching her from the other hotel bed, admiring Bonnie's commitment to keeping in touch with her loved ones. Something she herself has never been great at. All she ever wanted to do was escape and disappear into the world.

'Do you miss any part of your life from before you had kids?'

Bonnie tosses her phone onto the bed and turns to look at her. She shrugs. 'I mean, I'm not like you. My life wasn't that interesting before becoming a mother. I worked a lot, then I went to business school, then I worked some more.'

'So you wouldn't trade any part of your life for what you had then?'

Bonnie considers this. She slides down into a horizontal position on the bed and stares up at the hotel room ceiling.

'No. I mean, I just feel so much more settled now, more rooted. And my kids? I love them like nothing else in this world. I know it sounds like a cliché. But it's like . . . you become a parent, and it unlocks this whole other meaning to your existence. At least it did for me.'

Alex wonders what this could possibly feel like. A portal into another world.

'Why? Are you . . . unsure about having a child?' Bonnie levels this question at her carefully.

Alex feels caught, exposed. Until Nya, her sister has always been better at reading her than anyone else. 'Me? No. I mean, the kid hasn't arrived yet. But I'm worried, I guess.'

Bonnie turns onto her side to face Alex, propping her head up on a crooked elbow. 'Anxiety is definitely part of being a parent. But you're so chilled out, maybe you won't be as anxious as I was. What are you worried about?'

Alex looks away, her finger tracing a sinuous journey on the hotel duvet. 'That I'm not parent material. You know me, I'm no good at commitment—'

Bonnie interrupts her. 'But you're in a committed relationship now. You've always been committed to acting, right? And to travel. You've been committed to the stuff that's important to you. And once you have kid, that kid is gonna become the most important thing in your life.'

'You think? But what if it – What if she doesn't?'

Bonnie comes over to her bed, sits next to her and squeezes her in a sideways hug. 'She will. It's hard to imagine right now. But she will.'

Alex admires her sister's certainty. 'I guess Mom must have been like that with us. Like, we were her whole purpose for living?'

'Yeah,' Bonnie answers after a moment, releasing Alex from the hug. 'And then we all moved away.'

They sit side by side, stewing equally in their filial guilt.

'But honestly, her anxiety, all that worrying about us?' Alex offers this up, almost as an excuse. 'I couldn't take it. I mean, it was suffocating.'

Bonnie, as ever, tries to defend their parents. 'Yeah, but they were young. They were raising kids in a new country with no family around, and not much money. It must have been hard.' She pauses. 'You know, after they moved here, Mom only got to see her own mom once again in her lifetime.'

Alex looks at her sister, aghast. How had she not known that?

'Grandma came over to help out after I was born,' Bonnie continues. 'But Mom never felt like she had enough money to fly back to Taiwan to visit. And then when she did, it was decades later, for her mom's funeral.'

'Oh, Mom . . .' Alex feels a belated sorrow for the grand-mother she never knew, for what her own mother had to give up. For the personal histories she has never bothered to learn.

106

In comparison, her own decision to escape to London feels spoiled, selfish. Awash with guilt, unsure of what else to say, Alex stands up and heads to the bathroom to end the conversation.

'How's Nya been with the pregnancy?' Bonnie asks, solicitous. 'No scares or anything?'

Alex turns around. 'Good, I guess. First trimester was pretty rough, with all her nausea. But she's better now.'

Bonnie nods. 'It can be a scary time. The biology of becoming a mother and all that. But it's worth it in the end. Trust me.'

The next morning, the three of them ride in silence, as the tram climbs higher and higher up the vertiginous curve of Gateway Arch. Kevin watches St. Louis shrinking below him like a miniature board game: more neighborhoods, more highways and waterways filling his field of vision, the higher they rise.

His sisters are next to him, pressed up against the glass. Their eyes wide with wonder at the endless brown ribbon of the Mississippi, coiling its way across the Midwestern plain.

He remembers riding this same tram at a very different time in his life. Fifteen years ago, Jessica had clasped him in this tram car, charging him with a singular electricity. It was their first weekend away, in their heady early days of dating. Kevin had painstakingly researched all the tourist sites to impress her with, and the local culinary specialties: frozen custard and toasted ravioli and this thing all the Chinese restaurants served, called the St. Paul Sandwich. They ate it all on that trip. They ate and had sex and wandered this unfamiliar city, the flush of discovery intertwined with this other wondrous human being. He had wanted to stitch every one of his waking and sleeping moments to Jessica's existence, amazed that here at last was a woman who loved being with him, who did not question or mock him. He could ask for nothing more.

In the Gateway Arch tram car, Kevin recalls the delicious pressure on his arm when Jessica had clung to him, anxious but also thrilled to have an excuse to touch him. A phantom sensation for him now, which leaves him feeling bereft.

*

This is still on his mind as they stand on the green lawn afterward, posing for a group shot. Bonnie of course has engineered this, knowing Mom will want a series of framed photos for their living room. Historically in their family, Bonnie has always masterminded the group photos, sometimes even booking a professional photographer's studio for a torturous posed shot. But those days are long gone. Today, she simply asks a fellow tourist to take a photo on her iPhone.

'Say cheese!' the man chirps at them.

Kevin puts his arm around Alex, musters a smile momentarily, then steps away, trying not to think of Jessica. Above them, the silver span of Gateway Arch bisects the blue of the summer sky. A thin silver ribbon, virtually impossible in its symmetry.

* * *

'So tonight we're in Tulsa, right?' Bonnie asks, wiping her mouth with a napkin.

Kevin nods, aloof behind his sunglasses. 'Yeah. It's about a six-hour drive. Should be straightforward enough.'

They are seated outside an Italian restaurant on the Hill, a wide umbrella providing them shade against the hot June sun. They are soporific after an unusually early lunch. Bonnie had wanted to try toasted ravioli before leaving St. Louis, which she admits were heavenly morsels of cholesterol. She glances askance at Alex, silently sorry there weren't any vegetarian options.

But Alex stews behind her mirrored aviators, hardly acknowledging her brother's presence. She is at least perusing the map in front of them with interest, her finger tracing down the I-40 across Missouri. She gives a sharp intake of breath.

'What is it?' Bonnie asks.

'I didn't realize we were passing so close to the Ozarks,' Alex says.

'The Ozarks?' Bonnie shrugs. A place she's heard of, but which rarely comes up in conversation for her.

'Well, the area just sounds kind of interesting,' Alex says. She taps a spot on the map. 'Especially this place called Branson.'

Bonnie tries to recall what she associates with the Ozarks, but only a sense of some rural backwater, hillbillies, moonshine, and, well . . . these are probably all horrific stereotypes.

'Tonight's hotel is booked in Tulsa, so the main thing is we just need to get there,' Bonnie states. And no one seems to object. Alex is engrossed in the map and Kevin in his phone. Bonnie looks between the two of them, like magnets that repel each other. She sighs, hoping something will shift.

'Well, I guess we better hit the road. I'm going to the bathroom. Alex, wanna come?'

Alex slides out of her chair. Any excuse not to be with Kevin.

'Kevin!' Bonnie shouts, as she and Alex head inside. 'Can you at least pay the bill?'

She's not going to cover every meal, and surely he's in a better position to pay than Alex.

He glances up from his phone, unsmiling. *What is his problem?*

'Yeah, yeah.' Kevin leans over casually to pick up the receipt.

But Bonnie senses the slightest of hesitations. If he weren't her brother, she wouldn't have noticed.

* * *

Kevin pays with his iPhone, relieved that the St. Louis prices won't make a significant dent in his credit card balance. Walking slowly back to the table, he pauses over the group photo at Gateway Arch, which Bonnie has already sent to his phone. He considers texting it to Jessica, with a brief message: *Remember this place?*

But no, there is too much unspoken sadness, too big a gap between where they were then, fifteen years ago, and now. She might even get angry, think he was mocking her.

He flicks the photo closed and pockets his phone. Better not to send it.

* * *

'We all ready to go now?'

At their lunch table, Bonnie is excited for the next leg of their journey. St. Louis was surprisingly pleasant. What's next on Route 66? She reaches back to shoulder her handbag – when her hand touches empty air. In a moment of panic, she swivels around. But there's nothing hanging on the back of her chair.

'Shit,' she says, her voice strained in a high pitch. 'Shit shit shit shit shit!'

Adrenaline shoots through her body, as the dread seeps in. 'Kevin, have you seen my bag? My handbag? And my wallet?' She scans the table, but there's nothing – just crumpled cloth napkins and crumbs.

Kevin stops. 'Your what? Didn't you have it with you?'

'No, I—' She stares at him wide-eyed. 'I must have left it at the table. But – you were here the whole time, right?'

'I, uh . . .' Kevin is rooted to the spot, a shadow of guilt on his face. 'No, I took the bill inside to pay at the cash register. Thought it would be faster that way.'

'Kevin, what the fuck?! Can't you just be—' She swallows the rest of the sentence: *useful for once.*

'What, so it's my fault?' Kevin starts.

'No – just. Aaaargh! I can't believe this.' Bonnie collapses

111

back into her chair, her head in her hands. Her heartbeat quickens, and she's flooded with despair.

She glances around frantically to see who might have taken it, but there is no one near, just normal-looking pedestrians. No one who looks suspicious.

It couldn't have been more than five minutes ago that it was stolen, yet still . . . Someone fleet-footed could have run anywhere in those five minutes. Or jumped into a waiting car.

'Did you have a lot of money in there?' Alex asks.

'Some . . . a few hundred in cash, maybe. But all my credit cards. And . . . shit, my driver's license. And my house keys were in there . . .' A tide of nausea swells in her. She needs to call Chris. They probably need to change the locks, because her address is on her driver's license.

'And your phone? Do you still have that?' Alex presses.

Another jolt of panic, but Bonnie reaches back and feels the reassuring rectangular lump in the back pocket of her slacks. A temporary moment of relief.

'I've got it. I've got *that*, thank god.'

Kevin starts toward the restaurant. 'I'm gonna ask the restaurant staff, see if they've seen it.'

Bonnie closes her eyes for a moment, willing her mind to stay still, to stop spinning. *Of all the fucking things that could happen on this trip . . .*

When she opens her eyes, Alex has crouched down to her level, hands laid calmly on hers.

'It's okay,' Alex says quietly, in control. 'Here's what we're gonna do. If we don't find your wallet here, you're gonna cancel your credit cards. Then call Chris to let him know. And in the meantime, we'll find the nearest police station and report the theft. And you probably want to call your insurance, too.'

Bonnie knows these are all the logical steps to take, but it helps to have them spelled out to her. For once, she doesn't have to be doing the thinking and the planning. She can just follow instructions, like a child. There is a strange relief in this.

'But that'll take hours,' Bonnie moans. So much for leaving St. Louis soon. She slumps and puts her head in her hands again. 'I can't believe I was that stupid. Turn your back for a second, and that's all it takes.'

All the security that comes with her credit cards, what they enable her to purchase, how she can buy her way through the world. All of that gone now.

She knows exactly what her mom would say if she heard about this.

One of the most dangerous cities in America.

It's not like she hadn't been warned.

'Okay . . . I'm just repeating this again, so I've got it all down. One handbag. Beige, leather. Brand: Banana Republic. One large pink leather women's wallet. Brand: Paul Smith. Containing approximately three hundred dollars in cash, five credit cards, two debit cards, several other membership cards, and a Massachusetts driver's license made out to Bonnie Chu Prescott. Is that correct?'

Bonnie sits forward in the wooden chair in the police station, listening intently. In her lap, her hands clasp each other tightly.

'Yes, that's it.' She shapes an imaginary rectangle. 'I'd say the wallet is about . . . nine inches long by four. One of the ones with a zipper that goes all around three sides.'

The police man nods, as if humoring her.

'Are you gonna . . . write that down?' she asks.

He raises his eyebrows and says nothing. Then half-heartedly scrawls '9 x 4 in' next to the description.

'You should probably call your bank and cancel your cards,' he adds dryly.

'Yeah, I've done that already.'

'And then, um ... the contents of your handbag. One tube of lipstick. One bottle of hand sanitizer. Two face masks. One ChapStick. One packet of tissues. One small tube of hand cream. One small tube of sunblock. One bottle of eye drops. One packet of sanitizing wipes—'

'Two. Two packets of sanitizing wipes,' she corrects him.

'Two packets,' he says. 'Two ... tampons. One maxi pad. One packet of chewing gum. One box of raisins. A key ring with six keys on it. One sunglasses case, empty ...'

Bonnie is relieved her sunglasses had stayed on top of her head. They are Derek Lam, after all, and she had paid at least two hundred dollars for them. And in this heat and glare, she will need them.

'One small notebook. Two or three pens. One fold-up paper fan. One blue squeezy stress ball. One ... small toy race car ... ?'

Bonnie smiles sheepishly. That had been a present from her boys a few years ago. They had secretly, unbeknownst to Chris, decided to pool some pocket money to buy her a birthday present. And Milo had chosen a bright green race car, thinking it would be just the perfect gift for their mom. With a Sharpie, they had drawn in five figures in the car's window, to represent their family.

'Anything else? You forget the kitchen sink?' the policeman asks, deadpan.

Bonnie smiles back out of politeness, hiding her irritation. As far as she's concerned, all those items were perfectly justified. 'Hah. No, I think that's it.'

'Thank god. Think my hand was close to giving out.'

'You can't ... type these reports in?' Bonnie suggests.

'Trust me,' the cop says. 'You don't wanna see me typing.'

Seems fair. She is reminded that there is a whole sector of the population who don't know how to touch-type.

'So . . . what now?'

The cop leans back and looks at her, not unkindly. 'You're a competent little lady, aren't you?'

She wrinkles her brow slightly. Is he trying to be patronizing? Sergeant Marcel Thompson. A middle-aged Black man, with a trimmed mustache and dabs of gray hair at his temples. There is no hint of a leer. She feels none of the unease she has felt in the past when receiving similar comments from unknown men twice her size. She decides he is simply trying to be friendly.

'I'm used to running a household with three young sons,' she finally says, in an attempt to justify her competence. She's not going to mention her Harvard Business School degree or her once promising career in corporate America.

The cop grins, a wide bright smile. 'Just like my wife, then. When I get home, she's the one in charge. For all I know, she got just as much stuff in her handbag, too.' He stops and rubs his chin. 'I should probably offer to carry it more often.'

'I'm sure she wouldn't mind.'

'Damn, you know what that'd look like? Me, carrying my woman's handbag around? I wouldn't hear the end of it from the boys.'

They both share in a warm laugh.

'So . . . what are the chances of actually finding my handbag again?'

Sergeant Thompson looks up at the ceiling, then at Bonnie. 'I'd say a one in fifty chance you'll get it back. Probably more like one in eighty.'

'Oh.' The disappointment crests inside her, but somehow,

she's not surprised. She wonders what kind of data there is to actually back up his guess.

'These guys . . . They know how to operate. They'd be selling on the handbag and wallet, taking the cash, getting the most out of the cards. So if I were you, I wouldn't wait around hoping to get it back.'

'Well, thanks for being honest.' By the way he's glancing at her, he's probably surmised she doesn't need the money anyway. And it's true: she'll get a decent reimbursement from travel insurance, once she files the claim.

There's a pause, as she looks around and takes in the busy police station: cops sitting alone at their desks, making notes, others interviewing civilians and possible criminals. Everyone going about their own business.

'I guess this happens pretty often, right? Naive tourists getting their handbags stolen, right at their lunch table?'

Thompson tilts his head to one side. 'Not that it's an excuse or anything, but there's some pretty desperate folks in this city. Tourists can make easy targets.'

Bonnie senses he wanted to say: *Rich* tourists.

Serves her right for swanning around town with a fancy-looking handbag and a two-hundred-dollar pair of sunglasses on her face. Then she realizes the three hundred dollars in cash is worth more to someone else than to her.

'Y'all from out of state, right?' Thompson asks, shifting the tone of the conversation. 'Massachusetts is a looong way from here.'

'Yeah, we're all . . . doing this road trip together. Me and my brother and sister.' She explains her mom's situation, their ultimate endpoint in California.

He gives a long, low whistle. 'Your sister flew in from London for this trip? Damn. And where you folks off to next?'

Bonnie considers how much she should tell him. Then again, he's a cop. It must be safe. 'Tulsa, but uh . . . you heard of some place called Branson?'

Thompson nearly spits out his coffee. 'Y'all going to *Branson*?! My god.'

Bonnie balks, curious now. 'Wait, why? Is it . . . weird?'

Thompson shrugs. 'Let's just say, Branson ain't a place *I'd* take my family to on vacation. But it sure is popular with other folks.'

After St. Louis, Alex offers to drive. There was some trepidation at first – it had been years since she's driven on a US highway – but she pushes that out of her mind. She's ridden open-top Jeeps in Africa, camels in the Arabian desert, rickety motorboats through crocodile-infested waters in Malaysia. Handling a Mazda on Interstate 40 should be no problem.

Besides, there is an exhilarating sense of discovery that comes with sitting behind the wheel. Alex follows the brown Historic Route 66 markers, occasionally detouring off the broad, thundering interstate onto two-lane highways labeled by letter, not number. State Road U winds between isolated farms, through thickets and orchards, past general stores and restaurants, many of them shuttered up. They pass a giant red rocking chair, at least four stories tall, certified as 'The World's Largest Rocker' (according to a sign). They roll on. Route 66 entwines itself with the interstate, sometimes curving north of that wide concrete river of traffic, sometimes dipping south, but always heading westward into the gilded afternoon light.

No one wants to talk about it, but now with Bonnie's wallet stolen, circumstances have changed. Without her driver's license, she technically can't drive anymore. She had canceled her credit cards, but replacing them was another matter. The credit card company had assured her that as a Platinum Elite client, she *should* be able to receive her new card the next day. But there was a slight chance she might not, especially since tomorrow's hotel was in Tucumcari, New Mexico, in the middle of the desert.

'I mean, if it doesn't arrive tomorrow, we can't afford to hang around another day for my credit card, can we?' Bonnie asked. 'We need to get to the Grand Canyon and then Mom and Dad's.'

'We'll be at Mom and Dad's in five days. Just send them there,' Alex said. 'I'm sure we can last until then without your credit cards.'

'You sure?' Bonnie was uneasy.

Alex wondered if Bonnie was the most uncomfortable with the idea. Stripped of the ease that comes with her purchasing power. No longer able to simply present a piece of plastic or wave a few bills to solve any problem.

'Most of the hotels have been booked and paid for, right?' Alex reminded everyone. 'That means just covering food and gas and whatever else. Is that so tough?'

The three of them looked at each other for reassurance.

'I mean, come on.' Alex rolled her eyes. 'I backpacked through Southeast Asia on fifteen dollars a day. We can do this, people.'

'Well, we're not *in* a developing country, are we?' Kevin shot back. 'So that's hardly a useful comparison.'

Alex had to admit there was some truth in Kevin's statement. 'All I'm saying is, I've got my credit cards, so does Kevin. So what are we even worrying about?'

Her brother lifted his palms up, admitting defeat. 'Yeah, sure.' Though he certainly didn't sound very enthusiastic.

Bonnie finally relented with a shrug.

'C'mon, Bonnie Chu Prescott,' Alex teased. 'I bet this is the worst thing that has ever happened to you in your charmed life. We'll help you get through it.'

And Kevin had laughed along with her, while Bonnie took the joke gamely and retreated behind her Derek Lam sunglasses.

* * *

Bonnie realizes that to Alex, her life probably appears shiny and luxurious, free of worry, gifted with undeserved ease. As if loss is not a thing that can happen to Bonnie Chu Prescott – or if it does, that loss can easily be replaced by something new, just like her credit cards.

And it's true. The anxiety that she'd grown up with, which she'd somehow inherited from Mom, had begun to slowly melt away when she married into Chris's family. The Prescotts, with their ease and their confidence, swanning through life with their trust funds and vacation homes and long list of social and professional connections. In contrast, her mom would spend all of Sunday perusing the supermarket circulars, clipping coupons and compiling lists of where to buy milk, bananas, canned spaghetti at the cheapest price that week. Mrs. Prescott just rolled up to the nearest Trader Joe's, plucked whatever items she wanted from the shelves, and paid for them without a backward glance.

It was that kind of security which at first seemed so foreign to Bonnie. But which, in time, she grew accustomed to, the more her life became entwined with the Prescotts'.

But every time she returned home, there was that familiar anxiety. Her mom commenting on how much things cost, worrying endlessly about her, and then her sons, about Henry and Milo and Max.

When a neighbor invited the boys to come over and play on their Xbox, was it safe for them to walk around the neighborhood at dusk? You never knew what bad people might be waiting in the dark.

'What the hell are you talking about, Mom?' Bonnie asked, annoyed. 'It's *Irvine*. We're not exactly living in Compton or anything.'

'But you never know. Your boys don't know this area. Anything could happen to them.'

'They're just going for a walk around the block!'

This suburban labyrinth, where the sand-colored residences with the red-tiled Spanish roofs clustered around quiet cul-de-sacs.

But Mom would shake her head, uttering her tsks. '*Anything* could happen.'

And in some ways, Mom was right. Anything *could* happen to shake you out of your middle-class complacency. Handbags could get snatched, if you weren't careful. And other kinds of losses, Bonnie reflects, were even crueler, more irrational.

Watching the Missouri farmland roll past, reflecting on her conversation with Alex last night, she thinks of that other loss – when she and Chris had been trying to get pregnant. Before Henry, her oldest, she'd lost a child at eleven weeks. It seems strange now to call it a child, when it was hardly even a fetus. Bonnie had gone only two months without a period. But still, she had mothered a future life, and she had lost that life. A sorrow that she and Chris kept to themselves, because they'd been trying on and off for over a year. For a couple glorious, heady months, they'd sequestered the joy of knowing they were finally pregnant, making sure to wait the requisite twelve weeks before telling anyone.

And then, at eleven weeks, the pain in her abdomen. The blood in her panties.

The seeping dread that what she'd feared most was happening right now inside her body, and she had no control over it. She'd never been religious, but now she prayed fervently to God to save this baby, this child who barely even existed – and if he did, she would be good, she'd donate to more charities, she'd even join a church. But he didn't listen. The blood kept coming. So much that she had to cancel a client site visit, call in sick, even though her performance review was next month. Bonnie lay in bed in their Copley Square apartment, staring at their immaculate white wall for an entire day. She had done everything right in her life. Gotten all the As, graduated from impressive schools, committed long hours to her job, married the right kind of man. But no one had ever warned her that this – the ability to become a mother – had nothing to do with hard work and noble intentions. That the outcome could be so cruel, despite all the hope and love you had imbued in this little flicker of life.

When Chris came home from the office, he joined her in bed, his arm around her stomach where it hurt, Big Spoon to her Little Spoon. He didn't say much, his nose and mouth buried in her unwashed hair, his lips gentle on the back of her head.

'It'll be okay,' he said. He felt the tears on her face, dabbed at them gently with a tissue. 'We'll have plenty more chances.'

She lay in bed crying the entire weekend, and on Monday, she was back in the office, pretending nothing had happened. Ready to apologize to her clients for her absence, promising she'd fly out to meet them that week.

Six months later, she was pregnant with Henry.

Bonnie knows there is no particular tragedy to this story, because for her, everything turned out fine. She went on to have three boys, all perfectly healthy. Her sadness was soon replaced by joy and never-ending responsibility. But if she stops and thinks back, she can still access that anguish, so all-encompassing that weekend in her thirtieth year, and for many months after.

So Bonnie has felt loss in her life, she's just rarely spoken about it to anyone. Because loss and imperfection is something she cannot make visible. Somehow, if she did, she would be letting her parents – and everyone else – down.

She looks at Alex and Kevin in the front seat, the back of their heads remind her of watching Mom and Dad on childhood road trips. She wonders if she can share this story of miscarriage with her siblings, or if they will simply laugh it off as a non-tragedy, a forgettable blip of bad luck in Bonnie's otherwise perfect life. She'll keep it to herself for a little longer. It's probably safer, she thinks, as the rhythmic hum of the interstate lulls her into a slumber.

* * *

Kevin sits in the front, watching Bonnie drift off to sleep in the back seat. Maybe she needs it. Driving from Boston to Chicago in two days, then getting her handbag stolen – enough to tire anyone out.

He and Alex settle into an awkward, mutual silence, not wanting to wake Bonnie. As they cross Missouri, he notices billboards advertising Branson. *Dolly Parton's Stampede Dinner Show! Performing eight times a week without fail!* Men in red-white-and-blue cowboy outfits gallop astride white horses while waving a giant American flag. Equally abundant are road signs of more a Christian nature. Quotes from the Bible, comments writ large about Jesus: *Jesus Died for Your Sins. Jesus Loves You. Doubts in Jesus? Call 1-800-JESUS-4U.*

Near Springfield, Kevin is baffled when Alex makes a definite turn off the I-40, south onto the 65.

'Alex, what are you doing?' He hisses at her in a low whisper, still conscious of Bonnie asleep.

'Huh? What?' Alex looks at him innocently, and he wants to slap her.

123

'Route 66 goes that way.' He points to the interstate they just left.

'Well, I thought we could use a detour to see the Ozarks.' She grins. 'We'll just swing through Branson, dip into Arkansas, and meet up with the 66 north of Tulsa. Relax. It'll only add on another half hour, max.'

'You sure?' Kevin is skeptical, and hardly thrilled to be leaving the 66.

'C'mon, Kev,' Alex taunts. 'Off-script. Off-grid. The best way to travel! Plus, aren't you curious about Branson?'

Kevin wants to fume. This is the kind of chaotic behavior Alex was always subjecting everyone to when they were younger. Last-minute decisions. A sudden change of heart. She couldn't be normal like everyone else. She always had to push everything – and everyone – to the absolute limit, expectations be damned.

Being with Alex was like sitting next to the living embodiment of chaos: a vibrant, scintillating miasma of energy. When he was a child poring over astronomy books, Kevin learned about massive stars (that was the actual term) and often thought of his younger sister as one: enough energy to light up a room or stage, if she felt like it, but also so unstable. Ready to explode into a supernova of fury, before collapsing in on herself.

Most other stars – average stars – didn't explode. Over time, they decomposed into planetary nebulae, giving rise to planets and solar systems. Then they became white dwarfs. And when viewed from millions of light-years away, they were cold, distant pricks of light: safe, stable, if a little boring. Identical to all the other stars in the night sky.

Kevin was content to be like one of those unremarkable, identical stars. Why couldn't Alex?

*

'Are you mad at me?' Alex asks Kevin, turning her head to look over at him.

'Huh? What?' Kevin starts. It's rare for Alex to show any self-awareness like this.

Alex leans in closer, trying to keep her eyes on the road. 'I said, are you mad at me? For doing this . . . little detour. I just wanted to see what the Ozarks are like.'

Kevin snorts. 'I mean, I shouldn't be surprised.'

'What is that supposed to mean?!' Her voice prickles with aggression.

'You're always pulling this kind of shit.' He says this coldly, unapologetic. 'Making some reckless decision without taking anyone else into consideration.'

There's a pause before she answers.

'That's not true,' she finally says. He can hear the hurt in her voice, and somehow, that gives him a perverse, adolescent delight.

He sighs, 'Yes, it is. How about that time in Disneyland when you decided last minute that you didn't want to go on Space Mountain. After you, me, and Dad had been waiting in line for over an hour? All of a sudden you were too scared to go, but also too scared to get out of line on your own. So Dad had to go with you. And *who* ended up having to ride Space Mountain all by himself? I'd been looking forward to riding it for *years*, and then everything was ruined.'

He can still remember the Disneyland ride attendant looking down at him with pity. *'You don't have anyone else to ride this with you?'*

'Kevin, I was six years old when that happened,' Alex murmurs in disbelief. 'I was young and scared, so I'm sorry you had to ride Space Mountain on your own. But that was almost forty years ago. Get the fuck over it now!'

125

'Oh, but *your fear* matters more than mine?! I almost vomited riding Space Mountain alone, I was so scared. But I was too embarrassed to tell Mom and Dad, and I know they would have only cared about you anyway.'

There's another silence from Alex. 'Is that what you think? That Mom and Dad only care about me?'

He never should have brought up the Disneyland story. It made him sound weak and pathetic.

'Kevin, answer me.'

He exhales loudly. A sign announces thirty-seven more miles to Branson. 'You were the baby of the family. They were always talking about your art projects and how talented you were. They never said that kind of stuff about me.'

'But you were the only son in the family. You were automatically perfect no matter *what* you did.' Alex's voice is shot through with an unmistakable resentment. 'Aunts and uncles would fawn over you, ask you about your life goals. They gave you red envelopes with more money, took you out to watch ball games. But I had to be creative to get noticed. If I wasn't singing or dancing or painting up a storm, I'd just be some overlooked little sister.'

Kevin stares at the passing hills as he considers this. Alex, overlooked? Alex, having to fight for attention? That hardly seems plausible.

'You were never overlooked. From the moment you were born, all they ever worried about was you.' He can even recall it now. Being four years old and peering in on his parents, hunched over Baby Alex in her crib, checking her temperature and wringing their hands in worry. Forgetting about him, or only slipping out to read him a cursory bedtime story, before turning the light off on him. Leaving him in the dark on his own.

126

Alex sighs. 'That's the whole point. All they ever did was *worry*. I was always weak and little and fragile to them. They never had a sense that could I look after myself. So that's why I had to make stuff of my own. To be taken seriously. To show them what I *could* do.'

Kevin has rarely ever spoken to artists; like his sister, they've always seemed self-indulgent to him. For the first time now, he wonders if maybe artists *do* harbor some deep-seated need to create. To strike out and prove themselves to the world, in order to satisfy something inside.

'Listen, art was how I could be different from you guys. I was just as good as you at soccer, but Mom and Dad never took my soccer seriously. Girls weren't supposed to play soccer. I was supposed to be like Bonnie and do ballet and gymnastics and win piano competitions.'

Kevin snorts. 'We *all* had to win piano competitions ... thanks to Bonnie.'

They both look back at their sister, asleep and oblivious, her head leaning against the window.

'Except Bonnie was the only one who actually won anything.' Alex chuckles. 'I always got too nervous and messed up in the finals.'

'And I just ... wasn't very good at piano. So I never practiced.'

'So thanks, Bon!' Alex gestures toward their dozing sister. 'See, she set us *both* up for failure.'

They both share a laugh at this, and the conversation feels new, different. But not uncomfortable.

'Hey,' Alex says, her voice hinting of mischief. 'I bet she's getting an awful crick in her neck from sleeping like that.'

'Think we should wake her up?' Kevin nurses a bemused grin.

'Yeah, go on. We'd be doing her a favor.'

Alex taps a button, and Bonnie's window slides partly open. Her face tips sideways into the sudden rush of air and the roar of Route 65.

Bonnie jerks awake and gasps. 'Huh? What?' She looks around in shock, disoriented. 'What's happening?'

Kevin and Alex burst out laughing.

'We're entering the Ozarks,' Alex says. 'Didn't want you to miss it.'

Branson, Missouri

Maybe some of Alex and Kevin's conversation filtered into Bonnie's sleep, because she had been dreaming of Mom. A very early memory of Mom, glowing and pregnant with Kevin, while a young Bonnie watched, excited to have a baby brother. Or was that a real memory?

Bonnie is disoriented, stretching her neck and pondering this scrap of a dream, as she gazes out half-asleep at the Ozarks, whatever they are. Aren't they meant to be a quaint and charming backwater? Or a sanctuary for hillbillies?

Instead, they are on a modern concrete highway, coursing through forested mountains that gleam bronze in the afternoon sun. The carpet of tree cover is interrupted by massive billboards advertising country music revues, Christian rock concerts, the occasional touring Broadway musical. She glimpses shopping outlets and luxury resorts, roller coasters and water park slides tucked away on various spurs of these hillsides.

On one hillside to their right, an enormous white cross stands, at least five stories tall. It is aglow with bright fluorescent lighting and decorated with large, sky-blue tears.

Bonnie gapes.

If she had been anticipating the solitary pluck of a banjo when entering the Ozarks, the appropriate soundtrack here seems to be loud, commercial country rock, blasted from stadium speakers with razzamatazz sparklers spraying upward.

Perhaps Alex was right. Another country, another culture. Is this the America she knows?

'Are you guys hungry?' her sister asks. 'We haven't eaten since St. Louis.'

'Starving,' Bonnie answers, still bewildered.

Kevin shrugs. 'Well, let's see what kind of food we can get in the Ozarks.'

* * *

The answer is steak, as they cruise the streets of Branson, looking for somewhere to eat. Alex is too hungry to grumble about vegetarian options: mozzarella sticks and a side salad will have to do. Scarfing down their dinner in an Americana-themed steak restaurant, she is very conscious of how much they stick out among the clientele. Multigenerational white families, their faces red from the afternoon sun. The children occasionally sneak a look at the three Asians in a nearby booth.

Living in the middle of cosmopolitan London, it's been a while since Alex has felt this self-conscious about her race. But the waitstaff are friendly enough. No microaggressions here, just simply a feeling of being distinctly out of place. And that is something Alex has felt for most of her life.

Outside the restaurant on the Strip, they pass shops offering moonshine tastings, homemade fudge and Victorian dolls, model train sets and Jesus and his apostles figurine action sets. There is the usual tourist tat of T-shirts, shot glasses, mugs, magnets – most of them made in China, but all proudly emblazoned with 'Branson, MO.' Though less than twenty years old, the strip malls are designed with the false fronts of Western towns from the pioneer era. All this old-school Americana, evoking the glory of what this country used to be.

It's more than displacement that Alex feels now, but a discomfort, an unease.

Because the past, Alex thinks, is nothing this country should be celebrating. Massacres, slavery, Jim Crow laws, the Chinese Exclusion Act. Perhaps that is why, when she sees a town draped in a celebration of Americana, cowboy hats and Old Glory, the message to her is clear: she is not welcome. She is not someone who ever belonged in America's past. She, a Chinese American lesbian, is not wanted here. And never will be.

Driving through Branson, Alex follows Highway 76 up a hill, past low-budget motels and kitschy museums, elaborate go-kart tracks and Ferris wheels. There's a three-story-high chicken wearing a star-spangled vest, a recreation of the *Titanic*, giant meatballs advertising Italian food. In and among all of this, there are veterans memorials: American flags and carved stone markers commemorating the fallen.

Alex marvels at the miles upon miles of tourist development: so much construction, so much investment, just to entertain families on vacation. Then near one intersection, they hear chanting and horn-honking. A change of scene here: an angry crowd of people cluster around a strip mall, waving signs and banners.

'Whoa, what's that?' Kevin asks.

Alex slows the car for a better glimpse.

In fact, there are two bristling crowds of people facing each other, with thirty feet of tarmac between them. One group gathers under a Confederate flag, shouting and whooping. They wear cowboy hats and baseball caps, and a speaker on a flatbed truck amplifies a man's voice: '*We are proud children of the Confederacy. This is our heritage. We owe it to our forefathers.*'

131

Opposite them, on a stretch of sidewalk, the other group of protestors is largely Black, wearing black T-shirts, and waving homemade posters that say:

Black Lives Matter
Human Rights Are Not an Option
Dixie Should Be Dead

Both crowds are bunched outside a store with a large sign bearing the Confederate flag, advertising 'Southern heritage' souvenirs.

'Black Lives Matter! Black Lives Matter!' one crowd chants.

This, Alex thinks. She needs to see this. She turns into the parking lot.

'What are you doing?' Kevin seethes.

Alex parks the car nearby, stares out the window at the protestors.

'Don't get out of the car, Alex,' Bonnie warns. 'It might not be safe.'

'It's just a protest,' Alex grumbles. 'Besides, there's police right there.'

Two policemen stand off to the side, hands resting on holsters.

This is more than simply a spectacle. This is America in the modern age, and the very problem lies in people wanting to ignore the fissures – especially comfortable, compliant people like her well-to-do sister.

'Why are they protesting?' Kevin sounds like the usual ignorant idiot he always is.

Alex glares at him. 'Because it's the twenty-first century, and Confederate flags shouldn't be sold as souvenirs?' A dose of sarcasm for his cluelessness.

She reaches to open the door, but Bonnie snaps at her.

'Alex, don't! We need to reach Tulsa tonight, and I'm tired, and there's four more hours of driving.'

Alex fumes. How can they want to miss this? She's reluctant to leave; she wants to see the protest. But she also knows that Bonnie's right; she's already added on hours to their journey by detouring to Branson.

Her disappointment mixes with something else: a sense that she will always be alone in her family, weighed down by the awareness that comes with Nya's race.

'At least let me take a photo,' she insists. Something to document what she witnessed here. Opening the window, Alex leans out with her phone and zooms in to take a shot of the pro-Dixie crowd, then the Black Lives Matter protestors. Just then, a Black man looks up and frowns to see her photographing him.

Shit. He's gonna think I'm just another Asian tourist, here for sightseeing.

Alex curses her poor timing.

But is that so far from the truth?

Embarrassed, Alex fires up the Mazda, watches the protest recede behind them in the rearview mirror. For all she knows, these two groups have been demonstrating for days, weeks. There will be no resolution to the conflict, and the chanting will eventually peter out, only to flare up somewhere else, at another souvenir shop or statue or commemorative plaque, fueled by another group of protestors.

A quiet guilt creeps inside her: Was she merely there to gawk at this spectacle, an onlooker with no real skin in the game? What would Nya have wanted her to do?

She felt the urge to step out, to add her voice to the clamor.

But even now, the directive from her family was the same: stay in the car, lock the doors, don't get involved.

1991

The two men didn't exactly look like criminals, but they were the kind of guys you wanted to steer clear of. They were like something out of a Western, cowhands or whatever kind of guys just hung around outside, letting the sun and the dust settle on them, because there was nothing better to do. But they were content to just *be*. Kevin could never imagine being that comfortable simply sitting outside, staring at the world. And letting the rest of the world stare at you.

He and Dad approached the gas station shop – more like a shack made out of wood.

'We pay first, and ask about the bathroom there,' Dad had muttered to him, like a football coach whispering a plan of attack to his team, at least the way they did it in the movies.

They were getting closer to the two men, and he saw Dad and Mom exchange a nod – barely noticeable, before Mom and Bonnie veered off to the side, to look for the women's bathroom. Dad urged him to march up the steps into the building.

They passed the two men, sitting on the stairs.

'Got your gas?' one of the men asked Dad, almost as a challenge.

Dad nodded nervously. He slowed down to acknowledge the men but kept walking. 'Yeah yeah, thank you very much.'

That seemed to set off the two men, who sniggered. The same kind of laugh that had passed between the white boys in the locker room, when it was just them and Kevin. Nothing spoken aloud, but the traded looks, the silent teasing.

Dad opened the door to the shop, and the bell on the door rang. It wasn't one of those modern glass doors that slid open automatically when you approached. This was an older sort of gas station. No security cameras. You couldn't be sure if everything worked here.

But the man behind the counter was already waiting for them.

He smirked, tilting his head. 'Those're just my friends, making sure no one drives off without paying.'

'Yes, we here now, ready to pay.' Dad attempted a nervous smile, taking out his wallet.

Dad looked small and slight, and kept his eyes downward.

The man stared at the wallet. 'You don't want nothing else? Pepsi or chips or nothing like that?'

'Is . . . there . . . a bathroom key?'

'Oh, there's a key. But you don't need it. If you need a piss or a crap, you can just walk round the back and let yourself in the men's room.'

Kevin squirmed. The way the man just said it, so direct, with no shame . . .

The man stared out the window at Mom and Bonnie walking past, and gave a long, low whistle. 'That your wife and daughter?'

'Yes, yes, that's them,' Dad said, but he still had on that faltering half smile, and Kevin wanted to smack it off him. It was so embarrassing. The man was being so gross toward Mom and Bonnie, and that's all Dad could do, that stupid half smile?

'Them Oriental girls of yours sure are pretty,' the man said.

135

Kevin's eyes widened. Did he just say that about Mom and Bonnie? Gross. You weren't even supposed to use the word 'Oriental' anymore. You were supposed to say 'Asian.'

Dad quieted down, motionless like a cat, and just looked at the counter. 'Can I pay now?'

'Sure you don't want nothing else?'

Dad didn't reply, only shook his head.

'I seen your boy looking at the beef jerky. You want some beef jerky, son? I can add that on, you know. The gas comes out to fourteen thirty-three, and the beef jerky's two dollars. So let's just call that... an even twenty, how 'bout that?'

What was going on? The man had completely added it up wrong.

'I think twenty sounds about right. Don't it?' the man said. He glared at Dad, hard and unsmiling. Slowly, Dad's eyes crept upward until he was looking at the man. But Dad still said nothing.

Kevin spoke up, his heart beating fast: 'But the total is sixteen thirty-three—'

The man cut him off, and planted two meaty hands on the counter, drawing himself up to full height.

'Mr. Chan, tell your boy he don't need to be perfect at math every time.'

Kevin flinched. Chan wasn't their last name...

The bell rang again, and the two men from outside drifted into the shop. Silently, they walked up to the counter and leaned on it, one on either side of him and Dad. Fixed around them in a triangle, the men all glared at Dad, wordless.

Kevin was reminded of the fights at school, which always ended up with some boy punching another on the floor, a teacher arriving to break it up. But before the fists, there was always that moment of stillness.

No one said anything. The man behind the counter cleared his throat.

'This here gentleman was just paying his bill. Comes up to twenty, right?'

Dad nodded, his voice barely audible. 'Yeah, yeah, twenty.'

'What's that?' the man on the right asked loudly, and cocked a hand to his ear, mocking.

'Speak up!' the man on the left said. 'You wanna show your son here how a real man talks.'

The man behind the counter held his hand out for payment. It was thick and massive, and Kevin could see his fingernails were rimmed black with dirt.

Dad put a twenty-dollar bill on the counter. Then he grabbed Kevin's hand and headed for the door.

'Don't forget the beef jerky.'

Kevin stopped. He didn't even like beef jerky, but now Dad had paid for it. He looked at the rack of packets, which were gathering dust.

'I like this one here,' one of the men said. 'Extra-spicy, if you can handle it. Which I'm sure you Orientals can.'

The man grabbed a packet off the rack and tossed it to Kevin. There was a brief, terrifying flash of panic, like all those times in gym class, when Kevin prayed that he'd be able to catch the baseball as it arced toward him in the outfield.

He caught the beef jerky and held tight.

'Oh ho.' The man laughed. 'The kid can actually catch.'

Kevin headed for the door, the packet clutched to his chest.

With Branson behind them, Kevin watches as they cross Table Rock Lake on a wide suspension bridge. It is a picturesque crossing: forested hills and purpling sky reflected in the calm expanse of the water. In spirit, a million miles from what they'd witnessed back there: the fraught chanting, the ugly jostling of protest signs outside a strip mall.

'So was that worth swinging by Branson, to get your fix of redneck culture?' He meant to deliver this as a sarcastic joke to Alex, but instead it sounds mean and chiding.

She does not take it well, her hackles already on edge.

'I felt it was worth seeing,' Alex is defensive. 'That was America in a nutshell. The two halves.'

'Huh.' He's not sure he agrees. It must be easy for Alex, living on the other side of the Atlantic, to swoop in, witness a political protest outside a Confederate souvenir shop and pronounce that 'This is America.' But what if you're just going about your everyday life in Chicago and find yourself drawn to neither of those sides? Not the Black Lives Matter signs or the Confederate flag. Surely, there were more than the two halves, adding up to a bigger whole.

But Alex has always been given to reading some larger meaning into any random occurrence. When she was eight and about to go to a piano recital, she broke down in tears because she found a dead butterfly on their patio table and was convinced they would all die in a car crash on the way. They didn't, of course. They were fine. But delayed by Alex's sobbing, they all had to rush, and Dad nearly got a speeding ticket. Classic Alex. Causing chaos for everyone else, on account of her airy-fairy whims.

138

WHAT WE LEFT UNSAID

So America in a nutshell? He wasn't sure.

The car dips down into a valley, burnished golden in the evening light. At the far end of a field sits a large barn with a huge metal cross erected above it, a string of lights sparkle around a sign: Crown of Holy Thorns Chapel.

'I don't get why they're making such a big deal about a store anyway,' Kevin mutters. 'So they sell the Confederate flag, so what?'

'Did you actually say that, Kevin?' Alex raises her voice, irate.

Now I've done it. Kevin prepares himself for an hour-long lecture on intersectional something or other.

'That flag symbolizes the institutional enslavement of an entire race of people,' Alex says, her finger jabbing out the window. 'Every time it's worn or flown somewhere, it's an endorsement of slavery.'

'Are you sure?' Kevin asks, trying to play devil's advocate. 'Maybe people are just proud of being Southern, so they want to fly the Confederate flag? You know, Chicagoans root for the Bulls. Southerners wave a Confederate flag.'

'Except you would never in a million years find a Black Southerner flying that flag,' Alex pronounces with severity. 'But all those people supporting the shop? Proud to endorse a racist ideology.'

Kevin shakes his head. 'Yeah, but why do you even care? It's not your fight.'

'Kevin—' Alex says, but then suddenly stops short.

'What?' he challenges her.

'Never mind,' she croaks.

That was weird. Normally Alex is always gunning for a fight, but maybe she just ran out of steam.

Kevin sighs. 'I think people just dig in their heels. They say:

139

this is my way of life, and I'm not budging from it. Maybe it's not any more evil than that.'

'Well, *I'm* glad I live in Boston,' Bonnie remarks from her side of the car. He didn't realize she had been listening in.

'Why? Because New England is so enlightened?' Alex turns on her. 'It's pretty white there, last time I checked.'

Bonnie wisely ignores this comment. It is true, after all. 'At least we don't have shops that sell Confederate flags.'

'Guarantee you there's some racists in New England,' Alex mutters. 'They just hide behind a veneer of educated liberalism.'

Bonnie rolls her eyes and smacks her thigh in a sudden, unexpected motion. 'Listen, Alex, you can get angry at the world and think everyone's out to get you. But that's fucking *exhausting*. Most of us are just trying to live a life with as little conflict as possible. To raise our kids, make sure they're happy, and hope that we have some time at the end of the day to ... I dunno, watch an interesting documentary or read a good book or go to a yoga class or something.'

Alex snorts. 'Great, yoga ... But that's the whole problem! We're all so caught up in living our own nice comfortable lives that *we don't care anymore*. People will overlook institutional racism and the bombing of children and the disaster that is the US healthcare system, so long as they've got a good TV series to watch and a nice place to go on vacation, so they can forget about their miserable working lives for a few weeks of the year. That's what's so sad about it all.'

Alex seems to be visibly shaking with anger as she rounds a hill, emerging onto a plain of green-gold fields edged by pine forest. Kevin's annoyance with her mellows unexpectedly into something else. He is reminded of a faint memory: Alex as a little toddler, intrigued by a bee one minute. And the next minute, on the ground bawling, her face reddened in agony after the bee stung her. At six, all he felt for her then was concern. And love. She was so little, so tearful, and he just wanted her to be happy again.

Where has that protectiveness gone now?

He feels none of it. And is all the sadder for it.

Bonnie leans forward from the back seat and squeezes Alex's shoulder. 'Hey,' she says, soothing and kind. 'Wanna take a break from driving?'

Alex nods and exhales melodramatically, the weight of centuries. She dashes tears from her eyes as she pulls off onto the shoulder.

The car rattles to a halt on gravel, and one by one, the three of them climb out. They are in a wooded glade, and a stream trickles past, sliding past weeping willows that sway in the breeze, indifferent to the human frustrations and anxieties and resentments that pass by hundreds of times a day, in each of the cars on this highway.

They lean in silence on the wooden beam of a fence, each lost in their own thoughts. Horses whicker in a field nearby.

Suddenly, Alex speaks up, with her trademark sarcasm. 'Hey, does this count as bonding? Mom would be proud.'

Kevin and Bonnie laugh, grateful for some levity.

His sister Alex is such a mystery. Always has been, always will be.

Kevin tosses a stone into the stream. He watches as it sinks through the clear water, glinting golden in the late evening light before reaching the bottom.

Arkansas

They drive through the Ozarks in a deepening twilight. Aware of the miles they still have to cover, Kevin pushes down on the gas, speeding past farms and clapboard churches and closed general stores. They drive through another small, one-stoplight town, where a hand-painted wooden sign at the gas station announces: 'You Are Now in Arkansas.'

Bonnie doesn't mind this extra detour from the interstate. She has been quiet for most of the afternoon, the green pastures and secluded valleys of the Ozarks giving her reason for contemplation.

Instead of mere hours, it feels like a lifetime ago that she sat across from Sergeant Thompson in that St. Louis police station, embarrassed to list the excessive contents of her handbag: the designer wallet with its membership cards to art galleries and yoga studios and ice cream parlor loyalty schemes (*Get 10 stamps for a free double cone!*) Why was she carrying all that with her anyway?

It is the loss of the toy car that bothers her the most. All the other stuff, even the three hundred dollars in cash and the expensive Paul Smith wallet – all those are replaceable.

But she can still remember the moment when her three boys proudly presented her with that green toy car on her fortieth birthday, explaining who each of the drawn-on faces were. All five them in miniature form, engaged in an imaginary road trip.

Losing that car, Bonnie feels like she's lost a little bit of herself, a tiny but very essential failure as a mother. She could have kept that little car in her suitcase, or safely at home on her desk. But no, she'd insisted on bringing it with her as some kind of talisman on this ludicrous cross-country trip, and now it's been tossed out like trash by some grubby street-thief interested only in making a quick buck. Ignorant to its emotional value.

Or maybe, on second thought, that car will end up in the hands of a younger brother, some poor city kid who will find joy rolling it on the floor of the cramped apartment where he lives. Maybe he will imagine those hand-drawn faces to be his own mother and father and brothers.

Bonnie feels a bit better when she imagines it that way. What is cast off can still be loved by someone else.

With this sentimental balm, her middle-class guilt is allayed.

And she is all too aware of it. Because the guilt of being liberal and affluent is never-ending, once you venture outside the policed borders of your moneyed comfort zone. Here in the Ozarks, Bonnie sees ramshackle farmhouses, yards strewn with vehicles in various states of disassembly and rust. What would these people do in a medical emergency, miles from any hospital, with no private healthcare policy? And what would they do, to access even a fraction of the funds that her fourteen-year-old holds in his bank account?

Perhaps that is why the rich stay inside their gated communities and their private membership clubs. Not from the fear of being robbed — because if that did happen, you could easily replace what had been stolen from you. But the fear is in being reminded that others out there have so much less, due to a simple trick of fate. That they are willing to risk arrest, a police record, even jail time, all to make a profit which you would hardly notice if it were to be subtracted from your bank account balance.

And yet, you would feel outraged if this stranger were to take it from you.

* * *

In this dusky drive through the Ozarks, they are getting what Alex had hoped: a glimpse into another corner of America, previously unknown to them. Passing through the quaint main street of Eureka Springs, Alex notices rainbow flags above art galleries and organic cafes. This is a place she'd love to explore more, when she has more time.

A quick Google search tells her that this is a resort town for LGBTQ tourism, in the middle of the Ozarks.

Excited, she reads to her siblings from her phone screen.

' "Starting in the sixties and seventies, Eureka Springs attracted hippies, counterculture radicals, and lesbian separatists"... Wow!'

She keeps scanning. ' "But it had already been a Victorian resort village... The Osage, Shawnee, and Delaware knew about the healing properties of the springs... Then in 1879, Judge J.B. Saunders claimed his crippling disease was cured by the spring waters, leading to a boomtown... African Americans moved here and set up businesses for Black tourists... but after Plessy v. Ferguson, they were banned from all the springs but one." '

Alex absorbs this, as the 62 takes them away from the historic center, into the wooded hills. Indian removal, crass commercialism, racial segregation, all in one Ozark resort town.

'That's a potted history of the US right there,' Bonnie remarks.

144

'And then the lesbians took over!' Alex shouts with mock delight, pumping her fist in the air.

The others can't help but laugh.

Alex wonders, is this the kind of place where she and Nya might take their daughter on vacation, somewhere down the line? And how will she explain to their daughter the rainbow flags posted proudly along the main street of Eureka Springs, while an hour's drive away, Confederate flags are sold en masse to Branson tourists? 'They're just flags,' she would say, in a weird echo of Kevin. Yet they mean so much more.

Everyone flocking to their own tribe, even on vacation.

In Bentonville, they find a brass band playing an open-air concert in the picture-perfect town square. Compared to the run-down farms and hand-built churches of the Ozarks, downtown Bentonville seems like a movie set, scrubbed clean and manicured to recreate an idyllic American town of yesteryear.

The brass band is playing *Appalachian Spring* by Aaron Copland, as concertgoers sit fanning themselves on chairs by the wide steps of the town hall, the clock tower rising above them.

'What the . . .' Kevin mumbles.

'Is this place for real?' Bonnie asks.

And then Alex remembers: Walmart.

Bentonville, Arkansas, is the home of Walmart. Therein lies the affluence. And the manufactured retro facade.

'Stop, stop, stop,' Alex says. 'This is where the first-ever Walmart opened up.'

'So what, you want to pay your respects to Walmart?' Kevin snorts, sarcastically.

'No!' Alex scoffs. She recalls watching a left-wing documentary about questionable business practices and paltry health

145

insurance packages for their employees. 'But it's worth seeing just for a minute, right? Plus, I'd love to find a bathroom. I'm sure they've gotta be clean in this town.'

Kevin finds somewhere to park, and they skip out into the town square, passing a recreated 1950s soda fountain shop and, next to it, the Walmart Museum, the site of Sam Walton's first five-and-dime store.

A placard outside reads: *Sam Walton was a frugal man, who wanted to keep prices low, saving his customers money so they could live better.*

'You know, I still shop at Walmart from time to time,' Bonnie admits.

Kevin and Alex stop in their tracks, their faces alight with amusement. 'Bonnie Chu Prescott, who would have thought?'

Bonnie shrugs and keeps walking. 'Come on, I was raised by Mom and Dad. Part of me still *feels bad* if I spend money on something I can get cheaper elsewhere. Even if I can afford it.'

Ah, to be raised by frugal immigrants, Alex thinks. Bonnie can climb the heights of New England society, but she'll never fully escape her budget-conscious roots.

'There you go, always making Mom and Dad proud,' Kevin jokes.

They stand, smiling at each other in the balmy summer air, with a shared knowledge that doesn't need to be spoken. The brass band fires up another patriotic tune, and they saunter off into this strangely curated, postcard vision of small-town America.

When they return to the car, there's a cop standing in front of it, inspecting it. A sliver of rebellious fear creeps into Alex's stomach. The three of them exchange glances, unsure of what to do.

'Um, sir?' Kevin steps forward. 'Everything okay with the car?'

The policeman stands up. He is white, tall and unsmiling, younger than all of them. She watches him size Kevin up.

'You the owner of this vehicle?' the cop asks. A thin patina of politeness, and underneath, the demand.

'I am,' Kevin answers.

'You know you're not supposed to be parked here, right?' Phrased like a question, but of course it's not.

Shit, are they illegally parked?

'Oh, I'm so sorry,' Kevin says, his tone suppliant. 'I'm really sorry; I didn't realize that.'

'Yeah,' the cop answers, pointing to a nearby sign and then a yellow stripe on the tarmac. 'This is a no-loading zone. You're supposed to be on that side of the line. But on this side of the line, it's cause for a penalty.'

'Really?' Alex speaks up. 'But it's evening. There's no other cars around, and no one needs this space—'

'That's not the point,' the cop cuts her off, severe. 'We have rules for a reason.'

What reason? she thinks. *So you can go on a petty power trip?*

But she knows better than to voice that.

The cop studies her and Bonnie: two slight Asian women, one with a defiant voice and punkish hairstyle. Obvious outsiders.

'I could issue you a penalty for this, you know.'

Kevin moves into groveling mode.

'Listen, we're very sorry, Officer,' Kevin repeats. 'We've driven all the way from St. Louis and need to reach Tulsa by tonight, so we're pretty tired. I didn't see the sign.'

'You from Illinois?' The cop gestures to the license plate.

'Yes.' Kevin nods. 'Chicago. We're doing Route 66 but wanted a detour to see this part of the country.'

'Bentonville's a lovely town,' Bonnie adds, simpering. Alex wants to smack her.

The cop nods, as if this mention of all-American Route 66 makes them more acceptable somehow. 'And you don't have any drugs or weapons in the car?'

'N-no,' Kevin says, but looks away quickly.

The cop pauses for a moment, folding his arms in a military stance and staring at Kevin. Completely unnecessary, Alex thinks with anger. Honestly, how dangerous can someone like her brother really be?

But Kevin seems to shrink visibly, his eyes look down, then flick up briefly as if to beg the policeman: *Don't hurt me, please. I'm just an innocent Asian man.*

'Okay,' the cop finally says. 'Just move the car and be on your way.'

'Thank you, Officer,' Kevin says apologetically.

Thank you?! Alex is silently irate.

'And next time, pay more attention to where you're parking,' the cop adds. 'Bentonville's very proud of its historic down-town. But we can't have people parking all over the place, disregarding the rules.'

Historic, Alex scoffs internally. *As in, eighty years old and completely artificial.*

Kevin unlocks the car, and the three of them move to open their respective doors. All of their movements deliberately slowed down for the cop to see and approve of.

'Bunch of foreigners,' the cop suddenly mutters, aware he can be heard. The three of them freeze. But none of them dare say anything.

Wordlessly they get in the car and drive away. Alex shoots a furious look back at the cop, through their rear window. He's standing straight and watching them suspiciously, as if waiting for them to disappear.

* * *

'Well that was fucked-up,' Alex pronounces, as Kevin accelerates out of Bentonville.

They pass a giant blue billboard that still says 'Trump', years after the presidency has changed. The three of them sit in silence.

'Are we gonna talk about this?' Alex finally asks. 'Or just pretend it didn't happen?'

Bonnie shrugs. 'So what? The guy was an asshole. Lots of cops are. At least we didn't get fined in the end.'

Kevin agrees silently. Plus, with everything else going on in his life, he doesn't need any kind of penalty on his driver's license, even from another state.

'Yeah, but it's not about that,' Alex says. 'It was such an obvious power play on his part. And if we weren't Asian, would he have treated us like that?'

'He definitely wouldn't have said "bunch of foreigners" at the end,' Kevin grouses.

Bonnie sighs. 'Well, we're never gonna know. So what's the point of getting so worked up about stuff like that?'

Easy for Bonnie to say. In a week she'll return to her blue-blood New England lifestyle, as the wife of Christopher Prescott, the one acceptable Asian blip in a family that is the very definition of WASP.

But for Kevin? He thinks back to all the times he has encountered 'stuff like that' in his forty-odd years. The condescending white authority figures – sports coaches and managers and yes, policemen – with their offhand remarks. The boys in the office who would boast about sales targets and scoring hot girls on a Friday night, and then look at him with a muted pity, as if he would never be able to play in their league. The pretty white girls who laughed in his face at college when he tried, even remotely, to start a conversation with them, or showed just the slightest hint of attraction to them.

The unspoken disdain with which he was habitually treated, like he was a nonentity, a meaningless Asian face: just someone to follow orders, pay his bill, insert his credit card, and be gone.

From time to time, he had wanted to grip someone by the lapels and shout in their face: 'You know, I have feelings, too! I have interests and hobbies and ambitions!' But always, he was just another Asian guy, a law-abiding, khaki-wearing citizen.

His male colleagues and friends would make offhand remarks about sexy Asian women, occasionally joke if he had a cute sister to introduce them to. ('Uh, no. One is married, and the other one is crazy and lives in Europe,' he would say.) But he knew the same conversations were not happening among American women about the sexy qualities of Asian men, unless they were Keanu Reeves, or some other half-Asian actor with chiseled cheekbones and a chiseled chest. Ordinary-looking Asian men like him, round-faced and meager of muscle, did not register in their eyes.

And the jokes – god, the jokes about small penis size. Muttered casually, amiably, 'all in good fun.' He did not need to hear them, and yet they were always told somewhere on the edges of a conversation, at a party. What was the point of these jokes? To humiliate Asian men like him? To make the teller feel that little bit better about themselves, while he, the listener, had to laugh along and be cool with it?

Kevin had grown so accustomed to this kind of teasing that he realized it was better to tamp any emotion down. Appear stone-faced, unbothered. And in that sense, to become what they were expecting all along: an emotionless Asian face, barely human, anything but unique.

*

'That's just the thing.' Alex is now banging the woke drum for what feels like the twentieth time that day. 'It's easy enough for us Asians to let all those microaggressions slide off our backs. But if we were Black, who knows what would have happened?'

She has a point, as much as he hates to admit it.

Kevin knows all too well how differently he would have been treated in any scenario if he was a tall, broad-shouldered white guy. To be just 'one of the boys.'

'You're right,' he says. 'We should probably consider ourselves lucky.'

There's a silence in the car, and not a dissatisfied one. Perhaps it's Alex's surprise at hearing Kevin agree with her. He smiles inwardly.

But also there is the deeper, more hidden relief. That it never got as far as the cop searching the car for drugs or weapons. Because he'd lied about the gun in the glove compartment. Knowing full well that no one would ever suspect this nonentity Asian man from Illinois of owning a firearm.

And for him, there is a certain, unfamiliar thrill in lying straight to a policeman's face – and getting away with it.

Oklahoma

Somewhere in Oklahoma a couple hours later – after they've driven thru the Cherokee Nation, after miles of wide, flat farms and lakes – they regain the interstate and then Route 66.

To Bonnie, this leg of the trip seems never-ending. Atop Gateway Arch this morning, she marveled at how far she could see across the Midwestern plain. But now they've far outstripped that view from St. Louis, crossed the Ozarks and lake systems and state borders, and only now does she start to comprehend the breadth of the American West: this huge, endless expanse of land.

She's already imagining the plush comfort of her Tulsa hotel bed, its clean white sheets and outsized pillows, when Kevin inexplicably parks the car off a darkened section of the 66.

'God, do we really have to stop? I'm so tired.'

'One last stop,' he assures them. 'We haven't been on the 66 in a while, and I really want you guys to see this.'

The next minute, they stand staring at a strange roadside sight: inside a stagnant, mosquito-ridden pond, sits a giant grinning whale, painted an artificial turquoise. Its mouth yawns open, beckoning humans to step inside. In the evening light, the three of them are the only ones around.

'The Blue Whale of Catoosa,' Kevin informs them.

'This roadside stuff gets weirder and weirder,' Alex mutters.

But Bonnie can see the appeal. It's something her youngest would still love: the whale so elemental and welcoming, a cartoon brought to colossal life.

'Let's take a photo,' she says. 'I wanna show this to my kids.'

'You want us in front of it? Or inside the whale?' Alex asks.

They step inside this echoing whale, and Kevin taps the sides of it. Seems sturdy enough. Bonnie is reminded of that story from Pinocchio, or at least the version she knew from the Disney film. His devoted father, Geppetto, had gone searching for him but was swallowed by a monstrous whale, trapped there for days. So it was Pinocchio who journeyed to find his father, and who engineered their escape together from the belly of the whale.

Some distant chime rings inside her. Children coming to the rescue of their parents. A parent who had sacrificed everything for his child, who then escaped into the world, a wooden-limbed innocent, hardly deserving of his father's love . . .

Bonnie is thinking this as she snaps a selfie of her, Alex, and Kevin in the eerie twilight. The huge, gleaming whale rises behind them.

'You know, there's something I haven't told you guys.'

'What?' Her siblings' faces turn toward her, surprised in the yellow glow of the sodium lights.

Bonnie catches herself. *Why had she said that?*

'I . . .' She panics for a moment, wondering if she should backtrack. But Kevin and Alex look too expectant. She has to tell them something.

'It's nothing; it's small. But Alex, earlier you joked that my bag getting stolen was probably the worst thing to ever happen to me.'

Alex shrugs. 'It was just a joke. I didn't mean—'

Bonnie cuts through. 'Well, one bad thing did happen to me. Once.'

And she begins to unspool her tale. She was twenty-nine, she and Chris had been trying for a child . . .

* * *

'Oh, Bonnie, I had no idea,' Alex is saying, her eyes moist after she's heard Bonnie's story. She wraps Bonnie in a long, heartfelt hug, feeling, for the first time, an unfamiliar note of pity for her older sister.

Bonnie sniffles and dashes a tear from her eye. It's the most emotion her older sister allows herself to show.

'Well, there's no way you would have known about the miscarriage. Chris and I decided not to tell anyone.'

'And I was a self-absorbed twentysomething at the time,' Alex reflects. 'I wouldn't have known the right thing to say anyway.'

She glances at Kevin, who is standing apart from them, studying the stagnant water around the giant whale. Speaking of self-absorbed . . .

She knows Bonnie's story is not an unusual one. So many hopeful mothers-to-be over the years have lived that unspoken grief, betrayed by their own bodies. She wonders if the men have had any clue about that hidden sadness, experienced by the women in their lives.

Kevin turns to peer at her in the dark.

'Alex, are you *crying*?' He asks in disbelief. Almost contempt.

'My eyes are watering, yes,' Alex confirms, with defensive sarcasm.

'Why—' Kevin starts, but she cuts him off.

'Because it's sad, okay? It's sad that it happened to Bonnie all those years ago, and none of us ever got to comfort her about it.'

'Guys, it's not that big a deal, really,' Bonnie says.

'No, don't minimize it,' Alex warns her, the feminist right-eousness beginning to bubble forth.

Kevin scoffs. 'You really still cry at everything, don't you?'

'Is it any surprise, then, that I went to drama school?' Alex shoots back.

'I guess not.' Kevin shrugs. 'You must have won awards for crying on command there.'

Alex wants to add that in fact, she often *was* praised for this particular talent of hers, but she doesn't want to give Kevin the pleasure of confirming his suspicions.

'Guys.' Bonnie raises her voice, and suddenly Alex feels guilty for wresting the attention away from Bonnie, who has just bravely shared her story. 'It's late; I'm getting eaten alive by mosquitos out here. Let's just get to Tulsa, okay?'

She's about to offer some apology when – wonder of wonders – her brother beats her to it.

'I – I'm sorry that happened, Bonnie,' Kevin turns to Bonnie awkwardly. 'I'm glad you were able to have your boys in the end.'

So he *is* capable of apologizing. Or maybe just to Bonnie. Alex nurses her bitterness and broods.

'Thanks, Kev.' Bonnie smiles in the chiaroscuro glow of the streetlights. 'I'm glad I was, too.'

* * *

Kevin drives in silence, chastened by Bonnie's story, by the grief he could still hear in her voice, decades later. He thinks of that time, ages ago, when he and Jessica had been trying to get pregnant. When they were having sex a few times a week – something unheard of in his present-day marriage. (It's been nearly two years since they've had sex.)

He wonders if Jessica had ever miscarried. She had prayed a lot during that time, more than usual. There was always a Bible on her nightstand, and if she *had* lost a pregnancy . . . maybe she chose to keep it between her and God. Perhaps that is how ignorant he has always been, in this marriage. He, Kevin, would have fathered a child, lost it, and he would have never known.

* * *

They drive west in the summer night now, Tulsa a yellow-orange gleam ahead of them on the flat, darkened plain of Oklahoma. Bonnie had thought she was finished with her story, but another memory, even more submerged, has come to the surface.

With the heaviness of the previous conversation, she almost doesn't want to bring it up. But it's a story somehow related to her siblings. She leans toward their dark silhouettes, says something she has never told them before.

'You know, I think Mom also had a miscarriage. When I was really young. Before the two of you came along.'

'What?' Kevin is in shock. But his hands remain on the steering wheel, his eyes on the interstate.

They ride along in silence for a moment, the near full moon rising in the sky.

'Wow,' Alex says, a strange note of awe in her voice.

Bonnie considers. 'Mom never really spoke about it, but I remember.'

'What do you remember?'

'I would've been . . . I dunno, two? Maybe even younger.'

Bonnie thinks back. She has no coherent memories of those years, just snatches of feelings, faded images that she can't trust as either memory or invention.

156

'I just remember . . . Mom and Dad were smiling. They said I was going to have a baby brother . . .'

She does her own calculation. Sex of a fetus is generally determined at twenty weeks, so Mom must have been at least four months pregnant. She remembers Mom's body swelling, her belly so weird in its roundness. Resting an ear on that curvature of skin, wondering if a baby could really be living inside there. More than four months, then, if her belly was that round. Five at least.

'But it wasn't me?' Kevin asks.

'No, because it went away . . .'

Next, she remembers Mom doubled over in pain on the couch, then a neighbor coming over. Suddenly Mom and Dad were gone, and she was scared, confused. It must have been her first night away from them. Auntie Teresa stayed over to look after her and gave her chocolate milk, which she'd never had before.

Then, when they came back, Mom was in bed a lot. She never smiled. Her belly wasn't round anymore.

Bonnie asked Auntie Teresa if she could listen for her baby brother again in her mom's tummy. But Auntie grew angry and said *never* to ask about him.

So she didn't.

'And then, later on, Mom was pregnant again. With you. So I . . . got confused. I thought you'd gone away for a while and decided to come back.' She laughs wryly at her mistaken childhood logic.

It's too dark now to see anyone's faces, but she leans forward into the gap between her brother and sister, trying to gauge their response.

'I never knew,' Kevin says, downbeat.

'They probably thought I was too young to understand, so

157

why bother explaining. It was just a strange, vague memory that a baby brother was going to arrive long ago. And then he didn't.'

'And then he did,' Alex adds.

'And then he did,' Bonnie repeats, and squeezes Kevin's arm. Kevin is bizarrely nonresponsive, nor does he flinch. There are tears in her eyes, but she knows in the darkness, her siblings won't be able to see them. And she is grateful for this.

Bonnie thinks of her own miscarriage and tries to map that understanding, that grief onto her own mother. Her three boys and the frantic plunge into motherhood eventually crowded out that first, inexplicable loss. Mom, too, eventually had her longed-for son, and another daughter. But if she herself had felt such sadness miscarrying at eleven weeks, what must it have felt like for Mom, to lose a future son at five, maybe six months? An unborn son you had already introduced your daughter to. A son, who in Chinese culture, would be the greatest source of pride for a mother and a family.

When she herself had first learned she was pregnant with Henry, there was excitement, but also the fear of another miscarriage. That dread had underscored Bonnie's entire pregnancy, then her first few years with him ... and then maybe she had just transferred that fear onto her next child, and her next. Maybe she had never lost that fear, only felt it lessen slowly as she watched her sons grow stronger, smarter, more prepared to take on the world.

And she and Chris had all the security that came with the Prescott name and family assets that would never let them down.

What would it have been like for an immigrant like Mom, in a country where you had to survive in a new language, where you were scorned and patronized and fetishized, if you ever set foot outside of your safe, familiar zone of Asian American suburbia? Your fear would be intensified – and your anxiety for your children.

Mom clung desperately to the idea of Kevin when she became pregnant with him, even more so to the newborn himself when he arrived. Lavishing so much attention on him, that of course, Bonnie grew resentful. Of course, like any older child, she felt neglected.

But Mom had said that she was *jie-jie*, the big sister. She was relying on Bonnie to be grown-up and always look after her little brother. And Bonnie, wanting never to disappoint her parents, had eagerly taken up that mantle of responsibility.

Then when Alex arrived, there was that maternal clinginess again. Mom held baby Alex close, introducing Kevin to her, showering them both with kisses, whispering to them how happy she was to have them here with her. That she would never leave them, and they should never leave her, too. Bonnie would watch from afar, knowing that it was her job to be the good, responsible one. That they were weak and young, and they needed Bonnie to watch out for them.

Mom needed her to be like this, even if Mom also scared her, the sharp words that would come if she ever got a B on a report card, the silent disappointment if she ever disobeyed.

So Bonnie never did.

1991

I hope the bathroom isn't gross. I hope the bathroom isn't gross.
Bonnie had been thinking this since the car first pulled into the
gas station, and now Mom (still stone-faced) gave the door to
the ladies' room a nudge. It creaked open, and Bonnie held her
breath, expecting it to reek. She stayed back as Mom flicked
on a switch.

The light sputtered to life, a dim bulb that buzzed above
them, then flickered haphazardly.

Mom grunted in disapproval. 'So yucky.'

There was only one toilet and sink, and no stall, so the two
of them crowded inside and Mom slid the rusty bolt in place.
Bonnie felt a lot safer then.

But the bathroom *was* gross. It just smelled unclean and
rotting, and there were stains in the toilet bowl where someone
else's shit had crusted over, above the waterline. Bonnie
squeezed her eyes shut in disgust.

'You want me to go first?' Mom asked. And it was a repeat of
how they'd always done this in public toilets. When Bonnie was
young, really young, she was always afraid of public toilets, of
all the germs waiting to attack her, and Mom always offered to
go first, to show her it was okay. Nothing bad would happen.

Bonnie nodded, although she was certain the bleeding had already begun.

Mom screwed up her face, tore off two lengths of toilet paper, and laid them gingerly on the toilet seat in a V.

When Mom started to tug down her shorts, Bonnie turned her back to give her privacy. She stared in the bathroom mirror, smeared and dirty, and she wished her nose weren't so flat. She wanted a nose with a bridge, or one of those cute button noses that the cheerleaders had, so that when they wore their hair up in a high ponytail, their face had the right kind of profile. Perky and pretty. Not hers, with the flat nose and the mouth that curved out, like a chimpanzee.

She heard the trickle of Mom's pee, then the flush behind her. Thank god the toilet actually flushed.

'You okay, Bonnie? You enjoying the vacation so far?' Mom asked.

Bonnie shrugged. 'I guess.' She didn't understand what the big deal was about the Grand Canyon. She was missing Karen Choi's sleepover because of this family trip, and Chrissy and Jen would tease her about this, all the gossip she'd have to beg for.

'Don't sound like you're enjoying it.' Mom always picked up on these things. 'How 'bout Las Vegas? That was fun, right?'

'I dunno. I wish I could just . . . Kevin and Alex are so annoying to have around sometimes.'

'Hey, they're just younger. They don't understand as much as you. That's why they so lucky to have you as a big sister. You always looking out for them.'

'Well, maybe I don't want to sometimes.' She'd swapped places with Mom now, and hovered over the toilet, carefully taking down her shorts so that they didn't touch the gross toilet.

Only a couple spots of blood on her underwear. Phew.

'You need a pad?' Mom asked. She always knew somehow.

As Bonnie fixed the pad onto her underwear, she resented the mini-lecture Mom was giving her.

'Bonnie, in just three years, you going off to college. Then you don't have Kevin and Alex around all the time to annoy you. So be nice, look out for them while you can.'

She couldn't wait to be free of them. College sounded so grown-up and exciting, but what if she didn't get into Stanford and what if—

'Three more years?' she grumbled. 'That sounds like forever.'

Mom laughed. 'It's not forever. It go by like that.' She snapped her fingers, then paused, her hand in midair. It came to rest on Bonnie's hair, tucking a stray lock behind her ear, the way her mom had always done. She smiled at Bonnie. 'In three years, you'll be a pro with maxi pads. You'll be all grown-up, you'll start a life of your own—'

Mom suddenly stopped, her voice caught small, like she was about to cry. Bonnie was almost embarrassed. 'Mom?'

'Oh, Bonnie, silly me. I'm thinking ahead too much.'

Mom smiled again, but in the dim light of that flickering bulb, Bonnie thought she saw tears shining in her eyes.

'You finish up here and wash your hands. This place so filthy.' Mom sniffed. 'I go check on Alex, okay?'

'Okay.' Bonnie nodded, grateful to have a minute to herself in the bathroom.

Mom unbolted the door and stepped out. The desert sun flashed for a moment, temporarily blinding her, before the door swung shut again.

Everything after, happened on the other side of the door.

Photo Message sent 10:32PM, Central Time

Hey Mom and Dad, here's us at the Arch in St. Louis. We're in Tulsa, Oklahoma tonight. See you in a few days!

Bonnie taps away efficiently on her phone to her parents. Touristy photo of them beaming, very suitable for Mom and Dad. The stolen handbag, the nasty cop in Arkansas? Definitely not anything they needed to know about.

* * *

Photo Message sent 10:47PM, Central Time

Hey Schnopes, sending this from Oklahoma! Big skies out here, lots of stars. Me & your aunties went up the St. Louis Arch this morning. Maybe show this to your mom. She might like to see it.

Kevin curses himself and his utter weakness. He can't bring himself to text this directly to Jessica? He has to rely on their ten-year-old daughter as a go-between? What a loser he's become.

He flicks off the light switch, and lies spread-eagled on his hotel bed, staring straight up at the blank ceiling, despondent.

* * *

Photo Message sent 11:19PM, Central Time

G'morning! How are you feeling?

163

Bonnie's handbag got stolen in St. Louis. Kevin's still a dick. Here's a giant whale by the side of Route 66. Told you America was weird!

Alex suppresses a laugh as she hits send on her text to Nya. Over in London, the sun would have been up for hours, coaxing heat out of the sidewalk and macadam, before the morning commuters built up. Here in Tulsa, the city – if you can call it that – seems dead, empty streets on a weekday night. Far beyond the buildings, past the glow of urban lighting and oil refineries, the Oklahoma plain continues on toward a darkened horizon. Here she is, smack in the middle of America, a foreign country on either side of her.

Tulsa, Oklahoma

'All right, let's see what Google can tell us about Tulsa,' Alex says the next morning over breakfast.

She and Bonnie are drinking smoothies at an outdoor table in the Art Deco District of Tulsa. Kevin said he needed some time to himself in his room, so they are enjoying a leisurely breakfast surrounded by elaborately decorated buildings that rise up into the bright blue sky. Tulsa has skyscrapers and a grid of perpendicular streets and a sizeable sports stadium and all the usual trappings of a large American city, but somehow it feels remarkably laid-back, even empty, compared to Chicago or St. Louis.

Bonnie listens as Alex quotes from a webpage: 'Second largest city in Oklahoma . . . Located on the territory of the Muscogee (Creek) nation . . . Was nicknamed the "Birthplace of Route 66" . . . oh and, check this: Once held the name of "Oil capital of the world."'

Alex reads this out with surprise.

'I thought that'd be Dallas or something,' Bonnie admits. 'Or Riyadh.'

'First oil well was established in 1901 and . . . Wow, the population grew to over 140,000 by 1930 . . . Crazy.' Alex says. She's scanning down the page, then she stops short.

'What is it?' Bonnie asks, registering her shock.

'Uh... did you ever hear about a race massacre here in 1921?' She stares at a collection of words on her phone's screen, grasping the horror that they outline.

'Is that the same thing as the Tulsa Riots?' Bonnie wonders aloud.

Alex feels a low-level nausea rise in her gut, slowly mounting as she continues to read.

' "In the early twentieth century, Tulsa was home to the 'Black Wall Street,' one of the most prosperous Black communities in the United States at the time... Located in the Greenwood neighborhood, it was the site of the Tulsa Race Massacre, said to the be the single worst incident of racial violence in American history..." '

This country... She imagines telling this history to Nya, and the gravity of her wife's reaction, her eyes widening.

' "... a newspaper printed a false accusation of sexual assault of a white woman by a Black man... Mobs of White Tulsans killed Black Tulsans, looted and robbed the Black community, and burned down homes and businesses... Estimates suggested as many as three hundred died, many of them Black." '

The two of them sit in silence, absorbing this.

'Jesus Christ,' Bonnie says. 'They called that a riot?'

'Why have I never heard about this before?' Alex pronounces slowly, angered. 'We sat through years of American History classes, but there was no mention of it. How could they just erase something that big?'

They sit there, surrounded by the urban elegance of the Art Deco District, carved terracotta flourishing against the bright blue sky, and Alex is quietly sickened. She tries to recall what she had been taught about the history of Black America in school.

The slave system, the triangle trade, the Civil War. 'Forty

Acres and a Mule,' Jim Crow laws, segregation, Rosa Parks, Malcolm X, Martin Luther King Jr. – and then, that was it: as if King's famous speech, resonating over the Reflecting Pond that day in Washington, DC, had solved the problem. His vision of multiracial harmony achieved, cemented by the election of Obama. Everything since then had been conveniently glossed over, a neat division between America's racist past and its harmonious present. And yet . . .

Growing up in affluent Orange County, where there was not a single Black kid in her high school class, Alex had had no reason to question that. The present-day lives of Black people remained unknowable to her, yet a mere thirty-minute drive into South Central L.A. would have taught her something. But, like every Asian kid growing up in Orange County, she'd been told never to set foot in South Central L.A.

Some places, some peoples would remain forbidden to them, even though the stories were right there to be learned.

Alex feels only shame and regret at her smothered, sheltered childhood. In high school, she had never even noticed that Asian American history appeared so infrequently in her history textbooks, despite the fact 50 percent of the students in her school were Asian. Their own history would remain unknowable. A community shuttered from its past and its neighbors, compelled only to look forward, into the shiny future.

To her surprise, Bonnie is on her phone now, navigating her way through Google Maps. 'Look at that: Greenwood is like a twenty-minute walk from here.' She points to the screen, a blue arrow snaking at right angles around city blocks, like in a video game.

Alex stares at it for a minute, and a primal impulse trembles in her. An impulse that, in all her years of traveling, she has

167

learned to follow. Some places call to you. They beg for you to discover them.

'Let's go there,' she says, determined.

'What?' Bonnie looks at her in shock.

'Come on, it's only twenty minutes away. We don't have to meet Kevin till a bit later.'

'Yeah, but we've got another long drive ahead of us today.'

Always the same excuses. Why are they even on this trip, if not to explore?

'Listen.' She fixes Bonnie with a meaningful look. 'Nya would want me to go. To bear witness to this place.'

Her sister nods, reverent, believing. 'Okay.' Because what would Bonnie know of racism, really?

But in her line of work, Alex has come to learn these things. Acknowledging that collective trauma carves deep lines into our psyches and our histories. That setting foot physically onto a landscape is sometimes needed to honor the past.

* * *

While his sisters are learning the history of Tulsa over smoothies and croissants in the Art Deco District, Kevin is in his hotel room, hunched on the bed, listening to a voicemail.

He has heard this message several times already, but now he replays it again – as if some hidden clue might be noticed this time around.

But no, it is the same automated memo:

'Mr. Kevin Chu. This is the fifth message we have left you. Your payment of $252,917 is now overdue. If you do not pay this amount by July 8, we will be forced to move to the next phase of debt collection. We have also sent another letter detailing this to your home address.'

This isn't news, although he never likes to hear the amount

168

WHAT WE LEFT UNSAID

spelled out that starkly. But it's the last sentence that gets him: *We have sent a letter to your home address.*

The past few months, Kevin has been scrupulous, checking the mailbox every day before Jessica could, discreetly concealing any incriminating envelopes addressed to him. These letters on white, then yellow, then red paper announcing the amount owed, the deadline for payment, the consequences.

He had tucked these away in that locked drawer in his filing cabinet, allowing them to pile up as he researched more loans, more transfers, more possible ways of satisfying that terrifying debt.

But now, Kevin is not at home. And he won't be for another week and a half. Which means Jessica and her mother are the only adults checking the mail.

Perhaps he should call up Arabella, give her specific instructions to probe the mailbox every day, and sequester all letters addressed to him. But she's too sharp not to consider this request suspicious. Even if he lied and said it was a surprise for Mom, Arabella would suspect something.

Because he knows it's not just letters. If they've left voicemails on his cell phone, who's to say they aren't leaving the same kinds of messages on the landline at home.

What will happen when Jessica innocently sees the blinking red light on the answering service and presses play?

He squeezes his eyes shut, imagining her reaction. Her widened eyes, her snarl of rage and disgust . . . But maybe, contained inside all of that, a certain relief. The end of their pathetic sham of a marriage.

In a panic, he checks his apps to see if Jessica has tried to reach him. Not yet.

So as cowardly as it is, Kevin decides to take the path of least resistance: to do nothing for now. Let the knowledge reach her eventually. But for the time being, rest in the queasy silence of the world not knowing.

Because when he looks at the figure he owes, he knows he would just have to ask Bonnie, and she and Chris might lend him the money, possibly interest-free, to pay off that deficit. But then he would be in debt to his own sister.

If he asked his parents to help him, they'd do the same – *if* they had that kind of money. (He's never been entirely sure of their finances, because they always operated with such frugality). They might not even ask to be paid back. But it would be the greatest dishonor to Asian parents: to have a fully grown son, employed with two kids of his own, who couldn't even pay off his own debts. Because to them, the very definition of adulthood meant earning a paycheck, saving responsibly, supporting your family, supporting your elderly parents. Children became adults in order to look after the older generation. It should never be the other way around.

Just then, his phone pings. A message from Bonnie.

> Hey, we're gonna check out this place called Greenwood. You should meet us there. We'll be there in 30 min.

Kevin frowns. They're meant to be hitting the road. But he also needs to escape this hotel room, where he is going certifiably crazy.

He puts his phone on silent and tucks it in his back pocket. Unseen, but most certainly felt.

* * *

On Greenwood Avenue, Alex kneels down and lays her hand on the concrete. She wonders if she would feel it emanating from

170

the ground in this place. This legacy of bloodshed and fire, broken glass and smashed brick – can that kind of history be *felt?* Like tuning into a frequency that continues to reverberate across the decades. To be able to say you connected with this place, felt the horror with your own body.

But there's nothing. Just concrete, like any other city block. If it weren't for the bronze plaques and green banners fixed to lampposts, she would have walked down Black Wall Street completely oblivious to its tragic past.

'Are you all right?' Bonnie asks, peering at her with concern.

'Yeah.' But maybe also a little disappointed. That she couldn't vibe with the suffering of this place.

She knows what Nya would say. *You don't need to take on every trauma out there.* Sometimes it's enough to acknowledge and to listen.

Alex closes her eyes. *I was here. I wanted to learn.*

I am trying.

When she stands up, there's an older Black lady and a man hovering nearby. They watch her and Bonnie with some curiosity.

'You know, there's a museum right there if you wanna know more about this place.'

The lady points to a modern white building on a nearby corner, its long clean architectural lines in contrast to the historic redbrick buildings around them.

'Is it open?' Alex looks at it, excited.

'Yeah, we going there ourselves. Come and see. You look like you want to know.'

* * *

Kevin is dripping sweat by the time he finds himself standing in front of the Greenwood Rising museum. He's been circling

Tulsa's grid of wide, unpeopled streets, its concrete buildings shimmering in the heat, as he followed Bonnie's dropped pin on Google Maps. He wonders why anyone would choose to live out here on this endless, heated Western plain, baking in the Oklahoma sun.

The neighborhood he's in now seems to be primarily Black, judging from the pedestrians around him. Why would his sisters want him to come all the way out here?

Don't worry, it's cool, he tells himself. Bonnie wouldn't ask him to walk anywhere unsafe. Plus, it's the middle of the day.

If he were his mom or dad, surely he'd be panicking by now. But *they* live in a state of constant anxiety, forever insulated in their little Californian Asian enclave. They are terrified of setting foot in a Black community. But he, Kevin Chu, is not so cowardly.

He stands in front of this space-age-looking museum, and watches as a knot of Black tourists filter out, blinking into the sun. He nods at them from behind his sunglasses.

Where the hell are his sisters?

A moment later, they emerge from the black glass doors in a whoosh of air conditioning. 'Hey, you found it.' Bonnie attempts a grin at him. She and Alex look bleak, somehow, downtrodden.

'Yeah, I'm here. But . . . what is this place? Why'd you drag me out here?'

Alex seems taken aback. She breathes out, her annoyance already palpable.

'This is the Greenwood District, Kevin,' she says in that condescending voice of hers. 'And this is the museum about what happened here.'

'A museum? We don't have time for sightseeing. We have seven hours of driving ahead of us!'

'Okay, it can wait a few minutes, yeah?'

And then before he can protest, Alex launches into the history of this neighborhood. Something about a historic injustice against the Black community, innocent lives taken, all the catchphrases she is always spewing.

But Kevin can't keep track of another soapbox tirade. He can only think of those letters burning a hole in his filing cabinet at home, the envelope that Jessica inevitably will find herself opening . . .

'So basically there was a big massacre and a lot of people were killed right here?' he finally deadpans.

'Yeah,' Alex answers, like it's a challenge.

'A century ago?'

Kevin doesn't want to be an asshole, but he can't see why Alex is getting so worked up about it.

'Alex, that was a *century* ago. What does it have to do with us? That's history: people get massacred.' He seems to remember his US history class was always about wars: the Revolutionary War, the Civil War, then World Wars I and II, then Vietnam.

'Listen, if you want to go around to every single massacre site commemorating the dead, that's your choice. But not on this trip, when we have fifteen hundred miles to cover before we reach Mom and Dad.'

Alex glares at him for a moment, hatred in her eyes. 'You're a terrible person. Did you know that?'

Yes, he did know that. But he didn't need his own little sister reminding him.

'Alex, come on,' Bonnie tries to reason.

He cuts her off, frustration mounting inside of him.

'*Why* do you suddenly care so much? Black Lives Matter and now this.' He gestures wide to the museum, the street around him, shimmering in the heat. A bead of sweat trickles toward his eye and he dashes it away. 'I mean, since when have you ever cared so much about being Asian?'

That shuts Alex up, because he knows she has no response to that. Disappearing off to London for decades, hardly bothering to keep in touch with their parents. And Bonnie, too. So perfect she had to become white.

Alex opens her mouth, tears in her eyes as usual. She is about to say something, when the museum door opens and an older Black woman calls out to them.

'Alex! Bonnie! We going to Wanda J's for lunch after this. You wanna join?'

Oh, for god's sake. Did she make friends with the locals already?

Alex flashes them a hasty grin, while Bonnie calls back, diplomatic and fake as always. 'Oh, that's so kind of you, Mavis. But we really need to hit the road. We've got a hotel booked in New Mexico tonight.'

Mavis squints and comes over to them, curious. *Great. Just what we need.*

'Sure you don't want some fried catfish? It's world famous.' She smiles like someone warm and grandmotherly out of a commercial. 'You must be their brother,' she asks, direct but friendly.

Kevin gives a half-hearted wave. 'Uh, yeah, that's me.'

Mavis studies him, this white-haired, weathered Black lady, like so many he would have passed on the street in Chicago and never spoken to. She nods, satisfied. 'Y'all driving to see your mama in California, is that right?'

'Yup,' he answers, chastened by the thought of his mom. 'We're aiming to get there by Monday.'

'That's good, that's good.' She nods. 'Y'all are good kids. I'm sure she's gonna appreciate you going all this way for her.'

She better, he thinks. And grins back.

1991

In the men's room, Kevin wanted to ask his dad about what had happened with the three men at the cash register. How could they make Dad pay twenty dollars, and why did Dad just hand it over that easily? But somehow, he knew. It was in the way the three men planted themselves around his dad. Full of menace. The way they could have edged closer, three against one, and Kevin ... well, he knew he didn't stand a chance helping Dad out. He could barely stand up to Ryan Sanchez and Jeff Howie in school.

So the two of them stood next to each other, each emptying their bladder into the stained urinals in front of them. Kevin stood awkwardly, trying to pee with the packet of beef jerky tucked under his arm. There was nowhere clean enough in the bathroom to put it down. The urinals were scummy, ringed with brown like they hadn't been scrubbed in years. Mom would throw a fit if she saw them.

Dad still didn't speak. Just zipped up his fly and went to wash his hands. The trickling faucet was the only sound in the bathroom.

Kevin felt like he had to say something, just to fill the space. 'How much longer till we get to the Grand Canyon, Dad?'

'Huh? Oh . . . I think another hour maybe.' Dad sounded vague, like his mind was elsewhere.

Kevin nodded. He couldn't wait for the driving to be over. He wondered what the Grand Canyon would actually look like. How the stars might spread at night above that vast, dark chasm.

The urinal didn't flush properly, and Kevin shuddered at the thought of all those years of men stepping into the bathroom, pissing down into the bowl, with nothing to wash it down. No wonder it stank in here.

'Can you hold this?' Kevin held out the beef jerky to his dad, to free up his own hands for washing.

Dad studied the packet. 'Extra-spicy,' he said. 'You like beef jerky?'

Kevin shrugged. 'Not really. The guy made us buy it.'

Dad nodded in agreement. 'Better eat it. We pay for it, we need to eat it.'

And suddenly Kevin resented everything about this stupid trip. Having to eat this stupid beef jerky that Dad had somehow been duped into buying. How Dad didn't even put up a fight. Just nodded and said okay. How those men had stared at Mom and Bonnie, their eyes lingering the same way older boys watched the pretty girls walk past. And how there was nothing they could do about it. They could just stare and stare and make Dad pay twenty dollars, and no one was going to stop them.

'Dad,' Kevin started to ask. 'Why—'

But then he didn't know how to ask it. Why do they have to be so mean? Why do you let them do it? Why are you so embarrassing sometimes?

And he knew he couldn't say that, so the question just wilted into the stinking air of that dim bathroom.

Dad opened his mouth as if to say something. But then they heard it – a sound from outside, impossible to distinguish at first.

A high-pitched wheezing, almost a smothered squeal, ragged and terrified but somehow familiar. Filtering through to them, from outside the building.

He and Dad stared at each other, puzzled, trying to place the noise. But then another sound cut through the air, from farther away – and this one was unmistakable.

Three loud, insistent blasts from a car horn. And then again, beeping and beeping, as if trying to send a message.

'That's our car!' Kevin said, recognizing the sound of the horn.

And then the realization dawned on them in a moment of alarm.

'Alex.'

Alex is at the wheel as they drive out of Tulsa into the sunbaked Western plain. She needed something to do – even just the mindless mechanics of pressing the gas and passing the odd truck – to lessen the blow of her fight with Kevin in Greenwood.

She is still reeling from his last accusation. For once, he's right.

All her adult life, all she's wanted to do is get as far away as possible – from the petty anxieties of her mom and dad and their Asian American circles in Orange County. Where success was measured by the prestige of a child's college education, their annual salary, their box-ticking conformity to the safe, prescribed conventions of adulthood.

By the expected standards for an Asian American daughter, she's been terrible. Unstable career in the arts. Unmarried for years. Only comes home to visit once a year.

So no, she hasn't done much to embrace her heritage, because she's always associated it with those impossible expectations she would never be able to fulfill. A gap that drove her farther and farther afield, to carve out a life as radical and different as she could, thousands of miles away.

How could Kevin understand any of this?

And yet, he never will, if she continues to stay silent.

'Kevin, you there?'

Kevin turns to look at her. Bonnie opted for the back seat, advertently leaving them to resolve their spat. He's been watching open fields streak past, as the Oklahoma landscape stretches out, broader and flatter as they drive west.

'Yeah.'

Alex feels the apprehension building inside her, swelling to a breaking point.

'Nya's Black.'

A moment of silence from Kevin – she has to keep her eyes on the road, so she can't sense his reaction.

'Your . . . your wife?' he asks.

She is surprised he was able to piece that together. Or that he used the word 'wife.'

'Yeah.'

'I had no idea . . .' he says. 'I mean, I never would have guessed—'

'Well, why would you?' she admits. 'You only found out two days ago I was even married. I haven't exactly been forthcoming about my personal life these past few years.'

She can sense Kevin searching awkwardly for words, wondering what is acceptable to say and what isn't. She steps in to offer a bit more.

'You asked why I suddenly care so much about places like Greenwood. That's why.'

Kevin nods. 'That makes sense.'

'It does and it doesn't,' Alex muses. 'It's kind of hypocritical that I only care about that stuff now. Now that I have a partner who's Black.'

She thinks of white guys who consider themselves experts in Japanese culture, just because their girlfriend is Japanese. The affectation of it all. The superficial claim to knowledge, when faced with the weight of centuries, the long histories that have gone unknown.

'Yeah but, at least you care about those things,' Kevin says after a moment. 'That's a lot better than me. I've been too caught up in my own shit.'

Alex pauses, tempted to ask Kevin how he is, what's been going on in his life. He's seemed distracted these past few days, more defensive than she's ever known him. And particularly frazzled this morning.

But Kevin gets his question out first. 'Do Mom and Dad know?'

'About Nya?' She shakes her head. 'They don't even know I'm married to a woman. Let alone someone Black. So, um, I've got a lot to tell them in person when we get there.'

Kevin exhales slowly. 'Yeah. That'll be – that'll be a lot for them to take in.'

For an instant, she expects him to suggest maybe she shouldn't tell them, and she gears herself up for an angry response. But he says nothing. He leaves his statement like that, neither suggesting nor admonishing. They pass open fields baking under the summer sun and forlorn windmills spinning against the vast blue sky. Alex doesn't mind the silence this time.

They pass a brown sign, and the place name sparks a memory in her mind. The old thrill of travel: a map coming into its own. She starts to slow down, looking for the turnoff.

'You stopping somewhere?' Bonnie asks, leaning forward.

'Yeah. Here,' Alex says. 'It's a ghost town I read about. Just thought it'd be fun to check out for five minutes or so.'

* * *

Kevin stands on the deserted main street of Depew, Oklahoma, in a hushed awe. An actual ghost town, the faded shop fronts ranged next to each other, silent in the sun. Not a single business open, just a handful of cars parked here and there, and curious tourists wandering around, snapping photos on their phones.

'It was an oil boomtown about a century ago,' Alex explains. 'Then the oil ran out.'

There's nothing else to say as they stare down the sunbaked stretch of neglected buildings. A town that once had a life of its own, a population of human lives buzzing and thriving, but now abandoned to the unrelenting heat and dust.

Kevin takes a few steps in one direction, peeks through the sandy, cracked glass of a former general store. Nothing inside, just empty shelves and stools overturned. His mind drifts to the long history of get-rich-quick schemes: oil wells sunk and depleted, and all the fools who wasted their lives panning through muck for a flash of gold.

Don't. He forces himself to think of something else.

So Alex's wife is Black. Should he be shocked? Beyond the initial surprise, maybe not. He'd never stopped to consider what race his sister's partner would be, just that she'd be a lesbian. And in that sense, as different as he could imagine. So this is just a further version of different.

He knows virtually nothing else about Nya, and she appears as little more than a cipher in his mind. But he also knows that Nya must be someone remarkable to have tamed the intense roaming energy of his younger sister. And for that reason alone, she deserves to be more than a blank space.

* * *

Near Oklahoma City, they stop to fill up their tank. After following the quieter path of the 66, past fields and forgotten towns, they are back on the great concrete causeway of the I-44, a steady stream of cars and trucks rumbling past.

Alex unscrews the Mazda's gasoline tank, inserts the nozzle into place. There is the reassuring chug of fuel pouring through, and she looks up at the neon numbers advertising the price of gas.

$2.74 a gallon.

'We definitely don't get prices like that over on the East Coast,' Bonnie remarks as she emerges from the convenience store. She is slurping on a blue slushy and grins, her lips already stained an alarming turquoise. 'Hey, remember these?'

'Ah, the taste of childhood.'

Alex leans over for a slurp of her own, her mouth tingling at the touch of the ice. She recalls the pure delight of summer afternoons, when her dad let them share a blue slushy from the gas station, cold artificial sweetness tracing a trail down her throat.

'How was the bathroom?' Alex asks.

'Clean enough.'

Alex feels a trace of déjà vu, like she's asked Bonnie that before, in another lifetime. But she pushes the ghost of that feeling away.

They watch as Kevin wanders out of the men's bathroom now, down to the far edge of the forecourt. He gazes out at the unending rush of the highway, the skyline of Oklahoma City rising in the distance.

'Do you think he's okay?' Alex asks. 'He seems a bit on edge.'

Bonnie shakes her head slowly. 'Maybe. We only speak every few months, you know.'

'That's it?' She is surprised. She'd have thought Kevin and Bonnie have more in common, both living in the US, both raising kids in the suburbs.

'Yeah,' Bonnie sighs. 'I mean, Kevin and I were never... well, he was never the kind of person to share much about his life, anyway. And then, the past few years... I guess even less so.'

What could be going on with her brother? Behind the

uniform of polo shirt, khakis, white sneakers, behind the pretense of normality and his childlike excitement over Route 66, is Kevin actually content with his life? Her mind hovers around the issue of money. Previously her brother was always so proud to show off his spending ability, often snatching the restaurant bill before everyone else, in that Chinese game of financial one-upmanship. Who gets to pay, who gets to be the generous one.

'Did you notice he's hardly paid for stuff on this trip?' Alex is loath to say it, it makes her feel like a tattletale. And yet . . .

Bonnie nods. 'I hate to *make* him pay, but it's so weird. We all know he earns more than you.'

She adds as an afterthought: 'Sorry, I didn't mean—'

But Alex waves her away with a laugh. 'Don't worry, it's fine. And it's true.'

Kevin is headed their way now in the noontime haze, a pensive look on his face. He's taking off his sunglasses, wiping his brow – and in that instant, Alex glimpses something she doesn't normally see in Kevin's expression. A certain vulnerability. A little boy lost.

'Let me handle this.' Bonnie resumes her usual take-charge attitude, and Alex acquiesces out of habit.

'We ready to roll?' he asks when he reaches the car. He seems tired, dark circles under his eyes. But his face lights up when he sees the blue slushy.

'Want some?' Bonnie holds the cup out to him, and he takes a grateful slurp.

Bonnie waits another moment, then continues. 'Is everything okay, Kev?'

God, Bonnie. Couldn't approach anything casually if her life depended on it.

Kevin picks up on Bonnie's tone and looks from her to Alex,

trying to parse the conversation that has just passed between them.

'Uh . . . Why?' Another pause. 'What's up?'

Alex takes a half step toward Kevin. She thinks of her drama training. A single step to reposition yourself in the dialogue. Establish a greater intimacy. 'Don't worry about the gas. I've paid for it already.'

'Oh.' Kevin nods uncomfortably. 'Thanks.'

Alex clears her throat. 'And I also paid for all the gas yesterday. *And* dinner last night.'

Kevin exhales and closes his eyes for an extended minute, as if he's been caught out. 'Thanks. You been keeping tabs?'

Alex ignores Bonnie's warning look. 'I'm used to being frugal. I guess we all were at some point.'

He doesn't take the bait.

'Kevin.' Bonnie tries a softer approach. 'Do you mind . . . Is there anything you want to share with us? About why you're not paying . . .'

Alex can sense how awkward Bonnie is, speaking about money. Ah, the luxury of the affluent. To never have to raise the issue of finances because it's never an actual issue in your life.

Kevin stops, hunches over, doesn't look at either of them. There's something dejected in his posture. A kind of surrender.

'Oh god,' he finally says. 'I don't even know where to start.'

So there *is* a story. Alex starts to wonder what it could be.

'Just whatever you're comfortable with.'

'Sure. I'll . . . tell you sometime today. I need somewhere quiet.'

His voice is glum, almost inaudible in the roar of the highway nearby.

'Good.' Bonnie nods, encouraging. 'Honestly, we're not angry about the not paying ... We just want to make sure you're all right.'

Alex frowns. Actually, she is a little miffed about the not paying. But now is not the time to broach that. Instead, she holds the car keys out to Kevin.

'Wanna drive?'

'Yeah.' A single word as she tosses him the keys, then crosses over to the passenger side.

Just as the three of them are about to get in the car, there's a honk and some shouting. A large Jeep, shiny white with music blaring, squeals past them.

'Fucking chinks! Thought we got rid of you after Covid!'

A flash of fear, and Alex whips her head to see three young men, white and bearded, hanging out the window of the pickup. One of them raises a muscled arm and something wet explodes on the hood of Kevin's car.

SPLAT! It's another slushy, red this time. The liquid drips down the car's blue siding.

Then the white truck is gone, burning rubber down the highway, the young men laughing with glee.

'Assholes,' Alex fumes.

The melted slushy slides down, its drops tracing a sticky path down the bonnet, through the dust of the interstate.

* * *

Two hours later, Bonnie finds herself in the Oklahoma Route 66 Museum on the far side of the state. Though they still have four hours of driving that day, they've agreed that an hour of wandering through a museum might do them all some good. A temporary reprieve, something to distract their minds from the heavy conversations they've had, and which still await them.

'Oh wow,' the perky museum attendant had trilled, after

learning they hailed from Chicago, Boston, and London respectively. 'I thought you might be brother and sisters. You guys look so much alike! Make sure you sign the visitor's book before you leave!'

Bonnie cringed inwardly upon hearing that. She and Alex were similar, but Kevin bore little resemblance to them in facial features. Still, she smiled politely.

As she drifts into a sepia-toned display on the origins of Route 66, she muses on the subtle but very perceptible change in how others treat her when she is not with Chris and the boys. With her husband present, there was always a certain deference toward them: this well-to-do white man with his Asian wife and three good-looking, albeit slightly exotic sons. Respect would always be shown to him – and by extension, to Bonnie.

But with her siblings on this trip, it is a decidedly different experience. There is always the slight hesitance from others. The lurking suspicion that maybe she doesn't speak English, that she will be difficult to understand – and the disproportionate relief when her American accent comes through.

'Hey.' Alex nudges with a mischievous grin. 'Let's play a game: spot the person of color in the museum displays!'

'What?'

Thus far, they've seen pictures of cowboys, plastic mannequins of strapping blond men and redheaded housewives. In another room, Bonnie encounters a collection of mid-century Route 66 advertising, and there are Native Americans aplenty on tourist posters and souvenirs. Imposing chieftains in feather headdresses and demure maidens in braids. Ah, the noble fate of the Indian tribes: their identity conscripted into selling cigarettes, cooking oil, baking soda.

But she seems to recall seeing old advertisements with Black people or Chinese people portrayed in a similar way to hawk other products. Pickaninnies, golliwogs, Uncle Ben, Aunt Jemima. Chinamen, coolies, Confucius Say buy this cereal. Centuries of caricatures, printed on labels, billboards, advertisements. Exotic enough to brand consumer products. Forced to purchase their own stereotypes.

Distaste mounts inside her. She walks past an antiquated Greyhound and a VW bus on display, speakers blaring Frank Sinatra and Dinah Shore. She glances at a compilation of home movies from Route 66, running on an endless loop. Waves of Okies and hippies, families and bikers, all exploring the Mother Road – and all only of a certain skin tone. A version of American history where people of color don't exist.

Bonnie sits down on a nearby bench. She watches a young family pass through the museum: a towheaded boy, marveling at the model cars and gas station pumps; a little girl more interested in the plastic doll she's brought along.

The girl stops and stares at Bonnie, staring as if she's never seen an Asian person before. The girl's eyes widen, and then the mother glances over, notices Bonnie, and gives her a brief, cursory smile. Bonnie nods back. *I'm a mother, too,* she wants to say.

She drifts back through rooms of Route 66 road signs and tourist posters, a recreated VW hippie camper van, a shining 1950s diner interior. Is she, Bonnie Chu Prescott, meant to feel some nostalgia for an era that she never lived through? Because try as she might, she feels no connection to these rooms of treasured memorabilia. And in that sense, perhaps she has failed in being American.

Bonnie finds her sister taking photos of the racist advertisements.

'Can you believe this stuff?' Alex gestures to the posters.

'I guess I can,' Bonnie says, grateful that she never lived in an earlier America. She pauses for a moment, imagining what it must have been like for her mom and dad to make their way through this confusing country in the 60s and 70s: all its promises of success and melting-pot equality, all its prejudiced reality. To know this was your future, this was the strange place your children would grow up to call home.

She looks around, wondering where Kevin is.

'Come on, let's get out of here,' Alex says, staring at the grinning mannequins of a young mid-century couple at the wheel, the woman's plastic blond hair framing her painted face. 'This place gives me the creeps.'

1991

Bonnie heard the car horn honking. It had shaken her out of her reverie, her relief at not needing to leave a used maxi pad – a small part of her – here among all the unspeakable grime of this public bathroom.

Who was honking the horn like that, over and over again?

Bonnie hesitated, on tenterhooks, leaning toward the door as if it would give her answers. It seemed safer to stay inside.

But then she heard the screaming, more like a wailing – and she recognized Alex's voice. The way she often sounded when she threw her tantrums, but this time louder, more unhinged.

What the heck was happening?

Alex sounded like she was in pain – or angry. Bonnie had run to her sister many times before when she hadn't cried as loudly. Some protective instinct reared up in her.

It's okay, she reminded herself. *Mom and Dad are out there, too.*

Assured by this, she pushed out the door and around the corner.

'Alex? Mom?' she called. She held her hand up, shielding her eyes from the desert glare, and stopped short when she saw them all: Alex in tears, bawling like she'd witnessed the end of the world, and Mom curled around her in a defensive hug, the way she'd always done.

Dad, Kevin, and the three men from the gas station stood in a bizarre semicircle, all of them staring at Alex, almost aghast.

'What's happening?' Bonnie asked, trying to take charge.

'Nothing, Bonnie,' Mom answered, her voice adamant. 'Alex was just very upset, right?'

But Alex kept on crying, bawling like a trapped animal, her rage undirected. She glared at the three men, as if demanding something from them.

'D-Dad? Kevin? Is everything okay?' Bonnie turned to them, confused. They just looked back at her, wordless.

'Everything okay, Bonnie,' Mom continued. 'These men just make Alex cry. But she so young, you can't blame her.'

'Oh, Alex,' Bonnie went over and cuddled her. 'Maybe we shouldn't have left you in the car on your own. But it's all okay now.'

She was so accustomed to saying this, stroking Alex's hair and calming her down, all the times she was upset, that it didn't occur to her to think otherwise.

But Alex kept sobbing furiously, almost hyperventilating. An unspoken alarm sounded in Bonnie. She had never seen her little sister this upset before.

Mom stepped forward, her face serious, and looked at Dad, and then Kevin. Nodded to them.

'Come on, we go now.'

Like a robot, Mom headed toward the car. She glanced once at the men, as she passed them. A peculiar shift of her eyes, flat, with no emotion.

Bonnie didn't know what to make of that glance.

Texas

'Honestly, there's nothing else,' Alex says as she fiddles with the car radio again, eventually settling on the plaintive male warble of a country music ballad. For hours, she's been alternating between country and Christian rock, a soundtrack that they have inevitably surrendered to. 'Let's just listen to this.'

With Kevin at the wheel, they enter Texas.

More open road, more blue sky, more ghost towns. The I-40 unspools under the summer sky, and they pass well-preserved diners and abandoned gas stations, murals fading along empty main streets, and huge, futuristic wind farms. Long rows of windmills turn vacantly in unison against blue sky, standing guard high above the flat red earth.

As they approach Amarillo, they are beset by a series of relentless signs for a cowboy steak restaurant, which has definitely cornered the market on long-lead advertising in this part of Texas. *Twenty Miles Away!* Then fifteen, then ten, as announced by billboards with an outsized cowboy hat and an outline of the Lone Star State. *Home of the 72 oz. Steak Challenge! If you can eat it all in an hour, it's free!*

Jesus Christ. Alex shudders at the thought: four-and-a-half pounds of cow flesh, waiting on a plate to be devoured.

How far she's wandered from home. And yet, she reminds

herself, this is the very purpose of travel: leaving her comfort zone.

When they finally reach said steak restaurant, the line of waiting customers snakes all along the building's wraparound clapboard porch. One peek inside, and Alex sees long wooden tables, animal hides and Indian blankets, and ceiling fans attempting to stir the closed, fetid air above the rows of hungry diners. Mounted heads of buffalo gaze down as tourists gorge on steak, ribs, burgers, and mounds of deep-fried side dishes.

Alex's stomach lurches at the sight of it. For a vegetarian, it would just be mozzarella sticks and potato wedges again.

'The wait time is forty-five minutes,' Bonnie reports, looking aghast.

Kevin shakes his head. 'If you guys want to hear what I have to say, there's no way I'm going in there.'

In the end, they opt for Tex-Mex. They sit at an outdoor table, grateful for the shade under its faded red umbrella, as traffic streams past them. And while she wolfs down her bean and cheese burrito, Alex waits patiently. Sensing that Kevin is gearing himself up to tell them something, hoping to off-load the unspoken weight that has kept him quiet all day.

'So, Kevin,' Bonnie ventures, speaking carefully. 'Tell us what's going on. We just want to help.'

It's late afternoon, and the lowering sun casts a reddish tint on the land around them. Kevin turns to avoid the glare, uncomfortable. He looks at his sisters and starts to speak.

* * *

Kevin can't even explain how it started. Okay, fine. Investments. He'd been investing his savings since college, slowly watching their value grow over the years. But it wasn't very exciting, was it?

Mom and Dad always said to check your interest rates. Make sure your money's working as hard as possible. Because hard work, for them, was the answer to everything.

But he'd grown tired of things steadily accruing interest. Frankly, he'd grown tired of his life. Commuting to the office, doing what the boss wanted, reminding the kids to do their homework, doing what his wife wanted.

Was that it for the rest of his life? What could he possibly get excited about?

Then, a few years ago, the guys at work started talking about cryptocurrencies. Jared had bought Bitcoin earlier on, and now it was worth something like twenty times its original value – all in a very short period of time. Now *that* was exciting. Here was a whole new product that evaded the reach of the financial institutions, that transcended national boundaries. You could get in on the ground floor, make more in a couple of years than if you'd had that same money sitting in a CD or stocks over decades.

'Yeah, but they're unregulated—' Bonnie starts, but Kevin cuts her off.

Of course he knew they were unregulated. He'd done enough reading to know cryptocurrencies were considered the Wild West of the investment world.

Kevin pauses here, reflecting on the abandoned ghost town they saw earlier that day. The fading storefronts, the empty streets. The oil that ran dry all too quickly.

But who cares? He wanted excitement. Maybe even a sense of risk. None of this waiting for safe, boring IRAs to come into their value.

So Craig was going to this seminar after work about cryptocurrencies and he went along. That's how it started. Online, there was endless information you could soak up. YouTube videos and WhatsApp chat groups and something called TikTok ... online seminars, Twitter streams, a community of strangers giving the lowdown on which products were about to rocket in value.

He downloaded an investment app onto his phone, then another one. And he kept checking their value every few minutes. No wonder Jessica started to hate him. He never put down his phone.

Soon, he made good money on a few products, and it all seemed too easy. Click here, swipe there, put your thumbprint on your phone – and just like that, you were on your way to a healthy return. For the first time in a long while, he had accomplished something new.

Kevin pauses here, reluctant to continue.

And then things got weird. He'd bought a cryptocurrency which everyone said was going to skyrocket, once they went public. But that never happened. The company kept delaying the date that the currency was going to 'enter the real world,' and in the meantime, every time he checked his investment's value on their website, it kept going up and up.

'So it was a complete scam,' Bonnie says.

Yeah, it was. And he fell for it. It was hard not to get excited by what their website said: that his investment was shooting up in value. That for once, something exciting was actually happening in his life.

The crypto company was clever. First, they said he just needed to invest this little bit more to get an even higher rate of return. Then, when he started asking about the payout, they kept talking about more elite investor circles. Commit this much more to get platinum benefits ...

In the meantime, some of his other investments hadn't panned out the way he'd hoped. He lost money there, and thought, okay, let's make it all back on cryptocurrency. By that time, he'd already invested so much, he didn't want to lose it all. He wanted to make sure he got *something* in return.

But he didn't. It became a downward spiral, bad investment after bad investment. Then he started to panic.

'So over the course of three years . . .' Alex ventures. 'Kevin, how much money are we talking about here?'

Kevin hesitates, looks from one sister to the other.

'In total? Around two hundred and fifty thousand.'

He is nauseous just thinking about the figure. Because finally telling another person has solidified what he's done, made it very real. Inescapably real.

Alex is looking at him with huge, saucer-shaped eyes, ready to bug out of her face. She doesn't say anything, just exhales a breath, slow and portentous.

'You blew a quarter of a million dollars on cryptocurrency?' Alex shrieks. 'I don't even know what cryptocurrency is. How could you lose that much money?!'

'I ended up taking out some loans to be able to invest more. And I . . . I've paid back some of them, but I still owe a lot. And I – I'm overdue on some of the payments already.'

He looks to Bonnie, savvier older sister, praying she will not wear that same look of outrage, even though she most likely is thinking it.

'Was that – Was that *all* of your savings?' She finally formulates a question, practical as always.

'Everything I had access to, yeah,' he says. 'And I – I refinanced the house to get more equity.'

'Your house?' Bonnie cuts in. 'Does Jessica know?'

Kevin shakes his head. 'I don't – I don't think so. I don't know.'

He slumps downward, his face in his hands. 'Jessica has no idea. I've been hiding everything from her. She's gonna kill me when she finds out.'

When she finds out. Not if. Because that fact is a given. One of those urgent collection notices will find their way into her hands. Or she'll hear a voicemail left on their answering machine. Or a knock on their front door one day.

'How soon do you have to pay them back?' Bonnie asks.

'Like, yesterday,' Kevin answers. 'And there's another deadline in less than two weeks.'

'So if you can't make the payments, they might foreclose on the house?'

'Something like that, yeah.'

He knows how weak that sounds, this casual possibility that he and his family might be out of their home. But he's been in such denial that he hasn't even bothered to research the very real consequences of his unpaid debt.

'Do you have paperwork? Emails? Anything in writing you can forward us? I can get Chris to look into this. Maybe there's some way to prove they've been scamming you.'

But can you call it a scam if you've willingly, happily invested your money, fooled by this mirage of striking gold?

'I've got all that somewhere.' Stashed away in his locked filing cabinet in Wilmette, Illinois. The metallic rumble of a drawer containing his deepest, darkest secrets.

Suddenly he feels the urge to vomit. He staggers across the macadam and spews his half-digested enchilada onto a patch of scrubby weeds.

Kevin squeezes his eyes shut as he leans over, all too aware his sisters must be staring at him in shock. The late-afternoon sun is warm on his back, and he feels the dust sift into his nostrils. He's told them now. They know.

*

'Kevin?'

He turns around, squinting at them, into the sun.

'I just got a text from Dad. He wants to do a call tonight.' Bonnie holds up her phone.

Kevin nods and starts to walk back. They're looking to him for an answer, like he still has some semblance of authority, when clearly he's lost all human respect in their eyes.

'How long until Tucumcari?' Alex asks.

And then he realizes: he's the only one who really knows their driving itinerary.

Kevin looks at his watch, calculates a few things. 'Uhh ... it should be less than two hours' drive ... Plus the time zone change ... maybe tell them six thirty their time? Can they do that?'

Bonnie nods, and in another moment, she is on her feet, hugging him. Kevin registers this with a mild shock. He's the last person to deserve a hug right now.

'Hey,' she says. 'I'm glad you finally told us. It's terrible, but—'

'Really fucking dumb, Kevin!' Alex shouts.

'It's terrible,' Bonnie continues. 'But it'll all be okay.'

'You think?' Kevin looks from one sister to another. He doesn't know if he can believe that.

* * *

'*We'll figure something out,*' Bonnie had assured Kevin. But now, headed west with Alex at the wheel, Bonnie silently contemplates her brother's stupidity.

A quarter million dollars.

How furious would Mom and Dad be knowing that their son had strayed this far from his thrifty upbringing?

197

She can think of several other, better ways to be spending that amount of money.

Property. A car for each of her boys when they get their licenses, with plenty to spare. Mom's hospital bill. Or vital medical costs in some developing country: antibiotics, vaccinations, prosthetic limbs. Even those harelip operations on small, smiling children in tropical places – the kind of charity campaign she often sees advertised on glossy inserts, slipped into lifestyle magazines. Or perhaps simply food for starving families – but instead Kevin has wasted it in a foolish bid to score even more money for himself.

And if he had succeeded, to what end? So he could have a higher figure in his bank account. And then what?

Bonnie knows she and Chris are hardly saints in this regard, squirreling their money away in a range of long- and medium-term investments, choosing luxury vacations and second homes or fourth, fifth vehicles, before more altruistic uses of their money.

She knows what Alex is thinking. The insularity, the arrogance that comes with wealth.

Yes, she and Chris have worked hard at their various corporate jobs, putting in the long hours on business trips, at client sites, in boardrooms. Yet Bonnie can't say they really *deserve* this money compared to her parents, who worked just as hard, only to earn much, much less. But money begets more money. Her career and Chris's career have been about making wealthy people and businesses even wealthier. And she has always reaped the benefits.

So yes, maybe this is her version of philanthropy. Saving her own brother from financial ruin. There are wiser, more humanitarian uses for this quarter million dollars. But if you have family, there are some duties you can't walk away from.

Bonnie sits up as Alex pulls the car off the I-40 and onto a slip of road that crosses under the highway.

'Where we going?' she asks. They're now driving along a smaller road on the other side, opposite the flow of interstate traffic. 'We need to get to New Mexico tonight.'

Alex points up ahead to their left. To an unfamiliar series of shapes in the distance, emerging from the flat Texan plain.

'Just a quick stop,' Alex tells her with a grin. 'Something I think we'd all get a kick out of.'

Alex steps out of the car, gravel crunching underfoot, and squints at the unfamiliar site on an otherwise unremarkable field. She waits for her brother and sister before speaking, wind whipping at their clothes and hair.

'So *this* is Cadillac Ranch,' Alex announces, gesturing ahead.

She had read about this famed landmark, seen photos in the guidebooks. But now, standing on this windswept plain, with the evening sun bright in her eyes and the dust pricking her nostrils, it seems too surreal. So out of place and unexpected.

Ten impossible shapes, planted at a strange angle into the earth.

Seen from this distance, they are like ancient monoliths, mysterious and alien, standing guard over the flatness of the land.

'I don't get it,' Bonnie says. 'What is it?

'It's art, darling.' Alex affects a British accent. 'In the sixties, some millionaire recluse funded an idea from an artist's collective. Which was to take ten Cadillacs and sink them into the ground here. Was it some kind of anti-capitalist statement? Who knows?'

'But what are those people doing?' Bonnie points to the visitors crouching close to the cars, holding something up to them.

'It became a collective piece of art,' Alex continues. 'People started coming out here and spray-painting the cars. And now, decades later, there's layers and layers of paint, sprayed on by who knows how many people over the years.'

'So all those people are spray-painting?'

'I remember reading about this,' Kevin says softly, more to himself.

'That's the coolest part about it.' Alex says. 'That you can come, leave a message or a coat of paint, and then be on your way.'

To think, these ten luxury cars, status symbols from an earlier America, have now been transformed, imbued with an almost mystical significance. A shrine for travelers and wanderers and artists. Everyone leaving an offering or a prayer.

She shoots a glance at Kevin, who seems lost in his own world, the sunken Cadillacs reflected in his sunglasses.

'I'm gonna buy a can,' Alex announces, pointing to a shiny silver truck parked nearby. 'What color should I get?'

Her siblings look at her, surprised. It's the kind of question you'd ask a child choosing a toy. But adults?

'Uh ... green?' Kevin suggests.

'I like it.' Alex grins. 'Green for growth. For regeneration.'

As she turns to the makeshift spray-paint shop, she knows that her siblings would have traded a look behind her back: *Ah yes, their little sister, always finding some ridiculous symbolism in the most mundane of details.*

She doesn't mind. This entire trip is about shaking them out of the mundane, isn't it?

Moments later, Alex returns, holding her newly purchased can of spray paint aloft, triumphantly, in the bright evening sun.

'What are you guys waiting for?' She turns back to her brother and sister, taunting. 'Let's go deface some Cadillacs!'

She races on ahead and breaks into a run – hoping that they will follow.

Alex pounds the dusty ground, and behind her, she hears their footsteps, too.

She gives a whoop, causing other tourists to turn and stare, and she doesn't care.

The wind carries her cry over the flat, unbroken landscape. The three of them run headlong across the field, charging toward the monoliths, and the evening sun gilds their backs.

* * *

They are out of breath by the time they reach the Cadillacs. But it feels good, this breathlessness, this adrenaline pumping through her veins and arteries. Bonnie hasn't gone for a run in weeks, and here, in the Texan heat, with the sunlight and the dust, running feels more elemental. A brief test of survival, in different terrain.

The three of them lean over, hands on thighs, panting.

They all grin at each other, their previous worries thrown off temporarily by their spontaneous sprint.

The last time she'd run side by side with her brother and sister, they were children. Before teenage Bonnie no longer wanted to be seen playing with them, more interested in appearing grown-up than in silly, juvenile diversions.

The other visitors stare at them, these three Asian adults beaming after their impromptu run. A pair of stout white women smile at them. A trio of young redheaded kids gape.

What are you looking at? Bonnie wants to shout at them defiantly. But she's too busy regaining her breath.

'Shit, do you have any water?' Kevin croaks. 'Cardio in your forties. Ouch.'

Bonnie and Alex crack up.

'Oops, no water.' Alex coughs. 'I could use some, too. But you know what? I think you'll survive.'

They all laugh, and Alex jogs on, down the line of sunken Cadillacs, leading the way.

Up close, Bonnie explores the Cadillacs in awe. They are barely recognizable as cars. Appearing more like strangely familiar geological formations, the sleek straight lines of metal hidden under mineral-like layers of spray paint.

Some of the cars you can walk through, slipping between the roof of the cabin and the chassis. Finding a little sacred spot, to hide from the rest of the world.

They wander amid these curious architectures, aware of the thousands of lives that must have filtered through here in the past. Bonnie places her hand on the weathered hood of one car, searching for some cosmic vibe, the way Alex sought one in Greenwood, Tulsa. But there's nothing: just cold metal, sitting on that windswept plain for decades. She knocks on it, and a dull ring trembles in the air for a moment.

'So . . . right here?' Alex asks.

She shakes her spray-paint can and holds it poised in front of the hood.

Bonnie shrugs. 'What are you gonna spray?'

'No idea.'

But then Alex leans into it, a steady spray of fluorescent green speckling the bumpy surface below her. Bonnie and Kevin watch as she keeps spraying, a fantastical curlicue of

WHAT WE LEFT UNSAID

green emerging, tendrils like an Art Nouveau vine, or the curving arms of an underwater octopus.

The green creeps up one side of the bonnet, encompassing all the other colors that came before it. But the pattern is vibrant, arresting even amongst the outlandish sight of these sunken sedans.

She'd forgotten how artistic Alex was, how bold with each of her creations.

'Not bad,' Bonnie approves. 'What is it?'

'No idea.' Alex shrugs, with a laugh. 'But I had fun making it. Kevin, your go.' She tosses the can to Kevin, who looks up, catches it just in time.

He turns the corner of a car, hunting for a relatively bare patch of white. Then he leans over and sprays: *Chu's 4-EVA*.

They all burst into laughter.

''Cause, y'know, we want that to be the definitive statement of our family,' Alex jokes.

'And you?' Alex turns to Bonnie. 'Come on, collective art, Bon . . . Join in.'

Bonnie scoffs. 'I can spray something, sure. But it's just gonna get sprayed over in a few hours.'

'That's not the point.' Alex rolls her eyes. 'The point is to have made a contribution. To leave a part of you here. Like a penny you throw into a fountain.'

'Fine,' Bonnie says, as Kevin presses the can into her hands. She wanders off, wanting to be on her own with these strange, storied objects on this sunstruck plain. She studies the last Cadillac in the row. Every last inch of its surface is covered, but she finds a spot, on the curve of a tire, with just enough of a monochrome patch to spray onto.

For a moment she hesitates, thinking what kind of message

she could possibly leave here, in this windswept place. Then she sprays: '*We love you, Mom.*'

Bonnie gets up, the dust sifting between her toes. Probably no one else will read that scrawl; it will soon disappear under someone else's paint. But Bonnie will know it's there, one of countless spray-painted devotions, waiting beneath the Texan sun.

* * *

Kevin faces the western sun, with Cadillac Ranch to his back. He is grateful for this temporary reprieve from his situation, grateful that there is no cell phone signal out here. The wind and immense distances leave him bereft but temporarily free.

Bonnie edges up next to him, and they both look at the reddening sun, the shadows lengthening.

'Hey, you okay?' she asks.

He shrugs, wordless. He feels like he's told them everything by now.

'We should probably get going,' she says. 'You said it's another hour and forty to Tucumcari, right?' She pauses. 'And Dad wants to talk after that.'

Kevin swallows, and the nausea returns, threatens to floor him. Part of him would be relieved to just perish right here in Texas, his bones picked clean by vultures and the wind.

'Kevin.' Bonnie lays a hand on his elbow. 'I . . . I can lend you the money.'

He turns to stare at his sister. Inside him, a wave of commingled relief and gratitude is poised like a breaker frozen in midair, ready to fall. 'Are you sure?'

'I want to help. Of course, I do.' Bonnie's words are concentrated, considered. 'But I need to speak to Chris first. I mean . . . we've got the money.'

The wave crashes down. 'Oh my god, that would be incredible. I've been so stressed, and I—' Kevin pauses. Maybe she doesn't want to hear an emotional outpouring from her loser younger brother. 'I'll need to pay you back.'

Bonnie nods. Of course. Because no one borrows a quarter million dollars from their sister and expects not to have to pay it back.

'We'll work something out.' She turns from the sun and looks directly at him. 'But honestly, Kev, what were you thinking?'

He squeezes his eyes shut. The inevitable scolding from his older sister.

'I wasn't thinking, that's the problem. I was just so tired of my life. I wanted to change things up, make enough money to retire.'

He thinks of his parents, working every day until their pensions kicked in at the end of their sixties. Uncomplaining, content with their lot in life and their regular, unexciting paychecks.

Bonnie sighs. 'Those get-rich-quick schemes, they never work. I thought you knew that.'

Kevin grimaces at the lesson. *Easy for you to say.* The Prescotts have had multiple generations to compound their assets. Chris and Bonnie never needed to risk their life savings.

Then again, neither did I.

'I've got two conditions,' Bonnie says.

Kevin's gut lurches. This will be the greatest humiliation: to be beholden to his older sister. 'One is you keep us posted on your financial situation, pay us back little by little. Don't take out any investments without running that past us.'

Ouch. Sure, treat your own brother like a baby. But Kevin nods, humbled. 'And?'

'The second condition.' She pauses.

205

'What?' Kevin prods, impatient.

Bonnie sighs. 'I don't know how I feel about you . . . making this huge mistake, and me fixing it for you, and then that's it, problem solved. You can't just lose a quarter million dollars and expect there to be no consequences.'

Consequences? Like he's a dog she's trying to train. Or one of her own children deserving punishment. Kevin balks.

'What, do you want to publicly humiliate me? You want me to tell Mom and Dad, so I can lose everyone's respect? So they can know how much of a fool I am?' And how generous and angelic Bonnie is. Kevin crumples his face in his hands, just thinking about it.

'Kevin.' Bonnie leans in, her voice stern. 'I'm trying to figure out what is the right thing to do here. Would you rather owe money to some impersonal debt collection agency that'll make your life hell, or would you rather owe money to me?'

For a moment, he's tempted to answer: 'Some impersonal debt collection agency.' But then he thinks of a lifetime of collection letters sent to his address, chasing him down into old age.

'You at least need to tell Jessica. She's your wife. And the mother of your children. She deserves to know.'

Kevin imagines Jessica, her mouth opening in disbelief, that terrifying rage mounting in her. Something starts to die inside him.

'I mean, frankly speaking as a wife myself . . .' Bonnie adds. 'I would rather be told something like this by my husband than have to find out on my own.'

'Do you think she'll ever trust me again?'

'With money?' Bonnie considers this. 'I wouldn't blame her if she didn't.'

'If this were Chris, would *you* forgive him?' Although

everybody knows Christopher Prescott would never make a foolish investment like this.

Bonnie's answer surprises him. 'I'd have to. He's my husband. We have a family together.' She looks into the middle distance, piecing the reasons together as she speaks. As if she were gazing into their past or imagining possible futures. 'And if I couldn't learn to trust him again, then our marriage would be doomed.'

It dawns on him then: how difficult the road ahead is, if he wants to keep his marriage and his family intact. Jessica had already begun to resent him the minute he downloaded those investment apps, grew addicted to following them on his phone. The rot has only worsened since then.

'Come on,' Bonnie says, draping an arm over his shoulder and giving him a welcome squeeze. 'Alex is waiting. And so is Route 66.'

He turns for a moment and glances almost thankfully at Cadillac Ranch. Those alien shapes, sunken into the ground, nonjudgmental, whispering their secrets into the Texan plain for all of eternity.

1991

Alex remembers the car ride afterward. They kept driving south, away from the Grand Canyon. Away from the gas station and the men.

Everyone kept asking her if she was okay. Bonnie's big, worried eyes; Kevin a little more diffident – but of course she was. She'd just been sitting in the car the whole time.

She wanted to say, 'You should ask Mom, not me.'

Yet Mommy never mentioned anything about herself. In fact, she kept saying 'Alex just upset we left her in the car for so long.' And everyone looked at her the same way they always had: Little Alex, always crying.

She was tired of everyone coddling her like she was a baby. She didn't always cry now when she was upset. She'd learned how to control her tears, when to hold them in, when to let them out.

In fact, she felt the opposite of a baby, when she thought about the gas station, and what she'd done there. Those men had been scary. Bigger than Daddy, and mean-looking, even when she saw them from a distance. And yet, when she had run up to them screaming, they had stopped. They almost looked shocked, like they didn't know what to do.

Could it be that easy?

All you had to do was channel your anger, put it on display, storm onto the scene like you owned it. Scream and shout and – what was it they said? – put on a performance. Let everyone see, and they would believe.

That is what stays with her during the seven-hour drive back, as the desert mellows from gold to a rosy dusk. And it stays with her for weeks and months and years after. That there was a way to turn fear into anger. There was a power in performing. Mommy and Daddy never showed their feelings; they kept everything below the surface.

But scream and cry and you could call attention, surprise people, control the scene.

And that is how Alex learned to act.

In later years, after drama training, Alex came to realize that acting was never just about performance. There was always some kernel of truth to your emotions. You just had to amplify it, believe it in that single moment.

So it was there, the moment she stepped out of the car.

That afternoon in the desert, when she had acted brave and done a grown-up thing, her family had refused to see it. But maybe, one day, they would.

New Mexico

Less than four hours after entering the Texas panhandle, they exit it, crossing over into New Mexico in the amber glow of sunset. *'New Mexico – Land of Enchantment'* reads the roadside sign, and Alex finds herself open to it, seeking a spell of magic.

The Texan plain, featureless and pancake-flat, has begun to wrinkle, throwing up mesas and hills that gleam golden in the far distance.

'Ever been to New Mexico?' she asks the car.

'Nope,' Kevin answers from behind the wheel. (She is surprised her brother is responsive.)

'My first time, too,' Bonnie says.

By the time they reach Tucumcari, Alex is reminded of an oasis she once came across in the Sahara. An impossible cluster of palm trees and moist ground, surrounded by the endless, unforgiving sand.

Here is the Route 66 version.

Tucumcari is a strange, retro town. As if someone had preserved a slice of 1950s Americana – all flashing neon lights, Day-Glo motor lodges – and deposited it, largely forsaken, in the middle of the desert for the sand and the sun to blast through.

' "Once a vital stop for motorists in the heyday of Route 66, Tucumcari was bypassed when the new interstate was built five miles away. Without a steady flow of tourists, businesses began to suffer and the population declined." ' Alex reads this aloud from her phone, and she can't help but feel a little sad. The classic American story. Always build faster, newer, flashier. And leave other communities in the dust.

But she reminds herself not to judge, as she squints into the desert, seeking out the glow of neon amid the otherwise unmarked stretch of darkness. Kevin has been particularly excited about tonight's hotel. And surely she can tap into that excitement to present a cheery demeanor in their call tonight with Dad. That is a performance she has been accustomed to her whole life.

* * *

You can do this, you can hold this together.

This is the first thing on Bonnie's mind when Dad's call flashes up on her phone. They are sitting in their cozy queen bedroom in the Blue Swallow Motel in Tucumcari, the motel that Kevin enthusiastically reserved weeks ago. The furnishings here are all vintage, dating from the heyday of Route 66, and the honeyed lilt of 1950s crooners drifts from the motel's outside speakers into the nighttime desert air.

Bonnie reminds herself she's used to holding things together, isn't she? Three energetic boys to look after and Chris working sixty-hour weeks. Or calming her perpetually anxious parents and covering for her younger brother and sister and their foolish adolescent choices, all throughout their teenage years and into their twenties.

But this – *this* – her brother losing a quarter million dollars out of his own idiocy, this is on a scale she's never imagined before.

'Hey Dad! How are you?' Bonnie chirps in a preternaturally cheerful voice. 'We're in New Mexico.' *Take charge of the call. Pretend everything's normal.*

'Bonnie! Bonnie! Hi! Hi!' Dad's face is pixilated, but she can just about make out his nose, the glint of his wire-framed glasses.

'Hi Dad.' Alex leans in toward Bonnie's screen.

'Oh, hey Alex! Hi Kevin! Good to see you!'

Dad seems genuinely pleased, and Bonnie imagines for a moment what his life must be like, narrowed to his everyday existence of supermarket trips, neighborhood walks, and ping-pong sessions at the local senior center. And an ailing wife, who isn't on this call. She considers asking about Mom but senses the conversation will lead to her in the end.

'So . . . where are you guys? Did you say New Mexico?'

'Yeah,' Alex answers, bright and enthusiastic. 'We left Tulsa, Oklahoma, today, drove through the Texas panhandle, and now we're in Tucumcari, New Mexico.'

There's something undeniably performative about Alex's answer, and she wonders how long they have been playing this charade, pretending everything is positive and happy so their parents can worry less about them.

'Wow, so much driving,' Dad says. 'And what do you think of Oklahoma and Texas?'

'It's very big,' Alex says. 'Hot and dusty. Very spread out.'

She pulls a face and shrugs to Bonnie and Kevin. What else is she supposed to say?

'Wait till you get to see more of New Mexico and Arizona.' Dad nods. 'Very beautiful.'

'Have you been here before?'

'We drove through there once, before you all were born.'

'You did?' Bonnie is surprised. She didn't know that. She recalls her dad had traveled for work when he was younger. Before his job in telecoms had stabilized, along with their family income. But the thought of her dad – young, nervous, with his broken English – driving past large, indifferent trucks on the

I-44, somehow strikes an unfamiliar note of concern in her. There is a strange desire to reach back and protect her own naive parents, earlier in their immigrant lives.

'Yeah, when we moved from my PhD program in Tennessee to a postdoctoral position in California. Your mommy and I were young. Younger than all of you now.'

Bonnie strains to place that in the timeline of recent American history. That must have been in the late 60s, early 70s. What would it have been like to road-trip through Oklahoma and Texas back then, as skinny Asians, in their horn-rimmed glasses, with their timid driving and obvious accents?

'Mommy didn't like it,' Dad says, as if hearing her question spoken out loud. 'It was too dusty for her. She didn't like the food, either.'

The three of them laugh, because they can all imagine the way Mom would wrinkle her nose up at a menu listing only hamburgers and greasy all-American fare.

But this mention of Mom casts a new sobriety to the conversation.

'So . . . how is she, Dad?' This is the first time Kevin has spoken up, leaning in toward Bonnie's iPad to show his face.

Dad pauses, and she can feel his discomfort as he searches for the right English words to describe the rupture in their humble everyday lives. 'She's sleeping right now. Gets very tired these days. Even though, you know her, always want to do so many things. But she needs more rest.'

There's an uncharacteristic quaver in his voice as he says this.

'Oh.' Bonnie pauses for a moment. 'But we'll be there soon, only a few more days!'

'How much longer?' Dad asks. And he sounds lonely. Almost desperate, his voice shrunken.

'We should be there by Sunday night,' Alex answers.

'I think your Mommy would be very happy, knowing you all were here. And I would be happy, too.'

He offers it like that, a simple sentiment laid bare, so unlike their dad.

'We'll be happy, too, once we get there,' Bonnie assures him. Or will they? There is the dread of seeing her mom so much weaker, being wheeled down a hospital corridor for her impending operation.

'So listen,' Dad says. And now they are finally reaching the reason he wanted the call in the first place. He says the next question awkwardly, stepping slowly word by word. 'When you get here . . . your mommy is feeling unwell . . . Maybe better you don't say anything that will upset her too much.'

They sit and absorb that request.

'What do you mean?' Alex asks. There's the slightest edge of rebellion in the way she says this.

Dad sighs. 'She's not in good condition, your mom. I don't want her hearing anything that might shock her.'

'Like what?' Alex challenges. Bonnie shoots her a warning look, but her sister doesn't look up, her eyes trained on the iPad screen.

'Like the last time you and Kevin fought in front of her.'

Bonnie is surprised Dad even remembers. In all the years since, neither of their parents had mentioned that horrible argument or commented why Alex and Kevin never came home for the same Christmas.

'Do you know *why* we fought?' Alex asks. Her jaw is growing more set, her look hardening into a glare.

'Please don't be like that, Alex,' Dad says.

'Be like what?' Alex shoots back. 'Be angry? Be a lesbian?'

'See, exactly this. The way you raise your voice. The things you say that can shock her.'

Alex huffs.

'Well, what are you waiting for, Dad? For Mom's condition to improve so she can finally accept that *I'm a dyke*? And what if it doesn't improve? What if she goes her whole life without knowing that I'm actually, for the first time, really *happy* right now with my personal life—'

'Shh!!' Dad hisses at them. 'Don't say things like that! She will get better.'

But he doesn't sound very convincing. And Bonnie knows he said that mainly to ward off the rest of Alex's sentence.

'You don't understand, Alex,' Dad continues. 'Your mommy . . . she's spent so much of her life worrying about you.'

Alex rolls her eyes. 'I'm forty years old now. She can stop worrying.'

'Bonnie and Kevin, they're married. They own their homes; we don't worry so much—'

'Oh no,' Alex says, shaking her head slowly. There's a bitterness in her voice that sounds new, uncompromising. 'Do *not* compare me to Bonnie and Kevin. All you fucking do is compare us. What, like, *Kevin* is the paragon of financial solvency? *He's* the perfect family man?'

Alex's voice is thick with sarcasm, and Kevin looks to Bonnie in alarm, terrified of what she'll say next.

'Why you bringing me into this?' Kevin warns Alex.

Dad speaks. 'Of course we don't worry so much about Kevin—'

A caustic laugh from Alex. 'Just because he's got two kids, a job he hates, and a suburban home doesn't mean he has his shit together.'

'But see how responsible he is. You've said it – all the things he's been able to provide his family.'

'Aren't you still *renting* a place to live, Alex?' Kevin chides.

She glares back at him.

Kevin, what are you doing? Bonnie thinks with dread.

'Right,' Dad continues, oblivious. 'When you own your own home, Alex, that's a big milestone. Your jobs haven't paid well, so you're not there yet.'

'Haven't paid well . . . ?' Alex's voice is about to crack. ' Is *that* what matters?' Bonnie can sense the hurt in her, and she prays to her to keep up the façade.

But the anger flashes out in a torrent of words.

'Here's a newsflash, Dad: *I'm* not the only irresponsible one. Kevin might lose his house. He owes a lot of money. He fucked up on an investment, and now Bonnie is bailing him out. Don't tell Mom because it'll upset her,' – she says this singsong and bitter – 'but it's time one of you knows the truth. I'm sick of you all thinking *I'm* the fuckup.'

Dad is shocked silent for a moment, but then turns his head, his gaze searching for his son.

'Kevin, is that true?'

Kevin coughs. 'That I . . . what? That I owe money?'

They all look at Kevin, and the room is quiet, the sound of a Vic Damone track filtering in from outside.

'Yes.' Kevin speaks in a subdued voice. His hands twist against each other, his knuckles pale.

'How much?'

Kevin closes his eyes and hesitates. But Bonnie suddenly leans in. 'Dad, the amount doesn't matter. I'm lending him what he needs to pay it back.'

Alex growls, furious that Bonnie's stepped in to save Kevin.

Dad stops, confused by the turn in the conversation. 'That's – that's very good of you Bonnie. Always such a good *jie-jie*.'

God. Bonnie can imagine both her siblings groaning inwardly right now.

216

'So that's it?' Alex asks. 'Kevin gets away with it scot-free, and you don't even want to know more?'

'What is your *problem*, Alex?' Kevin shouts, his face red.

'Alex, Kevin,' Dad calls out in a weak attempt to calm them down. 'Don't. I don't need to know right now. You go visit the Grand Canyon together, then you come home, and we talk about it.'

'But not in front of Mom,' Alex mocks. 'Because god forbid we upset her with the truth.'

'No,' Dad says, missing Alex's sarcasm. 'Not in front of Mom.'

Alex works her jaw furiously, her mind on something.

'Dad,' she asks, her voice sharp. 'You know that time we tried to visit the Grand Canyon, the road trip we went on all those years ago?'

Bonnie senses the slightest of hesitations from Dad before he answers. 'Yes?'

'Why *did* we turn around when we were so close? Do you know?'

Bonnie pales when she hears this question. There's a trickle of apprehension into her gut, though she can't explain why.

Dad sighs. 'I don't know, Alex. That's not something I can answer. Maybe Mommy can tell you. When she's better.'

Alex stares at the iPad, disappointed. The tension in the room slowly deflates. From outside, they can hear Dinah Shore chirping one of her golden-age hits, and beyond that, the cars and trucks coursing along the interstate.

* * *

After they've ended the call with Dad, Kevin rears up, livid.

'You happy now?' he shouts at Alex, jabbing a finger at her.

She's never seen him this angry before. Not since she painted that portrait of him in middle school. But now there is also a tragic desperation to him, a sense that everything in his life is close to crumbling.

'You happy I've finally lost face in front of Dad? That he sees me for the loser I am?'

She almost regrets exposing him like that. 'Kevin, it wasn't about that. That's not why I said it.'

'Then why did you? So you could make yourself look better?'

'Because it's not fair!' she explodes. 'I get so much flak from them, just for being – for being gay and different. And here you are, throwing a quarter million dollars down the drain, and they still think you're the perfect son. It's just not fair.'

'Life isn't fair, Alex.' His voice is cutting, vicious. But it's the condescending tone that infuriates her the most.

'You think *I* don't know that?' she seethes back. 'Try telling the Native Americans that. Or all those Black people in Tulsa. Or the women I work with—'

'Oh, I get it.' Kevin's voice drips with contempt. 'This is all part of your "let's make the world a more equal place" campaign, right? Black Lives Matter and LGBTQIA whatever rights, and let's level the historically unequal playing field. Make Kevin the heterosexual man suffer.'

Alex bristles now. The way he belittles her worldview like there's no merit to it.

'No, Kevin.' Her voice is low now, quiet. She reminds herself to control it, to build, build to the big reveal. 'This isn't about that. But it's maybe, just *maybe*, about the fact you've never apologized for what you said to me that Christmas when I came out.'

And even though she doesn't want to, even though she wasn't planning on it, her voice cracks now, riddled with tears and anger.

Kevin is staring at her, eyes wide – either from dread or outrage, she can't tell.

'Do I have to *remind* you what you said?' she pushes on.

'You already reminded me,' Kevin seethes with sarcasm. 'As usual, I said something ignorant and insensitive.'

'That's a fucking understatement. You said me being a lesbian was "just a phase" I was going through. I needed to grow up. I needed to be an adult.'

'Alex, you *do* need to grow up.'

'Come on, Kevin,' Bonnie says, trying to intervene.

In a fury, Alex picks up a quilted pillow and heaves it at him. She doesn't care if it's vintage and lovingly preserved. 'I *am* grown-up! My version of adulthood may not look like yours, but I'm not some irresponsible kid. Do you have any idea how much it *hurt* to hear you say that? In front of Mom and Dad?'

'Oh, boo-hoo-hoo,' Kevin taunts her, exactly the same way he would when they were kids.

'Fuck off,' Alex fumes. 'You've always just *mocked* my way of life or anything I care about.'

'Because it's ridiculous; it's reckless, the way you live.'

Alex turns on him, eyes blazing. 'Speaking of reckless, who the fuck loses a quarter million dollars of life savings on *Bitcoin*?'

'Cryptocurrency,' Kevin corrects her.

'Whatever. You can't even fucking apologize, when you're so clearly in the wrong.'

They both seem to have run out of breath, and they pause for a moment, their argument at an impasse.

Finally, Kevin speaks up. He takes a step closer.

'Listen, I'm sorry, okay?'

Alex studies him, unwilling to trust this as sincere, half expecting him to renege on his apology.

But Kevin looks defeated, his anger souring into something like misery. 'But why do you need my apology so badly anyway? Why does it count for so much ... when you obviously think I'm such a loser? I'm sorry I voted for Trump.'

She doesn't know what to say, baffled by this confession.

'I'm sorry,' Kevin continues, his voice rising, curdling between sarcasm and anger. 'I'm sorry you have me as a brother. I'm sorry to Mom and Dad that I never became a doctor. I'm sorry I can't hold on to my money. I'm sorry I'm such an embarrassment to the family. I'm sorry I was ever born! Okay?'

'Kevin, I—'

His face is contorted, miserable now. His eyes shining with unshed tears. Alex is shocked to see so much self-loathing in him. A trickle of empathy finds its way into her heart.

'Are you happy now? Is that enough of an apology for you?' It comes out as a shriek, Kevin choking on his words.

Broken, he rushes for the door and slams it behind him. Desperate, Alex knows, not to cry in front of his own sisters. That kind of shame would be more than he could bear.

* * *

'Kevin? Kevin!' Bonnie steps out of the motel room, looks at his figure retreating quickly down the main street of Tucumcari, hotfooting it down Route 66 into the night.

She doesn't know if she should chase after him, then reasons he probably wants some time on his own. The same way Max does, when he gets too upset.

'Just let him go,' Alex says. She's sprawled on her bed, staring up at the ceiling. Deflated like a balloon that's let out all its air. 'He's an adult; he can figure out how to calm himself down.'

Uncertain, Bonnie flops down on the other bed. She realizes she is incredibly tired. 'You didn't have to push him so far.'

'He didn't have to be so stubborn about apologizing.'

Alex has a point. Neither of her siblings have been flawless in their behavior toward each other these past few years. Or in fact, ever.

She can understand Alex's anger, though. A rough calculation tells her that a quarter million dollars probably equates to three years of both Alex and Nya's salaries combined. Imagine working that hard at a job you actually believe in, one which helps others, only to see Kevin blow that same amount of money on a bad investment. And then to be bailed out that easily by your big sister, with no consequences.

'Do you think I'm a complete sucker, putting up my own money to save his ass?'

Silence from Alex's side of the room, before she finally speaks.

'If I had that kind of money, I'd probably do it, too. He is our brother, after all.'

Bonnie turns onto her side, props her head up, and faces her little sister. The same way they would in their bedroom at home decades ago, trading stories and gossip at bedtime. Before she became a teenager and insisted on getting her own room.

'*You* would do that?' she teases Alex. 'After the way he's treated you?'

Alex muses. 'I might need to subject him to some diversity and inclusion training before he gets the money.'

They both cackle. 'I'm not sure that would have much effect.'

'It probably never does,' Alex admits.

Bonnie sighs, listening to a Frank Sinatra ballad crooning on the evening air. Does this town ever stop blasting the golden oldies? 'What do we do now?'

Alex sits forward, staring straight ahead with a sullen resolution. 'I don't know about you, but I could sure use a beer. Should we see if there's any vintage bars open?'

Kevin steps out into the dark desert night of Tucumcari. It's past 10 p.m. and the streets are completely deserted. No cars, no people. Just the neon lights of their motel and the Teepee Curios gift shop, an illuminated teepee and cactus flickering noiselessly from green to red and back again, for no one but himself to see. He walks a long block to the next streetlight, then walks another block to the next one.

In the distance, a dog barks. Followed by another dog, and then a long, lonesome howl farther out. *A coyote?*

Kevin shivers. He thinks about his gun.

But then he wonders, why? So he could shoot at the empty air, the stars? He's already lost all his savings and his family's respect. There's nothing to be gained by shooting at a phantom dog.

And has he ever, in all his five years of gun ownership, ever actually shot that gun outside of the safe, well-lit confines of a shooting range? He's been too chicken to even join Brad Malloy on his hunting weekends with the boys.

He steels himself. *Be like Alex.* She wouldn't be scared by the nighttime and a few dogs baying in a strange town. (As much as it pains him, he has to admit this.) She'd probably walk into the dark and start howling with them.

He keeps walking in his stupid white Nikes, which are probably visible from a mile away. Maybe they just need to get dirty. Maybe he should just keep walking and disappear into the night.

* * *

Alex is submerged deep in a dream – something about Nya and a deserted gas station, but this time in the middle of South London – when Bonnie gently shakes her awake. Alex sits up, disoriented. The fragments of her dream linger for a moment, before dissolving into the dark of the motel room around her.

'Alex,' Bonnie says, half whispering, urgent.

'What is it?' Alex flinches as Bonnie flicks on the lamp. Suddenly, she sits bolt upright. 'Is it Mom?'

Bonnie shakes her head. 'It's not her. But . . . I have no idea where Kevin is.'

Alex breathes out with relief. Just Kevin. 'What time is it?'

'It's like two in the morning. I heard him go out a few hours ago. But I haven't heard him come back. And the car's still here.'

Alex feels something in her gut. 'He's not in his room?'

'I've knocked a few times. I've called his phone. Nothing.'

She sits back and rubs her eyes. 'Where the hell could he have gone?'

Bonnie gestures helplessly out the window. 'I mean, this town is completely dead at this hour. There's nowhere to go.'

Alex thinks for a moment. 'I dunno. Maybe there's a local backwater bar somewhere that's open late.' Though she has trouble imagining Kevin in a place like that, rubbing shoulders with the locals. Kevin with his polo shirt and khakis and iPhone addiction.

'What do we do? Should we go drive the streets and look for him?' She doesn't actually mean this, but is at a loss for any other ideas.

Bonnie shakes her head again, despairing. 'He's got the car keys. Or they're in his room. Which we can't get into.'

Alex wonders if maybe Bonnie is blowing this all out of proportion, but then again, he's their brother. She thinks of the pain and self-hatred in his face, just before he ran out on them.

Then she remembers something the motel proprietor had said when they checked in. *If you get locked out of your room, we have a spare key. You just need to knock on our door and wake us up. Whatever the hour.*

2:07 a.m.

She grimaces inwardly, then looks at Bonnie. 'Is this an emergency? Should we wake them up for the spare key?'

Bonnie sighs and sits down on the bed, her head in her hands.

'Listen, I'm worried about him.' Her voice is smaller, quieter. 'You don't know – We didn't – Kevin's got a gun in the glove compartment.'

Alex stares at her sister, the shock etched on her face. 'A *gun*? This entire fucking time you haven't told me?'

She thinks of her brother, his embittered anger, the self-loathing when he finally apologized. And somehow it all makes sense.

* * *

Kevin. Out of Bonnie's two siblings, it's always been Alex she's worried about her whole life. Alex with her thrill-seeking, her high emotions, her overactive tear ducts. Kevin was never a cause for concern because he always took the more normal route in life, never stepped out of bounds. Never tried anything out of the ordinary.

But she must have been blind this entire time. *Kevin* would have foolishly lost that much money on investments? *Kevin* would have staked his own family's home, their financial security, for what? A feeling of glory that comes with striking gold?

She's seen this in Chris, every time one of his portfolios 'makes a killing,' as he likes to say.

But for her own brother to be that stupid with his own hard-earned savings . . . For him, the consequences are more dire, heightened by disappointment and middle-age ennui. She hadn't realized he was this unhappy. How low is he willing to sink in his despair?

So Kevin's gun is on her mind as she explains the situation to Alex, as they walk with guilty steps across the gravel forecourt, as they knock on the mint-green door of the motel proprietor, and sheepishly explain to him about their missing brother, their need to access his room at this hour.

'It's just . . . we're worried about him. And he's got the car keys in his room, in case we need to take him anywhere.'

'You sure he's okay?' the proprietor, Dan, asks. An implant from Chicago who bought the motel a few years ago. A retirement dream for a lifelong Route 66 fanatic.

'He's been a bit down lately,' Alex explains. But there is a subsequent silence and a weight to her words that communicates something to Dan.

He nods, his paunch rounding out his striped pajamas. 'You two are good sisters,' he chuckles wryly. 'Wish mine cared as much about me. Let me get you the key.'

* * *

Kevin doesn't know how long he's been walking for. There is something hypnotic about the cool of the desert air on his skin, his own feet treading the asphalt, over and over, as he walks through miles of unmarked darkness. He is compelled to keep walking, keep putting more and more distance between him and the neglected oasis of neon that is Tucumcari.

The moon rises high above him, a white disc, nearly full, in the desert sky.

225

He has worked up a sweat, and he knows that if he were to stop, the desert chill would set in, and he would start to shiver.

So he continues walking, driven only by a desire to keep going, not to stop and face what he has left behind.

* * *

Alex's heart is beating as she inserts the key into the lock and turns it. She hopes to see Kevin flat on his back on his motel bed, asleep with his mouth open and a half-eaten pizza next to him on the chenille bedspread.

But nope, the room is nearly as untouched as when they checked in. His suitcase sits unpacked, and she casts about looking for some clue to where he could have gone.

'Is his wallet here?' Bonnie asks.

'Yep, right here.' Alex spots it on the 1930s side table. And right next to it, the car keys.

'What the fuck, Kevin?' Bonnie says to the empty room.

And Alex is thinking the same thing. With no car keys and no wallet on him, what the hell could Kevin be doing?

* * *

It feels like hours have passed, when he finally turns around.

He is not prepared to see all the darkness surrounding him.

Tucumcari is now far in the distance, a cluster of lights somewhere on the way to the horizon. The tourist businesses must have turned off their neon this late at night, or their blinking colors aren't visible from here. He can only see the yellow sodium wash of the streetlights, an alien gleam completely dwarfed by the vast darkened desert.

What time is it anyway? He glances at his Apple Watch, presses it alive. *2:34? Jesus, how did it get to be this late?*

He must have walked miles in the past few hours. No wonder

the town looks so far away. He suddenly feels the ache in his legs and contemplates if he has the energy to walk all that way back. Or should he just stop right here and wait for whatever befalls him.

There's no signal on his Apple Watch. It doesn't surprise him, this far out in the desert.

If he closed his eyes and took ten steps off the asphalt, he would not be able to distinguish the road from the wilderness. He could wander forever and be lost in the lightless desert, with no road to guide him and no source of drinking water.

Normally, such a thought would scare him. But on this night, at this moment, there is simply a calm acceptance of his fate. This is how far he has wandered. If he dies from neglect or stupidity or carelessness, it's only because he deserves it.

He thinks of scorpions and rattlesnakes, shriveled corpses discovered in the noonday sun. Briefly, an image of Arabella flashes through his mind, her curious eyes looking straight at him – and the thought of his family, Brian, and even Jessica, softens him for a moment.

But it's too late. And there's no point. He keeps walking into the night.

* * *

With a flick of a button, Bonnie unlocks the car remotely. The beep is disarmingly loud in the surrounding silence. The motor lodge was built for 1930s cars, and their SUV barely fits inside its designated solo garage. So she squeezes around to the driver-side door, worms into the seat, and unlocks the glove compartment.

Please be there, please be there, please be there, she prays, as she pats around gingerly inside.

When she feels the hard case and flicks it open, she is flooded with relief.

'Is the gun still there?' Alex asks.

Bonnie nods. 'Thank god.'

Then on second thought, if Kevin is out there on his own, she wonders if he's really better off without it.

* * *

Kevin thinks he's hallucinating when he sees another light in the distance ahead of him. This time much closer, not along all those miles of highway, but to the left of him, out there in the middle of the desert. Off-road.

He creeps closer and realizes it's a campfire, burning red-orange and crackling. Not like the cold, empty lights of the town.

The fire throws a pool of light around it on the desert floor, sparks rise into the night sky, and as he approaches, he hears voices, mumbling. Then occasionally rising to a whoop and holler.

He squints, trying to make out who's there. Four figures. No, five. No, seven. Sitting on the ground around the fire or ranged around it. Passing a bottle between them, then an occasional glowing spark.

There is the easy camaraderie of men who know each other, who are comfortable enough and masculine enough to drive this far into the desert and sit around a campfire together in the middle of nowhere.

Men who don't know him. Men who will only treat him as a stranger.

A cold chill passes through him, and he wonders if he should turn back.

But it's too late.

'Yello?' One of the men shouts, standing up and staring out into the dark, straight at him.

'Someone out there?' Another guy calls.

The easy camaraderie is broken, and instead a sharp, alert suspicion cuts through the group, everyone trained on the darkness, staring in Kevin's direction.

He gulps and takes a step back. Should he make a run for it . . . ?

A light is swung toward him, blinding Kevin in a spotlight. He squints and holds his hand up.

And a familiar fear, one from over thirty years ago, washes over him. The desert setting, the glaring light, these white guys who seem so at ease with their environment, a product of the wind and the sun themselves.

All seven of them are standing up now, frowning at him.

'Who the fuck is out there?'

* * *

'What are we supposed to do now? Drive around the desert, shouting his name?' Alex asks this as she wheels the Mazda onto the broad, desolate main street of Tucumcari at 2:45 a.m.

'Listen, I don't know!' Bonnie throws her hand up, exasperated. 'You're the intrepid traveler, you tell me!'

Alex snorts. 'I'm used to traveling *solo*. Specifically so I don't have to deal with situations like this.'

She realizes that comes across as harsh, but for her, that was always the point of solo travel: getting away from any kind of obligations or responsibilities. Be your own, self-sufficient person, alone in the world. In the cool desert chill, it strikes her how lonely, and even sad, that attitude is.

Alex makes a random right turn and takes the car down

darkened streets, an abandoned downtown area that resembles a post-apocalyptic movie set.

'So what do you think we should do? What do you think Kevin is capable of?' Bonnie asks. It occurs to Alex how unusual that sounds, to have Bonnie be the one asking for advice, unsure of what to do.

'Do you think he was capable of doing something desperate with that gun?'

Bonnie gives a strangled murmur and shrugs helplessly. 'I don't know. I didn't think he was capable of gambling that much money. I didn't think... I guess maybe we don't know Kevin so well after all.'

Alex absorbs that comment in the dark and says nothing, because she can't refute it. Two, three decades on, they hardly know their own brother. Or each other. The truth of that gap opens up in front of her, and she sees it now, as the car headlights pick out a blasted concrete wall, a crumpled poster for a yard sale that took place a week ago.

'Well,' Alex finally admits. 'I know him even less than you do. I mean, I never would have guessed he'd own a gun.'

'Mom and Dad are gonna kill us if anything happens to him,' Bonnie says.

Alex muses on this, then bursts out laughing.

'What are you laughing at?'

'You've been saying that same exact phrase as long as I've known you. "Mom and Dad are gonna kill us" if we don't get straight As. If we don't clean our rooms. If the rice overcooks...'

Her sister can't help but laugh, too, a wry admission on her part. 'I guess you're right.'

'Bonnie, you're *forty-six*. Do you still live in fear of what Mom and Dad are thinking?'

Bonnie sighs. 'Kind of sad, isn't it? I guess I can't ever

escape feeling like I have to be the responsible one. It's just so ingrained in me, every time I'm with you guys.'

'Well, I think you can step away from it at this point. We're middle-aged. We're responsible for our own lives.'

Bonnie doesn't say anything, but Alex knows she's heard.

'And besides, Mom and Dad aren't gonna kill us. We're their children. They just want to see more of us.'

They're back on the main street again, and Alex pulls up to a red light. They wait there at the vacant intersection, the red light and the streetlamps the only things visible in the night.

'This is fucking ridiculous,' Alex exclaims. 'I'm not waiting for this light.'

She stamps on the gas, and the Mazda blazes down the street.

'Alex!' Bonnie reprimands, and Alex rolls her eyes.

'It's three a.m. There's no other traffic. Do we want to find Kevin or what?'

* * *

They squint into the night. They've left the town and are driving slowly along the 209, their eyes trained for anything lying by the side of the road.

Bonnie shudders, wondering what they would do if they found Kevin in a heap on the asphalt, unconscious or bloodied or something worse. She tries to push that image out of her mind, while also preparing herself for it.

How far could he have possibly walked? Alex said there were three roads leading out of Tucumcari. If they trawl every one of them, there's still a good chance they'd miss him. It occurs to Bonnie how hopeless this search is. If he really wanted to disappear, the desert would be the perfect place to do it. You could vanish so easily here and never be found.

She thinks for a moment of her own three boys and Chris,

231

sleeping safely back home in Massachusetts, and she wishes she could call them now, speak to them and hear their voices in reply.

'How much farther should I go?' Alex asks.

'Oh, I don't know . . . How could he be so fucking stupid?' Bonnie moans, but there is more despair than rage in her voice.

This is impossible, Bonnie thinks. *Every single stretch of road looks exactly the same at night.*

Alex is about to wheel the car into a U-turn and double back, when Bonnie spots something in the distance.

'Wait wait wait,' she says. She points into the darkness to their left. 'What's that?'

Not too far from the road, there's the reddish-orange glow of a fire – a campfire, most likely, though they can't tell from this distance.

Alex nudges the Mazda forward till it crunches onto the margin. Their headlights illuminate a pickup truck parked off-road in the darkness, then another one. Most definitely a campfire.

'Shit,' Alex says. 'Well, they might know something?'

Bonnie doesn't say anything for a moment, just stares at the campfire, flickering like a taunting mirage.

Should they venture out and say hello to those people? Is that even safe? She is fully aware they are two women – two petite Asian women – on their own, in a remote desert late at night. And no one, save the motel proprietor (who is most likely asleep) knows they are here.

On the other hand, the campfire is the only sign of waking human life they've seen in a five-mile radius. If anyone's come across Kevin, these people are their only hope.

'Fuck it,' Alex mutters. 'Let's just go. You've got the gun, right?'

Bonnie looks at her in horror. 'Uh . . . why?'

* * *

Bonnie has probably had as much experience as Alex with guns – which is to say, none at all. But Alex instinctively knows that if anyone is going to use the gun between the two of them, it's going to be Alex.

She picks it up, the hardness and heft of it feeling surreal in her hand. Is it this easy? Just lift the gun, squeeze the trigger, and – bam! – end a life. She hesitates.

'Is the safety on?'

'I have no idea,' Bonnie answers.

'Me neither.'

Alex pauses again. She can't bring herself to carry something like that around. Just knowing what it's capable of.

'You know what? Let's just leave it here.'

'Yeah, probably better,' Bonnie agrees, uncertain.

Whatever happens, happens. But she for one doesn't want to be responsible for accidentally – or intentionally – killing anyone.

So she places the gun back carefully, flicks the case shut, and returns it to the glove compartment.

They slowly step down onto the desert floor, their eyes adjusting to the shades of darkness around them, now that the headlights are off.

One step. Then another. Alex almost stumbles over a clump of scrub. The going is torturous, sightless, but bit by bit, they are able to distinguish shapes in the darkness, and the campfire draws near.

As they approach, they can see that their arrival hasn't gone unnoticed. Parking an SUV in an otherwise empty desert at night would do it.

233

They see a few figures standing up, silhouetted against the flames, facing in their direction.

'Hey, who's there?' shouts a male voice.

Of course, a guy. Alex feels an instinctive dread and hopes that there might be at least a woman or two in the group.

'Hey,' she shouts back, pitching her voice lower than usual. She has a low voice, which can often be mistaken for a man's.

'You looking for your friend?' the man says.

She hears Bonnie's breath catch in her throat. 'Do they have him?' her sister whispers, hopeful.

It wasn't threatening, the way the man said it. But she can't see what these people look like; they're just shadows against the flames.

'Yeah, we're looking for someone,' she bellows back, trying to be as nondescript as possible.

There's some mumbling ahead, and then she sees a figure stagger up from the ground, where it had been lying. What the heck is going on?

'Bonnie? Alex?' Kevin's voice rings out weakly.

'Kevin!' Without hesitation, Bonnie runs forward before Alex can warn her to be careful.

Sure, she just blew their cover there.

Alex runs to catch up with her – and there he is: their brother, waving at them in recognition, before slumping back down on the desert floor.

Sprawled around him on the ground are a bunch of teenagers. Maybe twentysomethings. But not the gruff, meaty men she had been fearing. And no one seems injured. They just seem kind of . . . stoned. Staring up at the sky.

Alex feels a flood of relief – concern for her brother morphs into amusement.

'Kevin, what are you doing out here?'

Bonnie sounds exactly like their mom when she asks this.

'Hey.' The shape that is Kevin says vaguely, welcoming, and holds out an arm, waving. He sounds like he's drunk. Or high.

'Oh, is that your sisters?' someone asks.

'Hi! He said you might be coming!' Another person shouts, waving them over. It's a woman's voice, and Alex's fear turns into instant relief – and a sense of foolishness. Kevin isn't in danger. He's just hanging out with a bunch of locals, getting high.

'Have you been here this whole time?' Bonnie asks, when they arrive at Kevin's prostrate form. There is a note of annoyance in her voice, akin to scolding.

Kevin sits up, squinting at them. 'I've been walking. Then I found them.' He gestures to the kids. Twentysomethings. Hard to tell in this flickering firelight.

'Hey, I'm Chase,' a rangy, beardy young guy says this.

'I'm Vanessa.' A girl with a pierced nose.

'I'm Alex, and this is Bonnie.'

'Man, you guys look exactly like your brother.' *Not racist*, Alex reminds herself. Just trying to be friendly. And probably a little bit true.

'This guy is crazy! He was just walking. Walked all the way from town out here. Scared the shit out of us when he came up to us!' Another guy laughs, then takes a drag from a joint. As an afterthought, he holds it out to Bonnie and Alex. 'You want some?'

'What is it—' Bonnie starts to ask, but Alex nudges her in the ribs, talks over her.

'Sure,' she leans forward and takes the joint. Sucks in a drag, and nearly chokes from laughter when she sees the look of shock on Bonnie's face. Ahh, the delightful loosening that

235

comes with marijuana. Alex breathes out, content, and holds her face out to the cool night air.

She offers the joint to Bonnie.

'Your turn.' Alex is 98 percent sure Bonnie has never smoked marijuana before.

Bonnie stares back, aghast.

'Kev.' Alex points to Bonnie, who has taken the joint and is holding it gingerly, examining it. Surely this is a bonding moment, witnessing whether their law-abiding older sister will smoke a joint or not. A shared look of mischief passes between them.

'You gonna smoke it?' Chase asks.

'Uh, sure,' Bonnie says. She quickly holds the joint up to her lips and inhales uncertainly.

Bonnie Chu Prescott has just smoked a joint, everyone. This is an announcement Alex wants to make to the world, but instead she and Kevin keep it to themselves.

Alex puts a steadying hand on her shoulder.

'Breathe in, hold it as long as you want. Then out.'

Bonnie suppresses a cough, looks up in alarm at Alex.

'You know it's legal in New Mexico, right?' Alex winks at her. 'Wait a few minutes and it'll kick in.'

* * *

Ten minutes later – or is it three minutes later, who knows – they are all lying on the ground, staring up at the sky.

'So your bro was telling us all about the stars,' Travis is saying. 'He knows like every single one of them.'

Kevin hears this and floats on a cloud of hazy satisfaction, dreaming away.

'Really?' This is from Bonnie.

'Yeah, it's like he's memorized the whole universe. I been

living here my whole life and don't know shit about the stars. I can tell you the Big Dipper and Orion and that's about it.'

'You grow up here?' Alex asks.

'Yeah, born in Tucumcari. Lived here my whole life. It's boring as fuck. Nothing to do.'

'Is it weird growing up with all this neon and old-time music being played around town?'

'I mean, I dunno. It's just stuff for the tourists, but it's normal for us. It's only a certain part of town, anyway.'

It's been decades since Kevin's smoked pot. It was mainly a thing he did with his college buddies. But here with the crackling campfire and the impossible, wondrous display of stars above him, it feels like he was always meant to lie here on this particular spot in the desert and look up. The surrounding conversation slides past Kevin with an easy serenity.

'Yeah, my dad runs one of the hotels.'

'My mom manages one of the big diners and my dad works at the museum, and is a part-time electrician and does a bunch of other things.'

'And what do *you* guys want to do?' Alex is asking this. She's always been good at talking to random people. Way more casual than him or Bonnie.

'I dunno ... get out of here as soon as I can?'

The others laugh in agreement.

'Where would you go?'

'Albuquerque maybe, or Denver. Some place with some kind of action. Or more to do than just smoke up and stare at the stars.'

'I dunno, I'm okay with it,' one of the other guys says, almost sheepishly. 'I can just hang out here and play video games and ... y'know, that's cool with me.'

'Where you guys from?' Chase asks. 'Kevin said Chicago or something.'

'No, no, we're all from California.' Bonnie seems to be saying this. 'But we all live in different places now. I live near Boston, and Alex is in London.'

'Shit. London, like England?!' There are some gasps from the kids and yeah that makes sense, because Alex is getting the attention she always wants, and heck, maybe she deserves it, too . . . Kevin doesn't mind. The resentment is leached from him right now, replaced with a gentle fondness for everyone, including his sisters, because all he cares about now is staring up at the stars.

'Man, London is far . . .'

'. . . farthest I've gone in my life is Tulsa . . .'

And Kevin thinks how weird, because they've just driven from Tulsa today. That kid could just get in a car and drive for a few hours and – poof! like that – exceed the entire radius of his existence so far.

'Hey Kevin. Kevin.' Chase or is it Travis is asking him about the sky. 'Where's that thing called a nebula again?'

'It's up there, near Orion's Belt. Do you see those three stars in a row? And there's that kind of shimmery cloud just below it – that's the Orion Nebula.'

'What's a nebula?' Alex asks.

'Well, *that* nebula is a star-making nursery . . . That's where stars are born.' The others murmur with a hushed awe. As a kid, Kevin always liked the idea of a star nursery, a place where the early, pulsing origins of stars were nurtured and grown until they could develop and emit a light visible all the way across the universe.

'But other nebulae are the remnants of stars that have died,' Kevin continues. 'Like after a supernova has exploded.'

'Woah,' Vanessa breathes. 'But you said something about the light is really old . . .'

'Yeah, if a star explodes, it still takes time for the light to travel all this distance through the dark to reach us. So a supernova is something that really happened hundreds, maybe thousands of years ago. We're just seeing it now here on Earth.'

'*That* is a trip,' Travis murmurs.

'But they look the same from here?' Bonnie asks. 'The star-making nursery and the supernova?'

'Yeah, still that same kind of shimmery patch in the sky. Like stardust.'

Before life or after life, they all look like stardust.

There is something comforting in the thought, the uniform beauty of it all, filtering across the light-years toward us . . . It's the last thing Kevin thinks before he drifts off to a satisfied sleep.

* * *

In the brightening predawn, the sky streaked with gold and the promise of sun, Alex drives north. Back toward Tucumcari, to their vintage motel beds, which they've hardly slept in.

Kevin and Bonnie sit in the back seat, bleary-eyed. Each staring out at the reddening desert, the land slowly revealing itself, as the shadows lessen with the approaching sunrise.

'How'd you guys find me?' Kevin asks, breaking the silence.

'We just drove and drove,' Alex says. 'There wasn't any strategy, really.'

'We thought you were lying dead by the roadside some-where,' Bonnie says to Kevin. A reprimand, but also a joke.

'We had to wake up the motel owner to get into your room for the car keys,' Alex adds.

'Aw shit. Sorry, guys. Yeah, I don't know what came over me . . .'

Kevin trails off, but Alex can imagine. Being that deep in debt, keeping that kind of secret for so long. Then being outed in front of Dad. It would be enough to drive her into the desert by foot.

'Anyway, thanks,' Kevin says. 'For finding me. You didn't have to.'

'Well . . .' Bonnie starts. And Alex can tell she's trying, in her half-awake state, to parse the right words, ones that aren't condescending or bossy. 'You're our brother, after all. We've only got one of you.'

No one speaks after that, and no one needs to. They keep driving, the horizon glowing to the east, while all around them the land waits, still and hopeful for the coming daylight.

1991

Bonnie remembers being surprised by the sudden change in direction.

After the gas station, her mom and dad sat in the front seat, looking forward intently into the sun.

She didn't think it was any different from the previous eight hours of driving, but then Kevin had said: 'Wait a second, didn't we just pass this place?'

Her parents didn't say anything, just kept driving. But Kevin got louder and louder, convinced they were wrong.

'Dad! You're going the wrong way! The Grand Canyon is that way!'

Dad did have a tendency to get lost sometimes, but usually he admitted it early on. Yet this time, neither he nor Mom said anything.

'We're gonna end up back where we came from,' Kevin complained. And then, after no reaction from the front seat, he shut up and slumped into an adolescent mope.

Did she remember her parents acting differently, as if tiptoeing around a thing not to be discussed? Bonnie is ashamed to admit she didn't notice anything. She was just relieved she hadn't bled through her shorts.

They sat in silence as the flat, dry landscape rolled past. Even if they *had* come this way before, she wouldn't have known the difference.

Finally, Dad cleared his throat and spoke up.

'We're not going to the Grand Canyon anymore.'

What?

Bonnie sat up in shock. They must be kidding.

'What do you mean we're not going to the Grand Canyon?' The outrage in Kevin's voice was shrill. 'We drove all this way!'

'Mom? Dad? Are you serious?' Bonnie was majorly annoyed. She had missed Karen Choi's party for *this*, and now they weren't even going to see the Grand Canyon? 'We've been driving forever!'

'Why aren't we going?' Alex had been uncharacteristically quiet next to her, given her tantrum at the gas station, but now she spoke up. 'Is something wrong?'

'I told you, nothing's wrong!' Mom suddenly snapped from the front seat. 'But we're not going.' Her voice was firm, a concrete wall she knew not to challenge.

'That's so unfair!' Kevin howled.

'Yeah, really?' Bonnie said. 'You dragged us all the way out to the desert, just to turn around when we're almost there?'

'But why?' Alex asked again, her eyes wide, like some catastrophe had happened. And maybe one had. Because Mom and Dad were so careful about spending gas money, surely they wouldn't have wasted that on nothing.

'Your mommy doesn't want to go,' Dad announced. Just then, she caught the briefest of glances between her mom and dad but didn't know what to make of it. 'She doesn't think it's safe.'

That didn't make any sense.

'Oh, but it was safe yesterday and this morning, when we were driving all the way here?' Bonnie was furious. What a waste of a weekend. *Everyone* was going to be at Karen Choi's sleepover. There might be boys, too; maybe even Jason Feeney. She'd missed out on a chance to kiss Jason Feeney for this joke of a family vacation?

'Your mommy just wants to go home,' Dad said. 'We're all going home.'

So they were being serious. There was no way to convince them otherwise. Bonnie was aware of how hot the sun was now, blazing through the car window, onto her shoulders.

A sudden anger rose up in her, but she tried to bat it away. She couldn't wait to get away from her family, away from all these ridiculous rules. Her parents made no sense at all sometimes. At college, she'd be free of all this.

Alex spoke up. 'Mommy, do you need to go to the . . .'

But then her question trailed away, as her big eyes studied the back of Mom's head.

'What, the bathroom?' Kevin snorted, mocking. 'We all just went, dummy.'

'No, I meant . . .' Again, Alex's question withered.

'Mommy just needs to go home,' Dad said, after another moment of silence.

Bonnie thought it odd that Mom herself didn't speak up. But then again, her family was always weird like that.

They sleep late. Bonnie left a note on the motel owner's door-step – scrawled on the motel stationery, weighted down with a rock – asking if they could please have a late checkout at 1 p.m.? They could pay extra, and they would be very grateful.

It must have been okay with Dan, because she wakes up at twelve thirty to her phone alarm, the noontime sun slicing through the chenille curtains onto her face. Seven hours of sleep.

Certainly more than she gets at home with the three boys.

Still, she feels like she's been flattened by a truck after yesterday, and her siblings must feel the same.

'Sure you don't need me to drive?' she asks Kevin and Alex over a late breakfast of huevos rancheros and coffee.

'No.' Alex waves a hand to bat away her suggestion. 'You don't have a license on you. We'll be fine.'

Bonnie wishes she could. She misses driving, the wheel under her fingertips, the fine-tuned control. But she concedes to her siblings.

Kevin's looking at his map, the dark circles evident under his eyes. Yet he somehow seems at peace, more placid than before.

'What's the plan, captain?' Bonnie asks with a smile.

'So I figure since we're getting a late start today . . . and yesterday was a long day . . . maybe just four and a half hours of driving today. To Gallup, New Mexico. Should be plenty of hotels there. We can stop in Albuquerque for lunch or dinner, or whatever you want to call it.'

Gallup, New Mexico. Albuquerque. She's heard these names before, in a song or on television. But they were always abstract, mere ciphers. Now with each mile driven, each footstep outside the car, these places are made real to her. She is starting to understand the excitement Alex feels about travel, the unknown rendered knowable.

Bonnie stands up, energized. 'Let's hit the road, then.'

* * *

Nearing Albuquerque, Kevin drives. Enjoying the great, wide expanse of the land around him, the alien rock formations and escarpments that swell from the ground, accompanying them for several miles along the interstate, only to fade into the distance. The sky, which offered such a miraculous display of stars last night, is now a bright, cloudless blue.

'Hey Bonnie,' Alex says, teasing. 'Was that your first joint last night?'

Kevin laughs. He remembers the shared look of glee when they watched their sister attempting to smoke up.

'Uh, probably,' Bonnie confesses, but a wry smile plays across her lips.

'You enjoy it?'' Alex jokes.

'It was . . . different from what I expected. I just felt really chilled out. At peace.'

'That's the point,' Kevin says. And he thinks about those days in college, when he and his buddies spent entire lazy weekends stoned in front of their Sony PlayStation, eating pizza in their pajamas. God, if only he had that kind of freedom now.

'I can see the appeal. Did you guys do a lot of pot when you were younger?' Bonnie asks. More out of curiosity than as a policing older sister.

'Mmm,' Alex mumbles, noncommittal. 'From time to time. It was impossible to avoid in the theater scene.'

'How old were you guys when you first smoked pot?'

245

'I was in college,' Kevin says.

'I was in high school,' Alex answers.

'Wow,' Bonnie muses. 'I really *am* way behind you guys, aren't I?'

'I mean, it's not a competition about who's cool or not,' Alex says. 'I'm just glad you got to experience it.'

And Kevin thinks about his youth, the illicit thrill of who was smoking pot, who was drinking alcohol, what you were able to get away with. How much of that parental discipline was invented just to keep you in line. Because what do parents really know anyway? He's a parent now, and he's a complete fuckup.

His own parents are old now and they know so little about his actual life. Only what he's curated for them, selecting the best, most presentable bits of his existence, like one of those glossy Instagram grids that Jess was always obsessing over—

'So, Kevin,' Alex asks. Her persistent questioning reminds him of Arabella. 'How long have you had a gun for?'

'You know about that now?'

Bonnie leans in. 'I had to tell her. Last night. I mean, we wanted to make sure—'

'That I hadn't blown my head off?' Kevin says with a dry sarcasm. But he contemplates the idea impassively, like a spectator standing at a distance from a museum exhibit. What would it take to hold that definitive weight in his hand, hold it up to his temple and – He shudders. Last night he was willing to lose himself in the desert, but that other kind of choice, the decisiveness of it . . . He knows he's not capable of it.

'I've got three kids,' Bonnie continues. 'I just get worried sick about the thought of them out there . . . in a world with so many guns.'

Kevin has no answer to this. There's a reason why he keeps

his gun locked up in the glove compartment, a secret from his family. But also a reason why he has one in the first place.

'Yeah, why *do* you have a gun, anyway?' Alex asks, her tone verging on accusative.

Kevin thinks for a moment, as the desert around them stretches in the golden afternoon light. It's a question he's never had to answer before, because no one, not even Jessica, knew until now.

He thinks of another desert afternoon, decades ago, and the gun he saw strapped to a man's belt. The helplessness he felt in that moment.

'I guess . . . I dunno. I just felt safer owning one.'

'*Safer?*' Alex scoffs. 'Knowing you could blow someone's head off?'

Yesterday, Kevin might feel defensive. Today he's calmer, more contemplative.

'Safer knowing someone wouldn't be able to threaten me in the same way.'

And there is an undeniable sense of power, a hidden strength in knowing his gun is there, waiting to be taken up and wielded. Sensing the automatic authority that comes with it.

'This country,' Alex mumbles, looking out the window.

'Easy for you to say,' Kevin says. 'No one owns guns in England, so you don't feel you need to defend yourself in the same way.'

'You're right about that,' Alex admits.

'Do you even know how to shoot it?' Bonnie asks.

'Yeah,' Kevin answers, annoyed. 'I took gun-handling classes; I go to a shooting range from time to time. I'm not a complete idiot.'

'Could you teach us how to shoot it sometime?' There's a

sudden note of enthusiasm in Alex's voice, and Kevin can't help but smirk.

'What, one minute you're lecturing me about owning a gun, and the next minute you want to shoot it?'

Alex shrugs. 'I mean, since we have one, we might as well learn how to use it.'

Bonnie is silent, a disapproving look on her face.

'Sure,' Kevin says, relishing Alex's turnaround. 'I'll teach you sometime.'

He glances at Bonnie. 'How 'bout it, Bon? You wanna learn to shoot a gun, too?'

Their older sister fixes them with a look of death. 'Okay, Mom and Dad? They're definitely *never* hearing about this.'

* * *

At the Laguna 66 Pit Stop, Alex is finishing another grilled cheese sandwich (her third in as many days), while Kevin and Bonnie polish off their burgers with hatch green chili (a New Mexico specialty, apparently). They sit at a polished chrome counter and watch the traffic blaze by on the I-40 West.

'This is a frickin' good burger,' Kevin says, wiping up a drop of chili with a spare fry. 'You're really missing out.'

'Shut up.' Alex glares at him. She recalls, for a brief moment, the hedonistic delight of a good burger – the greasy patty, the melted cheese – and pushes it out of her mind. 'What I would do for a salad around here.'

'Don't worry, we'll get to California soon enough,' Bonnie jokes. 'I think my cholesterol level's quadrupled since we started this trip.'

'Whatever.' Kevin balls up the waxed-paper wrapper of his burger. 'I walked like ten miles last night. I deserve it.'

They all laugh.

'So how long till Gallup now?'

'Well, actually,' Alex says. 'Route 66 does a little diversion from the interstate here, so I just wanted to check something out.'

Bonnie and Kevin look at each other and shrug. 'Sounds good. What is it?'

'We're right on Laguna Pueblo land, and there's an old mission church around here.'

'Like how old?' Kevin asks, as the bill arrives. He looks at it askance, and Alex glances for a moment at him, then takes it. She guesses by now that she's the default purchaser. Ironic, for the sibling with the lowest earning power.

'I think late seventeenth century?'

'Jesus, that's old,' Bonnie exclaims. 'But I guess the Spanish were out here colonizing that long ago.'

'Well, there were people here before them, too,' Alex reminds her, as they walk back out into the bright sun. 'Still are.'

* * *

The Native American tribe out here is called the Pueblo, Alex explains, and they are divided into nineteen communities. Driving into the Laguna community, Bonnie can't help but feel like she's trespassing. That maybe this community is tired of having foreigners coming onto their land, first with guns and Bibles, then with cameras and tour guidebooks.

She also notices the road surface here is considerably more broken up, the sidewalks nonexistent, the signs and storefronts in need of fresh paint. The houses are low adobe buildings, virtually indistinguishable from the land. Behind them stretches a ridge of mountains, while children play on scrubby patches of grass. Three toddlers cluster around an older child on a rickety tricycle.

Bonnie thinks of the lush green lawns of the Boston suburbs, each family with a leafy backyard, hers with a trampoline, a tennis court, a private lake. Are they even in the same country?

'Technically, each Pueblo community is its own nation, distinct from the United States,' Alex says, as if reading her mind.

'It's like we're in a Third World country. Do they have enough money to repave their roads?' Kevin asks. It's a rhetorical question, which no one bothers to answer. And it strikes Bonnie as odd, how just a few miles away, the great modern interstate is repaved year after year with federal funding, but here on Pueblo territory, the one road in town is riddled with potholes.

'Actually, I read somewhere that the Laguna are one of the wealthier Pueblo communities around. There's a uranium mine near here.' Alex says this as she wheels the SUV along the one paved road in town, climbing the hill toward a rectangular white church at the top. She stops and backs up a few times, confused by what is a road and what is not, before finding the right place to park.

'Are we supposed to be here?' Bonnie asks.

'I think they offer tours of the church, so I guess tourists are okay,' Alex says, lowering herself from the Mazda. There's no one else around.

They approach Mission San José de Laguna through a doorway in a white adobe wall. It has a plain white front, topped only by a white cross against the bright blue sky.

The church is not particularly large, certainly not compared to cathedrals she's seen in Europe or the modern mega-churches of the American suburbs. But it is simple and self-contained, its own kind of fortress against the sun and prying outsiders.

Bonnie finds herself transported to a more elementary time, when a building was really just a place to shelter you from the sun and wind and rain, not equipped with elaborate security systems, high-speed broadband, home entertainment with a thousand TV channels to get lost in. All that seems so distant, standing here on this sunbaked church doorstep.

Alex knocks on the weathered wooden door. No answer. She tries the rusted metal door pull, but it's locked shut.

'Huh,' she says. The three of them stand there, unsure of what to do. There's no sign about tours or visiting hours anywhere.

'You know, maybe we should go,' Bonnie says. She feels that anxiety about being in the wrong place, unwanted.

'I wonder if there's someone around,' Alex mutters, and ventures along the building, looking for another door. Bonnie watches her younger sister, recognizing the same adventurous spirit that drove her to explore so many countries over the years, the massive backpack on her slender frame. She's always been secretly envious of the places Alex got to see.

Suddenly a group of men round the corner, in conversation with each other. Three Pueblo men, in white shirt and jeans, and an older white man in priestly garb. Bonnie feels distinctly self-conscious and wonders if they should leave now. Or if that would be even ruder.

But the men glance and nod, undisturbed, at Bonnie and her siblings, before continuing their conversation. One of the men carries something in his arms, flat packages wrapped in clear plastic. And before two of the men head off, he hands a package to each of them. They nod, then make their way down to their respective trucks and drive off.

Bonnie watches them go in the afternoon light, her eye tracing the road they follow out of the town, toward the mesas and open land.

'Hello,' the priest says to them. Bonnie is shaken out of her reverie.

'Hi,' Alex smiles back.

'If you're looking for a tour of the mission, I'm afraid we've already had our last tour for the day.' Bonnie feels a slight disappointment, now that her own curiosity has been piqued.

'Oh, okay, that's fine,' Alex answers. 'We were just driving by.'

As if anyone just casually makes a detour to a Native American community.

'We don't want to intrude or anything,' Bonnie adds.

He introduces himself as Father McAllister, the resident Catholic priest. He's been stationed out here for eleven years, but there's been a Catholic presence at this church since it was built in 1699. Bonnie calculates that's roughly as old as the churches in Boston, founded by English settlers in a very different landscape. Not that either of those traditions have any specific relevance for the children of Taiwanese immigrants who only came to the US a few decades ago.

But just being on this landscape affects the soul. You can look out for miles and feel like you're the only person from here to the horizon. She can see how a church might serve a rarefied purpose in this place.

'This is Joe,' Father McAllister gestures to the Pueblo man holding the plastic-wrapped packages.

'Hi, hi.' They wave and introduce themselves. Bonnie considers how weird it is that as an American, she's grown up knowing about an entire race of people who are seen as ancient and inseparable from the land, the original inhabitants of this country – yet she has never actually met one until now.

She smiles, trying not to stare. He just looks like any other dark-haired middle-aged guy.

'We've just had a council meeting,' Father McAllister explains.

'Actually, we have some extra bread here, if you want some.' Joe offers them a package: it's round flat bread wrapped up in paper, inside a plastic bag. 'It's still warm.'

'Oh wow, that's very kind,' Alex says. 'Are you sure?'

Surely these people can use the bread more than they can. Then Bonnie chastises herself for automatically assuming they're poor.

'Yeah, yeah, we have plenty,' Joe insists. She takes the package, a warm bundle that she holds close to her body. Her mouth starts to water at the thought of fresh-baked bread.

Father McAllister explains the bread has been baked in traditional clay ovens, which are used communally. They can even see the oven, right around the corner. The same oven that's been used for centuries by this community.

Joe leaves them and they watch as he walks down the hill, dust puffing up behind his footsteps. Father McAllister glances back up to the church. 'You know what? I can give you a quick peek inside the mission,' he says. 'No photos, though.'

'Really?' Bonnie asks, her eyes alight like a child's.

He shrugs. 'You seem like nice enough folks.'

They look at each other, elated.

* * *

They step inside the darkened interior of the mission with a certain reverence, as the priest flicks on the light switch. Alex holds in her breath, then gasps. 'Oh wow.'

The mission holds the same quiet peace she has witnessed in old churches elsewhere, a refuge from the outside world. But she's never stood in a church like this before. The smooth adobe walls are painted white, with red and brown indigenous designs – waves and crests and zigzags – marching down the wall, above the wooden pews to a busy altar. Yet it's the ceiling that's most striking: laid across with simple plain timbers, left to right, enclosing this sacred space.

Alex thinks of all the services, masses and baptisms, weddings

253

and funerals, that have transpired here over the centuries, on this weathered rock under the vast desert sky. Through the American Revolution, the Civil War, two World Wars, and now in the age of Wi-Fi and Netflix and Instagram, everyone mesmerized by insubstantial images flicked away on a screen, while here sits this solid adobe church, under sun and star-dusted night sky, still drawing parishioners to its secluded interior.

The three of them nod, taking a step or two down the aisle, staring up at the timbered ceiling.

'That is something,' Kevin says. And he sounds genuine. None of his usual snark.

'It is, isn't it?' Father McAllister says. 'The community are very proud of it.'

Even though it's their own colonization, a foreign religion brought down upon them. But then Alex thinks, *So what?* She knows plenty of Koreans and Chinese and Blacks for whom the church is a vital part of their everyday lives. Is it still colonization, if it gives them something they can believe in?

Back out under the desert sky, they stand in the shade of the mission and look out through another doorway in the wall, at the shadows lengthening across the rocky landscape.

Alex has a lot of questions for the priest. About the community, how many people live here, what their main source of income is. She doesn't want to appear too nosy, but she can't help it. What would it be like to live out here, fully aware of the legacy of the past? The land that was taken from you, the religion that was forced upon you, but then became part of your culture, like a tree grafted onto another.

Father McAllister explains Pueblo isn't actually the tribe's name for themselves. 'Keresan' is their word for their language. Pueblo is Spanish for simply 'town' or 'people.' A completely generic word.

'But they don't mind being called Pueblo?' Alex asks. She is slightly enraged that for centuries these people have been going by the name given to them by their colonizers.

Father McAllister replies. 'They've got their own language and their own name. They know who they are.'

Alex considers this and looks out at the wide, desert landscape, the red mesa in the distance unchanged for millennia. Maybe that is the wiser approach to take. What do names matter if you know who you are?

She watches the interstate race past, trucks and cars and mobile homes on their way to some other place. You can barely even hear it from here, although it's only a few miles away. It appears as a concrete ribbon in the middle distance, threading its way to the horizon.

She has another thought, weighted with a note of sadness. This is the same interstate that her mom and dad drove in the 1970s on their way to California. She knows for certain they never would have stopped off at this lonely spot on Laguna Pueblo land. Because her parents didn't do that: they didn't venture into the unknown, they didn't take intentional detours. They never stepped off the established path because they didn't feel like they *could*. That it was safe enough for them. So they would have missed witnessing this timeworn mission, the sacred interior, its singular peace. And for that, for all the unseen wonder that her parents never experienced, she mourns.

* * *

Gallup, New Mexico, is one of those towns Kevin knows he's heard in a song somewhere. In reality, it seems to stretch for ages along the I-40 in the western part of the state. Judging by the highway signs that accompany their approach, every single two- to four-star hotel chain has a presence in Gallup.

'I guess we didn't need to worry about finding a place to stay,' Bonnie concedes as they turn off the interstate ramp, onto the sunbaked streets of downtown Gallup.

A mid-century movie theater, liquor stores, hipster coffee shops. Native American community centers jostle up against kitschy Indian 'trading posts.'

Kevin cruises down the grid of downtown streets but keeps going.

'Kev, what are you doing?' Alex asks. 'Our hotel was back that way.'

'Just doing some exploring,' he answers with a mischievous look.

A smile ripples across Alex's face. Her own brother, finally scoring points in her book.

They pass tracts of low clapboard houses, weatherworn cars and pickups parked nearby. Soon the houses peter out to barren scrubland, desert dotted here and there with shacks and unmarked roads. The road climbs higher, passing piles of scree sitting on featureless flatland.

'You taking us somewhere in particular?' Bonnie asks.

'I wanted to show you something,' Kevin says with a mysterious smile. 'Just looking for the right place.'

Behind his back, he's sure his sisters are exchanging wary looks, that same eye roll they've traded around him since childhood. But this just pleases him more. They won't be expecting this.

Finally, he turns the SUV down an unmarked road that looks suitable. The asphalt soon runs out. Kevin edges forward over gravel and dirt toward a cluster of boulders, then stops the car. Right here is perfect.

*

Kevin sets the five Diet Coke cans in a row along the boulder, the evening light glinting off them.

'What is this?' Alex jokes. 'Some kind of shooting practice?'

'Exactly.'

He stands next to his sisters and takes out the gun.

'Oh shit,' Bonnie shrieks. 'Put that back!'

'Well, Alex asked for a crash course in shooting a gun. So here it is.'

'I didn't mean, like, right away!' Alex says.

'You wanna wait till we get back to Orange County?' Kevin asks. 'Sure, Mom and Dad will love that.'

His sisters glare at him for a brief moment in a silent standoff.

'Okay, fine,' Bonnie finally says. 'You dragged us out here, you get fifteen, twenty minutes to show us how to shoot a gun.'

Kevin scoffs. 'This is not something you want to rush. So here it is. Hold it. Don't freak out. It's just an object.'

'An object that can *kill* someone,' Bonnie mutters.

'Bonnie Chu Prescott, if you're gonna have that attitude...' Kevin mimics a schoolteacher, hands on his hips.

Bonnie shakes her head and relents.

'So... Cylinder. Cylinder release. Safety.' Kevin indicates these parts of the gun one by one.

'How 'bout the trigger?' Alex asks.

'I'm getting there! Jesus.' They're worse than his kids.

He walks them through how to line up the sights, how to handle the safety, how to load up the bullets. Alex learns quickly, almost eagerly. And once Bonnie gets over her initial reluctance, she manages the mechanics of it just fine.

'And now, shooting time.' Kevin grins and gestures to the Diet Coke cans with a flourish. 'Sorry, I should have lined up cans of Miller Lite for a more authentic feel.'

'Diet Coke will do,' Alex jokes. 'We're cosmopolitan like that.'

Bonnie murmurs under her breath. 'I cannot *believe* that my own brother is getting me to shoot at a Coke can.'

'Come on, Bon.' Alex laughs. 'You've smoked your first joint. Now you're shooting your first gun. We're gonna make a man out of you before we're done!'

Kevin and Alex snort, while Bonnie glowers.

'Okay, I'll go first,' Alex volunteers. As much as she protests about being a pacifist and a vegetarian, Alex does seem remarkably interested in shooting a gun. Her aim is terrible, but then again, so was his, the first time he tried shooting. She goes through several bullets. None of them manage to hit a Coke can.

'Ever see me bowl?' Alex asks. 'It's kinda like this.'

Somehow, Kevin likes his sisters better when they admit her own incompetence at things. And there is an unusual, gratifying feeling in being the one teaching them, not having to trail in their wake for once.

'You'll get better with practice,' Kevin reassures her. Then he takes the gun and offers it to Bonnie. 'You wanna try?'

Bonnie grimaces. 'If Mom and Dad ever find out...'

Kevin snorts. 'They *won't*. We're in the middle of the New Mexico desert. How are they gonna find out?'

He gestures to the emptiness around them. But something about it – the clarity of light and the dust – somehow spooks him, reminds him of something else.

Still, he walks Bonnie through it. How to position herself firmly on her feet, how to hold the gun steady.

'Think of someone you absolutely hate. Then fire.'

Bonnie thinks for a minute. 'There isn't anyone. I'm not a teenager, Kevin. I'm a balanced adult. There's no one I actively hate.'

Kevin grumbles. He can think of several people he'd gladly

put in his sights, his boss first and foremost. 'Well then, pretend you're a teenager all over again. There must have been some annoying girls you hated back then.'

Bonnie nods. Closes her eyes for a moment, suppresses a smirk, then looks up. 'Okay, let's do it.'

Kevin gestures, the stage is all hers.

And how weird is it to see Bonnie Chu Prescott, his perfect, rule-abiding older sister, standing with her legs in a V, ready to shoot his revolver.

She holds the gun steady in her hands, squints down the sights at one of the Diet Coke cans, and fires.

Photo Message sent, 7:26PM, Mountain Time

I miss you guys so much. We're in Gallup, New Mexico now. The desert is really something. We should come out here sometime. Are you boys all behaving?

Photo Message sent, 7:51PM, Mountain Time

Check out the desert this morning. Saw so many stars last night. Big hug from me, Schnopes. Hope you & Brian & Mom are ok.

* * *

Photo Message sent, 8:23PM, Mountain Time

New Mexico tonight. The desert is gorgeous, primeval. Here's sunrise after a LOOONG night. Long story: Kevin disappeared, we found him. Bonnie smoked pot for the 1st time ever. Kevin has a fucking GUN, and I learned how to shoot it. Yep, crazy times.

* * *

Photo Message sent, 8:40PM, Mountain Time

Hi Mom & Dad. This is us in Tucumcari yesterday. Beautiful desert out here. We'll cross over into Arizona tomorrow – and then the Grand Canyon! See you soon. Much love from all of us.

Arizona

The next morning, the sign at the state line shouts out at them in primary colors: a bright blue rectangle, a gold star trailed by red and yellow streamers. *The Grand Canyon State welcomes you.*

'Woo-hoo! We're almost there!' Bonnie cheers.

Alex knows she should feel a sense of accomplishment – and perhaps relief – that they are so close to their destination.

But there is also a shadow of dread. A reminder of that afternoon, long ago, when she sat in the back seat of another car and looked out at a different tract of desert.

She wonders if the others have any memory of it, too.

1991

Everyone seemed to blame it on Alex. Why they had to turn around at the last minute, why they never got to see the Grand Canyon. The blame sat heavy like the heat inside the car, the entire journey home.

Kevin certainly blamed it all on her, and that was so unfair. Why didn't anyone consider what had happened to Mommy? But no one else had seen. And maybe even she had imagined it.

Early on, Alex realized — or maybe sensed — that she shouldn't talk about it. Because Mommy never talked about it.

In fact, Mommy became very quiet after that trip. She didn't laugh as much or take them out of the house as much. She stayed in her pajamas all day, and sometimes Alex would find her sitting in front of the TV, not really watching what was on the screen. Just staring at it.

But she kept cooking their meals, telling them to do their homework, driving them to piano and soccer lessons. So maybe everything was still all right.

In time, Alex forgot about most of it. Yet something about that gas station, the long episode of waiting inside the car, the creepy feeling she had about the men — those all lodged in her memory, like sharp, painful details, nailed hard to the wall but concealed behind layers of cobwebs and clutter.

She sometimes thought about one of her favorite books, where the little girl walked into a wardrobe, burrowing her way past all the long-stored winter coats and found a passage to another world. In that story, it had been a wonderful world, a magical one. But maybe in this story, the hidden passageway took you to a place you didn't want to enter. A dark and dangerous one. So Alex kept the door firmly closed.

Mommy clearly didn't want to open it – and perhaps, then, neither should she.

They are at an overlook point in the Painted Desert when it strikes Alex. She has seen this somewhere before, in a faded 1970s photo. The colors in that picture are muted and slightly overexposed, in the same way that everything from that decade appears. But the landscape seems familiar: this particular bluff of red rock, the dry valley with striated colors.

'Do you guys remember that photo of Mom and Dad from one of their old albums?'

Bonnie and Kevin both turn to her, curious.

'What photo?' Kevin asks.

But Bonnie perks up. 'Oh yeah, that one! The one where Dad's hair is shaggy, and he's got those seventies glasses.'

'Yeah, and Mom's hair is practically down to her waist! I think that photo was taken right here.'

Kevin shakes his head. 'I guess I looked at that photo album a lot less than you guys.'

And something – some sense of loss – twists inside Alex, recalling those pictures of her parents that she only glanced at from time to time in her childhood. There were two or three albums, stored on the lower shelf of the bookcase in the living room. Photos – many of them blurry or overexposed – lovingly pressed onto the self-adhesive pages that creaked as you turned them. Photos of Mom and Dad before they had kids, when they were young and carefree – a thought that is somehow jarring. They must have stopped at the Painted Desert on their drive out to California and stood at this very spot for a picture. Maybe a stranger offered to take a photo for them, this young Chinese couple who kept to themselves – or maybe they were bold enough to ask a fellow tourist.

At least then, they had seen the Painted Desert. And maybe they had wanted to show this same kind of red rock landscape to their own kids, when they'd decided to go on vacation to the Grand Canyon. Only they never had a chance.

'We'll check out the photo when we get to their house,' Bonnie is saying to Kevin. 'C'mon, let's take a photo here.'

They gather together, faces against the wind. But there's no one else around, so it's another selfie, their faces preternaturally wide, staring up at the lens while the rose-colored bluffs and canyons unfold behind them in the morning light.

Bonnie taps at her phone. 'There, I've just sent it to Mom and Dad.'

'They'll love it,' Kevin says.

They stand a minute longer, admiring the landscape in silence. The wind whistles.

'Well,' Kevin says. 'About four more hours of driving today. We should reach the Grand Canyon this evening.'

Alex thinks, then finally speaks. 'Do you guys ever think about that trip, when we didn't get to the Grand Canyon?'

Bonnie and Kevin pause. 'Yeah, what about it?' Kevin asks.

Alex can detect a faint note of reticence in his voice. But she presses on.

'What do you guys remember about it?'

1991

Kevin remembers the silence in the car, after the gas station. If the car ride there had seemed forever, the one back was even longer. They were supposed to have lunch at the Grand Canyon, and instead they ate at some stupid diner in the middle of nowhere, Alex poking at her uneaten grilled cheese sandwich, while everyone else in the diner – all the white people there – kept staring at them.

The entire way back to California, hardly anyone spoke.

By then, Kevin's fury at the situation had turned to hatred toward his little sister. If she hadn't kicked up such a fuss at the gas station, they'd be at the Grand Canyon by now. Mom always babied Alex so much, catering to her moods and tantrums, but this? This was just plain unfair.

'Hope you're happy,' Kevin seethed to Alex as they left the diner and walked out to the car. The parking lot was searing hot, and inside the car would be even hotter.

'What do you mean?' Alex looked at him, and he wanted to slap that innocent look off her face.

'You ruined the whole vacation.'

'No I didn't. I wanted to see the Grand Canyon, too.'

'Oh, shut up.' She always had some excuse. He was sick of her whining and attention-seeking.

Back in the car (which was boiling, but at least Dad turned on the air conditioning), Kevin decided to pinch and twist Alex's skin the way he used to when they were a lot younger. It had been gratifying then to get some kind of reaction out of this little, more vulnerable toddler, and it was still gratifying now. Wait until she wasn't looking, then pinch a spot on her arm and twist. Pinch and twist. Pinch and twist.

Alex whimpered, and that pleased him.

'Ow, what are you doing?' Alex asked.

But he didn't say anything. Pinch and twist. Let her learn her lesson that way.

'That hurts,' Alex cried. And then of course: 'Mom!'

For once, Mom didn't react. She'd been very quiet the entire journey back.

'Kevin, stop it!' Bonnie finally shouted, as if she were Mom.

No matter what, someone was always going to defend Alex.

Kevin stopped pinching. But his resentment only continued to grow.

Even as they drove west into the reddening sun. Even as the night descended and they journeyed on through the desert, the highway widening into four lanes, then six. The white lines on the road slipped past, unceasing in the dark, and Kevin's resentment grew.

Bonnie watches that afternoon as the vast red emptiness of the Navajo Nation stretches all around them. Alex had explained that there were two ways to reach the Grand Canyon from Flagstaff. The more touristed route was the 64, shooting straight north to Tusayan, the main tourist hub for the Grand Canyon. This was the route the tour buses followed, the campervans and the old-fashioned steam railroad for tourists. It was also the route they had driven on their road trip with Mom and Dad thirty years ago.

The less popular route was the 89, which cut through the Navajo Nation, approaching the Grand Canyon from the sparser east end of the national park, and running alongside the South Rim of the Canyon for several miles.

'That's the one we should take,' Alex said. No one objected.

And so now Bonnie finds them heading north through a landscape that is more barren than anything she has seen before. If the past few days have taken her through unending tracts of desert, this land – the land of the Navajo Nation – is another planet of desolation. An immense flat plain of red rock stretching all the way to the horizon, with virtually no roads visible. Just the 89 streaking north, and a cluster of buildings alongside it from time to time.

'Alex, didn't you say the Navajo ended up better off than the other tribes? They got more land or something?'

'That's what I read somewhere.' Alex turns to look out the window. 'The US government was more generous to them.'

'Yeah, but *this* is the land they got?' Kevin's sarcasm is thick.

'I don't even know how anyone could make a living off this land.' Bonnie shakes her head.

'Let alone maintain a community,' Alex adds. 'But somehow, they do it.'

'No wonder there's so many Native American casinos,' Bonnie says. 'May as well earn a profit from American greed.'

Alex barks out a laugh, but Kevin is silent.

Bonnie studies the back of his head. It is, after all, his own greed that drove Kevin to make those moronic investments – or maybe it was just a desire to have what everyone else seemed to have. The good life you saw on TV commercials: the five-star luxury vacations and immersive home entertainment systems, families piling into shiny SUVs and laughing on their road trips out to the desert. The life she has, Bonnie realizes with a deepening guilt. And the kind of life that no one could even imagine, here on the blasted terrain of the Navajo Nation.

* * *

Kevin is on his phone, flicking through Google Maps to find the next gas station on their way to the Grand Canyon. There's a no-brand one coming up in ten miles.

'Oh, I bet the gas is cheaper there,' Alex chirps from behind the wheel.

But something in her comment fills Kevin with a familiar dread. An unwanted echo.

'We're not going to that,' he says with a certain finality.

Alex smirks. 'Why not?'

Kevin has no time for her teasing. 'Just . . . there's a Chevron a few miles on.'

'What's the big deal—' Alex starts to ask. But she stops when she sees the look on Kevin's face. And perhaps an unspoken understanding passes between them. A light registers in his sister's eyes.

'Just go to the Chevron, okay?' Kevin says, his voice severe.

Alex nods. Message understood.

But even at the Chevron, when Kevin steps into the clean, well-lit store, with its reassuring white walls and panel lighting, he is confronted with a glistening rack of beef jerky packets – and a sudden surge of vomit rises in his gut.

Don't think of that, he reminds himself.

Yet the nausea remains, threatening to engulf him, even as he retreats back to the car, eyes squinted against the desert sky.

* * *

Alex doesn't notice it at first. She had turned left when she reached the junction of the 64 and the 89, after leaving the gas station. She's been driving for nearly an hour now through the Navajo Nation, this dry red desert, almost hypnotic in its monotony. So even the shadow that appears in the distance is just that at first – a streak of dark snaking across the terrain to her right, a ragged seam in the land.

But the seam draws closer as the road winds higher. It seems to grow wider, too, offering more than just a glimpse of shadow.

'What is that?' Alex asks her siblings.

Kevin is oblivious. 'What is what?'

'That . . .' Alex squints out the window, trying to catch a glimpse while keeping her eyes on the road. 'I dunno, it's like a crack . . .'

She trails off as it dawns on her.

A crack in the earth.

'Wait, is that the Grand Canyon?' Bonnie shouts.

'That's it?!' Kevin is disbelieving.

Alex looks ahead for a place to stop, but there's nowhere

convenient. She is jealous as her brother and sister lean over, stare in awe out the window.

'Yeah, I think that's it!'

'No way!'

She can hear the giddiness in their voices, like they're children all over again on the first morning of a vacation.

'Alex, you gotta see this.'

'I know!' she shouts. 'And I gotta find somewhere safe to stop.'

Finally, up ahead she glimpses a spot where the highway's shoulder widens into an advertised overlook, then a broad parking lot. They park, run down the path to where a blue guardrail fences the ground off from a vast chasm. And there: an opening in the earth, deeper and wider than anything she could have imagined. The ground disappears beneath them into a vertical drop. Clutching the guardrail, Alex stares down and across an impossible, intricate layering of shadow and rock, golden-brown cliff face and hidden nooks, the flat desert on top, air and blue sky above, shadow and river down below, and this is it. This is the Grand Canyon at their feet.

She stares down and down and down, like she is looking into deep time, a vertical corridor to a nameless past, long before the human species arrived.

'Oh my god,' Kevin says, standing next to her.

Bonnie breathes out, her eyes wide. 'I can't believe I haven't seen this until now.'

* * *

Just space and rock and sun and shadow. But the starkness of it all, plunging straight down. The sense that you could just step out into thin air – one, two more steps from where Kevin stands at this guardrail, and you would gift your life to the rock and the air below.

Kevin has no intention of doing that, but he can imagine the allure. To disappear, just like that. He could stand here forever, his eye tracing every nook and cranny, visually losing himself in the infinite stone labyrinth below. He can see why someone might want to plunge all the way in, abandon himself inside this kind of stark beauty.

All the worries of his adulthood: the resentments and frustrations, the expectations and debts. They all melt away; microscopic, petty concerns next to the immensity of the scene before him.

What does a quarter of a million dollars matter? What does foreclosure on a house matter, when he can stand here, on the edge of an impossible chasm, and be completely dwarfed by the land and the still desert air?

What if he were to lie here on this rock, the desert sun slowly leaching the life out of him, the stars shifting above him in their constellations? Even if he died here, he would be completely at peace.

* * *

Bonnie understands now why her parents wanted them to visit the Grand Canyon thirty years ago. She cannot believe she has lived her entire pampered life, nearly half a century of it, completely oblivious to this wondrous crack in the earth.

Today, she is content to stand here on the edge, marveling side by side with her brother and sister. But she wishes that someday she can return here with her three boys and watch

271

their jaws drop. Milo has always loved rocks and geology. He would adore being here. Henry would want to know the history of this place: how people first discovered it, who first explored the river down below. And Max would simply take in the colors, the shadows, the texture of minerals. Her peaceful little artist, content to stare at the beauty of it all.

Perhaps her own parents had similar thoughts about their three children when they planned that trip to the Grand Canyon, knowing it was somehow an intrinsic part of the American experience to witness its singular grandeur. Then, with a twinge of regret, she remembers she was a bratty fourteen-year-old at the time. She didn't want to go. There was some girl's sleepover happening that weekend, and she resented being dragged onto this family road trip when her period was about to start.

Her period.

Bonnie has a flashback to standing in the grungy bathroom of a gas station, squeamish that she couldn't change her pad somewhere cleaner.

A darker wave of discomfort rolls in when she remembers that afternoon.

And she feels the guilt again. That she wasn't a better daughter at the time, more grateful, less selfish. That she couldn't somehow help her own parents continue that trip – whatever had happened – so that they could drive that remaining hour to make it here, to the Grand Canyon. That her parents have never stood here, on this precipice, to witness the Grand Canyon in person. And probably, at their age, they never will.

* * *

Alex stares down into the canyon, and she has never seen anything more lonely or vast or timeless than this storied crack in the earth. She tries to imagine the accumulated millennia that created it: wind, rain, river, earthquake. So much time, layered upon itself, to carve this chasm a mile deep into the rock.

To think it was just here, waiting to be discovered. What did the pioneers think when they first stumbled upon the Grand Canyon? Nothing they had seen before in their lives could have prepared them for it. How far did the Native American folktales travel, in speaking of this impossible rift that split the very bedrock of the earth, somewhere beyond the mountains and the deserts on the far side of the continent?

It had been here and would always be here, for as long as humans could witness it.

Perhaps this is it. The great divide that separates America. Literal here, hewn into the very rock. But elsewhere, a more metaphorical chasm.

Black Lives Mattered or All Lives Mattered, or in fact no lives mattered to this implacable landscape, which operated on a scale so much broader than the measure of a human life.

And Alex realizes the irony. Because this geology doesn't care about people. Not herself or her siblings, or any of the other tourists perched here on the edge like miniscule ants. It didn't care about Manifest Destiny or the Louisiana Purchase or the Indian Removal Act or anything she'd had to memorize in history class: sections of the American continent demarcated in different colors, to indicate when they became part of this nation. Because the land was always here. It never cared about countries or borders.

The land didn't care about territorial wars or culture wars or world wars or police shootings or vaccines or recessions. Americans will weaken and die from lack of affordable healthcare, and this landscape won't care. Americans will exhaust their energy on zero-hour contracts and hashtag campaigns and torturously complicated tax returns, and this land will remain oblivious. They will drive themselves to extinction, shooting each other with assault weapons, or pouring pollutants into the rivers and the air, or eating themselves into a fast-food oblivion, and when the United States of America collapses – somewhere decades or centuries from now – this land will still be here.

There is no particular joy or sadness for Alex when she realizes this. Just an acceptance, an understanding of the colossal scale of difference between the land and the people that visit it.

Our lives are mere specks in the ever-evolving story of this landscape.

And yet that speck is all we have.

We do the most we can with what we are given.

Suddenly she longs for Nya, waiting for her in their London flat as her belly swells. She wants to speak to her, try to film a video here, so Nya can catch at least a faint glimpse of what she is seeing.

But really, truly, some things you can only see for yourself.

She looks to either side of her: to Kevin, leaning over the railing, toward the abyss; and to Bonnie, who stands gazing out with a slight smile on her face. She stands next to her brother and sister, the two people on this planet who have grown up in parallel with her, their lives stretching away in directions she could not have imagined – and she is glad that they are together here, on the edge of the Grand Canyon. A brief shared moment, lives lived together, in the vast chronicle of time.

At a Navajo jewelry stand, positioned conveniently at the Grand Canyon overlook, Bonnie watches Alex studying several turquoise and silver necklaces. Alex has always been a tomboy, never cared much for fashion accessories. And yet, she is examining an elaborate, feminine necklace, silver curlicues intertwined with turquoise and coral pieces.

'Since when are you so into jewelry?' she jokes.

'Oh, I wanted to get something for Nya,' Alex says. 'She'd love this stuff. Native craftspeople, bought at a roadside stand.'

Bonnie smiles. It is the first time she has seen her sister demonstrate this kind of care and love for another human being. She'll be fine as a mother.

A thought occurs to her.

'You know, we should get something for Mom.'

Alex turns. 'You think? She doesn't really wear jewelry. Says it gets in the way of things.'

Bonnie muses. 'Maybe she'll make an exception. A Grand Canyon souvenir from her kids.'

And so they look at the turquoise stones on display. Rock formed through the millennia, mined and shaped and worked by human hands into these necklaces and bracelets and rings. A memento for the ages.

* * *

Later, they are sitting at a more elevated lookout point above the Grand Canyon, inside the national park. Other tourists are scattered along the guardrails, posing for photos, admiring the view. Multigenerational families, couples in love, a fraternity group on a road trip, celebrating their college graduation.

It feels like they have been here for hours. Then again, you lose track of time when you look at the Grand Canyon.

Kevin and his sisters are perched on a plateau a little above and away from the guardrail, watching the human parade of tourists below, and the implacable abyss beyond. The shadows have lengthened, casting the canyon in a tapestry of blues and purples. The colors shift and deepen, as the sun sinks and the day draws to a close.

'It never really made sense to me,' Bonnie says, unprompted.

'What didn't?' Kevin asks.

'Why we turned around after stopping at that gas station. I mean, it was so weird... One minute they were all set on visiting the Grand Canyon. And then suddenly they changed their minds.'

A discomfort tugs at Kevin, one that he has buried in all the years since. His nausea from earlier in the day starts to return.

'I think they got spooked by those men,' he says.

'What men?' Bonnie asks.

Kevin and Alex stare at her.

'You don't remember those men?' Alex prods. 'The ones who were hanging out in front of the gas station?'

Kevin remembers. A bag of beef jerky in his hand, the plastic crinkling.

Bonnie shakes her head. 'No, I just remember using the bathroom. I remember it was really gross in there. And then you were honking on the horn for some reason.'

'Yeah, why *did* you do that?' Kevin turns to Alex, accusatory at first, but fueled by a fierce curiosity. 'Were you just bored or something?'

Alex recoils, silently outraged, and stares at her siblings. 'Do you honestly have no clue what happened?'

Kevin shrugs, unsure. 'Mom said you were upset about something.'

'*I* was upset?' Alex retorts.

Kevin thinks back. Yes, definitely. He can remember her eight-year-old face, screwed up and howling. And yet...

'Everyone asked if I was okay, but no one ever asked Mom,' Alex says.

The men. He forces himself to picture those three individuals, who exist more like ciphers in his mind, human-shaped outlines with cowboy hats – because he has been loath to dwell on them ever again.

He spies the group of frat boys posing for a photo in front of the Grand Canyon. Young men with athletic builds; tanned forearms around shoulders; jokey, masculine banter. A family walks past, their teenage daughter lithe in a strappy tank top and denim cutoffs. Kevin watches as the frat boys ogle her, trading lascivious looks between them. It's a leer he's seen all too often, passed between men when an attractive female is nearby, and yet—

A terrible connection dawns on him. A synapse firing three decades too late. 'Oh my god...'

'What?' His sisters look at him, alarmed.

'I just suddenly remembered. I *did* see something after I came out of the bathroom.'

Kevin shakes his head, disbelieving.

The sun has dropped low now, no longer visible above the rim of the earth. With the last of its light gone, the entire spectacle of geological color retreats into darkness.

'Kevin, what is it?' Alex asks. 'You have to tell us.'

1991

'Stay here,' Dad said, before bolting out the door.

And for a second Kevin did just that, standing like an idiot in that dirty men's room, holding the packet of beef jerky that he already hated.

The car horn kept puncturing the air, and then it stopped. And he was able to hear in that space, a low sort of scuffling, and a thump – was it against the wall? Or body to body, a punch thrown?

And then that wheezing again – and he remembered where he'd heard it before. From Mom, all those times she was upset and would shut herself in her room, but he still could hear her sobbing through the walls. That was what he heard now.

Kevin pushed out the door, panic flooding him. He didn't know what he could do, but he couldn't keep standing there in the bathroom like a baby.

The desert sun struck him full in the eyes, blinding him momentarily. He staggered around the corner of the building, and there, in the shade, he saw them. Alex was nowhere to be seen. Instead, it was four, no five adult figures, arranged along the wall. All dim in the sharp shadow of the building.

Dad was crouched down low. Bent over, like he'd been

punched. One of the men, the one from behind the counter, stood over him.

It took a while for his eyes to distinguish the other figures, but there was someone pressed up against the wall, arms shielding their face. That was Mom, shrinking back and back, even though she had nowhere farther to go. And on either side of her, the same way they had cornered Dad, were the two other men, eyes fixed on her intently.

Mom gasped when she saw Kevin.

One of the men took a step back from Mom – as if, an instant earlier, he had been closer to her.

And Kevin found his voice and croaked, 'Mom? Dad?'

All the grown-ups turned and stared at him.

'Kevin,' Mom said. Her voice at first was small and shrunken. And it was jarring to hear her like that. Normally Mom was so in charge, insisting that he do his homework, take out the trash, look after Alex.

The three men stood up straight, looking at Kevin, then at each other.

Mom straightened her clothes. But why were they rumpled in the first place?

'You here to rescue your Mommy and Daddy?' One of the men next to Mom said this, as a smile cracked across his face. An unpleasant smile. He took a step toward Kevin.

'Hey,' Dad said, but the man next to him laid a meaty arm on his shoulder. And Dad shut up.

Kevin's throat went dry. He was grateful he'd just relieved his bladder. Otherwise, his pants would be wet now. He remembered what the other boys had said about fights: 'Don't take a step back. Makes you look like a coward.' But the man approaching him was a lot taller than the boys at his school. Kevin gripped the packet of beef jerky.

'I was just – I heard something . . .' he started to say. And then he stopped, his eyes staring at the man's waist. Strapped onto that brown leather belt was a holster, and inside it, a gun.

The words died inside Kevin, and his stomach went numb.

'Don't touch him!' Mom shouted. Her voice was shrill and desperate, and he didn't know what he hated more: the man approaching him with the cold smile, or the way his own mom sounded so pleading, so pathetic.

'Oh, I won't hurt him,' the man said in a singsong voice that seemed to say otherwise.

Mom muttered to Dad in Taiwanese, a harsh, urgent tone that Kevin recognized, without understanding the words. Dad mumbled something back. And the man next to Dad, the one from behind the cash register, rounded on him: 'You two just *quit* jabbering.'

By now, the first man was in front of him, grinning, and he reached out a hand, patting Kevin on the top of his head awkwardly.

'Well aren't you cute. Little Chinese kid on his first trip into the desert.'

Kevin tried not to cower as the man's hand slid down, to rest on his shoulder. The man was so close he could smell the sour stench of beer, which he recognized from Dad. Kevin wished he could do something more, escape the man's grasp or even punch him – but he could only stand there, utterly useless. Waiting for the man to do whatever he was planning. He hated himself in that moment, and he hated Mom and Dad for standing and watching like dummies.

Then, the sound of feet pounding the ground. Light feet, small feet. And a voice, high-pitched, that screeched: 'Kevin???!'

Something barreled into him, pushing him and the man

apart. Kevin was knocked to the ground, momentarily dazed, while the screaming continued.

'You keep away from him! You keep away from all of them!'

Kevin looked up, squinting from the sun, and he saw Alex, tiny and furious, shouting at the men, circling back and forth. 'What are you doing? What are you doing?!'

Was she crying? Almost crying? He couldn't quite tell, nor had he ever heard her voice this loud and frenzied. There was a desperation in it, just like Mom's, but also a strange sort of power.

The men were in shock as they watched Alex bawl at them.

'Leave them alone! We're going to the Grand Canyon!'

Alex ran up to the man in front of him, and screamed at him, her fists balled by her side, her eyes clenched tight in her face.

What was she doing? This was even more embarrassing than Mom and Dad. She was way too old to be throwing fits like this.

But something in the air of the situation had changed. The danger that had shone, sharp like a needle in the moments before, had vanished.

'What the fuck...' one of the men muttered.

'Alex!' Mom shouted.

And Alex ran in a crazed circle, like a tiny rabid dog loosed upon the world, howling to the bright blue desert sky, before running to Mom.

* * *

'So you *had* seen something?' Alex says to him. Her eyes trained on him, intense.

Kevin seems to squirm. 'I was too young to really get it... And too scared.'

Alex stares at the far edge of the Grand Canyon, where a spur of rock has caught the last ray of dying light, gleaming across the darkened chasm. Her memory from that afternoon throbs like a vital pulse.

'But then,' she finally says. 'None of you actually know what happened. Or what I saw.'

Her siblings turn to her, half-dreading. 'What did *you* see?'

1991

She'd been stuck in the car so long, like a bug frying under a magnifying glass. Trying to hide from the desert sun, for what felt like forever. Bored, she'd watched the dust swirl up in little eddies hovering above the ground, before vanishing into the air.

She wondered what the Grand Canyon would be like, and tried to remember all the things she'd learned about it. That it was a mile from the top all the way down to the bottom. That the pioneers had come across it in their covered wagons and had no idea how to cross it. That people had died falling into it, from looking too hard and not paying attention to their feet.

All this stoked in her a sense of fear, along with awe. What would it be like to actually stand there with this mile-long drop at your feet? To be that close to certain death, while in the presence of something so beautiful?

Alex was thinking all of this when she noticed something move by the side of the building. Her mom walking with her usual direct pace, heading toward the car. To her.

Mommy. Her eight-year-old heart did a flip of joy. This meant they'd be leaving soon, getting away from this creepy gas station.

But then the men stood up. From where they sat on the steps in front of the shop. At one point the two men had wandered inside the shop, and then back out, after Dad and Kevin had gone around the corner.

And now it wasn't just two men. Here came a third, who must have been inside the store the whole time.

The three of them stood as Mommy passed, and she heard them whistle. Mommy kept walking. Then, suddenly, there was a shout from the men.

Alex sat up straight, her face pressed against the window, watching. For some reason, a sense of dread crept back into her stomach – the same feeling that had nested there ever since they pulled into this gas station.

Mommy stopped and turned to the men. They were too far away, and Alex couldn't hear what any of them were saying. But Mommy looked small, exposed, like she didn't want to be there.

The men took a step closer.

Mommy stepped back.

It was strange to see Mommy like that – tense, ready to spring away – like the neighbor's cat when someone raised a hand at it.

The men stepped even closer to Mommy.

Mommy, run, Alex wanted to shout. *Come here to the car.*

And a moment later, Mommy did. She turned toward the car, and Alex could swear Mommy was going to say something to her – but the men charged, like lions around that one zebra in that nature program she once watched on TV. One of them clamped a hand around her mouth and head, another around her waist. The last man almost laughed as they carried Mommy around the side of the building.

And then she was gone. Nothing but dust swirling up where those four grown-ups had once stood.

For a second, Alex wondered if she'd imagined it all. Some

trick of the heat and light, the way they say mirages happened out here in the desert.

But no — she'd seen it right in front of her. There was no denying it.

Her heart thumped, and she looked around the car. What could she could do, how could she get help? She felt a strange, desperate surge inside her: *do* something.

Stay inside, don't leave the car, Mommy had said. But now she was gone and no one else saw what had happened to her.

Count to twenty. See if Mommy comes back.

Alex counted to twenty, fervently, hopefully, her heartbeat pounding between the numbers. Eighteen, nineteen, twenty.

Still no sign of Mommy.

Help. Alex wanted to shout. But Daddy and Bonnie and Kevin were still inside the bathrooms; they couldn't hear her from here.

Alex leaned over into the front seat, trying to find something, anything.

And then she saw the driver's wheel. And the button on it with the shape of the horn.

Alex lurched into Daddy's seat, squeezing her body between the two seats, and leaned on the horn as hard as she could.

The sound of the blast cut through the desert air. She pressed the horn three times, just to make sure.

She hoped they heard it.

'Do you really think that could be it?' Kevin asks.

'*What* could be it?' Bonnie shoots back at him. Not a challenge, but she wants to hear him put it into words. She herself is so unsure about the hazy outlines of that particular afternoon, she hesitates to rely solely on her own imagination.

'That Mom was...' Kevin starts again. 'That those men did something to her.'

'Like what?' Bonnie pushes. 'Like they... raped her?' She whispers this word, reluctant to speak it in relation to her own mother.

The three of them sit in the descending twilight in silence, contemplating that possibility. A horrible truth that could have been a part of their lives this entire time – and everyone completely oblivious to it.

Trying to be practical, Bonnie does the math.

'Alex, after you saw the men do that, how long do you think they had her for? I mean, from when they took her around the corner.'

Alex is reluctant, but pauses to guess.

'I counted to twenty, just to see if she reappeared. When she didn't, I... wanted to count to twenty again. I was too scared to go out.'

'But you honked the horn?' Bonnie asks.

Alex nods.

'Okay, so twenty, thirty seconds and then you honked the horn. Which we all heard.'

'And then Dad rushed out,' Kevin says. 'But I came out soon after. And then Alex.'

'And then me.' Bonnie feels a wave of regret at her own ignorance; when she, as the oldest child, should have done something. But at least she can figure this out now. Bonnie thinks out loud: 'So fifty seconds or so. Maybe a minute when they had her.'

She doesn't want to consider the logistics, but she has to. How long does it take for men to get hard? To reach a state where they can... She thinks of Chris, all those times she's been with him. And the guys before. But she can't compare. Those were entirely different scenarios, romantic ones, where there had been a mutual attraction brewing for months – or at least a few weeks. She realizes how sheltered she has been – and how lucky – to have never experienced the nasty, violent side of male attraction, aside from odd comments and whistles and gropes. But to be a man, to have that potential to inflict pain, that need to penetrate...

'I can't...' She shakes her head, puts her head in her hands, faced with a reality she doesn't want to comprehend.

Alex puts an arm around her shoulders, and the feeling of her sister's warmth helps to lessen the chill in her bones.

'Maybe they just—' Kevin stops. But he can't bring himself to put anything into words.

'Look, it's not our job to piece this together,' Alex says slowly. 'We were just kids; we're going off fragments of memories here. The only way to find out what really happened is to ask Mom.'

The three of them stare at each other, aware this is almost impossible. How could one broach this kind of topic with Mom? Mom with her iron grip on anything about her own children, one that only loosened with long distance and old age. A memory Mom clearly wants to bury in the dust and heat of that long-ago afternoon.

Bonnie thinks of her own boys. If something like this had

287

happened to her, would *she* want them to know, at their young age?

If it was something minor, she would have brushed it under the carpet, done her best to minimize it. If it was more serious... to call attention to it, to involve the police and all the severity of that process... it would have taken too much away from the boys. Exposed them too early to the ugly realities of life.

How could you possibly force this kind of knowledge on your own children?

'I can understand why she'd want to keep something like that from us,' Bonnie says soberly.

'Really?' Alex looks at her, questioning.

'Come on. Mom?' Bonnie can't believe they don't see this immediately. 'With *her* hang-up around shame? *Her* perfectionist streak?'

She nearly stumbles on that last one. All too aware that these questions could apply just as easily to herself. The desire to mask. To achieve perfection – or at least the semblance of it. As if that was the only way to survive in this world.

* * *

The disquiet that Kevin has always felt about that afternoon has begun to swell. Expanding outward, trickling through every vein and capillary of his body, to assume its fullest volume of fear.

Could something like that have happened to Mom? In the few minutes that they were in the bathroom? With a certain regret, all he can remember was his own preadolescent feeling of shame and hatred. His father looking down at the counter, resigned. That stupid packet of beef jerky that he carried the entire time.

Mom barely registers in his memory of that gas station. And yet... he saw the two men crouching toward her, the way she

288

smoothed out the crumples in her clothing when his ten-year-old self showed up, confused.

The nausea of something like that happening to Mom. As a kid, it was ick because . . . well, Mom couldn't be sexual. Why would the men whistle at her like that?

But as an adult man now, he knows more.

'How old was Mom when we did that trip?'

He and Bonnie both calculate in their heads simultaneously, the familiar, all-too-dorky competition of who can add or subtract faster. He gets there first.

'Forty-two. She was forty-two.'

Forty-two is Jessica's age right now. From a distance, Jessica could still pass for being in her twenties. Up close, in her thirties. *Asian don't raisin*, as they say.

He's seen the way men eye his slim-figured wife in Chicago, when she's wearing a shorter dress or tight yoga pants. An observation that always brought him an element of pride as a husband. But now, with his own mother . . . He doesn't want to think about it.

Something in this stomach turns.

Sometimes, he genuinely hates being a guy.

* * *

They drive west in the dark now, on the road that takes them along the South Rim of the Grand Canyon. It had grown too cold after the sun went down, stealing with it all lingering traces of its warmth. The trees of the Kaibab National Forest rise up, a darkened mass to their left. To their right, they still catch glimpses of the Grand Canyon, ghostly and shadowed now, appearing now and then through gaps in the vegetation. A knowledge of that steep drop-off, only a few yards to their right.

Alex drives in silence, contemplating the enormity of what they have uncovered. *Mom, poor Mom.*

There is sadness, thinking of what her mom may have been hiding all these years. But also, her anger at men, at what they can do to women. So casually, so easily, without a second thought. And leave behind these kinds of lasting damages. She has seen this in her line of work, and had wanted her own life to somehow be free. But perhaps that was too much to hope for.

They exit the South Entrance of Grand Canyon National Park in darkness, the headlights illuminating now-empty lanes that are jammed with traffic during the day.

'It's just a short drive to Tusayan,' Alex says, as she turns the Mazda onto the 64, headed south.

With a wave of foreboding, she realizes this is the highway they were driving north on thirty years ago when their family tried to visit the Grand Canyon.

They are drained from their past few hours of conversation, all the small and big revelations, readjusting their memories and their understandings of the past. Alex longs for the bland assurance of a hotel room, the fresh sheets, and the TV screen that can numb you as you sit in an anonymous bed.

'Mom and Dad will probably want to talk to us, right?' Bonnie asks. 'Since we've actually visited the Grand Canyon today.'

'I mean, we spoke to them last night,' Kevin ventures.

Was that only fifteen, sixteen hours ago, when they found Kevin sprawled on the ground outside that desert campfire, blissfully stoned?

'I mean, they know we're all right,' Kevin continues. 'We can just text them a photo from the Grand Canyon.'

'Mmm, I guess it can wait,' Bonnie wavers.

Alex slows down as a cluster of deer step tentatively into her headlight beam. They watch as the animals move across the road, ephemeral shapes slipping from darkness back into darkness – made flesh only for that one instant in her headlights.

One deer – the last deer – stops for a moment and turns to look straight at them, eyes like brilliant pinpricks reflecting the light, holding their gaze. Then it scampers off.

Alex feels a frisson of the uncanny. A message she can't quite decipher.

'You know,' she says. 'One thing we should do tomorrow. We have to stop by that old gas station. We'll be driving right past it.'

Bonnie sucks in her breath. 'Do you think that's really necessary?'

'Yeah,' Alex says, steadfast. There's no doubt in her mind. To fix a geographic reality to that memory of hers. To confront it thirty years later, when they are wiser, stronger, more adult. 'It is.'

She speaks into the darkness. 'You guys can stay in the car. But I want to see it in person.'

To set foot there. As if stepping onto that forgotten ground could somehow hold an answer.

1991

The horn sounded for as long as she could hold it for. One long blast, then three more, insistent.

Alex felt very alone and very exposed, sitting there on her own in the car, with the bright blue sky and the flat, dusty land all around her. Doing her best to draw attention, to get anyone to notice.

But nothing happened. No one appeared around the corner of the building – not Daddy or Bonnie or Kevin. And not Mommy or the men.

Where had everyone gone? And what was happening to Mommy?

She knew it wasn't good. Mommy had tried to run away, but they hadn't let her. And when people try to stop you, they sometimes want to hurt you. She remembered those stories about Stranger Danger from school. And those men were definitely strangers.

Her heart hammering in her throat, Alex honked the horn again. Three more blasts.

But still no one came.

Somehow, Alex knew she couldn't keep waiting in the car. Mommy had told her to stay, but now Mommy was the one who needed help.

Alex looked around frantically. The cars on the highway just kept going past. No one else was pulling into this gas station.

She closed her eyes for an instant, told herself to be brave.

Pull up the lock on the door. Open it.

The dust from outside wafted onto her feet.

Imagine what would happen. If those men wanted to take away not just Mommy – but Daddy and Bonnie and Kevin, too. Everyone you know.

It wouldn't be fair. More than unfair. *Feel it.* A current of rage churned deep inside her. Alex found it and nursed it. A scream ripped out of her as she began running toward the side of the building. *Scream even louder. Cry.* And she did.

Her voice found form, cut through the haze.

Thinking only of Mommy and the men, hoping that they were still there, that it wasn't too late. That the blue sky around her would still hold up when she rounded the corner of the building.

Photo Message sent at 9:21PM, Mountain Time

Hey Mom and Dad – See, we made it to the Grand Canyon! Wish you were here.

*

Reply sent at 8:24PM, Pacific Time

So nice to see this photo. So proud you got there. Now come home safe.

* * *

Late morning the next day and they are blazing south on the 64. After breakfast that morning, they'd visited the Grand Canyon again. The haunted, indigo watercolors of the twilit canyon were replaced now with the dazzling reds and oranges of the morning. Still stunning, but with all the tourists milling about, the endless mugging for selfies, it was less mythic.

Mom and Dad should be here with us, Alex thought. And she looked at another Asian family posing on the edge of the canyon, the parents as old as Bonnie or Kevin, the children grinning for the camera – and she felt awash with regret.

So after the requisite photos and souvenirs, they'd hit the road again, that homing instinct drawing them to their parents. Alex is at the wheel, because there is something about this particular stretch of the journey that begs her to take control, to decisively turn onto that gas station forecourt.

Besides, of the three of them, she will have the best memory

294

of the place. It had seemed an eternity that she was stuck inside their dusty family car, staring at the gas station.

Nevertheless, a trepidation rises in her gut as she drives south. What if she can't recognize it from this direction? They will be coming from the north, but thirty years ago, they approached it from the south. What if she doesn't recognize it at all?

The night before, she had searched on Google for all the gas stations on the east side of the 64, between here and Williams. There were six on the fifty-two-mile stretch, four of them recognizable brands – the kinds Mom had wanted to avoid because they cost more. That narrowed it down to three gas stations, but by that point, Alex had felt overwhelmed by the precision required to pinpoint the correct place – and the emotions she had to hold at bay.

So she had given up, telling herself that she would recognize it. It would be impossible not to feel the psychic waves emanating from that forecourt, the ramshackle building.

Alex has been traveling for twenty-five years, from the moment she could strap on an overstuffed backpack and buy herself a Eurail pass. For her, the need to map experience onto geography is vital. And locating this particular geographic spot is the most vital of all.

'What are you planning to do when we find it?' Kevin asks as they head south into the blazing morning. Her siblings aren't nearly as enthusiastic about this plan as she is.

Alex is quiet for a while. 'I don't know,' she finally admits. 'I guess I won't know until we get there.'

It's less than an hour's drive from Tusayan to Williams to regain the I-40, and most of the gas stations are clustered at the halfway point at Grand Canyon Junction, where the 180 from

Flagstaff funnels tourists on their way north to see the great wonder. As they approach this clutch of fast-food eateries and motels, Alex watches the far side of the highway like a hawk. Exxon, Chevron, 76. Everything is chrome and illuminated plastic; wide, glittering parking lots. But where's the no-name run-down gas station? The tumbleweeds skittering over the cracked asphalt, haunting her memory, like a scene from a redneck horror film.

Where, where, where is it?

An unfamiliar obsessive thrumming has pulled her taut.

'Do you see it?' Alex asks, insistent.

Bonnie and Kevin are craning their necks, too, but they shake their heads. In another minute they've driven through Grand Canyon Junction and are on the wide-open road again.

'Do you think we missed it?' Alex feels distraught.

Bonnie sighs. 'I mean, there were three of us. We were all looking pretty closely.'

'Maybe it's a little farther ahead,' Alex mutters.

She keeps driving, but there's nothing, just more tract housing and flat, scrubby desert beneath the brilliant blue sky. The miles pass in silence.

It has to be there, she thinks. Somewhere on the left side of the highway.

She is on edge as she drives the rest of the 64 south, her eyes darting constantly to the left, searching, searching for that glimpse of the familiar. A Shell station, another Chevron, and then they are seeing signs to Williams, attempts at outer suburbs, industrial buildings, and a retail shopping outlet.

A growing disappointment begins to spread inside her.

'I don't understand. How did we miss it?' She is almost desperate in her confusion.

'Maybe it got built over,' Bonnie suggests. 'It was pretty

run-down when we were there, so maybe it got knocked down and . . . turned into something else.'

'Good riddance,' Kevin mumbles.

'But – No.' Alex almost wants to protest. 'Should I turn around?' If they head back north, they'll be on the correct side of the road to look for it.

'No!' Bonnie and Kevin both shout.

'Why the hell would you want to do that?' Kevin is annoyed.

'Well, I just—' Alex stops, unsure of how to explain this herself. What's essential is locating the actual place, fixing it onto a spot on a map. Pinning it like a dark moth that has been worrying the underside of her memory for decades.

'I don't know . . .' Alex struggles to find the right words. 'If we can't even see the place – If we can't stand there and verify that *this* is where that thing happened all those years ago . . . how do I know I wasn't just imagining it?'

She knows that's what Bonnie and Kevin are thinking, because childhood Alex with her outsized imagination was always dreaming up fantasies. She just wanted the three of them to stand there, like they had at the edge of the Grand Canyon last night, and confirm that yes, this was the place. This was the scene of that strange, unexplained change in Mom. And in their family.

Are you sure you weren't just imagining it?

The question she knows all too well from work, when women are disbelieved, their voices doubted. Accused of elaborating the truth.

Yet she would never *want* to imagine something like that.

'But Alex, you were sure you saw that happen to her, right?' Bonnie probes gently. There is nothing in her voice that suggests disbelief, just a quiet seeking of a confirmation.

'Yes, I'm sure,' Alex says, her mouth set, her eyes fixed on the highway ahead. 'I wouldn't have reacted like that if I hadn't.'

'And I remember feeling creeped out by those men, or at least the place. And Kevin clearly didn't have a good experience with them.'

Kevin coughs. 'Fucking racists.'

'So . . . yeah, I can see how something like that could have happened,' Bonnie concludes. 'I know I might have questioned it last night, but . . . I think you should trust your eight-year-old self.'

And maybe this is the absolution she needs.

The affirmation that eight-year-old Alex wasn't wrong. She, out of all of them, had seen the fullest version of the truth. She didn't need to stand on a gas station forecourt to affirm what had happened thirty years ago. She knew it in her heart of hearts – because once you accepted that truth, so many other things fell into place: not just the sudden decision to turn the car around, but Mom's reclusiveness, her anxiety whenever any of them left the house, her distaste for gas stations or garages or any place that smelled of gasoline or engines, the domain of intimidating masculine men. And then Alex's growing resentment, her impulse to rebel by escaping, by traveling as far as she could go.

With this realization, the tension in Alex dissolves. There is no need for a U-turn to locate a decrepit gas station in search of an affirmation. The affirmation is right here, in her heart. In this car, with her siblings.

'I wish I'd been paying more attention back then,' Bonnie is saying. 'I was such a teenage brat. But Alex, you were always observant. You saw what happened, and you did something about it. I don't think I would have, at the time.'

'I tried,' Kevin says after a moment. 'But I didn't ... I was scared.'

A sob chokes through Alex, and unexpectedly, she finds herself crying. Tears stain her face, fogging her sunglasses. She squints in order to keep driving, to get a clear view of the highway.

Poor Mom, she thinks. But then also, even though she hates the act of self-pity, *Poor me*. How one incident, glimpsed so many years ago, could haunt herself – could haunt all of them in these fractured ways.

'Are you okay?' Kevin asks gently, leaning in.

Bonnie places a warm hand on her shoulder, and Alex sniffles, a smile breaking through her tears.

'We can stop if you want ...'

But Alex shakes her head. There is something liberating now in blazing past that unidentified spot on the 64 and continuing on. Wherever that gas station was, it's now in the past. She knows it will live on in their memories; there's no need to revisit it in person. Alex presses on the gas, and the car kicks up to eighty.

'Let's keep going.'

The I-40 looms ahead, but the road they're on dips underneath it, following its own path west. A familiar brown sign tells them Historic Route 66 is coming up.

Alex can think of no better road to bring them home.

As the years passed, maybe intuitively, it all made sense to Alex.

Mom worried endlessly the first time she went backpacking around Europe, at the age of nineteen. It was just a three-week trip, but Mom wanted her to write down a schedule of where she would be each day.

'Can't you just tell me you'll be in Paris this day, Rome that day?'

'But I don't know, Mom!'

'How do you not know? Where you going to stay?'

'I don't know yet. I'll figure it out when I get there.'

'Why you have to wait until then?'

'Because that's the whole point of backpacking! You go where you feel like in the moment.'

Mom had looked at her suspiciously, like it was a ridiculous hoax, this chaotic form of travel.

'Besides, what difference does it make – if you know when I'm in Paris and when I'm in Rome?'

'Because then at least I *know*. I can check the weather report in those places; I can pay attention to the news.'

'For what? In case there's a terrorist attack? Or a freak tornado in France?'

'Just tell me! Just write it down!'

It almost seemed irrational, Mom's need to know these facts. But as Bonnie explained to her, maybe these small scraps of knowledge were somehow soothing to Mom. In the great wide unknown of the world, they helped anchor Mom's fear of the unpredictable.

So Alex wrote down a rudimentary itinerary, resentful of

having to put pen to paper and already start puncturing the joyous spontaneity of her trip.

On her next trip, she didn't offer as much information to her mom, because she knew it would freak her out. 'I'm going to Spain,' is all she said. And with each trip, she became vaguer and vaguer, not wanting to cause Mom any concern. Her mom's constant worrying only served to annoy her, to sour their conversations. So the less her mom knew about her travels, the better.

* * *

After Seligman, Arizona, Route 66 loops north, a single road arcing through the expansive desert.

Kevin is at the wheel, and they take in the red land and the blue sky, the Burma Shave signs that appear periodically, little jokes planted in the otherwise vacant landscape. They are digesting the lunch they had in a whimsical, kitschy place back in Seligman, all sorts of disjointed odds and ends cobbled together in a 3-D collage, repurposed toilet bowls and boots and radiators and reassembled mannequins, with the desert dust blowing through everything.

That same dust sifts outside their car, lining the bottom of the windshield, but Kevin doesn't mind. They are now a six- or seven-hour drive from Mom and Dad's. Keep driving, and they'll be there tonight.

They pass an Indian reservation, advertising 'the real Grand Canyon experience.' Kevin considers stopping for gas, but the road keeps calling to him, and he just wants to drive.

A railroad runs to their left, parallel to the highway. Kevin wonders what it must be like to drive alongside the shuddering train, pretending to outrun it.

More desert, then another small smattering of buildings, then more desert. How barren this land is, open to the sky, with nothing to plunder.

They see a sign advertising Kingman in thirty miles.

'Hey,' Alex says. 'This is the last stretch of the 66 for us. After Kingman, it's basically the interstate all the way home to L.A. We did it!'

Kevin smiles, feeling a rare sense of accomplishment, but also a certain sadness. Once they reach California tonight, this part of the trip will be over. The open road, and the endless sky.

With a sinking heart he realizes California means a reliable cell phone signal. No more excuses about evading Jessica and the inevitable confrontation with her. The reality of his debt – and its impact on his marriage – will be unavoidable.

'Do you wanna do, like, one last detour?' Alex asks, a glint of mischief in her eyes.

'What do you mean? Is there a place here the guidebook recommends?' Kevin meets her glance. And for once they are in agreement. His eyes scan the desolate landscape. Anything to delay the inevitable.

'No. I mean *really* off-road,' Alex snorts. 'Screw the guidebook, Kevin. Just turn off somewhere and explore . . . *That's* the real deal.'

'Can we do that?' Bonnie leans in from the back, hesitant.

'Come on, Bon, it's America!' Alex affects a Southern twang. 'It's a free country! Just look at all that wide-open desert for us to explore!' She gestures all around them.

'What is there to see?'

Kevin shrugs. 'We won't know until we find out, right?'

Alex points out the windshield to where a great, burnt-red mesa rises to their left, behind the train tracks. 'I mean, *that* looks interesting. What if we just drive out there and check it out? We're never gonna pass this way again.'

Kevin can sense Bonnie wavering.

'*Off-road*, Bonnie...' he teases her, singsong. 'Come on, go off-road... Tell your boys you went on an adventure.'

'And honestly, if it's boring, it's boring. We'll just turn around and head back,' Alex continues.

Bonnie looks at the two of them, the beginnings of a grin starting to play on her lips. 'Oh, all right. And you're right – when's the next time we'll be driving through the middle of nowhere together, without our kids? So yeah, let's do it.'

Kevin does a little whoop and points to an unmarked road that branches off the 66 to their left, heading toward the mesa. There's no other turnoff for long, arid miles.

'That one?'

'Go for it,' Alex eggs him on.

With a childlike glee, Kevin turns the wheel toward the blank, waiting landscape.

He glances briefly at the fuel gauge. Forty-five miles left in the tank. They should be fine.

Kevin never forgot that afternoon in Arizona. There was too much in those moments – the blinding bright of the sun, the holstered gun, the weight of the man's hand on his shoulder. The sight of Alex baying like a rabid dog, her face streaming with tears.

Every time he sees a packet of beef jerky, an underlying nausea lodges in his throat.

'*Little Chinese kid on his first trip into the desert.*'

He hated the condescension in the man's voice, even though he has heard that same tone over and over again from white men throughout his life.

Most of all, he hated how weak and wordless his dad had been. And how, when it came to it, when the man was standing

303

right in front of him, taunting him, he, Kevin, had done nothing. It was Alex who had come tearing through, disrupting everything. He remembers the flash of relief he felt when Alex showed up, deflecting the men's attention toward her. Always Alex, Alex, Alex. For ten-year-old Kevin, it was easier to think of it as all Alex's fault, the whole reason they never got to see the Grand Canyon. Blame it all on Alex, and everything resolved into a clearer, more acceptable shape.

But that sense of helplessness he has felt time and time again throughout his life.

Even now, at forty-two, it can wash over him when he least expects it.

He will pull into a near-empty gas station, and a brief flash of queasiness will return.

When he and Jess and the kids started going on road trips, he would make sure to only visit Exxons or Mobils or Shell gas stations – some recognizable brand that could be held accountable for poor customer service. And there always had to be at least one other car in the forecourt, preferably two, to ensure they were never the sole customers there.

Yet still, something about his kids asking to use the gas station bathroom, the feel of those clunky communal bathroom keys, handled by countless grubby hands, makes his heart lurch. *Don't go here. Wait until we're somewhere safe*, he wanted to say.

He has never told Jessica about this incident from his childhood, because it's almost a non-incident. And as a father of two, he knows this is not a story they would want to hear, when their own father was weak and fearful as a boy.

So purchasing that gun, storing it in his glove compartment, is his secret. These actions, at least, help to make him feel a little better about who he is now. A little less useless.

They rumble through this scorched land, the only car visible once they've turned off the 66. Deeper and deeper into the desert, driving closer to the mesa that rises between them and the horizon.

'Can we actually reach it?' Kevin asks, after their road starts to lose its asphalt surface.

Alex rolls down her window, leans her head out, and hollers joyfully.

'What was that for?' Bonnie asks.

'Because we're the only people around,' Alex says. 'Once I get back to London, I won't be able to see landscapes like this.'

Kevin smiles, then slows the car down.

'Good point,' he says. 'Look, I don't think we can get any closer. Let's get out of the car now, take it all in. One final hurrah in the desert.'

He knows this is uncharacteristic of him, and he is secretly proud of that. Perhaps Alex's spontaneity is rubbing off.

They step out into the silent desert: just the three of them, the car, and the vast, empty terrain, as far as the eye can see. They stand and contemplate the mesa, this huge mass of living rock, rising timeless and monumental. There is not a noise to be heard, not the rumble of any traffic, or the skitter of a creature. The world around them is entirely at peace. The sun baking the air around them.

In all his life, Kevin has never been in a place this serene. This is what the desert can offer you, if you journey far enough into it.

'Wow,' he breathes. 'So quiet.'

He closes his eyes, feeling the sun on his face. *Remember this,* he tells himself. *Once you return to the real world, remember this moment of peace.*

Alex squints into the distance and points to a faint pale line that crosses the immense red rock desert.

'Looks like there's another road we might be able to take, instead of backtracking the way we came.'

They all stare at it. In this boundless landscape, it seems as abstract as a line randomly drawn on a chalkboard. To follow it seems irrational, wild. And entirely tempting.

'Sure, let's try it.'

Kevin leans back against the Mazda and promptly yelps, jerking away.

'Hot?' Alex asks, grinning.

'Burning, ouch,' he says, squinting up at the sun. 'Then again, makes sense. All this desert heat, and one metal car to soak it up.'

As usual, his sisters laugh at his expense. This time, he doesn't mind.

'I think we must have made a wrong turn back there,' Bonnie is saying this as she peers out at the landscape, so dry and unforgiving in this sun.

'What do you mean, a wrong turn?' Alex frowns. 'You can't exactly get lost in this landscape. You can see in every direction.'

'Yeah, but you make one wrong turn, and then you're headed in that direction forever, unless you do a U-turn.'

'Are you saying you want me to turn around?' Kevin asks, annoyed, his hands gripping the wheel. 'What does the GPS say?'

'The GPS is fucked. No signal.' Next to him, Alex jabs at the screen. 'I guess we shouldn't have gone down this road.'

'What does your phone say?'

'I can't get a signal, either.' Alex swipes at her phone and grumbles.

Bonnie checks her phone, too. Nothing.

'We must be in some dead zone for cell phone signals.'

'That's reassuring,' Kevin mutters.

'So . . . where the hell are we?' Bonnie asks.

Alex flips through the road atlas, then scours the Arizona map.

'So . . . we were on Route 66, and then we turned off after Valentine. But the map doesn't show the smaller roads. So, once we get back to the 66, it's easy to find Kingman.'

Kevin eyes the fuel gauge. His dashboard display tells him he has thirty-five miles to go before empty. A quiet panic starts to throb at the base of his stomach.

'How many miles is it to Kingman?' Kevin asks.

'I think that last sign we passed said thirty, right?'

'Okay, well, we're low on gas. We don't really have much to spare.'

'Shit.'

Kevin feels his sisters biting back their reprimand, and he is glad they've opted not to say anything.

A wordless tension settles over the three of them as they continue rolling over the barely paved road, loose stones plinking against the sides of the car.

Bonnie sits up and points.

'Hey, there's some kind of farm up ahead.'

They all strain to see through the cloud of dust that surrounds them. Kevin can just about make out a collection of low buildings, hunched in the middle distance, away from the road. 'Maybe we can ask for directions there.'

Kevin's willing to admit they made a wrong turn. He'll stop, he'll turn around. But there's no way he's stopping in the middle-of-nowhere desert to ask the locals for directions. He's seen enough *X-Files* episodes and slasher films to know that's a bad idea.

They've reached the entrance to a barely noticeable ranch, a skeletal iron gate rising from the dusty desert floor. In the arch, the iron is twisted into letters to spell 'Old Scorpion Ranch' – or maybe it's Cold Scorpion, but the 'C' fell off.

Skulls of cattle and horse are fixed at various points along the gate. *How comforting*, Kevin thinks.

He swings the Mazda through the gates, and the road grows even bumpier. He trundles along, looking for an appropriate place to maneuver the car into a three-point turn. In such a remote location, he'd rather not go off-road. The last thing they need is a tire puncture. Nor does he know how to change a tire.

'Can you imagine having a ranch out this far from nowhere?' Alex muses aloud. 'I mean, can cattle even survive in this heat?'

Hence all the cow skulls fixed to the ranch gate.

At last the road widens temporarily, and Kevin starts to turn the wheel.

'What are you doing?' Bonnie asks, insistent. 'I thought we were going to drive up and ask for directions.'

'Turning the car around,' Kevin explains. 'The easiest thing is to backtrack at this stage.'

The Mazda is now straddled across the dirt road, and Kevin is about to reverse, when Alex speaks up. 'Wait, can you stop for a moment? We might be able to get a better cell phone signal if we step outside.'

Good point. He has to admit, Alex does have a practical

knack for traveling and navigating. That, plus he wouldn't mind the chance to relieve himself. For nearly an hour, he's been bursting for a bathroom.

He stops the car, and Alex and Bonnie jump out, holding their phones high in search of a signal.

'C'mon, c'mon Google Maps,' Alex prays.

Kevin walks some distance to the other side of the car. He faces away from the others, toward the intricate network of mesas stretching to their left, and behind them, the low brown hills that back the horizon.

You really can walk for miles in any direction out here and die of dehydration under the desert sun. Now he believes it.

Some large bird – maybe a vulture – sails overhead, screeching a lonesome call, and he sees its shadow drifting along the barren ground in front of him.

Kevin relieves himself with a temporary joy, watching his urine creep a snake-like pattern in the desert sand.

And then, he spies out of the corner of his eye, another vehicle coming toward them. From the ranch buildings up ahead. At first, it's just the cloud of dust, churning up in a straight line – then, gradually, he hears the rumble of the engine, growing closer.

Oh shit, he thinks.

He watches out of curiosity. But then he sees another vehicle – what looks like a quad bike – blazing up a storm of dust as it bumps over the scrub from another direction, straight toward them.

What the . . .? His heartbeat starts to quicken.

'Do you see that?' Bonnie asks. 'Maybe we can ask them for directions.'

'Uh . . . I'd like to get the hell of here,' Alex breathes, and she spins around, headed for the front passenger seat.

But it's too late, because in another moment, the truck arrives with a roar of its engine: a creaking brown pickup, more dust than metal. Even before the truck screeches to a stop, two men jump off it, running toward them with a focused fury.

'Get the fuck off our land!' one of the men bellows.

The other one stops and crooks his arm up, pointing a rifle at them. 'You got no right to be here. You're all fucking trespassing!'

Kevin stares. The two men are breathing hard from their run, and they look as dusty and worn as their truck. Creatures of the desert, just like the two men from the gas station. Kevin suddenly feels like he's going to be sick, but no, he begs, not here. Not in front of these people.

In another moment, the truck door slams and a middle-aged woman stalks out, her hair pulled back in a severe ponytail. There's a whine and a growl and clank of chains. By her side, a massive German shepherd strains at its leash. It lets out a volley of vicious barking.

Bonnie and Kevin flinch. But Alex stares at the dog, unshaken.

'Our dog doesn't like trespassers,' the woman announces as she pulls back on the leash. 'And no wonder. City folk like you.'

'Look at this,' the first man growls, staring at them. 'Bunch of chinks show up on our property.'

What the fuck, Kevin thinks. It's like they've walked into a horror film. He reminds himself: the racist cop in Arkansas, the campfire in New Mexico . . . His fear was always worse than what actually transpired. Still, the tension mounts in him.

The woman and the second man start to pace, circling them and the car. The German shepherd snarls.

A fourth person arrives on the quad bike. And when he dismounts, striding through the cloud of dust, Kevin concludes it must be the prodigal son. A man in his late twenties, massive and at least six foot two. His biceps bulge where the sleeves of his faded T-shirt have been cut off.

Kevin stares dumbstruck at the advancing foursome. Once again – like that afternoon thirty years ago – he is frozen in fear. For a second, the thought of his revolver flits through his mind, but it's tucked away in the glove compartment, impossible to reach.

The younger man now approaches, studying them. He doesn't seem as hostile as the other three, glaring with menace, and a dash of curiosity. His elders do the talking.

'The thing is,' the first man says, 'the government told us to keep our distance. Viruses and all that, pandemic, Chinese flu. But shit – no matter how far we stay away, we can't escape people like you.'

'What are you talking about?' Alex asks, incensed. 'We're not here to infect you, we were just turning our car around—'

'You shut the fuck up while you're on our land,' the first man bellows.

Kevin doesn't say anything. He's been in situations like this before, just not on a remote ranch in Arizona. Just stay quiet, don't react, and wait for the bullying to pass.

'*Your* land?' Alex challenges. She gestures to the incalculable distance all around them, the endless desert floor, the mesas and hills on the horizon. 'This is – What, you own *all* this land?' There's that note of sarcasm in her voice, and Kevin wants to warn her to tone it down.

'Everything this side of the road is ours,' the second man says. 'You drive through that gate, you're on our land. And it's our land, our rules.'

'And what are your rules?' Alex challenges.

Alex, shut the hell up.

Kevin can see the ranchers assessing his little sister in a new

311

light. Her short haircut, her boyish stance, her atypical defiance. Surely they never expected this slim Asian woman to speak like this.

'Christ, you're a ballsy one, aren't you?' the woman asks.

'Listen,' Bonnie steps forward, her hands held upward in surrender mode. She is trying the calm, diplomatic approach, smoothed over by her boardroom poise. 'We really don't mean any harm. We just want to turn our car around and head back the way we came.'

'That's right. You better get back to where you came from. Your own country!'

'Really?' Alex raises her voice, stinging with outrage. 'You're gonna use that? We're American, too. We were born here.'

Kevin and Bonnie look at Alex in alarm. What is she doing?

'We don't want none of you chinks coming over here, spreading your virus.'

'Look, we're sorry. We're going,' Bonnie says apologetically. And she turns to open the car door, staring daggers at Alex.

But the woman shrieks at the top of her voice. 'Hey! You don't get to go until we say you can. You're gonna bother us like this, rocking up to our place, uninvited? There's a price you gotta pay.'

Here we go. That's what it comes down to. He scans the barren ranch and realizes these people have nothing – just miles and miles of arid land. Kevin tries to imagine how much cash is in his wallet. How much will it take to buy their way of this?

'What do you want from us?' Alex asks, defiant.

The woman runs her eyes over them: assessing their car, their clothes, their footwear. No doubt estimating how much she can demand from them.

In the intervening silence, Bonnie attempts another escape.

'We've got friends expecting us in Kingman, so we should be in our way.'

'Five hundred dollars!' the woman finally barks, erupting into fury.

'What?!' Alex exclaims. 'Who even carries that much cash around?'

'I said five hundred dollars.'

'Cindy, doesn't have to be that much,' one of the men says.

'No way!' Alex scoffs. 'We're not paying five hundred dollars just because we drove onto your property to turn our car around.'

'Well, let's see the inside of your wallets, then,' Cindy challenges. 'Or Phil's gonna shoot one of your tires.'

Kevin panics. He is *not* getting stranded out here in the desert with these rednecks. He steps forward, gesturing to the front seat. 'Let me get my wallet. It's in the car.'

'Kevin.' Alex's voice is sharp. 'Don't forget: your *wallet* is in the glove compartment.'

She gives him an equally pointed look, and Kevin glances back. Message received. But is she fucking crazy? What exactly does she expect him to do with his gun? His stomach feels like it's going to fall through right now. Four ranchers with rifles, a dog, and two vehicles. There's no way he's holding up a revolver to them.

As he leans into the car and unlocks the glove compartment, Bonnie steps forward, her voice calm, her hands still up.

'Listen, I'm going to have a look in my wallet, too. But can you stop training those guns on us? It would make us feel a lot better. We *will* pay you. We will. We just want to get out of here safely.'

She issues this as a reassurance, yet also a bargaining point.

The ranchers hesitate, their rifles still cocked.

'What?' Alex says, sarcastic. 'You think my brother is gonna take out a gun and shoot you all?'

Kevin thinks he's going to pee in his pants right there.

But it works. Clearly, they have no such thought. 'All right, then,' Cindy says. 'Just give us that money.'

* * *

The rifles down, they enter a strange standoff while Bonnie and Kevin count out the cash from what they can find in the car.

Alex stands there in the desert sun, staring at the ranchers while they wait. They squint up at the sky, then down at their feet, avoiding eye contact.

'So, uh, you guys had this ranch out here for long?' Alex is genuinely curious; she also somehow wants to change the tenor of the conversation. *Flip the scene, establish rapport with your audience.*

Cindy frowns at this attempt to be friendly, but the men don't see the harm in the answering. The older man who's not Phil coughs and speaks up: 'Uh, our great-grandfather came out here in 1928, got himself some land . . .'

Phil looks at the other man and nods.

'Oh, so . . . you guys are brothers?' Alex asks. She feels the tension between them thawing, moment by moment.

'Yep, we are. Been seeing to this ranch all our lives.'

She thinks of all those decades living in such a remote place with your brother. To have him occupy such a large part of your world. And for the rest of your world to be so . . . empty.

'And what do you guys raise here on the ranch?'

'Cattle,' Phil answers. 'Mainly cattle, but the market's getting tough. They don't do so well in this heat, and the big cattle farms—'

'I've had just about enough of this,' Cindy juts in. 'We're not here to make best friends. Where is that money?'

'Guys,' Alex raises her voice to Bonnie and Kevin, keeping her eye on the ranchers. 'You counted the money yet?'

She hopes the two of them have figured out a plan, anything to get them out of here safely.

Bonnie pokes her head out of the car. 'Uh, so we don't have a lot of cash on us,' she begins. 'Really sorry about this, but . . . we've only got about a hundred and fifty here.'

Alex listens on tenterhooks, hoping that's enough to bribe them.

'I said five hundred dollars!' Cindy shrieks. 'That's nowhere near enough.'

Hearing the anger in her voice, the German shepherd rears up again, growling.

Alex flinches as it barks. Thinking how to turn this situation around.

'Give us your watches and your phones, and we'll call it even,' Cindy demands.

'What?' Bonnie says. 'No, we need our phones.'

'You can buy yourselves new ones when you get home,' Cindy barks. 'Signal don't reach out here anyway.'

'Don't you guys think a hundred and fifty dollars is enough?' Alex turns to Phil and his brother. 'I mean, the cash is yours; we haven't caused you any trouble.'

Phil hesitates. 'Come on, Cin, one-fifty is good, right?'

Cindy raises her shotgun to the air, her face livid. 'I don't think you're in any state to be bargaining, are you?'

And Alex jumps in her skin when the gun is fired, and a crack splits the sky.

* * *

315

And just like that, Alex is down on the ground, curled up. Groaning.

Alex. Bonnie panics, her heart in her mouth. She has flashbacks to her childhood and adolescence, always knowing little Alex had to be looked after. She had fallen and twisted her ankle; she was being pushed around by a bigger kid.

She had been shot in the desert, miles from nowhere.

Bonnie rushes to her sister, searching, searching for the blood, but Alex is wailing up a storm, her hand clenching her side.

'Oh my god, it burns!'

Bonnie stares in disbelief. A bullet. In her own sister.

Everything a whirlwind to Bonnie, telling her she will never, never forgive herself for letting this happen to Alex.

'Cindy, you shot her!' she hears Phil say at the edge of her awareness, but she doesn't care what they're saying. She only cares about Alex.

A deep guttural moan from her sister, who clutches her. 'Get me in the car! I need a hospital.' Her breath is ragged, almost sobbing, and Bonnie knows she needs to keep her head cool, think straight, be practical, the way she has had to be her entire life.

'Are you hurt, Alex? Are you bleeding?'

'The car. Get me to the car!' Alex moans.

In disbelief, Bonnie and Kevin stare at each other. A single horrified look, sharing the same unified thought.

Time to get the fuck out of here.

* * *

'Where is our money?' Cindy fumes. 'You can't leave without paying!'

Kevin is still frozen, watching as Bonnie attempts to haul

Alex into the back seat of the Mazda. Alex is wailing: horrible, bloodcurdling howls of pain that he hasn't heard from her since childhood.

Phil and his brother and the silent younger man gaze in horror, too.

'Go get them!' Cindy shrieks to the men. 'Get our money.'

And that's when Kevin moves. In one clean action, instinctual, unthinking, he raises his revolver, points it at all of them.

They stop, disbelieving.

'No,' he says. And his voice is calm but loud, projected with a confidence that he's rarely felt before and doesn't even feel now, as his heart hammers in his chest. What is it Alex says about assuming a personality? *Believe this is you. For this moment only.*

'Stay back,' Kevin continues, his voice still firm. 'I have your money right here.'

And again, miraculously, smoothly, he takes one hand off the gun, slips it into his back pocket and raises it high, holding the cash aloft so they can see it. The gun doesn't waver, the desert sun glints off the metal. The bills ripple in the breeze.

'Right here! The money's yours, as long as you stay back.'

And they do. They listen. Kevin can hardly believe it. This is what happens when you hold up a gun. Fear turns to power. He edges slowly to the front passenger seat of the car, his gun still trained, the money still held high.

'Just let us go,' he shouts, not as a plea but as a directive. 'My sister's hurt, and we need a hospital.'

He's at the open door now. Just a moment longer and he'll be inside. Is this actually working? How much time does Alex have left?

Finally, Cindy breaks. 'Get them!' she shrieks as she looses the German shepherd and it springs to life, teeth bared, raring straight at them.

Kevin squeezes the trigger.

The dog balks, stops short. But he hasn't hit it. He aimed for the quad bike, the easiest shot from this angle, and now the tire deflates, the body of the vehicle sinking to the ground.

He actually hit it! With a rare rush of elation, Kevin throws the cash as far as he can to the earth, leaps into the car, and slams the door shut.

Bonnie's started the car with a jolt, she reverses it at an alarming speed down the dirt road, tires crunching the gravel underneath. Kevin is flung against the door, bracing himself against the jolting. Through their front window, he sees the ranchers piling into their truck.

Is Bonnie driving backward?

'What the fuck are you doing?' Kevin shouts.

'It's called a J-turn!' Bonnie shouts back. She spins the wheel, and the car turns, does a 180. Kevin almost wants to vomit.

'Get your seat belt on!' she commands. 'I'm gonna floor it.'

* * *

You can do this, you can do this, you can do this, Bonnie thinks as she sits in the driver's seat, the adrenaline coursing through her body. *Alex Alex Alex is in the back, bleeding from a gunshot wound. You get her to a hospital now.*

Bonnie stabs the child lock button to secure the doors. Her right hand flies over the gearshift, while her right foot slams down on the gas pedal. Flooring it out of there, the dirt road jolts them mercilessly, the pebbles pelt the outside of the car.

She glances in the rearview mirror and sees the ranchers' truck rumbling up a dust storm behind them, chasing their tail. The quad bike remains stationary, receding into the distance.

But the pickup is building speed. They shot Alex; they'll shoot them all if they catch up.

'Faster!' Kevin shouts.

'I'm trying! But this road isn't paved!'

She pushes harder on the gas and the RPM dial jumps, the pebbles rain harder against the car.

More gunshots from behind them.

'Are they actually shooting at us?'

Bonnie glances frantically at the console, the gearshift, trying to refamiliarize herself with the Mazda's controls. In a moment of awe, she realizes that Kevin's car has something called 'sport mode'. Faster acceleration, she thinks. Has he never used this mode before? What a chump.

She flicks the button, and the car immediately responds. The engine roars, the dial jumps to six as the added pickup kicks in.

They're almost at the junction with the road, and in a blind panic, Bonnie shouts, 'Left or right? Left or right?'

'Left!' Alex bellows from the back seat, and Bonnie doesn't have time to ask if she's sure, because her sister's never been wrong with directions before, and she just has to trust her now.

She eases off the gas for a moment, deftly swings the Mazda left onto the road, and with the tarmac regained, the car gathers speed.

The truck is still on their tail, swinging into place behind them. As long as she keeps the speed up, as long as they've got enough gas, Bonnie feels fairly certain Kevin's car is the superior vehicle.

More gunshots crack the air around them; they all duck down instinctively.

'Alex, are you okay back there?' she shouts, frantic. 'Are you bleeding?'

'What the . . . ?' she hears Kevin say, incredulous.

Bonnie dares to turn around for moment to look at Alex in the back seat. What she sees shocks her. Alex is sitting up, perfectly fine, seat belt crossed over her chest.

'Eyes on the road!' Alex reminds her, and Bonnie turns back, swerves the SUV into the middle of the barren road.

But where's the blood? And the wailing?

'Alex, what the hell? You've just been shot!' she shouts, trying to make eye contact in the rearview mirror.

She feels Alex lean forward into the gap between her and Kevin. Her voice right by their ears.

'I wasn't shot,' her sister says, calm and casual. 'It's called acting.'

* * *

You've just been shot, Alex told. herself. *Now show the world your pain.*

And that's how she howled.

On the ground, clutching her side, writhing in the dust of the desert. In drama school, onstage, she was always able to summon the tears, and she feels them starting now, even as her eyes are screwed shut in feigned anguish.

They don't need to see the blood. They just need to hear your wailing.

And so she channeled the pain and gave it a voice. Pain for all those decades of strained connection with her family, the distance between them growing greater and greater. Pain for her mother, the shame she hid for thirty years, and the cost of her silence. Pain for all the secret losses, never known, and all the losses that are still to come.

And now, sitting in the back seat of the Mazda as Bonnie blazes through the sunburnt desert, Alex can't help but feel a little proud. A pretty good performance, wasn't it? Apparently fooled everyone, including her siblings.

'You *faked* it?' Kevin is shrieking. 'I genuinely thought you'd been shot. I was freaking out.'

'Look, I needed to throw them off so we'd get a chance to escape,' Alex explains. 'If you'd known I was faking, it wouldn't have worked.'

It occurs to her that since drama school, neither of her siblings have actually seen her perform live before – partly because they all live so far away, and partly because her professional jobs were so few and far between. Ironic that it took getting shot at by racist ranchers in Arizona for them to really appreciate her talent.

'Don't you ever tell me again that acting is a useless skill,' she quips. 'Speaking of, nice shot, Kevin. Their quad bike!'

'I know, wasn't it cool?!' He grins, pleased with himself.

Bonnie joins in, too, throwing out praise, even as the desert races past them.

'Hey, did you actually throw them a hundred and fifty dollars?' Alex asks.

Kevin snorts. 'It was more like ninety dollars. Which, I dunno, at least gets them a new quad bike tire.'

Bonnie cuts in, urgent. 'Alex, can you get Google Maps on your phone now? Where the hell are we? We don't have much gas.'

Alex flicks her phone on. 'Amazing! We have a signal finally. Okay . . . We are coming up to the 66. Make a left, and then Kingman in . . . about twenty-five miles.'

'Twenty-five?!' Bonnie repeats, agitated. She eyes the gas gauge. 'We're cutting it pretty close.'

* * *

Bonnie handles the driving deftly, blazing down the tarmac and consistently pushing the Mazda to eighty miles per hour, even ninety, along this sun-baked stretch of desert road. This entire time the ranchers' truck has been on their tail, but Bonnie has managed to stay ahead, her eyes scanning the road for any potholes or rocks that could disrupt their speed.

Bonnie glances in the rearview mirror again, and sees the pickup rumbling behind her, its metal hood glinting behind the cloud of dust. What are they actually going to do? Chase them all the way across the state?

With a swell of relief, she spies a two-lane road crossing the landscape up ahead. That must be Route 66. The only highway in all this lonely expanse of red rock. Their path back to civilization.

There are at least a handful of cars and trucks traversing its broad, gray length – another reason for relief. Since escaping the ranch, they have not passed a single other car – it's just been them and the pickup, ominous on their tail, racing under the sunstruck sky.

'Left here onto the 66,' Alex says.

The gas gauge now says seventeen miles left. Bonnie estimates, at this speed, it'll be less. But you can apparently drive for several more miles after the gauge hits zero. Not that she's ever cut it this fine before.

The pickup pushes closer to them, in a final bid to catch them before the junction.

Fuck that. Bonnie slams down on the gas, speeding up as they approach the highway.

There is a bump up ahead, as the train tracks cross the road. Bonnie doesn't slow down. The car races over the tracks, jolting them all on impact.

'What the hell are you doing?' Alex asks.

'Trying to get away from them,' Bonnie answers deadpan, and now she recognizes the surge of adrenaline she first felt when hit the accelerator in the rental Camaro, driving away from Boston.

To be entirely in control. Speed and motion at your disposal with the pump of a pedal, the nudge of the steering wheel. To be able to dodge, to outstrip, to negotiate disaster solely through the skill of your own hands and reaction time. Everything balanced on a knife edge, and her in command of it all.

Left turn. Left turn . . .

A flash of a mirror attracts her attention in the desert distance. There's a huge tractor trailer barreling down the 66 on her left, and if she times this just right, at the correct speed . . . She'll be able to turn just before the truck and shake off the ranchers.

She quells her instinct to put on the turn signal. No need to tell anyone where they're headed.

How fast can she take this turn without spinning out? Forty? Fifty?

She turns on her headlights, her hazards, anything to warn the truck driver that she won't be slowing down. *Manic driver up ahead! Trying to escape from psychopaths here!*

'Bonnie, slow down,' Alex seethes, keeping her voice low.

'Guys, hold on to something back there!' Bonnie shouts. 'I'm gonna take this turn a little fast.'

She double-checks: the child lock is on. Oncoming traffic on the right is a decent distance away. There's just enough space to clear the tractor trailer, which is now honking its horn, demanding she stop. Momentarily, she eases up on the gas. And then, in another flash, she jerks the wheel to the left, barely clearing the truck. The car spins out the far side of the lane, scraping over the rumble strips, and she's on the hard shoulder now, but keeps driving, her hands nimble on the wheel. She swerves the car back onto the highway, regaining her speed.

The truck driver blares its horn in anger. Bonnie doesn't care. She's elated, floating on a cloud of triumph she has never felt before.

She managed to cut off those crazy ranchers, and now there's just open road ahead.

The pickup is still behind them, waiting to make the turn, receding into the distance.

Bonnie glances at the gas gauge. Ten miles now.

Come on, Mazda. Get us to Kingman.

Bonnie operates on a high, threading her way past vans and trucks, gunning for the clear macadam just beyond. She's got her eye on the pickup, which still follows them.

'Ten more miles,' Alex announces.

The gas gauge is nearly at zero now, the bright red warning light flashing.

Maybe she should slow down a bit.

Just then, she sees it coming up on her right: a police car parked on the shoulder.

She's at ninety and pushes down on the brake, hoping she'll slow down in time. But in another second, she's passed the cop, and she hears its siren start up, its lights flashing as it races to catch up with her.

Fuck.

There's no way she's planning to outrun a cop, certainly not on an empty tank of gas. 'The police?!' Alex shouts in disbelief.

Bonnie presses the brake, puts on her righthand indicator to show her compliance.

'I'll handle this,' Bonnie instructs. She exhales slowly in an attempt to calm her heartbeat. *Channel your inner affluent white woman. You're Bonnie Prescott from Boston.*

There's a surge of relief as she realizes the presence of the police car will surely drive away the ranchers. And as she jounces over the rumble strips and comes to a halt on the shoulder, she can see the brown pickup racing past, slipping gratefully into the distance. No longer interested in the pursuit.

Yet still, any interaction that involves a cop pulling you over is, by default, laced with anxiety.

Has she ever been stopped by the police before? Bonnie racks her brain. There was that time in her mid-twenties when she was caught speeding, but the police officer, a middle-aged balding white guy, seemed to find her cute.

'You got a great smile, kid,' he'd said. 'So I'll let you off this time. Just watch your speed. Or I'll have to pull you over again.' He winked at her – and she can still remember feeling that creepiness, that this older white cop seemed to be flirting with her, toying with her.

But that was twenty years ago, and she can't summon up that Little Asian Girl Lost shtick anymore because she's got too many gray hairs.

Bonnie considers the best possible way to play this, when the tap comes on her side window.

The cop is wearing mirrored aviator sunglasses, which block any chance of eye contact. He looks middle-aged or a bit older, judging by the sparseness of his hair. He leans down, peers into the car interior.

Bonnie lowers the window, removes her sunglasses, and assumes a look of contrition. *We have nothing to hide*, she reminds herself. *I was only speeding.*

'Ma'am, I clocked you going at ninety,' the cop says. 'Speed limit here is seventy.'

'I know, I'm sorry, Officer.' Bonnie pitches her voice slightly higher to sound more innocent. 'I just got carried away. My first time driving Route 66, I guess.'

The officer cracks a wry, almost patronizing smile. 'Yeah, a lot of tourists get carried away by that. But just cause we're in the middle of nowhere doesn't mean there's no speed limits.'

Bonnie nods, a chastened child.

'I'm sorry, Officer. I really am.'

The cop leans in closer and studies Kevin next to her. Then peers into the back seat, curious.

In her rearview mirror, Bonnie glimpses Alex giving an agreeable wave.

'Hello.' Her sister grins.

We're not hiding anything; we don't have a gun, Bonnie repeats to herself. *We didn't just shoot at a group of racist ranchers who ran us off their property.*

'So ... Illinois plates, huh? You musta driven a long way to be here.'

'Yeah, we're, um ... This is my brother and sister.' Bonnie eases into a friendlier, more intimate cadence. 'We're driving Route 66 to see our mom, who's out in California. She's recently had a stroke and wanted to see us.'

'Ah, I'm sorry to hear that,' the cop says. She can't tell if he's being genuine or not, but at least he's attempting the hallmarks of civility. 'If you're really in such a hurry, you should have flown.'

They all laugh contritely, knowing they need to humor this cop's attempt at humor.

'Well, we're all from different parts, actually.' And for the twentieth time on that trip, Bonnie explains their mom's request and their respective geographies: Boston, Chicago, London.

The cop whistles. 'That is some story.' *It's not just a story*, she thinks. *It's the truth.* 'And what did you think of the Grand Canyon?'

'We just came from there this morning, and it was ... Yeah, it was pretty incredible, wasn't it?' She looks around at Alex and Kevin, and they nod enthusiastically, voicing the requisite awe.

'Amazing.'

'Nothing like that in Illinois.'

'Yeah, I wish our mom could have seen it,' Bonnie adds.

327

'It's something everyone in this country deserves to see at least once,' the cop declares. He pauses, then resumes his authority.

'What was your name, ma'am?'

'Uh, Bonnie.' *Don't tell him any more than he needs to know.*

'Can I see some ID?'

'Sure,' Bonnie answers automatically and nods. Then she freezes in a jolt of panic. She no longer has her license. It's somewhere in St. Louis, probably sold on the black market to an underage kid or illegal immigrant. Should she explain all that, or will it just invite more suspicion?

She swallows, trying to think her way out of this one.

'Ma'am?' the cop prods.

'Uh . . . I'm just trying to remember where I put my license,' she says with a weak laugh to buy herself more time. What's the penalty for driving without a license? On top of speeding? A fine? Jail time?

'Oh, hey,' Alex speaks up. 'I've got it right here. Remember, you asked me to hold on to it?'

What is she talking about? Bonnie thinks in a panic, turns around and stares at Alex. But then Alex produces a California driver's license and waves it at her. She places it firmly in her hands: Alexandra Mei-Jing Chu. And next to the name: a photo of Alex from five years ago. Before she cut her hair.

Bonnie senses a daring glimmer of hope. *Alex, you fucking genius.* They look similar enough. Besides, don't all Asian women look the same to most people?

The cop coughs, impatient, and holds out his hand for the license. Bonnie hands it to him. And stares straight ahead, although she's desperate to trade a winning look with Alex.

'I thought you said your name was Bonnie?' he asks.

Shit. A new flood of panic. 'Yeah, that's my nickname.' She smiles. 'I always hated the name Alexandra. I wanted some-thing . . . cuter. Like Bonnie.'

Say it with conviction. You believe it, they'll believe it.

'Drove all of us crazy,' Alex adds, then mimics a child's voice. *'My name is not Alexandra! Call me Bonnie!'*

Kevin adds a laugh next to her.

'Like Bonnie and Clyde, huh?' the cop asks.

'Well, maybe not as dangerous,' Bonnie says.

'You sure as hell *drive* like Bonnie and Clyde,' the cop jokes.

'I'm sorry. I really am.'

'Listen, Ms. Bonnie Alexandra what-have-you Chu. You seem like nice people, but I'm afraid I'm gonna have to fine you for speeding. Rules are rules. You know?'

'That's – that's perfectly understandable.'

'Well, so here in Arizona, if you're driving above ninety, that counts as criminal speeding. The fine is five hundred dollars and you can spend up to thirty days in jail for it.'

Bonnie panics anew. Five hundred dollars again? Vultures, wherever you go. She just gave him Alex's license, and now possibly incriminated her for something she didn't actually do.

'Oh my god, I've got three young boys,' she starts. 'I don't know if I can be in jail that long.'

The cop nods and waves her away.

'But, like I said, you seem like nice people. And you said your mama's in the hospital and whatnot, so I don't want to cause you any more stress. So if I *don't* call it criminal speeding, and say you were just going at *eighty-five* miles per hour, then that's just fifteen above the speed limit. And the fine is three hundred dollars. That sound all right?'

Bonnie's heartbeat calms in a wave of relief. 'I mean, yeah . . .' She looks to Alex for her reaction.

'Wow, that's very kind of you,' Alex cuts in, smiling at the cop.

Bonnie will ultimately pay the three hundred dollars, of course, but the fine will go on Alex's license. She glances at her younger sister, who shrugs, unbothered.

'Thank you, Officer,' Bonnie says. 'I really appreciate it. And yes, we'll pay the fine right away.'

'Just watch your speeding,' the cop says.

'Hey, I told you to slow down, *Alexandra*,' Alex says in a know-it-all voice, joking.

Bonnie shakes her head and jerks a thumb at Alex. 'Imagine a road trip with your sister taunting you all the time.'

'I wouldn't dream of it,' the cop says.

Alex hands over a credit card, one that says Alexandra Chu on it. 'Here, Officer, you can pay the speeding fine with this.'

* * *

'I don't want to hear any jokes ever again about Asian women being bad drivers,' Bonnie announces as they reenter the traffic on Route 66.

Alex cackles, watching her sister with a newfound admiration. 'Yeah, where *did* you learn to drive like that?'

'I've always been a good driver,' Bonnie says. 'Despite whatever Chris says. But uh, I took a tactical driving course last year. Sort of a treat to myself. That's where I learned to do the J-turn.'

'Wow,' Kevin says, impressed. 'Does Chris know?'

'No.' Bonnie smiles. 'And he doesn't need to. Maybe I'll surprise him one of these days.'

'Well, you definitely should.' Alex grins. 'Those are some crazy skills.' Bonnie the dark horse. What other hidden traits does her older sister have?

330

At Kingman, they refill their gas at a Mobil, then switch over. Kevin takes the wheel, as one of the two drivers currently in possession of their license. He'll drive them all the way to California. Alex is grateful to be done with her driving duties for the trip.

But she's grateful for much more than that.

She is grateful for money, that three hundred dollars is not life-or-death for her family.

She is grateful for their race, that the cop believed them. Knowing that if they were Black, they might not have gotten away so easily.

She is grateful she doesn't live in the US. Because a speeding misdemeanor on her California driving record means little to her. She won't need to pay car insurance in this country or worry about her premium going up.

Overall, Alex realizes, how lucky they were. How lucky they always have been, even though she rarely felt that growing up. It could have been worse. It could always have been much worse.

California

At just after 9 p.m. that night, they knock on their parents' door in Irvine, California.

Kevin recalls being a kid, knocking on that door at the end of the school day, waiting for his mom to greet them with a smile and sliced oranges on the kitchen table. Then, when he got older, he was entrusted with his own house key. How grown-up he felt, to slip that key in, turn it, and voilà – step into the house all on his own.

Now it is late at night, he and his sisters wait anxious and tired on that same doorstep, aware that it's possibly past their parents' bedtime. They've driven five straight hours since Kingman, stopping for a final dinner in Victorville, California. By then, the simple two lanes of the I-40 that had accompanied them since Missouri had widened to four, then six lanes of the I-15 headed west. The traffic grew more aggressive and congested the closer they drew to L.A. And when the 15 crested the Cajon Pass to breach the San Bernardino Mountains, they saw all of Greater L.A. spread out before them: a sprawling grid of freeway and shopping plazas and tract housing as far as the eye could see, glittering with thousands of watts of energy in the early evening, implanted on the land. Cities built on sand. From desert to metropolis in a matter of minutes.

Kevin felt his heart sink at the sight of all this civilization massed in front of him. He would miss the open road, the simplicity of it all. One direction, always headed west, without having to worry about lane changes or exits ramps or suburban labyrinths, because you knew where you were going. It was just you and the road and the open sky, reminding you of your purpose.

That melancholy persisted when they reached their parents' house. It sat in shadows, a ghost of the house he had known so well in childhood. Illuminated only by the porchlight that had been left on to welcome them.

The house looked so small, compared to his own home in Wilmette, Illinois.

And Mom and Dad themselves seem to have shrunk, when they finally open the front door.

There is none of the cheeriness and vigor that fueled his mom in his youth, every time she greeted him after school. Instead, she and Dad stand, thin and stooped in their older age. There are smiles on their faces, of course, and they open their arms wide for a hug.

As Kevin sinks into it, he is all too aware of how frail his mom feels. Her bones all too detectable through her cardigan, the thin layer of flesh and muscle that constitutes her body these days.

'Mom.' He studies her, his hands on her upper arms, as if that support is needed to keep her standing. 'How are you feeling?'

'Much better, now that you're all here.'

She smiles, radiating that same motherly adoration she has given him all his life, which he knows he does not deserve. This in itself nearly brings him to tears, but he stifles them at the source. Instead, he notices how exhausted she seems, the droop of skin above her eyes, the wrinkles at their corners.

'We were worried about you,' Dad says. 'It's a long drive from the Grand Canyon in one day.'

'Believe me, we know,' Alex mutters. Kevin and Bonnie both suppress a laugh.

'But you made it, that's what counts,' Dad answers.

'It's so good to see you,' Bonnie effuses, and she envelops Dad and Mom in a group hug, which then grows to absorb Kevin and Alex.

Kevin realizes how rare this feeling is, of being squeezed among four other people, his place among them unquestioned. He hasn't had this kind of group hug with his own kids and wife in ages.

They squeeze for a bit longer, aware that physical affection like this is so unusual in their family. Then slowly, almost sheepishly, they ease out of the hug.

'Come, come, I made some food for you,' Mom entreats them to the kitchen.

'Smooth trip?' Dad asks, hopeful.

'Um . . .' Bonnie looks at Kevin, then Alex, a conspiratorial glance shared by all three of them. 'Well, we got here in one piece. That's what counts.'

On their way up to their bedrooms, Kevin pauses at the turn of the stairs. There on the wall is Alex's portrait of him at thirteen, the source of so much resentment. He slumps in his adolescent gloom, glowering behind his Coke-bottle glasses. The brash orange and blue strokes of paint capture all the uncertainty he felt at that point in his life.

Kevin squints and can see himself in that storm of color. Gone is his adolescent anger at Alex for drawing it, only admiration for her artistic talent. He is glad someone painted him at that age, as much as he hated it at the time. He just wanted to get through those teenage years as quickly as possible, leaving no trace of the person he was.

'Pretty good, isn't it?' Alex jokes, cocky.

'That was always my favorite piece of art you did,' Bonnie says.

'Not mine,' Kevin grumbles.

And Alex laughs. 'Sorry, Kevin.'

'It's okay, I'll live.' They smile at each other on the landing, as that same clock from their childhood sounds eleven o'clock, marking the night with its familiar whirr and chime.

'But I can see why it won a prize,' Kevin adds with kindness. 'You should get back to painting.'

* * *

In her childhood bedroom upstairs, Alex flicks on the light switch and reacquaints herself with the bed, the desk, the chest of drawers that defined so much of her world growing up. Had there once been a time when these four walls demarcated her space of dreaming? The place where she imagined who she might become, the kind of life she hoped to live?

The walls and sides of her bookcase are still decorated with the art she made in middle school and high school: drawings, pastels, watercolors, etchings. She'd been prolific in art class. Above her bed stretches a map of the world, with all the pins stuck into it: red thumbtacks for the places she wanted to visit, replaced by white tacks when she finally did visit them. After a while, she'd stopped adding in the tacks. There were too many places to keep track of, especially as her visits back home grew more and more infrequent.

Otherwise, this bedroom remains just as she'd left it when she went away to college, so lovingly preserved by her mother. Alex staunches a tear when she realizes this room is all her parents really know of her life. Alex at eighteen, eager to conquer the world. But the twenty-two years since then? There's so little of it she's told them.

Alex promises that one day, when the time is right, she will come and visit with Nya and their daughter in tow, and they will see this room, too. The map that teenage Alex had dotted with all the tacks, the world with all the places still to visit.

An idea comes to her. She opens a drawer in her desk, rifles around in it, and digs up a white thumbtack. Standing on top of her bed, she studies the map, locates the United States. One uniform color from Pacific to Atlantic, but somewhere in the southwest – maybe right *there* – the Grand Canyon yawns. Alex sticks the thumbtack in, and steps back to survey her work, satisfied.

When she goes to close that desk drawer, she is confronted with a paint set of hers from high school. The pots are crusted over and dried, the paint decades past saving. Yet the brushes are still there. In need of a wash, yet still perfectly functional.

Maybe Kevin's right. Maybe these brushes deserve to be used again. But what can she paint? She picks up one paintbrush, tickles her chin with the bristles the way she used to as a kid, and a glimmer of an idea starts to form.

* * *

In the corner of Kevin's bedroom stands his childhood telescope. He can still remember his joy when opening it on Christmas morning, at nine years old. All those nights he peered through it in anticipation, hoping to spot a planet or a constellation that was in season.

He leans forward now and lines up his eye, readjusting the finder scope to try and focus on the night sky. Can he still recognize the patterns he eagerly memorized as a child? He

336

frowns, disappointed. Too much light pollution here in Southern California. But somewhere east of here, there is an unpolluted sky, where the universe of stars begs to be read and identified.

He can take the telescope back home to Chicago. Kevin imagines himself setting it up in front of Arabella and Brian, acquainting them with it, explaining all the parts. Maybe even taking them camping, to witness clearer skies.

'Here,' he would say. 'Look through here. And tell me what you can see.'

'There we go, that's the photo.'

The next day, Bonnie has leafed carefully through Mom and Dad's photo albums, the pages creaking like they hadn't been opened in years. There, underneath the clear cellophane, she's found the picture of them in the 70s – Dad shaggy-haired, Mom's hair nearly touching her waist – and stretching behind them, the Painted Desert, the colors now faded in the photograph.

'Wow,' Kevin says.

They look so young. Like skinny college kids she'd want to look after, to give them home-cooked dinners and a clean bed at night. They are smiling, excited, their hair whipped by the wind. And yet, she knew they lived in a world that battered and belittled them, a challenging place to carve out a niche for their three children.

Bonnie takes out her phone and places it next to the photo. On-screen is the picture of herself, Kevin, and Alex taken just two days ago, posed in front of that same bluff of rose-colored sandstone, the colors sharper and more vivid.

Alex leans forward with her phone and takes a photo of the 1970s snapshot. Then a photo of the two images next to each other.

'What are you doing?' Bonnie is curious.

Alex shrugs. 'Just had an idea for a painting.'

They study the two images in silence.

'Can you see a resemblance?' Alex asks.

Bonnie looks from one photo to the other, trying to map Dad onto Kevin, Mom onto herself and Alex.

'Mmmm, I'm not sure,' Kevin says.

Bonnie remembers a time in her teenage years when she grew angry if someone said she looked like Mom. Now, with her mom fading, she wishes the physical link between them were more obvious. But ultimately, what difference does it make? She knows where she came from; she knows who birthed and raised her. She doesn't need the rest of the world's recognition. She knows in her heart, and she is grateful.

Slowly, slowly, the familiarity of her childhood surroundings eases back into Bonnie's bones. Inside the house, she is confronted with her piano competition trophies and school certificates and first-place ballet ribbons. But it is the outside environment that calms her: the California sun, the tall palm trees lining the broad concrete streets, the abundance of Asian eateries that would put any New England town to shame. A few more weeks here, and Bonnie could forget she had ever abandoned this warmth for the redbrick and crisp bite of Massachusetts living.

Now, Bonnie's fingers work delicately behind her mother's skinny neck, as she fastens the clasp on the Navajo necklace they've just presented her. In the end, they decided on a simple teardrop of turquoise, encased in worked silver. It sits on Mom's gaunt clavicle now, a splash of color to enliven her otherwise functional wardrobe.

'We bought it at the Grand Canyon,' Bonnie explains. 'Thought you'd appreciate the memento.' She thinks again of the millennia of geological forces which shaped that stone.

'I do,' their mother beams. 'Makes me feel like I was there.'

Mom's operation is tomorrow, and they sit on their parents' couch, all too aware of what awaits them the next day. Yet there is so much to catch up on. So much her parents don't know. Bonnie wonders what is better left unsaid.

She did at least tell them about her purse being stolen, to explain why three of her credit cards had arrived at her parents' address.

'That's terrible!' Mom sniffs. 'I heard St. Louis is so unsafe.'

Bonnie shrugs. 'Well, I lost some money, sure. But I'll be able to claim most of it back on insurance.'

'So tell us about your trip,' their Dad begs. 'Route 66! Eight states in seven days. What an adventure.'

'Hey, you can blame Mom for the idea,' Alex ribs gently, and Mom smirks weakly in response.

'How was it? What was your favorite part?'

'Mmm . . . probably the Grand Canyon,' Kevin says. And the others nod in agreement, their eyes drawn wide, reimagining that glorious chasm, the untold colors and mineral layers buckled one upon the other.

Mom smiles. 'I knew you would like it. I always knew it was a place you needed to see.'

Bonnie exchanges glances with her siblings, and for a moment, they hover over the possibility of breaking open the truth. But Bonnie shakes her head infinitesimally, and they move on.

'There were some other cool parts, too,' Alex continues. 'Tucumcari, New Mexico, was a trip.' She sniggers. 'And Cadillac Ranch was really something.'

'I got a speeding ticket,' Bonnie volunteers.

'What?' Mom shrieks, then tsks in disapproval. 'You know better than that.'

'Bonnie, why were you speeding?' Dad asks.

'I was in a rush to see you guys,' Bonnie says. Kevin and Alex stifle a laugh. 'Don't worry – it's fine,' she tries to reassure them. 'I paid a fine. The cop let us off lightly.'

Mom shakes her head. 'You sure?'

'Yes,' Bonnie says, exasperated, almost regretting she told them.

'I'm ... in some financial trouble,' Kevin volunteers.

'What kind of trouble?' Mom asks in shock.

They aren't doing a very good job of avoiding upsetting news, are they?

Kevin shrugs. 'I'll tell you more later. The main thing is, I screwed up big time with my investments, and Bonnie saved my ass. She's going to help me out with the debt, and I'll pay her back.'

He grins at her in full gratitude, and Bonnie tolerates the comments from her parents about how good a big sister she is. 'And Alex?' She looks to her little sister, giving her the prompt she needs.

Alex clears her throat and leans in, an uncharacteristic display of nerves for her.

'Mom. Dad. There's something I haven't told you.' She glances around, apprehensive. 'I'm married. To a wonderful woman named Nya. And she's – we're pregnant. We're going to have a daughter.'

* * *

Alex waits for it, the words of disapproval, or the hidden remonstration. The disbelieving question from her parents: Not a man, but a *woman*? As she shares her news, bit by bit, she prepares herself for the outburst, the tears.

Only it never comes. Maybe her mom is too confused, her grasp of the world too tenuous for the truth to register. Or maybe she simply underestimated her parents, failed to realize that their view of the world was wider and more welcoming than she'd thought. Or maybe, nearing the end of her life, her mom recognized that there was no point in putting up barriers, in tightening her already narrowing margin of experience.

So instead, her mom looks at her with a newfound happiness, envelops her in a warm hug.

'A new grandchild. *Your* child.' She beams, gazing at Alex with moist, adoring eyes. 'I hope I get to meet her one day.'

* * *

They watch as their mom is wheeled down the hospital corridor, the wheelchair squeaking down the gleaming tiles to the operating room that awaits her.

Kevin has a lump in his throat, and he doesn't know if that's from anxiety over Mom's operation or the impending call with Jessica, or both. Probably both.

Once the rest of them dissolve into a silent, restless waiting, Kevin decides he can't put it off any longer. He finds a quiet corner of the hospital, a window overlooking the palm-lined parking lot, and the freeway coursing past.

He digs out his phone and calls home.

'Hello?'

His heart nearly bursts when he hears Arabella's voice, high and hopeful.

'Hey Schnopes, it's me.'

'Dad!' The joy in her voice brings tears to his eyes. 'How'd the trip go? Are you in California now?'

'It was good; it was such an adventure.' Kevin grins. 'I can't wait to show you pictures.'

'Send us some more! We've hardly heard from you.'

'I know, I know. I'm sorry.' He dwells on those words; he genuinely means them. 'How's Mom?'

'She's busy, stressed,' Arabella says. 'Probably a little angry at you.'

'Listen, can I talk to her?'

'Sure,' Arabella says casually, like she's not handing him over to the executioner. 'Mom, it's Dad!'

Kevin closes his eyes, preparing himself, running the sentences through his head again. *There's something I have to tell you. You're gonna hate me. And that will be totally justified.*

A click and scrape as Jessica holds the phone to her ear.

'Hello, Kevin?' At the sound of her voice, he wants to disappear.

'Yes, it's me.'

'About time you called.'

'I know. I'm sorry.'

And that's how he begins.

Alex sits and waits as her mom sleeps peacefully in her bed.

To their great relief, the operation was successful. But the doctor warned them that given their mom's age and medical condition, her health was on an inevitable downward trajectory. Future strokes – or future disruptions to her nervous system – could not be ruled out. They had to be prepared for that.

So Alex studies her mom's shallow breathing, her gaunt cheeks and closed eyes, with a deep sadness and a deep love. Aware that she may not have many chances to sit alone with her, just the two of them, in the future.

She has perhaps never seen her mother asleep before; it's always been the other way around. When she was an infant, her mom waited patiently for her to fall asleep. Or stood over her bed to rouse her in time for school. And then, when she grew older, her mom worried, waiting up late at night until Alex got home, always on the dot of her midnight curfew.

Alex silently apologizes for all the grief and all the stress she caused her mom in the past. She didn't mean to upset her. She was only trying to live the life she wanted.

She closes her eyes, puts her face in her hands, and takes a deep breath to soothe the swell of emotions. When she looks up, her mom is awake, studying her, those familiar eyes, kind now and patient.

'Alex.' Her mom smiles, her eyes full of love and adoration.

'Mom.' Alex takes her hand. 'How are you feeling?'

Mom coughs, then sips from the cup of water Alex holds up to her mouth. 'I'm alive,' she croaks.

Alex laughs through her tears. 'Yes, you are.'

*

'When you fly back to London?'

'Next week. Kevin and I have to drive his car back to Chicago, and I'll fly from there.' He needs to get his car home somehow, and Alex feels that there can be no harm in spending a few more days with her brother. Certainly progress, compared to where she was a week ago with him.

'Good – you two are back to normal.'

'Yeah, we're getting there.' Well, they were probably never normal.

'You look forward to going back to London?'

Alex wonders if this question is a test, trying to gauge how much Alex likes being at home.

'I do miss Nya. And I miss London. It is my home, after all.'

Mom nods, and a look of pain crosses her face.

'Are you okay?' Alex is suddenly hypersensitive to any slight shift in her mom's well-being. She is aware how different this is from the annoyance and frustration she always felt around her mom, ever since adolescence.

Mom turns her head, grimacing.

'It's not that . . . Not that.' She looks at Alex, somehow rueful. 'Oh, Alex, how'd I go so wrong as a mother?'

For a moment, Alex's heart sinks and she imagines a homophobic comment, her mom self-flagellating over raising a lesbian daughter. But then her mom continues.

'What did I do to drive you away? Why you go so far?'

And the disappointment turns to guilt now, submerging Alex, even as she feels the tears rising in her eyes. Lamenting all the years that have gone by, her mom aging and weakening in this house, while Alex was out forging her best life, breezily backpacking through far-flung continents.

Alex shakes her head. 'You did nothing wrong.'

345

As she says it, she realizes this isn't fully true – Mom's anxiety, her constant harping and worrying, certainly fueled Alex's need to escape. But she cannot say that. And she realizes how difficult, how impossible it is to raise a child and not impart some of your own fears and anxieties onto them. To not have your child react to this inheritance.

'Are you sure?' Mom asks, sensing doubt.

'You were an amazing mother,' Alex reassures her. 'We were all lucky to have you.' And in this, she is fully sincere.

'And you, Alex? You looking forward to being a mother?'

Alex is touched. She had been certain that with all the tumult around the operation, and her mom's increasingly tenuous grip on reality, that her news about being married and expecting a child would have gone forgotten. After all, it's not like she, Alex, is carrying the child. Her type of impending motherhood is entirely invisible.

'Oh, Mom.' Where can she start? Of course she is excited to be a mother. But she is also terrified of so many things. She confesses this to her own mom now.

'I was scared the whole time I raised the three of you,' Mom says, her eyes drifting, as if gazing into the past. And this makes perfect sense to Alex, even though she's never heard her mother admit this before. The pressure to get straight As, the warnings not to go out, the evils of partying and drinking. All of this embedded in fear. 'I was scared to mess up. Or mess you up. Scared something would happen to one of you.'

'You shouldn't have been so scared, Mom. You did a great job.' Far from any family or support, in a foreign country, living as frugally as they did.

'I know, I did, didn't I?' Mom grins, cheekily. And Alex is glad to see a flash of her earlier spirit. 'So now you, Alex. Don't worry so much. Enjoy it. You will be an excellent mom.'

This kind of blessing moves Alex in ways she hadn't expected. 'Me?'

She could understand Bonnie as a good mother. Her older sister has been playing responsible and attentive for as long as she's known her. But the Alex they all labeled as spontaneous, reckless, flighty? (Although she wasn't really any of these, yet these perceptions of her stuck, and they had always hurt a little.)

'Yes.' Mom nods, certain. 'Alex, you always unafraid. Not like me. More open and trusting. Your own mom? There's things I could have done better.'

'No, Mom, come on. Don't be so hard on yourself.' Alex clasps her mom's hands, as tears glisten in both their eyes. 'I mean, you always encouraged me to follow my passions. Even if you wanted me to be a doctor, you got me art supplies, piano lessons, drama lessons. You let me explore who I wanted to be. You let me travel.'

Mom snorts. 'No, that was all you. Alex, you always very headstrong and knew what you wanted.'

Alex shrugs. 'Well, you were, too. In your own way.'

They both laugh at this.

'I guess you got that from me,' Mom admits.

A silence falls on them as Alex studies her feeling of guilt again. Knowing that for her, the travel was partly about wanting to get as far away as possible, to prove all her mother's anxieties wrong. She lets go of Mom's hands, and sits back in her chair, gazing at her mother, not wanting to broach the next topic.

But it is inevitable. All roads – or at least the road they have taken – were destined to lead here, to Alex asking this question.

She thinks again to her drama training. *Soft voice, but firm. Own the silences. And fill it with love.*

347

'Mom, why did you want us to visit the Grand Canyon after all these years?'

Mom turns solemn, a frown playing across her brow and mouth.

'Ah, Alex, why you asking me this? You know why.'

'Do I?' Alex leans in, peering at her mom, hoping that in making eye contact she will open the channel that has been blocked for so long.

'Look at me. I ... I can't travel like this,' Mom admits. 'But I wanted you and Kevin and Bonnie to see it. I know we tried to, all those years ago. I'm sorry you never got to go.'

And the next question, edging even closer to the truth. Alex feels bad even asking it.

'Mom, what *did* happen at that gas station on the way to the Grand Canyon?'

Hearing this, her mom squeezes her eyes shut and shudders quietly.

When she speaks next, it comes out as a strained whisper, distraught and searching. 'Why you asking me this now? After all these years? Better to just forget.'

Alex swallows. 'I can't just forget. I was so young, but I still remember it so clearly ...'

Mom's eyes widen in horror. Perhaps it has never occurred to her what her own daughter saw that day. 'No one wants to think of those things ... What do you remember?'

And she relates it all: staying in the car with the doors locked, seeing the men drag a much younger Mom around the corner, out of sight.

Mom's eyes fill with tears, and suddenly, despite her wrinkles, her exhaustion from the operation, she looks much younger, lost and helpless.

'You saw that?' she asks, aghast.

'Yes. Why do you think I came out screaming?'

'Oh, Alex ... I ...'

And the strain of speaking becomes too much for her mother. Her voice breaks into sobs, her eyes press shut against the memories as tears trail down her face. Seeing her mother like this, Alex cries, too, wishes she could help relieve the burden for her somehow.

Mom shakes her head, whispers fiercely. 'I don't want to think about that day.'

Alex takes her hand again. 'Mom, those men. Did they ... hurt you? Touch you?'

Mom continues to cry, uttering tears but no words. And then, she nods.

Alex's heart deflates. Her dread confirmed, and with it, the doleful truth.

'What did they do?'

Mom sniffles, wipes away tears with the back of her hand. She finally speaks with a muted anger.

'Why you need to know? Can't I just keep some things to myself?'

'Because it's not ...' Alex flinches, mentally running through all the catchphrases she uses in her professional life. The cost to mental health, the damage to one's self-esteem, the impact of trauma, the burden of staying silent. But none of these can she say to her own mother.

'It's not good for you to bottle it all up.'

'If I want to, why can't I?' Her mom bristles. 'I'm your mother. Do I need to tell you everything?'

'No, I mean, it's your choice, of course. It's just ...' And Alex realizes she can't push her own mother like this. She has to respect her own choices, even this late in her life. Finally, she relents.

'I don't want to talk about it now,' Mom whispers.

'Well, I'm here. If you ever want to.'

But is she really here? In a few days she'll be driving back across the country, and then stepping onto a plane to London. And with her mom in this condition and her own baby on the way, Alex prays there will be more time. And maybe during that time, her mom will find the words to tell her, to find that release.

'Oh, Alex.' Mom's voice now is an echo of a scold, a reminder from her childhood. 'I told you to stay in the car and keep it locked! Why did you come out?'

She stares at her mom. Feeling again like she is a child, unfairly punished.

'Because I saw what happened to you. I had to do something.'

Mom tucks her mouth into a rueful smile, touches Alex on the cheek. The tears glisten in her eyes.

'My little baby. Already so grown-up back then.' They both chuckle through their tears. 'See, that's the difference between you and me. I'm a coward. But you, so little back then. You still came out screaming to try and do something.'

No, Alex thinks. *You would have done the same, too.*

And she has no doubt about it.

Ta-da! Me and some palm trees. Good to hear my driver's license has arrived. Can't wait to see you guys soon. 2 vacations we should do: the Grand Canyon (let me drive). And I think we should go to Taiwan. It'd be nice for the boys to know that side of their family. And good for me, too.

*

Two days later, they cluster around the sign on Santa Monica Pier, all five of them.

Unlike its counterpart in Chicago, the sign is white and scrubbed clean. It stands amid the ocean air and the cries of seagulls, standing guard over the wooden boards and all the tourists who stream past, taking in the calm blue expanse of the Pacific.

Santa Monica 66. End of the Trail

'You want a picture of just the three of you?' Dad had asked.

But no, they had insisted on their parents joining them. 'We wouldn't have gotten here without you,' Bonnie reminds them.

So now they stand together, arms around each other, and smile at a stranger for a photo.

At another time, Bonnie might have groaned at her awkward posture in the picture, asked that they take another one. And even though Dad is squinting, even though there's a random kid with a bright orange T-shirt screaming in the background – this photo is just fine. Perfect in its imperfection.

351

Mom is tired and needs to sit down on a bench, so Dad accompanies her, tells them to 'Go on ahead; enjoy the pier.'

She ambles along in the heat and sunshine, her brother and sister by her side. Later tonight, Bonnie will catch the red-eye to Boston, reunite herself with her husband and three sons. She cannot wait for that embrace, the excitement in their eyes, the firm constancy of Chris wrapped around her.

But this afternoon, she knows to dedicate the remaining time to her own parents and siblings. It may be a long time before they see each other again, all together.

They are at the end of the pier now, and lean over the metal railing, staring into the endless blue waters of the Pacific. She turns to her siblings.

'You guys really ready to drive cross-country all over again?'

Kevin grins. 'I think Alex and I can handle it. We're not taking the same route. This time it's the I-15 up to the 70, then the 80 back to Chicago.'

'So we're going thru Utah and then over the Rockies in Colorado. Then, like, Nebraska and Iowa,' Alex explains. 'It'll be fun! Thirty hours of driving, and we won't be able to stop much. But still fun.'

'Anything in particular you want to see?'

'There's some monument to Chinese railroad workers I'd like to check out. And maybe the site of a Japanese internment camp.'

Bonnie smiles at her sister's boundless curiosity, her urgent desire to explore and to witness.

'One thing for sure though,' Alex quips. 'I'm gonna miss all the vegetarian options here in California.'

* * *

Kevin marvels that there are still so many states he hasn't seen, despite living in this country for four decades. And he

352

is grateful that he'll be able to discover some more of them with his younger sister. Mountain ranges and open prairies still await them. He smiles, just thinking of the open road.

'I'm bringing the telescope, too,' he adds, excited. 'We gotta check out the constellations when we're out there.' Maybe they'll even see some nebulae up in the night sky.

'Everything go okay with Jessica?' Bonnie asks, more solicitous.

'Well, at least she couldn't throttle me over the phone,' Kevin says. 'By the time I get back, she'll have hopefully cooled down.'

His sisters trade looks and grimace.

'It certainly helped, though, that I said I was able to start paying it back, with your help.' He glances at Bonnie. 'You're like a patron saint now in Jessica's eyes.'

'Oh god,' Bonnie mutters. 'Listen, I don't deserve it. I'm just glad I can help somehow.'

They watch fondly as a young white family poses for a photo next to them, grinning in front of the Pacific, sporting Hollywood T-shirts and Southern accents. They're certainly not from around here.

Suddenly Alex turns to Kevin and Bonnie, her eyes alight. 'Hey, let's go for a swim!'

'Really?' They stare at her, balking at another one of her harebrained Alex ideas.

'We've all got our swimsuits, right? It's the Pacific; it's Santa Monica. We've done all of Route 66. Let's get in the fucking ocean and celebrate.'

Kevin can think of no good objection, and neither can Bonnie. And as they run down the pier, their feet pounding on wood, to tell their parents their plan, Kevin realizes this is just what his kids would do. And just what the three of them would have done when they were younger.

* * *

They race into the waves, blanching at first from the unexpected shock of the water. Her skin breaks out in goose bumps, but once her body is used to it, Alex realizes the water isn't cold at all. She dips her head down, submerges herself entirely. The tang of saltwater, the chill dancing across her skin.

'Are you crazy?' Bonnie shouts.

'It's not cold!' Alex resurfaces. 'Come on, let's go farther out!'

Bonnie frowns but keeps up with them. They swim out and out, past the young child learning to bodyboard with her father, past the teenage boys jostling and whooping. Bobbing in and out of the surf, while the elemental thrill of rushing seawater drowns all their adult concerns.

Sometimes a wave drenches them, and sometimes they're able to stay afloat.

When they have covered a decent distance, Alex doggy-paddles toward her brother and sister, and they drift there on the surface of the Pacific, squinting back at the shore.

'Hey look, there's Mom and Dad!'

Kevin points to where their parents sit on the sand, two small, slight figures. To anyone else, they're indistinguishable from the rest of the beachgoers. But to Alex, she can recognize her father's stoop, the protective way her mom adjusts her visor to ward off the afternoon sun.

'Mom and Dad! Over here!' Bonnie shouts.

They're too far away.

'I'm not sure if they can hear us,' Alex says.

And the three of them wave frantically, hoping their parents will see them. Only they can't be entirely sure. Mom raises her hand, or maybe that is only to block the sunlight from her eyes. *Is* there a moment of recognition?

* * *

354

Across the sand, across the seawater, Mei-Huey Chu squints into the Pacific, resigned to her failing eyesight. Earlier, as a young mother, she was convinced she could recognize her three children in any crowd, so attuned was she to their individual tics and movements, her own hopes and fears invested in their moods. But now, in her old age, she admits she cannot tell her own children from all the other specks in the sea. Yet she knows they are out there, those three human lives that she brought into this world. They may drift far, but like the tide, they will always find their way back home.

* * *

In silence, Alex, Kevin, and Bonnie bob in the swell of saltwater and watch their parents, growing smaller and smaller on the broad, golden stretch of sand.

Finally, when she has watched enough, when her heart has filled with an unfathomable sad affection, Alex turns west to face the sun and the rest of the ocean, glittering to the horizon.

There's a wave headed toward them. It rises higher and higher, and at the very top, where the wave is thinnest, the sun glints through it like glass. It is then that she sees the school of tiny fish, caught for a moment at the crest of the wave, illuminated by the sunlight. The fish glint like silver flecks, their miniscule fish-shadows etched crystal clear in the curve of turquoise water – and then, in another instant, the wave collapses, and the vision is gone.

Alex gasps at the sight, wishing that her mom could see this, could swim out this far to witness the inexplicable beauty that exists, transitory, at the crest of a wave. But that is impossible. Some things you cannot share with your mother. Yet she will be happy enough, knowing it is something her own daughter has seen. That ghost of knowing is enough.

Acknowledgments

I can't be sure if I sparked the idea for this book before or after realizing I had never done the Great American Road Trip – and was maybe missing out on some seminal life experience. At any rate, in 2020, while shackled by the Covid lockdown and a newborn, I felt a sudden desire for the open road – to drive vast distances and explore the wide desert spaces of a country I had felt separate from for so long. Planning this trip while living in the English countryside was an interesting exercise in stabbing a pin into thin air and hoping something might materialize out of it. But I suppose that is the essence of adventure, something that we often lack in our day-to-day lives.

The research that fueled this book would not have been possible, first and foremost, without my partner Sam, whom I convinced to go on a three-week road trip with our nearly two-year-old toddler in tow. So thank you Sam, for going along with my harebrained idea – and of course to our son Timo, for being so amenable to sleeping in new motel rooms every night and taking his afternoon nap on a different stretch of American highway each day. I hope you enjoyed the trip, too.

Wherever we went, the general friendliness of everyday Americans served as a rejoinder to the polarizing politics that so often divides America on the page and screen. I don't know if I have contributed to that polarizing through writing this book, but I hope not.

On the book side of things, I of course must thank my agent Robert Caskie for his invaluable support, encouragement, and industry savvy. This is the first novel I've ever written 'in contract' with existing publishers, so thank you to my editors Leodora Darlington and Emily Bestler for their patience, enthusiasm, and trust in giving me the space to write the book I wanted – and shaping it with their wisdom. Many thanks to Gretchen Koss of Tandem Literary, for her enthusiasm and expertise in spreading the word about this book. Thank you, too, to Francesca Pathak and Sarah Benton for their encouragement on early drafts. And to everyone at Atria Books/Simon & Schuster and Orion Fiction for supporting this third novel of mine, which takes a quite different direction from my previous two.

I must thank many great friends who were incredibly helpful and welcoming to us along the way. In Chicago: Susan Russell (who sourced a toddler car seat, travel cot, and invaluable toys for us), Jess Montalvo & Matt Henkler, Nancy & Bryan Chavez, Ali Golensky, and Lori Rader-Day. In St. Louis: Joe Gfaller, and Peggy & Bill Luth. In Colorado: Tamara Torres-McGovern, Piper Dumont & Tovi; Jen and Will Howard. In Arizona: Olivia Verma & Nick Smith. Other friends offered advice and support on the trip: Elizabeth Dotson-Westphalen and Sarah Matthew, Libby Luth, Kyle Graham, Vanessa Torres, and David Heska Wanbli Weiden. Robert & Dawn Federico at the Blue Swallow Motel in Tucumcari, New Mexico were great hotel proprietors.

Many thanks to all the kind folks we met and all the stories we heard during our road trip in the US. Thank you to Google

Maps for making it so easy to locate the nearest available playground, wherever in the Western world one happens to be.

There are fascinating pockets of American history dotted throughout the West, much of which I was unable to capture in this book. One such pocket is Amache, the site of the Japanese internment camp, near Granada, Colorado. Thank you to John at the Amache Preservation Society, whom I never actually met.

I am indebted to all the writers and filmmakers of road trip narratives, who have contributed to the genre over the years. I could name many of them, but *Blue Highways* by William Least Heat-Moon must be admired for capturing the humanity of an America that once was, and which may still exist in hidden corners. Edward Abbey and Ansel Adams influenced me early on in my life to appreciate the desert spaces of the American West, long before I ever set foot there.

I owe a great deal to my 'in-laws' Nicola and Bob Grove for their backing and encouragement, for providing a solid base to call home during the rocky years of Covid and early parenthood. Thank you to both sides of my family, both the Lins and the Li's/Lee's for the inspiration, their love and support.

And as ever, I would not be who I am without my sister Emmeline, my Dad, and of course, my Mom. I wish you could see all the places I've visited in my life. Perhaps writing about them is my way of taking you on the journey.

Credits

Winnie M Li and Orion Fiction would like to thank everyone at Orion who worked on the publication of *What We Left Unsaid* in the UK.

Editorial
Leodora Darlington

Copy editor
Fraser Crichton

Proofreader
Alex Davis

Audio
Paul Stark
Louise Richardson
Georgina Cutler-Ross

Contracts
Rachel Monte
Ellie Bowker
Tabitha Gresty

Design
Charlotte Abrams-Simpson
Nick Shah
Deborah Francois
Helen Ewing

Editorial Management
Anshuman Yadav
Charlie Panayiotou
Jane Hughes
Bartley Shaw

Marketing
Ellie Nightingale

Production
Hannah Cox
Katie Horrocks

Finance
Jasdip Nandra
Nick Gibson
Sue Baker
Tom Costello

Publicity
Harry Taylor

Sales
Dave Murphy
Esther Waters
Victoria Laws
Group Sales teams across Digital, Field, International and Non-Trade

Operations
Group Sales Operations team

Rights
Rebecca Folland
Tara Hiatt
Ben Fowler
Maddie Stephens
Ruth Blakemore
Marie Henckel

Help us make the next generation of readers

We – both author and publisher – hope you enjoyed this book. We believe that you can become a reader at any time in your life, but we'd love your help to give the next generation a head start.

Did you know that 9 per cent of children don't have a book of their own in their home, rising to 13 per cent in disadvantaged families*? We'd like to try to change that by asking you to consider the role you could play in helping to build readers of the future.

We'd love you to think of sharing, borrowing, reading, buying or talking about a book with a child in your life and spreading the love of reading. We want to make sure the next generation continue to have access to books, wherever they come from.

And if you would like to consider donating to charities that help fund literacy projects, find out more at **www.literacytrust.org.uk** and **www.booktrust.org.uk**.

THANK YOU

*As reported by the National Literacy Trust